Breeding Clinic

A HEATVERSE NOVEL

ALEXIS B. OSBORNE

Dark Moon
PUBLISHING

Editing by Lindsay York of LY Publishing

Proofreading by DerpyWickedFox Editorial

Cover, Discreet edition cover, Interior art © 2024 by Alexis B. Osborne

Alice's Adventures in Wonderland by Lewis Carol was originally published by Thomas Y. Crowell & Co., New York, Boston, 1893. Excerpts, quotations, and references are used in this work by right of public domain.

ISBN: 978-1-957341-27-9 (eBook)

ISBN: 978-1-957341-28-6 (Paperback)

ISBN: 978-1-957341-29-3 (Discreet Paperback)

First printing edition 2024

Published by

Dark Moon Publishing, Inc.

P. O. Box 2772

Poughkeepsie, New York, 12603

DarkMoonPublishing@gmail.com

*For everyone who read the tag line "it's the literary equivalent of a bunch of fetish gear covered in c*m, tossed into a dumpster, and set on fire" and 1-clicked, this one's for you. You definitely don't want to read this one in public.*

p.s. If this book gets you pregnant, name the baby after me.

Acknowledgments

A huge thank you to Bianca Stracquadanio for sensitivity reading, answering my many questions about Brazilian culture, and the translation of Portuguese phrases. This book would not have been the same without your help.

What is Omegaverse?

If you're unfamiliar with the omegaverse genre then here is a quick rundown of its quirks and tropes. Omegaverse, sometimes called A/B/O or OV, is a sort of alternate reality where humans are divided into 3 dynamics: alphas, betas, and omegas.

Alphas are physically bigger and more muscular than betas and omegas. They're natural born leaders who fiercely protect their loved ones, but they can become aggressive and their jealousy and possessive urges can sometimes get them into trouble. Each alpha gives off a unique pheromone / scent / perfume that attracts omegas as a lure. An alpha claims another person as a pack mate by biting a claiming bite into the juncture between the neck and shoulder. The base of an alpha's penis contains a knot which swells upon orgasm to stopper up an omega and tie the alpha and omega together for a short time for a higher chance of pregnancy. Alphas produce copious amounts of cum, and their cum is often highly nutritious to help feed an omega who doesn't eat during a heat. Alphas exposed to an omega in heat go into a rut and can become frenzied and combative against other alphas. Alphas purr to soothe distressed omegas, growl as a warning or threat to others, and bark to deliver a command. In a heterosexual OV, a female alpha often has a lock at the entrance of the vagina (the female version of a knot) that swells and locks onto a penis during her orgasm. In some LGBTQ OV, a female alpha's clit swells into a pseudo-penis, usually a smaller one than a male's, with a knot at the base and she can impregnate others.

Betas are the balanced citizens of the omegaverse. Their body size and shape vary from person to person. They don't experience the heats or ruts that omegas and alphas do and they don't have knots or locks. Sometimes they have pheromones like alphas and omegas do, but sometimes these are underdeveloped and faint. It varies widely from author to author. These are the average everyday regular humans of the omegaverse. Most OV books focus on alpha/omega pairings, but beta pack mates exist in many polyam romances, too.

Omegas are the smaller and often more slender and submissive dynamic. Instead of menstruating, they experience estrous/heats. Heats range from a monthly occurrence to a few times a year, depending on the author and the omega. Heats last for days to a week, similar to a period. While in heat, an omega becomes obsessed with finding a compatible alpha, nesting, and breeding. The delirium and increased libido of a heat may drive an omega to accept a strange alpha they normally wouldn't choose. Omegas produce a unique pheromone / scent / perfume like an alpha does. When in heat, this pheromone acts as a lure and becomes addicting to alphas and can send an alpha into rut. During heat, an omega produces excess lubricant called "slick" which helps ease the chaffing from a week-long sex marathon. An alpha's growl can trigger an omega to produce an extra gush of slick. Heats often make omegas physically warmer to the touch and sensitive to rough fabric. Omegas who have been bitten between the neck and shoulder by an alpha are considered claimed or mated. Mating is the OV equivalent of marriage and is usually permanent. Omegas are more fertile than betas. In some OV books, omegas are prone to having multiple babies rather than singles and sometimes the infants are called pups. While in heat, omegas rarely eat except for an alpha's nutritive cum. In heterosexual OV, the alpha's knot lodges behind her pubic bone to tie them together and trap the pool of semen near the cervix to increase the chance of pregnancy. In some LGBTQ OV, a male omega has a self-lubricating anus and accepts an alpha's knot anally or they may have two holes plus a smaller penis. Mpreg, or male pregnancy, is a topic you'll sometimes find in gay MM OV. The male omega either gives birth through c-section or delivers anally or through their mating hole. How MPreg works is author dependent and varies.

Pheromone preferences vary widely from alpha to alpha and omega to omega. The saying "one man's trash is another man's treasure" applies here. What smells amazing to one alpha/omega smells gross or bland to another. Many OV romances involve alphas and omegas looking for scent matches or their "fated mate" rather than dating. Alphas and omegas will scent mark each other through touch via pheromones, especially by rubbing their partner with their cheek or chin or touching their scent gland to claim their "territory."

Nesting is something that omegas in heat and pregnant omegas do. It involves gathering lots of soft bedding and pillows and creating a small, cozy space that makes them feel safe. The nest is where omegas spend their heat and it can be where they'll give birth and raise their young, too. Think of it like the coziest adult pillow fort you've ever built. Omegas in heat like to make the nest smell like their alpha or pack through scent marking and sex. It's not unusual for an omega to drag her pack mate's cast-off clothes into the nest. If you've ever stolen a boyfriend's hoodie and worn it to bed because it smells like him, then that's a good example of human nesting behavior.

Omegaverse books sometimes have shifters (like werewolves) but many of them don't. Some omegaverse books even take place with orcs or elves or in space with aliens!

The Heatverse is a non-shifter contemporary OV. There are no werewolves or shifters in this series.

Content Guide

A list of tropes and triggers may be found on the author's
website.
www.alexisbosborne.com

Breeding
CLINIC

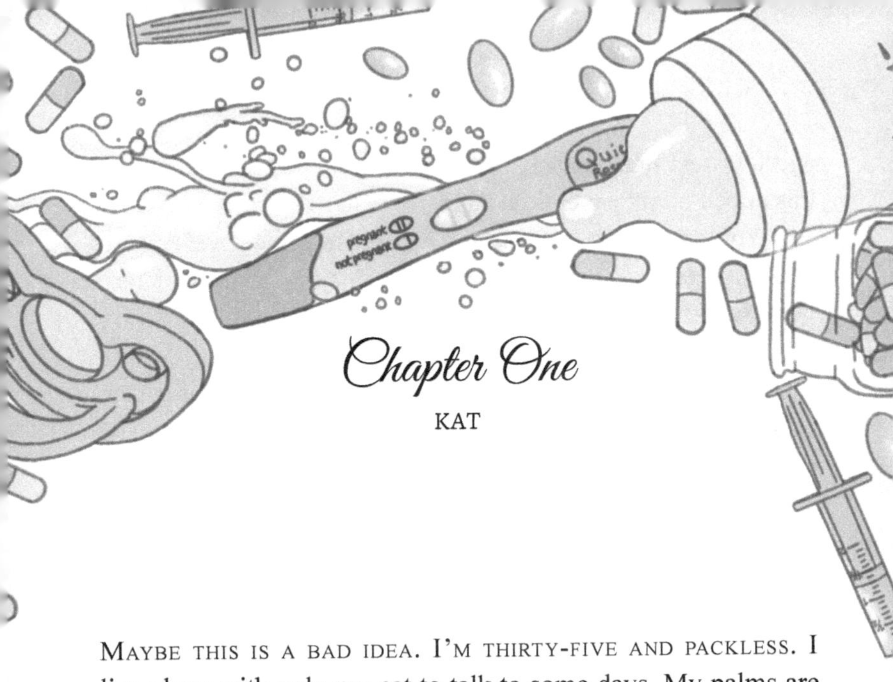

Chapter One

KAT

Maybe this is a bad idea. I'm thirty-five and packless. I live alone with only my cat to talk to some days. My palms are sweating, and I'm gripping the steering wheel too tightly while I sit in the clinic's parking lot. It's not too late to turn around and go home. Nobody but Jen knows I'm here.

As if my thoughts summon her, her name flashes across my car's dashboard display. I tap the green icon and wait for it to connect.

"How is it? Is it nice?" Jen asks.

"I haven't gone in yet."

The building is nondescript from the outside. White painted brick with a powder blue sign showing their medical logo. It could just as easily be a radiology office or dentist. Even their name is subtle. Family Solutions. It's a fertility clinic. One of the best. Word of mouth says that Dr. Fugo gets results. His success rate is twelve percent higher than his peers.

"Are you thinking of turning around?" she asks.

"Maybe. What if they turn me away?" Not all clinics or sperm banks allow single patients. But after a pack dissolution and four lost pregnancies, being thirty-five means if I don't do this now, I might never do it at all.

"You won't know if you don't walk in," she says. "But if you're not sure yet, then don't. You can wait for another heat cycle or two. And there's always adoption."

Adoption is an option, although it's a hard one if you're single. Part of me still wants the experience of being pregnant. Of growing my baby in my womb and giving birth. Nursing and looking at the child I made. One who looks like me. All I need is the sperm.

If I don't go in now, I'll never come back.

Resolved, I grab my phone off the charger and turn off my car. "I'm going in."

"Thatta girl. Call me the minute you're done. I want to hear everything." Jen's kids scream in the background, and she sounds rushed when she says, "I'll talk to you later."

"Bye," I say, but she's already hung up to deal with her kids. They're two and four years old and a handful. But their cute smiles and the sheer joy on their faces when they witness something exciting and new for the first time makes my ovaries twist with longing. I want a hellion or two of my own.

I slam my car door shut and press the button on my fob to lock it, then walk across the parking lot. Before I chicken out, I tug the door open. A blast of warm air hits me, making my light coat and sweater overly hot. It's only March, but it's unseasonably warm this Spring. It's supposed to be a scorching summer this year.

A pretty brunette beta receptionist greets me with a smile and asks if I have an appointment.

"Hi, I'm Kathleen. I have a one o'clock with Dr. Fugo. I'm a new patient."

She taps on her screen, then hands me a clipboard with new patient forms and a pen. "You're seeing his NP today. He's out sick for the week. Here, fill these out and bring them up to me when you're done. I've got you all checked in."

"Oh, okay." That's a bit disappointing. I'd wanted to meet the renowned fertility specialist. I take the forms and sit, then fill them out. The packet is seven pages thick and thorough, going over everything from pack status to demographics to previous pregnancies and a long family history form. Filling it out takes my focus until I'm done and I've handed it in.

Now there's nothing between me and my anxiety as I wait. A medical assistant eventually calls my name and I follow her, listening to her new patient spiel. She shows me to a room and grabs a set of vitals before leaving me alone.

Twenty minutes later, the NP comes into the room and looks over my chart. "Kathleen? Hi. I'm Amanda. So I see that you're here for a new patient evaluation. Can you tell me more about what brought you here today?"

"Everyone calls me Kat, and…" My heart pounds in my chest, vacillating between hope and dread. Will they say no? Turn me away? That's the worst part of all of this. The endless brief periods of hope between the long stretches of grief. "I'd like to have a baby."

She smiles and takes a seat, going over my paperwork more thoroughly. "Well, you're in the right place. That's what we do here. If you wanted a root canal, then we'd have a problem."

I laugh nervously at her corny joke. Relief washes over me and the tight knot in my chest unclenches. I'm glad I came. "So you think it's possible?"

"There's always a chance. I've read through the testing you've had at other practices. Seems like you've run through the whole gauntlet of tests and there weren't any significant findings. I understand you had four losses with your old pack? No births?"

I swallow past the lump in my throat. The lost pregnancies

are old, but the hurt never fully fades. Not all the way. Maybe if I'd been able to move past it, my pack wouldn't have rejected me. But I didn't know how. I still don't. Not when being a mother is the one thing I've always wanted since I was a girl myself. "That's right. They all happened early, even though the doctors said my progesterone level was fine."

"Most pregnancies that fail do so in the first trimester. It's a sensitive time period, and if things don't divide and multiply right, it won't stick. But after three years of trying to conceive with no live births, we have to assume there's something more going on."

I nod. It's nothing I haven't already heard. This is the third fertility specialist I've seen.

The NP continues, saying, "Unexplained infertility is an umbrella diagnosis for disorders we don't fully understand yet. But your heat cycles are regular according to their notes. Your old ultrasounds show you're ovulating fine. That means we have a few options."

I sit up taller in my seat, eager. "Okay. What are those?"

"There are three main methods. Natural insemination, intrauterine insemination, and In Vitro Fertilization. In IVF, we harvest your eggs, inseminate them in the lab, and transplant an embryo into your uterus a few days later. There are pros and cons to all of them, and the cost varies but goes up as more intervention is needed. Here's a pamphlet with our prices. Most insurance doesn't cover infertility services, so we offer bundle pricing and we have financing options too if you'd like to take out a medical loan."

I take the pamphlet from her, not shocked at the high price tag for some of their services. IVF can cost as much as buying a car. Thanks to my pack disbanding settlement, I have the money for it. But I don't think I'm ready for all the shots that come with IVF. What if Jen is right? What if it's Josh who had the problem?

"What are the success rates for each one?" I ask.

"Normally I'd recommend going straight to medicated IUI or IVF for someone in your age range. But you had bloodwork done six months ago and your ovarian reserve is good. Since omegas are hyper-fertile compared to betas, you could try a low-dose medicated insemination round. Our results show that we have a better success rate with this method when an alpha and omega are scent matched well. Your sensitive nose can tell a lot about the compatibility of a prospective alpha. If that doesn't work after your second heat, then you could consider more advanced options."

Hope renews me yet again. "Okay. Let's do that. So what's next?"

"We'll have you look through the books, pick out some sperm donors, and do a sniff test for compatibility. Unless you already have someone donating? No? Well, that's fine. We have plenty of wonderful donors for you to choose from. All of them go through criminal background, motility, and STI tests. In the meantime, we'll run some fresh blood work and call your prescription into your pharmacy. You'll need to test your urine at home with estrus strips. When the indicator says you're in preheat, call us to book your heat appointment, then start your medication. It's usually about five days of pills."

"Okay," I say, truly excited now. "My heat's due in a week or two."

She smiles at my enthusiasm and leaves me to order the medication and blood work. A medical assistant brings me to another area where they draw several vials of blood. Then she leaves me in a private room with a white glossy book of potential donors. There aren't any current photos, only baby photos and donor numbers. Each page has a list of basic demographic info, a health history, family history, and a brief paragraph about why they're donating.

Most of the donors are young, struggling college kids who are probably doing it for the money. Their essays glowingly praise how selfless the act of donation is. Each one sounds almost exactly the same as the next. While they probably have the healthiest sperm, I find it hard to pick from one of them. None of them feel right. When the first binder is a dud with only a few maybes, I grab another from the rack on the table.

The second binder has a better mix of donors. Some are in their twenties, most are in their thirties, and a few are older still. Their essays are more personal. Some talk about how they always wanted kids but never found the right partner. Others talk about busy, intense careers taking up their prime breeding years. From this one, I find three potential donors.

The first is a thirty-four-year-old lawyer. He's smart and successful. He enjoys hiking and jogging with his dog. But his pheromone sample smells terrible. My nose wrinkles as I seal his baggie and flip to the next donor I liked.

The second one is thirty-eight and owns a pub. His paragraph talks proudly of his family. How he'd always wanted a large family like the one he grew up in. How he never found someone to have kids with. On his days off, he enjoys being with his friends and family and watching movies. While his bio doesn't stand out among all the doctors, lawyers, and business executives, there's something sweet about it.

His scent sample is a dreamy mix of woodsy notes. It reminds me of that one summer when I was fourteen and my entire extended family went camping in the mountains. We ate blackberries straight from the vine and caught rainbow trout that we skinned and cooked.

The third donor is an engineer. His baby photo is of him crying while meeting the Easter Bunny. It's an endearing mix of cute and funny that makes me laugh. His scent is okay. An overly sweet mix of cinnamon and sugar that might be sickening in large doses. His bio hits all the right notes. He's smart, has a great career, has a cute baby photo, and I like his sense of humor.

I flip through the album again to make sure I didn't miss anyone. There's something about the second donor that I can't get out of my mind. Maybe it's how much he appreciates family or his scent, but my gut is steering me toward him.

She said to follow my nose. Besides, if the first time doesn't work, I can always pick a new donor. They might have more to choose from by then.

I make my choice, feeling satisfied that I'm finally doing this after months of thinking about it. I hand the binder with my choice on top to a harried-looking staff member sitting at a computer in the hallway, then head out.

My phone is in my hand and I'm dialing Jen as soon as the door closes behind me.

"Hey. How'd it go?" she asks.

"Amazing." I smile and head to my car, unlocking it and cranking the engine. "They took blood work, and I picked a donor. Once my next heat starts, I call them and take some pills. It'll probably be next week."

"See? That wasn't so bad. I—Bailey! Put that cat down *right now*! Because I told you so. Thank you."

My cheeks hurt from grinning. "I'll let you go. You sound busy."

"I can't wait for her to start kindergarten," she sighs.

"You'll be a crying mess the day she finally leaves for school," I tease her.

In the background, something crashes to the ground and breaks. Jen sighs again. "True. I gotta go. I'll call you when they're down for their nap."

I pull out into traffic and drive to the store. There are probably still some old estrus and pregnancy test strips collecting dust in the shoebox hidden in the back of my closet. But it might be best to start fresh. What if they expired? Besides, digging out that old box of dying dreams would make me sad.

The family planning section of the local big box store brings back enough painful memories as it is. For the first year after everything, I pretended it didn't exist. I never looked down the aisle while getting groceries. Now butterflies flutter in my stomach as I debate the blue one or the pink one like I've never done this before. There's a new digital test kit they didn't sell three years ago. Thin test strips go into a portable machine and the result pops up on a digital display. Its box says it does both ovulation and pregnancy tracking and it syncs to a smartphone calendar app.

I put the two-hundred-dollar machine in my cart and buy an extra box of refill strips. I grab a few more things I need so it won't be the only thing the cashier rings up. Not that the eighteen-year-old with the lip ring cares. The bored teenager scans my items quickly and rattles off the total. I throw everything into a bag and pay, then take my purchases home.

Waffles greets me at the door, rubbing against my legs and meowing, begging for his dinner like he's starving. "I fed you this morning," I remind him. He meows again and leads me to his food bowl as if I might have forgotten where it is.

I scoop some cat food into his dish and stroke his back, enjoying the way he arches into it. "You're getting fat." Waffles doesn't care. I make a mental note to switch him to a light formula for indoor cats. He's older now too, and his metabolism's slowing down.

After dinner, I set up the fancy machine in my bathroom and download the app. A few taps syncs it to my health app and it records my heat information. The instructions say it works best with first morning urine, so I force myself to wait to try it out.

I try to distract myself with a movie, but nothing holds my attention. My thoughts keep drifting back to baby fever. It's crazy to look up nursery photos, but I can't help myself. My old pack never understood my relentless need to plan.

Four potential nursery themes later, I finally call it quits when I can hardly keep my eyes open. The movie rolls to credits. I turn the television off and drag myself to the bathroom to brush my teeth, then go to bed.

In the morning, I wake up with energy. It's time to pee on a test strip. I read the instructions that came with it again, then pee into a cup and dip the test strip. The cap goes back on and it's the other end that goes into the machine to be read.

After three agonizing minutes, the display reads low fertility. Now that I've told the machine when I want to test, it sets an alarm for the rest of the cycle.

With nothing else to do but wait for my body to do its thing, I wait.

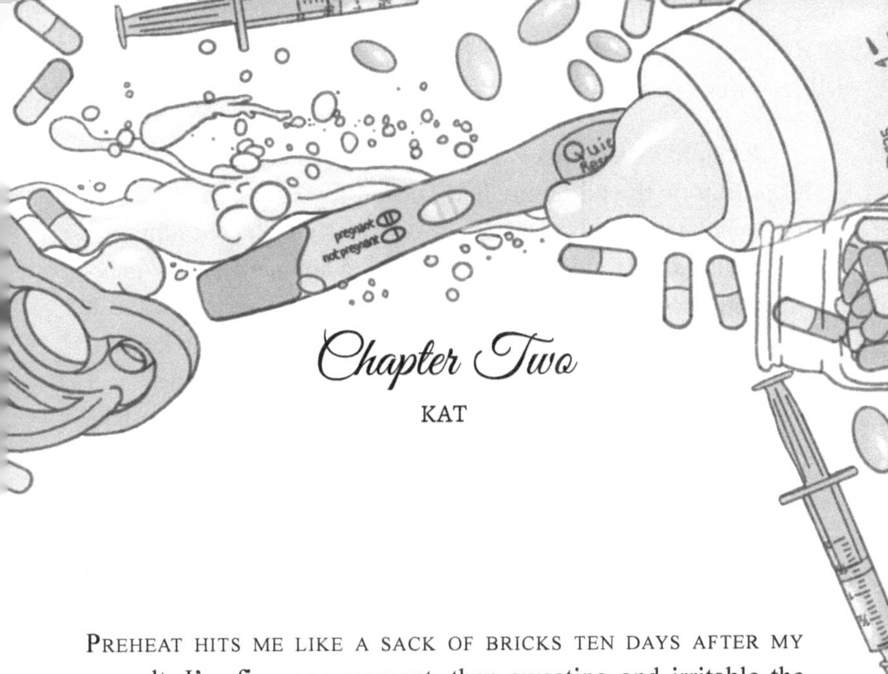

Chapter Two

KAT

PREHEAT HITS ME LIKE A SACK OF BRICKS TEN DAYS AFTER MY consult. I'm fine one moment, then sweating and irritable the next. A telltale cramp tells me it's coming on fast.

I turn the stove off and head to the bathroom to take a test, forcing myself not to stare at the timer counting down. The timer goes off and the fertility monitor's screen reads high fertility. My luteinizing hormone is rising.

I call the clinic and set an appointment for insemination. I'll take my first pill tonight. A few days from now, I'll drive to the clinic and stay there for a medicated heat cycle.

Waffles is going to need a pet sitter. I call the girl I normally use and make up a story about going out of town for a few days.

"Have fun!" she tells me, probably thinking I'm going on vacation. "I'll come over on Tuesday after my classes are done. If you need me earlier, let me know."

"I will. Thanks, Chelsea. I'll leave the money on the kitchen table. And don't feed Waffles too much. He's on a diet."

"I won't," she lies. We both know she spoils him rotten with treats. But he loves her and I like having someone in the house when I'm away.

Panic hits me when I realize I never picked up the medication. I throw the lid on my half-cooked food and run out to the pharmacy to fill my prescription. An elderly alpha checking out the arthritis aisle glances in my direction and smiles. The pharmacy tech tells me to wait while they fill it. They restocked it when I never picked it up. I wait, antsy to get it and go home. I hate leaving the house during preheat. People get so weird.

After twenty minutes, she rings up the prescription. I take the first pill while sitting in my car in the parking lot, then head home. By the time I'm at the house, my stomach is no longer interested in dinner. I toss the half-made spaghetti out and reach for a protein water and chocolate. Once I'm settled on the couch, Waffles jumps into my lap and I pet him while looking for something good to watch.

FOUR DAYS LATER, A WET BURST OF SLICK GUSHES BETWEEN MY thighs after a cramp. It's time to head to the clinic. I text Jen that I'm going in, then Chelsea to tell her that I'm leaving. I wheel my small suitcase out to my car, doing deep breathing exercises between agonizing cramps.

While I drive, I call the clinic to let them know I'm on my way. The woman on the other end of the phone gives me the address for their heat clinic. It's a signless brick building a few blocks away from their main office.

A worker brings me inside and shows me to a small office where they take my vitals. She pulls out a patient folder with paperwork and my sperm donor's profile. "This is the alpha you've chosen?" she asks.

"Yes." His chubby baby photo makes me smile, and the

pheromone swatch clipped to his profile makes my clit throb. My nose is extra sensitive during a heat, and I chose well. He smells delicious. My pussy clamps down on nothing and I stifle a whimper.

"Sign here. This is a standard waiver for patient care, a billing agreement, and a consent for natural insemination treatment. We have a credit card on file. Is that the one you want us to use?"

"Yes. That one's fine." I take the pen from her and sign, clenching my teeth as a spasm rocks my core. God, it's bad. I don't know if it's the medication or the anticipation but this is the worst heat I've ever had since I was a teenager. Knot hunger rots my brain and leaves me blinking extra slow, my thoughts sluggish. Betas will never understand how bad it is. How painfully desperate an omega becomes during their heat.

I would sit on the first dick presented to me if it made this horrible, empty ache go away.

Slick drenches my special heat panties. When I squeeze my thighs together and tense, my clit aches. It's swollen and ready for petting. I need this woman to leave so I can shove my hand down my waistband and bang out a shallow orgasm so I can think again.

I sign all of the papers and shove the pile at her. "Everything looks good. How long do I have to wait?"

"I'll show you to your room where you'll be staying for the duration of your heat. We'll hook you up to a monitor that lets us track your vital signs from the nurse's station. There are cameras and microphones in the room for your safety, but we won't be watching unless you call for help or we suspect you need emergency assistance. Your safety is our number one priority, and we take all preventative steps to make this heat as safe and satisfying as possible."

Safe? Oh, the meds.

"Do you want to get settled in your room?" she asks, heading to the door.

"Yes." I stand and follow her, wheeling my suitcase behind me. When my head spins, I lean my shoulder against the wall. I need to lie down.

"All of our heat attendants are betas," she says, tapping her keycard to a black square by the door. It beeps as a light turns green. The door's deadbolt unlocks. "They work in twelve hour shifts so you'll have several throughout your stay but we try to keep you with the same group. There are scent free toiletries in the bathroom. If you need a heat aid, new ones are in the nightstand. The charge will be added to your bill once the safety seal is broken."

She waves a hand to the TV mounted on the wall and the small desk where a computer could go. I feel bad for omegas who have to try and work through their heat. "There's cable if you're up to watching TV and you're welcome to use the wi-fi. Meals will be delivered regularly if you're up to eating. If you need anything, use this intercom button. The door will be kept locked for your safety."

The room is nicer than I thought it would be. It's more like a hotel room than a hospital room. There's a queen-size bed in the center with fresh white sheets and a plethora of pillows in different sizes. The duvet looks thick and fluffy. There are a bunch of laundered blankets displayed on a rack for nesting. I brought my own, but I appreciate their thoroughness.

The door on the side leads to a small bathroom. The only thing the room lacks is a window with a view. They've put a pretty stained glass film on the windows to let in light but provide privacy too. Abstract paintings of swatches of color hang on the wall. I roll my suitcase to the dresser and leave it to unpack later when I have a lull.

My thighs clench again and I realize I'm fidgeting. I tighten my fists to keep from relieving this awful, all consuming need with her still in the room.

She puts on a pair of blue gloves and opens a small package, then peels the paper backing off a sticker the size of my palm. "This is the monitor," she says. The sticker goes in the center of my chest below my throat.

The movement brings her close and a fog clouds my thoughts. All I notice is how shiny and pretty her hair is. How her fitted scrubs cling to her small waist and breasts. Her scent is a subtle floral blend underneath her fading null wash soap. If she drops her hand any lower than my sternum, I'm going to embarrass myself by moaning. The brief contact of her fingers against my hot skin is wonderful.

"There." She steps back and smiles. "All done."

"Thank you," I choke out. "I'd like to be alone for a bit."

She nods and heads to the door. "Of course." Before the door closes behind her, she pokes her head back in and smiles. "Good luck!"

I smile back until the door closes, an electronic locking sound buzzing. Then I shove my hand under the waistband of my stretchy pants and panties. I'm soaked, my arousal thick. My nipples tighten and rub against my sports bra. A sudden flush of heat leaves me panting.

It's so fucking hot. I'm burning up from the inside out and desperate for a cock. My middle finger rubs circles around my swollen clit and a shallow orgasm shudders through me. My pussy clenches repeatedly around nothing. It's enough to sate me so I can unpack, but it's a drop in the ocean when it comes to the needs of my heat.

I shove my sweaty hair away from my face, not caring that I'm spreading slick everywhere. There's no such thing as pride during a heat. Not when omegas become mewling, cum-drenched creatures.

Hold it together, I tell myself. It's only day one. My heats average about four.

With the orgasm, my head clears a little. I have enough time to unpack my suitcase into the dresser and add my blankets to the bed. I'll build my nest later when I have the urge. For now, my only focus is on finding my vibrator.

I pull the hot pink vibrator with the clit teaser and knotted base from my bag and plug its charging cord into the outlet by the bed. I'm naked in seconds. My sweat-soaked clothes are tossed onto the floor and forgotten.

The bed squeaks as I climb onto it and lie on my back. The moment the bulbous tip of the vibrator touches my pussy, I breathe a sigh of relief. It bottoms out inside me with a single thrust. Pulling it almost all the way out, I do that again. Working it in and out of me. I don't need the vibration function to come again.

My walls clamp down on hard silicone, and this time I let out the moan I've been holding. Are they watching me? Listening? Does my heart rate spike with every fluttering orgasm? The idea of a room full of betas crowded around a monitor makes my clit throb. Are they really not watching the cameras?

Omegas are made for crowds. For the safety of packs, the larger the better. The idea of an audience turns me on.

I spread my thighs wide and pull the vibrator out, plunging it back in again. It hits my cervix and my toes curl. I've always loved it deep and fast. Rough. There's something so primal and delicious about being rutted. Being pinned down and bred. The cold drip of cum down my thighs.

My toy is a poor substitute for a real alpha. I save the knotting feature until I can't take it anymore. Until the way it knocks against my cervix isn't enough. Desire swells inside my core, large and demanding. I want a knot. *Need it.*

It's too early to give into that urge. Instead, I edge myself. I flick the vibration setting on to my favorite, the deep pulse. The vibrator kicks to life inside me. Both the head and clit ticklers buzz. Another shallow orgasm rips through me. I throw my head back and use my free hand to play with my breast. Pinch my taut nipple until it aches.

My thighs squeeze against the toy and I rock, using the momentum to drive the vibrator in deeper. Three orgasms. Four. When the next one won't come no matter how much I whine or shove the toy in deeper, that's when I finally hit the knotting button. The base of the toy swells, pulling in air. It inflates inside me, the pressure growing right against my g-spot.

Eyes closed and pussy dripping, I come on the artificial knot. My walls squeeze down on inflated silicone, and the worst of the wave of heat passes.

A shudder rolls through me as I turn the vibrator off and lie there, my toy still buried deep. Sated, at least for a while. I drag one of my blankets over myself and close my eyes. Rest and sleep will come in fits and spurts for the next few days.

With a hand over my belly, I think of the baby I hope to make.

It's the emptiness that wakes me. Sitting up and rubbing my eyes, I blink at the unfamiliar room until I remember where I am. My vibrator slipped out while I slept once the safety mechanism disengaged the knot. The analog clock tells me I slept for two hours.

A tray with saran-wrap-covered gelatin, a cup of fruit cocktail, and a chilled protein water sits on the floor by my door. Someone dropped it off while I napped. I take advantage of my brief moment of clarity to crack the safety seal on the protein water and drink it down. The thought of solid food turns my stomach so I leave the gelatin and fruit untouched.

There's a small white cup with a pill in it that I didn't notice at first. More ovulation medicine? I swallow the pill with the last of my protein water, then go into the bathroom to pee and clean up. My thighs are crusty with dried slick.

I look at the shower with longing, but I'm not sure if I can get the sticker wet so I settle for washing up with a wet towel and brushing my teeth. By the time I'm cleaner, my need is rising again. I crawl into bed and kick the covers off, too hot to enjoy their softness.

I need dick in the worst way.

A whine builds in my throat as I fish around for my vibrator. I click the vibration setting on. It starts up, then dies a moment later. I click it again, but this time it doesn't turn on. It's dead. "Fuck." I was so distracted from the insane levels of medicated horniness that I forgot to charge it.

There's nothing to do except shove the charging cord into its base and set it aside, then problem solve this manually. Lying on my back, I spread my thighs and run my fingers up the sensitive inside. I massage over my swollen mound, sliding two fingers between my lips.

My clit aches, already swollen and ready. Always ready for more during a heat. I pinch my nipple and roll my clit in circles, rocking against my hand. It's not enough. Pushing in, I stretch my channel wide and plunge two fingers, then three, into my slick hole. A whine rips from my throat, and I toss my head back and arch into the pumping motion of my hand.

My nipple is rock hard, my breast soft. I imagine them swollen with milk. Leaking. Imagine my cunt dripping with cum instead of slick.

They're going to breed me. Going to shove healthy alpha

sperm deep inside me so my womb can be filled. By next week I might be pregnant.

I whine again, too needy for words. The door beeps and opens, but I'm too close to coming to be worried that they'll see me like this while they take the food tray away.

Let them watch. I don't fucking care. All I care about is coming.

My clit throbs in time with my pulse and I moan. My hand isn't fast enough. My fingers can't pump deep enough. It isn't enough. A needy omega sound pours from me.

A soothing alpha purr rumbles through the room in response. Slick bursts between my thighs, soaking my hand and thighs. Saturating the nest.

I'm startled enough to stop fingering myself and crack my eyes open.

An alpha, tall and broad chested with dark hair going gray at the temples and tan skin stands over me. He's wearing nothing but a pair of soft gray sweatpants.

What the fuck?

I freeze and whine in confusion.

His purr doubles, getting louder and faster. It's rusty, like he's not used to doing it. But he gains confidence the more he does it. The sound smooths out to a rolling, thunderous rumble that makes my concerned thoughts settle. He slips a hand in the waistband of his sweatpants and shoves them down. A thick cock springs free.

My nostrils flare as I drag in his scent. Thick, deep woods full of pine trees and evergreens. And underneath his scent, two more. A comforting smoky fire and cold, crisp snow. He smells like happy memories and wilderness.

The alpha undresses until he's naked, his big cock jutting forward in the air. A bead of pre-cum drips from his flared ruddy head.

Mouth watering and pussy weeping, I whine in confusion and need. *Why is my donor here?*

The alpha puts a knee on the bed as if testing the water, then crawls onto it. He reaches out and touches my ankle, closes his fingers, his grasp gentle but firm.

My mind shorts out the moment he makes contact. With his scent, his rumbling purr, his dripping cock, all I can think about is sitting on it. I need the deep, horrible ache inside me to *stop*.

A spasm wracks my core and my pussy clenches around my still buried fingers. Not enough. *More. Moremoremore.*

"Please," I moan, not sure what I'm really asking for.

His hand slides up my leg, over my knee, and traces along the sensitive skin along my inner thigh. Fingers wrap around my wrist and tug my hand out of my cunt. I whimper at the loss, then stare enraptured as he brings my hand to his face. He sniffs me, then tastes me. His pink tongue darts out to lick the slick off my fingers. It's wet and firm, and he purrs while he cleans me up. My pussy throbs, wishing his tongue was licking elsewhere.

The alpha stares at me with warm brown eyes. A short, trimmed beard covers his jaw. His nose is straight. His smile is even. He's handsome. A thrill shivers through me. I picked a good one.

He licks my hand clean, then settles himself in the hollow of my body. His knee moves, knocks mine wider, and I arch instinctively. Spreading myself for him.

I put a hand on his chest to push him back. To ask him what the fuck he's doing in my room. But then his cock brushes against my wet slit. I'm lost to the haze of my heat again.

My fingers dig into his skin to pull him closer. To line him up where I need him most. His head dips to the hollow of my throat, smelling me. His nose runs from my shoulder to the side of my jaw. My body tenses, going still on instinct. His teeth are dangerously close to my bare throat.

I whine with need. "Please."

"You smell so fucking good," he moans, his voice deep and rough. "Like fresh baked sugar cookies. I didn't know it would be like this. Didn't think…"

Me either. When they said natural insemination I thought they meant the medical version of a turkey baster. But this… *Fuck, this is so much better.* No wonder everyone whispers that Dr. Fugo is the best. How is this legal?

His hips flex with his next inhale and his cock rubs against my clit. Teases over my hole. Notches at my entrance without pushing inside.

I can't take the teasing any longer. He needs to either fuck me or get off so I can find my vibrator. My nails dig into his shoulder and my whine turns annoyed. "Please."

"You want my baby, sweetheart?" he asks.

Oh, fuck. Dirty breeding talk? My eyes roll back in my head. I flex my hips, trying to impale myself on his cock. But he denies me, leaning back enough that the angle isn't good. Here, spread out underneath him, I'm not in control.

"I want to hear you say it, sweetheart," he says. "Tell me you want me to put my baby in you."

"Yes," I pant, annoyed he isn't fucking me already. That thinking and speaking are a struggle. "Fuck me, please. I want your baby."

His cock nudges deeper, but torturously slow. The rough sound he makes in the back of his throat as he buries himself inside my hot, wet heat satisfies me. His hips pull back and thrust again with tentative movement.

It's been a long time since I had a partner who wasn't battery operated. A part of me doesn't like that he's taking his sweet time. Testing out the depth of my channel and how much of his cock I'm able to comfortably take.

I want all of it. My nails dig depressions in his back and my thighs squeeze his hips. "Harder."

He lets out a surprised breath, and his next thrust comes harder. Our bodies slap together and his cock batters at my cervix. He nips my earlobe between his teeth. "Like that, hellcat?"

I frown. "They told you my name?" That isn't fair considering I don't know his. Only his donor number.

"Hmm?" His thrusts pause.

"Kat."

He thrusts again, slow and deep. His weight is heavy as he settles himself on top of me. And his eyes stare into me, before dropping down to my mouth. "Can I kiss you, pretty kitty?"

I miss kissing. Maybe more than sex, outside of a heat of course. I nod, and his lips dip toward mine. They're soft at first. Then firm. When his tongue licks at me, I let my mouth fall open. He dips inside, stroking my tongue with his. The shallow thrusts of his cock match his tongue so he's fucking me from both ends. It turns deep and passionate, leaving me breathless. I moan into his mouth and he finally breaks the kiss, his lips sliding toward my ear.

"My name's Liam," he whispers. Is this not allowed? There's something thrilling about breaking the rules of anonymity.

Liam pulls away to sit up on his knees and adjusts me on his makeshift lap. My ass rests on his thighs as he uses my hips like handles. He pulls me down on each upward thrust, his cockhead hitting deep.

"Fuck. Your pussy feels so good, kitten."

I'd say the same of his cock if I were capable of words. My hands twist in the sheets as he surges deep. Using my pussy like a cocksleeve. Taking his pleasure. I'm stretched wide, my pink lips wrapping around his plunging cock. Sweat beads his brow, making his delicious scent thicker in the room.

"Don't stop," I beg him. I want this. I want his sperm. His baby. We're going to make a beautiful child together.

"I'm not stopping till you're dripping," he promises.

I'm lost to my heat as he ruts me. Fucks me deep and hard. Ignores my cries with each shallow orgasm until his swelling knot catches on my pubic bone. Until he can't pull out anymore.

He buries himself deep, his head dropped down to watch his cock pulse inside me. We both stare, enraptured, as he pumps me full. His knot fully inflates, stoppering me up. Locking all that healthy alpha seed inside.

"Come for me, kitten. Soak up all this seed." He grunts with satisfaction and thumbs my clit, rubbing me until I'm panting and writhing on his cock.

I come, walls fluttering weakly around his cock and knot. He kicks one more time inside me, one last rush of semen draining from his balls.

"That's a good girl."

He collapses on top of me, his weight heavy but nice. We're both covered in sweat. He strokes my tangled hair. That's nice. I haven't been held after sex in a long time.

I drift off, exhausted and satisfied. For now, anyway. A heat's never fully satisfied until it's over. I'm barely aware of his knot deflating and his cock disengaging. He pulls away, then spreads my pussy wide to watch his cum drip down the crack of my ass. It soaks into the bed, mingling with my slick. Satisfied I've been well seeded, he turns me on my side and collapses behind me, spooning me.

It's strangely more intimate than the sex, or even the kissing. But I'm too tired and happy to say anything about how odd it is for my sperm donor to cuddle me.

THE RUMBLE OF A PURR BETWEEN MY LEGS WAKES ME. LIAM licks my pussy, his tongue darting through my folds to clean away old slick and cum. Making room for a fresh load.

"Mmm." I arch into it, reaching down to play with his hair while he eats me out. His tongue rolls over my clit, and then he sucks me into his mouth. "Fuck, that's good." My hand tightens into a fist in his hair, trapping his head between my thighs.

He purrs, his mouth still suctioned around my clit, and I'm lost in my heat again. He works an orgasm out of me, then ignores my whining to surface for air.

"You need more cum," he tells me.

I let Liam position me how he wants me, content to stay limp and boneless as he puts me on my hands and knees. He takes up the traditional breeding pose behind me.

The bed sheets are cool and refreshing under my flushed cheek as he pulls my ass higher into the air. The mattress dips as he gets into position. His cock brushing over my slit, coating himself in my slick. Notching at my entrance, then plunging in deep.

"Oh, fuck," I cry out, squeezing my eyes closed and fisting my hands in the twisted sheets. He's deeper than before. Like he's trying to fuck himself directly into my womb.

Liam sets a rough, brutal pace. Rutting me. Our skin slaps together, making a filthy staccato. He grunts and fists an ass cheek in each palm, stretching me wide so he can watch his cock be swallowed by my eager pussy.

"Fuck, Kitty Kat," he moans. "I didn't know pussy could be so damn good."

His praise makes me blush. And the way his scalloped head rubs along my g-spot makes me come. My spasms push him out, but he forces his way back inside my pulsing channel. "No, you're gonna take it. Take all of it."

I squeeze down on purpose, enjoying how it makes him groan. "I want it."

"Yeah, you do. This pretty pussy is begging to drip with cum. Not much longer. I can't resist you."

He makes good on his promise, coming a few thrusts later. Liam pulls his swelling knot free with a wet pop, then forces it back in. The stretch borders on pain, and his next attempt fails. He swells, and swells. Stretching my pussy wide. Plugging his cum in deep. He pulses, his cock shooting thick ropes of cum all over my ripe, open cervix. If this doesn't put a baby in me, it won't be for lack of trying.

"Make yourself come, pretty kitty," he orders.

I work a hand down between me and the mattress and explore where he's buried deep. How his knot fills me completely. My gentle explorations of our tie makes him groan. He spreads my ass cheeks wide, and I feel him pulse inside me again. Another dribble of fresh alpha cum.

My fingers brush over my swollen, tender clit. I roll it in familiar circles, touching myself exactly how I like it. I come, pussy spasming around his too big knot, my face buried in the scent filled nest.

We smell right together. Like a snow covered wood and a warm fire. Like Christmas cookies and a decorated tree.

"That's good, sweetheart. Good job taking another load." He pats me on the ass and runs his hands lightly over my back, petting me.

"Will you purr for me?" I ask, shy about the request.

He purrs, that deep alpha rumble that makes me feel safe. It rattles through all of our points of connections. Massages deep into my bones until I'm boneless. My eyes close, and I sleep.

THIS TIME IT'S ME WHO WAKES HIM. I STUDY HIS FACE WHILE HE sleeps. He's big. So broad chested and hairy, like most alphas are. Faint laugh lines and the gray at his temples make me happy. I can't imagine doing this with a twenty-year-old. That would be so awkward.

His cock plumps in my hand as I stroke it to life until it's pointing up. He wakes up when I straddle him, his cockhead dragging over my slick pussy.

"I'm sorry," I say as I notch him at my entrance and slide down. "I couldn't wait." Lifting up, I slam back down and grind my needy clit on his base. "I need you." Need him deep, scratching this relentless itch. Need my empty pussy filled with cum.

Liam grabs my hips and holds me still, ignoring my whimper of distress. Then he plants his heels and fucks up into me, taking over. He bounces me on his dick, gripping my hips to keep me in place.

"I've got what you need," he promises.

I collapse on his chest and bury my nose in the hair between his pecs. His scent and the faint rumble I can feel but not hear soothes me. The thick cock in my pussy appeases the rest.

"Fuck, I can't get enough of you," he groans. "Of this pretty cunt."

"More," I demand. All I can think of is his virile alpha cum. Dripping white ropes of it. Filling me. Stuffing me. Dripping out of me. His sperm meeting with my egg and giving me the baby I've longed for my whole life.

I rake a hand through his chest hair and writhe against him, my desperation breaking his rhythm. "I need this." My hips rock against him in the pursuit of pleasure.

Liam's hand encircles my wrist, and he bends my arm behind my back, pinning it there. His hips buck, jarring me out of my focus. He wrests control from me, and resumes his pounding from below.

"Be a good girl and take it then," he warns me with a growl.

My eyes slide closed as I let him take control. He fucks me hard. Fast. More roughly than I could manage. I love it. Love being put in my place. Of having an alpha who's not afraid to rut me properly. I'm not made of glass. "Yes."

"Are you ready for me to breed you?" he asks.

My pussy tightens around his girth. "Yes. Put a baby in me."

His fingers tighten around my wrist, and the force of his thrusts bounce me, my breasts and thighs jiggling with each smack.

He comes, knot swelling, cock jerking, balls emptying. And then he grinds me on his knot. Rubs my pussy against his body until I cry out. When he lets go of his hold on my wrist, I collapse against his chest. I pass out draped over him.

THE NEXT TIME I COME TO, I'M BEING LOWERED INTO A WARM bath. "Shh, you're okay," he says when I startle awake.

My heat-slowed thoughts muddle along enough to string a two-word sentence together. "The sticker."

"It's waterproof," he reassures me.

Well, he would know. How many times has he donated? He bathes me, taking care between my thighs where the sensitive skin's chapped and raw. That's from his beard, I think. I have vague memories of straddling his face and making him eat me out again. Not that he complained.

I'd be embarrassed, but he's been just as demanding with his rutting. Heats make animals of us both.

His gentle washing leaves me hot and ready, and I moan, biting my lip, while arching against his hand. He chuckles. "Such a needy pussy."

"Yes." I wrap an arm around his neck and drag him into the bath with me.

He lets me, although the tub is barely big enough for it. It's oversized, but he's still an alpha. We end up flipped with him under me. I ride his lap, the water splashing over the rim of the tub with our thrusts.

Liam grabs one of my breasts and brings it to his mouth, laving the tip with his tongue before sucking. I groan and rock, rubbing my clit against his pubic bone. His abdominals tense as I use him.

When I come, pussy clenching, he bites my nipple. My mouth drops open with a ragged moan. He only lets go once my pussy's stopped throbbing. He sits up and leans me back, working me on his cock.

Our eyes lock, and the moment is more intimate than it has any right to be. He's my sperm donor. Not my lover. But when he comes and his knot swells, none of that matters.

"You're an insatiable little thing," he teases me once we're both panting and spent. "How do you pack all that horniness in such a small package?"

I rub wet hands over my body, teasing out the ache he bit into my breasts. They're tender from the heat and fertility meds.

"Afraid you can't keep up, old man?" I tease him back. He's older than me if I remember his profile correctly.

Liam grins, his eyes glinting dangerously. "Oh, now you've done it." He grips my ass and gets his legs under him, then stands.

I shriek with laughter as he carries us, soaking wet, to the nest. Our tie pulls at my core with every step. "Not the nest!" Ignoring me, he lays me down. "Now it's all wet," I pout.

"It was already soaked with your slick." He stays upright, standing between my legs as I lie on my back.

"And your cum."

He thumbs my clit and arches one brow, then looks to the side and grins. Twisting, he reaches for something. "If you can think enough to be sassy, then I'm not rutting you properly."

"What are you—"

Mechanical vibrations burst to life, and he brings my abandoned vibrator into view from where it had gotten lost in the nest at some point. *He charged it?* Liam brings the vibrating tip to my clit and I see stars.

"Oh, fuck. It's too much," I tell him, squirming. But I'm trapped on his knot. There's nowhere to go.

"You can take it, kitty cat. Come on my knot. Milk me. Show me how much you want my baby."

He's ruthless as he teases my clit with the vibrator. Even when I come, he doesn't stop. Pleasure turns into oversensitized pain, and still he doesn't relent. After two orgasms, my clit goes a bit numb.

"I can't." I can't handle another.

"Let me show you what I'm famous for."

He rubs the vibrator in circles and changes the rhythm to a rapid pulse. Impossibly, I come again. And again. I can't think. Can't speak. Can't do more than moan and writhe and come on his cock. Each flutter of my pussy makes his cock pulsate. Fills me with another spurt of cum.

Liam's hips pump, teasing his swollen knot at my entrance. He can't pop it free, can't push it deeper, but that doesn't stop him from rocking.

My belly is full and tight. The results of his insane efforts are physically visible. There's a small pouching of distention. And still, my body adapts. Stretches. Takes it.

I come again, gasping, while tears leak from the corners of my eyes.

"That's good, sweet girl. Just a little more. I know you can do it."

I can't. My heart is pounding in my chest. My breathing is ragged. My clit vacillates between throbbing and numb. And throughout all of this delicious torment, my pussy strangles his cock. How does he have any cum left in him? His balls have to be drained at this point, rut or not.

After orgasm number seven, he clicks the vibrator off and tosses it aside. I'm panting. Words are beyond me. All I can do is twitch with aftershocks.

A hand presses lightly on my lower belly. Over the bulge he made. I groan. I'm so full—it's a miracle I haven't burst.

Once his knot deflates, Liam pulls out and bends my knees to my chest. He's keeping the cum inside me for as long as possible.

If this doesn't do it, I don't know what will.

When a dribble of cum and slick drips down my ass, Liam scoops it up and shoves it back inside me.

"There we go, kitten," he purrs. "That's a good girl."

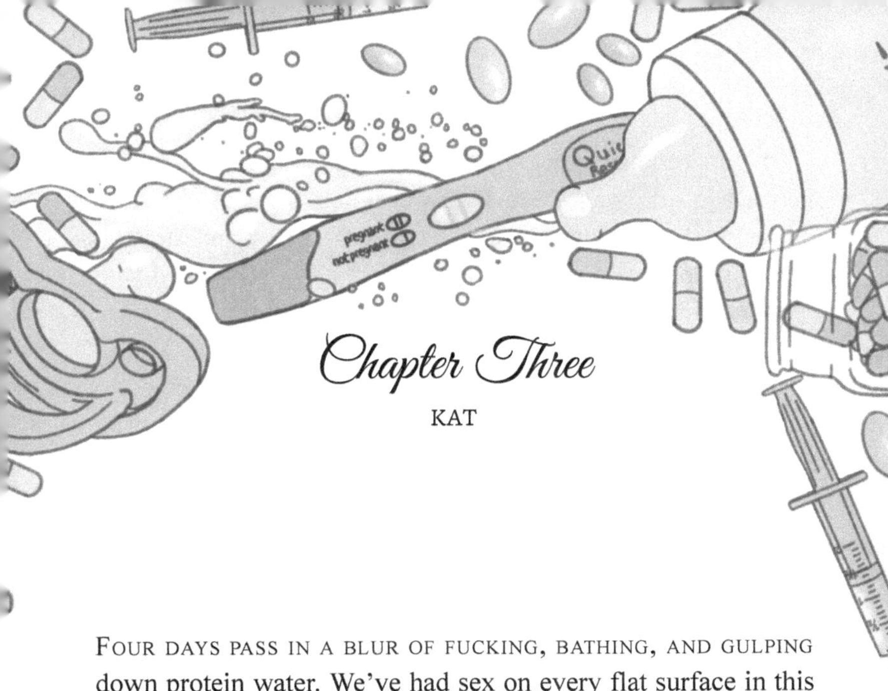

Chapter Three

KAT

Four days pass in a blur of fucking, bathing, and gulping down protein water. We've had sex on every flat surface in this room, and a few of the vertical ones. I'm less feverish and my thoughts are clearer.

So I do what I've been wanting to do ever since I first laid eyes on Liam and his beautiful cock. I slide down his legs and take him into my mouth. While he's soft, I can fit more of him inside me. I swirl my tongue around his head.

He tastes good. Like sex and sin, and decadent pheromones. His cock plumps in my mouth until I can't take him to the root anymore. When fingers card through my knotted hair, I notice he's awake.

"Kat, you don't have to," he says.

But this isn't for him. I've missed sucking cock. I always loved the velvety slide of skin between my lips. Playing with all that softness over such hardness. Pushing my tongue into a weeping slit. I palm his big, heavy balls and roll them gently in my hand.

"You don't… Fuck. That's good. You're good at sucking cock."

I pop off his cock, enjoying the way a string of saliva connects his dripping tip to my lower lip. "I want to. Your cock is perfect." It was made to be worshiped. Thick and straight, with a slight upward curve. His tip is red and well formed with a wide corona. I press his cock to his belly and trace his ridge with my tongue.

"Well… don't let me stop you then. If you really want to."

I let my eyes go half-lidded as he stares at me. I bring his tip to my mouth again and suck. His eyes flutter shut and his breath stutters into a low purr.

With a hand wrapped tight around his base, I suck his tip into my mouth and jerk his length. Use his excess skin to massage his shaft, making a tight ring of my fingers. Milking him. My jaw aches—I'm out of practice—but I keep going.

His breathing stutters and his purr gets deeper. His cock thickens, the knot at his base swelling against the heel of my palm. His balls pull up tight.

"I'm… Fuck, I'm coming."

Ignoring his warning, I take him as deep as I can and squeeze his knot. Pulsing. Mimicking a fluttering pussy. His perineum jerks, and the first lash of cum strikes the roof of my mouth. He's salty and musky with a hint of his pheromones. Crisp, herbal pine. The more he comes, the sweeter he gets. The more I like the way he tastes.

I gather it all in my mouth, swallowing every drop, then lick him clean. And I purr while I do it. Until he's a limp mess underneath me.

Once he's bone dry, I pull off his cock and give the split in his head one last swipe of my tongue to make sure I got it all.

"Fuck, kitten. That was so good. Come here. Let me return the favor. I want one last taste before they make me go."

I didn't suck his cock to get my pussy licked, but I won't say no. I crawl up his body and settle my knees on either side of his head. He nuzzles between my thighs, his nose sliding between my folds.

His mouth is warm and wet. He sucks my lips into his mouth and darts his tongue inside my core. He purrs while he licks, and I bury my hands in his tangled curls as he eats me out.

When his tongue moves to my clit, I'm ready. It's sore and swollen, but he's gentle as he sucks me, licking patterns around my clit. Almost reverent. Pressure builds in my pelvis, winding tighter and tighter. Desperate and needy, I ride his face. All concerns about his ability to breathe are gone. He'll figure it out. And I need to come.

Balanced on the precipice of release, I tense. And then pleasure washes through me. I cry out, riding the waves. Riding his tongue. He laps up my slick and licks me through my aftershocks until I'm clean.

Once my heartbeat and breathing have steadied, I climb off him and collapse into the nest.

He reaches over and drags me against him, our hot naked bodies pressed flush.

"You're pregnant." He lets out a shaky breath and smiles. "We made a baby."

I tense, and he sits up, his brow furrowed with concern.

"You can't possibly tell that yet. It's too early," I protest.

"I can," he says. "I'm an alpha. I can tell. Isn't this… This is what you wanted, right?"

Emotion overwhelms me. Of course it is. But also… it isn't. I was the girl who always dreamed of finding her pack. Getting mated. Having babies. The cliche omega who wanted to be a homemaker. Instead, my pack rejected me. I couldn't move past the lost pregnancies. Didn't want to give up. They were tired of the heartache. So they moved on without me. I never planned to be a single mother. But I'd rather have a baby alone than never have one at all.

"It is. I'm just nervous. What if it doesn't... stick?" I've lived through it before. Even when it hurt so bad I thought it might kill me.

His thumb makes circles on my thigh. He pulls me closer and tucks my head under his chin, and then he purrs. It's comforting. "Nobody can predict the future. But if it helps, they told me I have grade A swimmers."

My lips turn up in a smile while my head rises and falls with his breathing. His heart beats a steady rhythm under my cheek. "Is that so?"

"Yeah." He rubs my arm, my back. "They basically said my sperm are really smart. They know which way to swim. And if it doesn't work out, I wouldn't mind trying again. You know, I wasn't expecting this. To like you, I mean. But I do. Do you think..."

He doesn't finish his sentence.

"It's good to hear that I didn't pick stupid sperm," I say, trying to lighten the mood again.

We had fun, and I like him too. More than I should, considering I'm paying him for his sperm. He's a donor, not a hookup. He's not my alpha.

Am I really pregnant? I smile and sit up. My hand goes to my lower belly, though there's nothing to feel yet. "Will they tell you if it sticks or... doesn't?"

Liam frowns, his eyebrows pinching together. "Of course. I—"

The door lock buzzes, and I have enough time to grab a blanket and hug it to my chest as a nurse walks in. "Hi. Sorry to barge in, but if your heat's over, we need to turn this room over. We had another patient go into their heat cycle early."

"Oh, of course," I answer. The soft moment fades and grim

reality sets in. Liam isn't my lover, and this isn't my home. It's a fertility clinic, and he's my sperm donor. An enthusiastic one, but still only a donor. I got what I paid for, and now it's time to leave.

"I need to find my clothes." I get out of bed and run a hand through my snarled hair, looking around. The room is a mess. There are blankets and pillows scattered everywhere.

Liam extracts his gray sweatpants from the nest. I don't remember pulling them into it or building one. My memory of the last four days is spotty. I get dressed, grateful the nurse busies herself with putting on a pair of gloves and stripping the bed. I shove my blankets from home and vibrator into my bag.

He's already gone by the time I'm ready to go. A pang of disappointment hits me, but then I chastise myself for it. Of course he left. He's earned the break after what I put him through. I leave, thanking the nurses and staff as I go, my face tomato red. How many of them watched me get railed for four days straight? Listened to me come? Watched my heartbeat spike with every orgasm?

They're professional and friendly, but busy as I leave. This is another day at work for them.

I dig my car keys out of my purse and unlock my car, blasting the AC and rolling down the windows. My phone is dead. I plug it into the charger and start driving. When I'm halfway home, a bunch of text messages and missed calls come in. Most are from Jen, a few are from Chelsea with pictures of Waffles in amusing places or wearing funny outfits, and one is from my editor saying she finished the manuscript and sent the invoice.

The first thing I do is text Chelsea that I'm headed home and won't need her to come by after her classes today. The second to call Jen. My best friend answers on the second ring.

"Bitch, I am dying for details," she says.

"I'm driving home now. Can't wait to brush my hair and shower. I look like roadkill."

"How'd it go?"

There's a flash of memory of Liam purring for me when a cramp got bad. I can still smell him on my skin. Part of me wants to put off the shower as long as possible so I don't wash his scent off me. But the more rational part of me knows it's best to move on. I'll probably never see him again. Hopefully. If I do, it's because this cycle failed.

"It was great. Different from what I expected, but good. I got to meet my donor."

"Oooh. Is he cute?"

"He is. And nice, and funny." *And great at eating pussy, but she doesn't need to hear that.*

"I'm glad it worked out well for you. When will you find out the results?" she asks.

"Next week. I have to make an appointment to get blood work drawn."

I can hear her kids in the background, and sure enough, a minute later Jen says she has to go.

Waffles clings to my side when I get home. He follows me into the bathroom and sits on the counter while I shower. Once I'm clean and my hair is combed out, I take special care to put thick unscented lotion on my inner thighs where I'm chaffed.

After, I grab some broth and crackers and a ginger ale and plant my ass on the couch with a cozy blanket. Everything else can wait until tomorrow. Waffles joins me, settling in my lap, and we find something good to watch. Heats always take it out of me. And I have a lot of sleep to catch up on over the next couple of days.

THE FERTILITY MONITOR BECKONS ME LIKE A SIREN'S LURE every time I go to the bathroom to pee. It doesn't help that I work from home, so I see it constantly. The urge to pee on a stick gets so bad that I have to shove it into a drawer so I don't waste the expensive test sticks.

By the time the clinic sends me an automated appointment reminder for my blood work, my resolve breaks. Am I a bit nauseous? My appetite's been poor. Are my breasts more tender than usual? Every potential symptom becomes my latest hyper-fixation. They're probably all side effects from the progesterone supplement they called in for me. Although they don't think my progesterone is the problem, it's better safe than sorry.

Waffle meows and paws at the bathroom door, and I'm jarred out of my staring contest with the drawer. One test won't hurt. The appointment's tomorrow, anyway. And if it's not good news, I'd rather find out in private. That way I can spend all night crying and planning what to do for my next heat.

I dig the fertility monitor out of the drawer and find a pregnancy test strip, then pee and stick it in and wait. Minutes stretch into an eternity. By the time it beeps, I'm a nervous wreck. I glance at the screen.

There's a smiley face with the word pregnant under it.

"Oh, fuck." I stare at it to make sure it's real, then pinch myself to make sure I'm not dreaming.

It's real. I'm pregnant. For now, anyway. My happiness is cautious. But I finish up in the bathroom and text Jen to share the news.

KAT

I'm pregnant

JEN

OMG! Already?

Good job sperm donor!

I told you Josh was the problem

I don't know why he refused to get tested

I go to the clinic tomorrow for the official test

How often do you have to go?

Every day for three days then weekly

They have to make sure my hormones are doubling

Exciting! I'm so happy for you <3

When do you get to see the baby?

My OB made me wait ten weeks

It's torture

They do a scan at six weeks

Our discussion turns to other stuff. My new book, and her disaster playdate with a new mom from her local baby group. Her responses get slower, so I tell her I'll talk to her tomorrow. With three mates and two kids under five, her life is chaos.

I smile to myself and stare at the digital smiley face. I can't wait for a little chaos of my own.

Chapter Four

LIAM

I SMELL HER BEFORE I SEE HER. DIRTY, SEXY CHRISTMAS cookies. The cutout kind that's covered in a pretty smear of colored icing and sugar sprinkles. Her scent is thicker. I don't know how to describe it, but she smells pregnant.

My groin tightens as the door opens and the cloud of her thick pheromones punches me in the sinuses. Nervous, I stand up out of habit. My dad always taught me to stand when your date appears, even though this isn't technically a date.

She glances my way and appears startled, her eyes widening.

Shit, should I have stayed seated? Man, this is awkward.

Unsure of what to do, I sit back down. "Hi." It's a lame greeting after six long weeks of not being told anything except that her blood work was good.

"Have a seat on the exam table," the ultrasound tech says. She grabs a patient gown and paper blanket from a basket on a shelf. "I'll give you a few minutes to change. Everything from the waist down comes off."

"Umm…" Kat takes them.

The ultrasound tech leaves, shutting the door behind her.

I didn't realize she'd have to get naked for this. Don't they put the goop and stuff on the belly? I stand and wipe my palms on my jeans.

Kat hesitates. Like I haven't seen every inch of her already. Licked every inch with my tongue.

"I won't watch," I tell her. Turning around, I stare at the medical poster on the wall.

"Thanks."

After a brief hesitation, I hear the rustling of clothing, then the creak of the exam table. I wait until she tells me it's okay to look. She's cuter than I remembered. Expressive hazel eyes and brown hair. I wonder if our kid's gonna have her eyes. That thought makes me smile.

"How have you been?" I ask to break the ice.

"Good." she says, raking her hair out of her face. "Puking every morning and afternoon, but… That's a good sign. I'm sorry, I didn't expect you to be here for this."

"Why wouldn't I be?" I ask, puzzled. I wouldn't miss this for the world. My kid's first ultrasound. I hope they give me a print out so I can put it on the fridge for Gabriel and Matthew. The clinic wouldn't let them come.

She opens her mouth to say something, but the ultrasound tech's arrival interrupts her. The tech pulls her machine over and sits, explaining everything that's about to happen. I watch her put a condom on the ultrasound's dildo-shaped attachment. She lubes it up and puts it under Kat's paper blanket.

Oh. So that's why they had her change.

All three of us focus on the tech's screen. It looks like TV static to me, but the tech spends a lot of time taking snapshots and marking measurements with digital calipers.

"Is everything good?" I ask.

"I'm taking measurements for the doctor," the tech says. "He'll go over the results with you."

"Oh, okay." I deflate in my seat. I thought I'd see a tiny baby, but I guess it's still really early. All I can make out among the static is a blob and a smaller blob.

The tech hits a button on the machine, and then a rapid fluttering whooshing fills the room. Kat and I both perk up at the sound. "Is that—"

"That's a good heartbeat," Kat interrupts. "It's fast."

Fast is... good?

The tech takes a recording, then says she's done. She pulls the ultrasound probe out and disposes of the condom, then hands Kat a stack of napkins. "You can get dressed. The doctor will be in shortly."

At the door, the tech pauses and looks back over her shoulder. She smiles at me. "Good job, Daddy."

Kat sits up and pulls her heels out of the exam table's stirrups. "Oh, he's not the dad, he's the sperm donor."

My smile drops off my face, and the ultrasound tech freezes. "What?" I ask her. "I'm the father."

She better not tell my kid that I'm their sperm donor. I'm going to be there. For every baseball game and school dance. Each scraped knee and scribbled drawing.

Kat looks at me like I've grown a second head and sits up, her knees pressed together. "You're a sperm donor. I picked your profile out of a donation book."

Alarmed, I glance at the ultrasound tech for help. "No. I signed up for co-parenting. My pack doesn't have a breeding partner."

"Your pack," Kat says, her eyes getting bigger by the second. "No. What? You're mistaken. I came here for a sperm donor."

We both stare at the ultrasound tech. "I'm gonna go get the doctor. Wait here," she says, then dips out.

Kat jumps off the exam table and scoops the gel from

between her legs, then chucks the napkins in the trash. This time I don't bother to turn my back while she changes. She pulls on her panties, shorts, and sandals. Then she takes the patient gown off and throws it into the wicker basket in the corner.

"What are you talking about?" she asks.

"I didn't sign up for sperm donation," I tell her. "That baby's half mine."

"No. Oh, God, no. What the fuck? This is not happening." She drags her hands through her hair, pushing it away from her face. The color drains from her, and she wobbles where she stands.

"Sit down before you pass out." I put a hand on her arm so I can grab her and keep her from hitting her head if she faints. I put a little alpha command in it so she knows I'm serious. This woman has my baby in her belly. Her wellbeing is my highest concern.

Kat plops her ass into the chair next to me. I try to talk to her, but nothing I say to her stirs her out of her shock. It's like she doesn't hear me.

A while later, the door opens and an older, balding man with glasses appears. "Please follow me. We'll talk in my office."

We follow him into his office where he shuts the door then motions for us to sit. He takes up his padded leather chair behind the desk. "I'm Dr. Fugo, and I'm sorry to have to explain that there's been a clerical error with your paperwork."

A lump forms in my throat and I swallow past it. "What exactly does that mean?"

"Ms. Daniels came here for sperm donation as a single parent. She matched with you, a co-parent seeker, by accident. We're investigating this to find out what happened. Our computer system is designed to prevent this type of error. All of our donors are codified by donation type. Co-parents go through a rigorous meet and greet before their match is verified. Ms. Daniels, can you tell me about your initial visit here? Is Mr. O'Donnell the donor you picked?"

"Yes." Her voice is faint, like she's barely aware of what's happening. "The binders…"

Dr. Fugo pulls two files from a cabinet behind his computer. "I found your paperwork from the day you came in for treatment. The consent forms you signed are for co-parenting."

Kat frowns and leans forward. "No. I… I was in heat. Whatever she gave me, I signed."

A sick knot of dread builds in my stomach. They can't. They can't take my baby from me. It's half mine. I didn't sign up to be some anonymous sperm donor. I point at her still flat stomach and stare the doctor down. "That baby is mine."

She looks at me, her expression turning murderous. "You can't have my baby. You have no idea what I've gone through to have it." Kat asks him, "what does this mean for me?"

"Legally, this baby belongs to both of you," Dr. Fugo says. "I know this is a shock. This isn't what anyone planned. And we'll be investigating our computer system and talking to the staff who were here that day. To make sure this never happens again. For now, why don't you go home? Your baby is healthy and developing perfectly. You can switch to your regular OBGYN at this point in the pregnancy, Ms. Daniels. The girls up front will call you to set up the appointment. Here's the packet I give to all new parents. Read it. Sleep on it. And most importantly, talk to each other."

We're shown the door. Once we're outside and standing on the sidewalk, I study her. She's small. The top of her head comes to my chest. She's petite but curvy with nice, wide hips. Good babymaking hips.

She glances at me with a mutinous expression like I planned this or tricked her. If anything, I'm the one who feels tricked.

She's carrying my baby and there's nothing I can do about it. I feel powerless. What am I supposed to do? Watch her leave with my kid? A child she didn't mean to share with me?

What if she decides she doesn't want to be tied to me and my pack?

"Please don't do anything to hurt my baby," I beg her.

She makes a disgusted face. "God, I would never."

"Good." Relief washes over me, easing the knot in my stomach. "Because I'm Catholic."

"Oh, fuck my life," Kat says, running her hands through her hair again. "This is a fucking disaster. I have to go."

When am I gonna see her again? "Give me your number so we can talk about this." The clinic wouldn't give it to me. It's been driving me up the wall.

She hesitates before she gives in. We add each other's numbers in our phones.

"We should sit down and talk," I say.

"Not today." She rubs at her head like she has a headache. "I need to go home and vomit."

Right. She did say that she'd been puking a lot. That's normal. I think. "Okay. You'll tell me if you need anything? I don't care what it is or what time of day it is. If you and the baby need anything, I want to know. You're eating healthy, right? I think there's stuff on that list you can't eat."

"I know." She sighs and fishes her keys out of her purse. "We'll talk… later. Right now I just can't."

I watch her walk off with that promise and hope that I won't regret letting her go. But I can't do anything about it. It's not like alphas kidnap omega brides from rival tribes anymore. Once her car, a nice and safe sedan, leaves the parking lot, I head to my truck.

How the hell am I going to explain this clusterfuck to my pack?

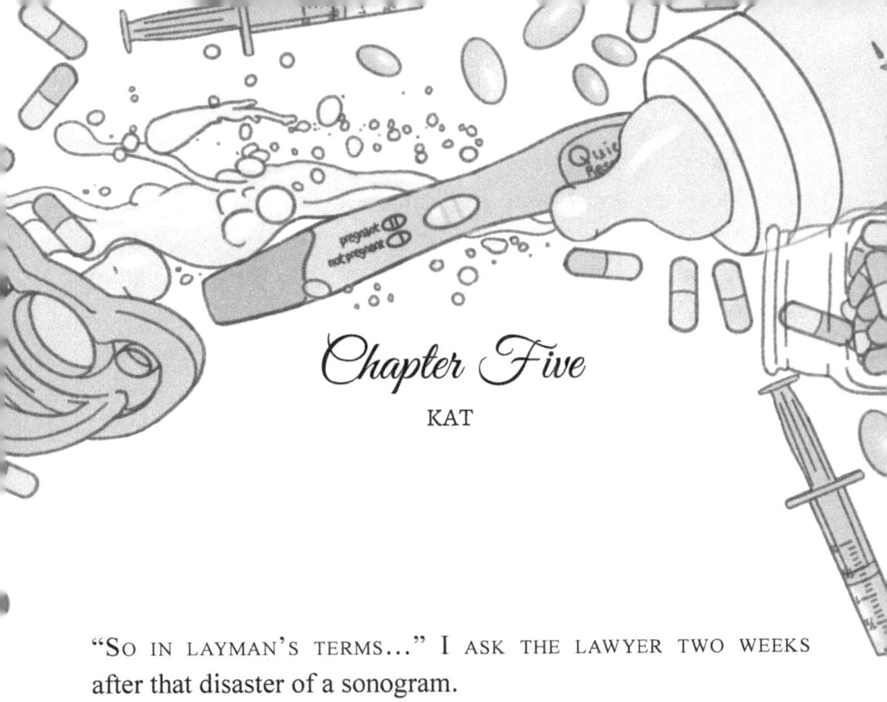

Chapter Five

KAT

"So in layman's terms..." I ask the lawyer two weeks after that disaster of a sonogram.

She puts her pen down and settles back in her chair. "It would be an extremely difficult case to win, and it would take a lot of time and money. I'm willing to represent you and try, but I can't guarantee the outcome. The courts don't like to take parental rights away if a parent will fight for partial custody of their child."

"But he was only supposed to be a sperm donor."

"I know." Her eyes soften, but her frown is grim. "And I'd start by arguing that a contract signed while in the throes of estrus isn't legally binding. Your mental state was altered. But they'll counter that the mistake was yours at the initial appointment when you were not in estrus. That you picked a match from the wrong binder."

"But they weren't labeled."

"Which is a system error on the clinic's fault. If you wanted to sue them for damages, that would be a much easier case to argue. Their negligence and system issues caused you real emotional distress."

I shake my head. "They refunded me the fees. And I don't need more money. I want my baby. He can't take my baby from me."

"He can't," she agrees. "But he can sue you for partial custody. A judge will probably grant it. I looked into him and his pack. No arrest records. A solid work history. The alpha owns his own small business, which employs about twenty people. And his packmates are clean. The Brazilian beta's family immigrated here legally, and he's a permanent resident. He works at the hospital. The other beta has several lawyers in his immediate family. Their lawyer will argue they're all model citizens and pillars of society. I can't find any angle to dig into them. I wouldn't advise bringing a suit against his pack for full custody if you believe they'll fight it."

They will. "So I'm fucked."

"Think about it and decide what you'd like to do. If you decide to sue the clinic, I can start that paperwork."

Defeated, I take the business card she offers me and head out to my car. I sit in the shade and let the air blast my face. Then I grip the steering wheel and scream. People walking down the sidewalk stare, but move along. Nobody stops to ask the crazy, screaming omega why she's losing her damn mind.

My phone rings, and Jen's name flashes across my dash. I answer it.

"What'd the lawyer say?" she asks.

"That I'm fucked. He owns half of my baby and he can sue me for partial custody."

"Motherfucker."

All the steam goes out of me, leaving me depleted. "It's not his fault. It's the clinic's."

And a bit of mine, I guess. I didn't realize I grabbed a binder I shouldn't have. And I barely glanced at the paperwork I signed. But who expects an omega in heat to read fine print legalese? It's ridiculous.

"You should sue them," Jen says.

I don't have the energy to deal with a lawsuit. The pregnancy has sapped my strength and brain cells. I take three or four naps a day and going through my editor's suggestions is like pulling teeth. Her notes are good, but I can't focus well enough to think straight before my mind wanders or I need to puke again.

"I don't want to sue them." I rub my flat stomach absent-mindedly.

"I can't believe you got dicked down by an alpha and didn't tell me," Jen says, sounding offended.

"I thought it was the reason why everyone says his clinic's the best!"

"Like a secret menu?" she asks. "But instead of fancy coffee, it's dicks?"

The sheer ridiculousness of it makes me laugh, and then Jen joins in. The harder she laughs, the harder I laugh. Until my eyes water and I can hardly breathe, I rest my forehead against my steering wheel. None of this is funny, but if I don't laugh, I'll cry.

"You know what I think?" Jen asks.

"What?"

"You should go talk to them. Find out what they want. What if it's not that bad? You do three days one week, they do four, then it switches. Could be nice. Sometimes I'd kill to have a long weekend alone with my pack."

But that's the difference between us. She's got a pack of wonderful men who adore her. Me? All I have are my books and my cat.

Hot tears prick at my eyes and I sniff them back. I hate the idea of handing my baby off to strangers every week. But she's right that I can't avoid them forever. Ignoring this problem won't make it go away. "You're right. I need to talk to them."

"Let me know what they say. And this time, don't leave out a single detail. Okay, I'll let you go. Bye."

"Bye." Glancing in the rearview mirror, I pull out of the parking lot. The lawyer might not have been able to help me, but she did find the name of the business he owns. O'Donnell's. It's the Irish pub on Main Street.

I drive across town and pull into their parking lot and stare at their sign. The outside is painted white and dark green. The gilded wooden sign with a green shamrock hangs over the door. Music pumps through their doorway as an older beta couple leaves with a white box of leftovers in their hands.

The waitresses are wearing work shirts and black pants. They look up from their dry erase seating chart to ask me if I want to sit at the bar or a table.

My eyes snap to Liam instantly, despite the crowd. Like an invisible string connects us. He's standing behind the bar, a black towel tossed over his shoulder. He smiles at a patron while he pours them a beer, putting it down so the foam can settle. He's as handsome as I remember.

"The bar," I tell them, walking past the hostess stand. I find an empty stool and settle onto it, then wait for him to get to me.

Liam makes his rounds around the bar, pulling beers and mixing cocktails. He takes a plate of food from a runner and sets the gravy-covered fries down for a customer. He works quickly and efficiently, his large hands palming several stacked plates at once.

I'm only now realizing that coming here like this was a mistake. I should have called, not ambushed him at work. But if I'd thought about it for too long, I'd have chickened out. Like I did every other time, I considered picking up the phone and calling him all week.

He texts me good morning and good night. He's sent me links to pregnancy-safe recipes. And mommy blog articles about staying cool in the summer while pregnant. I haven't texted him back. Not a single time. And that makes me feel guilty.

When he finally sees me, he freezes. Liam recovers quickly, setting a clean glass full of ice in front of me. He taps a button on his soda gun and ginger ale fills the glass. Bubbles pop and fizz in the dark liquid, clinging to the glass wall. He drops a straw in and slides it across the bar.

"How are you?" he asks.

I palm the glass and rub a bead of condensation away. "Good. Shocked, tired, and sick to death of vomiting." I know what he's really asking. "We're fine."

He smiles and his right cheek dimples. It makes him alarmingly attractive. "Good. I'm glad you're both okay."

This isn't his fault, and I realize how unfair this all must be for him. He didn't get what he wanted, either. Now, somehow, we have to figure out how to make this work. "I'm sorry. I shouldn't be bothering you while you're working. I wasn't thinking." I hike my purse up on my shoulder to leave him alone while he's working.

"No, sit! Please. I'm glad you came. We can figure this out. But not here. Come on. I live upstairs. We can talk there." He sets his bar towel down and takes off his black apron. "James, take over for me."

I lean back on my stool. "Wait, you live above the bar?"

"Yeah?"

Is he insane? "You can't raise a baby in a bar!" In my shock, I'm too loud. The people around us stop their conversations and stare. I blush from their scrutiny.

"Good thing I don't live inside the bar then." He opens the hatch that separates the bar from the restaurant and comes around to grip my elbow. "Bring your ginger ale. I think I have some crackers. I read that helps."

He's too bossy, as alphas often are. But I'm eager to get away from his staring patrons. Liam brings me to the back of the pub to a door he unlocks with his key. Behind it, there's a staircase leading up. I follow him. He unlocks another door at the top with the same key.

The apartment above the bar is nicer than I expected. The building is old, but it has a worn, vintage vibe to it that's charming. Thick rugs pad the squeaky hardwood floors. The walls are painted a pretty sage green. Large windows let in light.

"It's not as loud up here as I thought it would be," I say, looking around.

He raps a knuckle on one wall. "The walls are plaster. Good for sound insulation." Then he leaves me in his living room to rummage through his kitchen cupboards. "O'Donnell's was my great-granddad's. Patrick O'Donnell. He immigrated here from Dublin with his parents when he was two. That's a photo of him there right after the pub opened."

I look at the wall beside me, studying his family photos. Most are recent, but some are old. I'm most interested in the ones in black and white and sepia. The oldest is a photo of this bar, but from the 1930s, judging by the clothing and cars. A tall alpha in a brimmed hat lifts a beer up in celebration under the pub's iconic sign. It's a different sign than the one that hangs now, but the symbol carved into it is the same. The photo isn't crisp, but the man has the same dimple as Liam.

"He built it?"

"Bought it near the end of prohibition. Got it for pennies on the dollar after prohibition drove the English-style pub that used to be here out of business. Renovated everything to the studs with his own two hands. Ran it as a social club for all the Irish immigrants until they legalized alcohol again. I'm still untangling his electrical work. Now I know why my dad and granddad never touched it. Can of fucking worms."

I grimace. Bad wiring rises to the top of my concern list. But the other photos on the wall soon distract me. There's Liam standing with two other men, all of them dressed in suits. One has pale skin covered in freckles and curly brown hair, and the other is taller with golden brown skin and perfect white teeth. They're hugging each other and smiling at the camera. The image is too intimate for them to only be friends. His pack?

A cabinet slams shut, and I jolt out of my snooping. He hands me the crackers, and he's right, they do help. I've been living off crackers, toast, and baked potatoes for weeks. I can't wait for the first trimester nausea to subside.

"Thanks." I pop one in my mouth and chew slowly. He looks so happy to have done something for me. I don't have the heart to tell him they're stale. A sip of ginger ale washes it down, and another gets the after taste out of my mouth. "Are these all photos of your family?"

He turns his attention to the wall of photos and I set the stale crackers down on an end table while he's distracted. "Yes. That's my grandfather. This one is him with his pack. That baby is my father. I'm the oldest of five. Those are my brothers and sisters there. And these are my mates, Matthew and Gabriel."

From their height and builds, I'm guessing they're betas. I recall him saying they didn't have a breeding partner.

"How'd you meet?" I ask.

"Matthew and I went to the same college. We shared a math class and I'm terrible with algebra. He offered to tutor me. Not that it improved my grade much. After a few weeks of tutoring and hanging out we spent more time fucking around than studying. I still failed the class. By the end of the semester I didn't care because I'd found my first packmate. Later, we met Gabriel at a world cup tournament. The tickets were a

Christmas present from Matthew's parents. Make sure that in front of Gabriel you call it football, not soccer, or he'll give you a long lecture about it."

My heart twinges with old wounds. Josh plays soccer professionally for the USL. I sat and watched a lot of his games, but I never quite fit in with the other spouses.

"Are you into sports?" Liam asks.

"No." I'm quick to change the subject. "So you own the bar? What do your packmates do?"

"Gabriel is a physician's assistant. Matthew is a banker."

Oh. Those are all very normal jobs. I'm not sure what I was hoping for. Some sign that this pack can't take care of a baby. But a stable pack with triple employment versus a single mother... One who's self-employed with a variable income... Even with my savings, I know which way a judge might lean. The lawyer was right. The stale cracker sits like lead in my stomach.

"What about you?" he asks.

"I'm a writer," I say, keeping it vague.

"Oh, that's so cool. Fiction? Nonfiction? Anything I've read?"

"I doubt it. I write romance novels." I cringe saying it, considering how we met. I'm painfully aware that my personal love life has been a failure. My characters always meet the right person, fall in love, and live a happy life full of bliss and as many babies as they want. But real life doesn't always follow the script. Sometimes happily ever after isn't forever.

His eyebrows shoot up and he smiles, his cheek dimpling again. "Well, now I definitely have to read one. I could learn some tips."

He doesn't need any tips. "I'm not sure you're ready for what I write."

His smile widens into a grin. "You don't know what I'm

into. Is it butt stuff? Kinky? I probably have a pair of fuzzy handcuffs from a bachelor party somewhere."

The fact that his handcuffs are probably fuzzy covered plastic tells me what I need to know. "Something like that."

"Wow. You're really not going to tell me. After I told you all about my family too." He pretends to be hurt, placing a hand to his chest. "The mother of my child is cruel."

His off-the-cuff remark reminds me that I came here for serious reasons. "So… we should talk."

The phone on the wall rings, interrupting what he was about to say. Liam answers it, listening to the voice on the other end. His easy expression becomes serious. "I'll be right there. No, don't call the cops yet. Let me talk to them."

He hangs up and gives me an apologetic look. "I have to go downstairs for a bit and deal with two drunk idiots. Stay here. I'm going to lock the door behind me to make sure you're safe."

He leaves and locks it. I strain to listen for the sounds of a fight or yelling, but the sounds from the bar downstairs are muffled. All I can really hear is the traffic noise from the road out front. I take advantage of his absence to snoop.

There are two bedrooms, a small kitchen, and a bathroom plus the living room. It's small, but cozy. The second bedroom looks like a guest suite that doubles as an office. *Is this where they planned to put the nursery?*

There's nothing egregious. No devil worshiping altar or insect-riddled piles of filth. If anything, they're tidier than me. I have the bad habit of letting dirty dishes pile up in the sink until I remember to load the dishwasher.

After twenty minutes, I'm somehow both bored and anxious. I sit on their couch and pull out my phone, checking my socials and scrolling through the photos and feeds of old friends and older coworkers. My aunt posted another set of really badly angled selfies and pictures of her food. Looks like she's in Miami right now.

The sound of police sirens wail outside. Seems like they ended up having to call the cops. The sun drifts toward the horizon and the boredom makes my eyes harder to open. I try to read a book, but every time I sit down this is what happens. I fall asleep.

A few minutes won't hurt. I'll just close my eyes. His key in the lock will wake me.

The old brown couch smells like them. Like the woods, and a campfire, and the crispness of freshly fallen snow. I lie down, pressing my face into one of their pillows to breathe in the blend of their scents. Minutes later, I'm asleep.

THE SCENT AND POP OF COOKING BACON WAKES ME. CONFUSED and groggy, I sit up. A patterned quilt falls off my shoulder. I grab it before it can slip to the floor. My shoes are gone. Where are my shoes? I find them lined up neatly underneath the coffee table with my purse and phone sitting above them.

"Are you hungry?" a man asks from the kitchen.

I wipe drool off my cheek with the heel of my palm and blush. How the fuck did I not hear him come in? I blink at the beta who's still waiting for an answer. Gabriel. The Brazilian PA. He's wearing fitted black scrubs that show off the breadth of his shoulders and the size of his muscular arms. He flips the bacon with a spatula.

He's cooking breakfast. Shit, what time is it? I glance outside, but it's still dark out. It could be ten at night or four in the morning.

"Breakfast for dinner?" he asks, pointing to his frying pan with his spatula.

Dinner. Thank God. "Where's Liam?" I ask, still waking up. How long was I asleep?

"Dealing with the cops. Nothing big, only a broken stool and some bruises."

That doesn't sound like nothing. "Is that typical?"

He stirs the contents of his pan and grinds salt and pepper over it. "No. Once or twice a year, someone decides to act foolish. But most of the patrons are regulars. They come for the food and a beer after work, not shots and fights."

An actual kettle whistles, and he clicks the burner off, pouring hot water into a mug. He adds a spoonful of honey and a bag of tea and brings it over to me. The label is a popular brand of pregnancy tea. A blend of caffeine-free white tea, ginger, and aromatics that are supposed to soothe nausea.

"My sister swears by this," he says. "She drank it with all three of her babies."

"Thank you." Did they buy this specifically for me? In case I came over? That's sweet.

I blow on the tea to cool it and take a sip. It's a bit spicy but also sweet, and the odd combination goes down easily.

Gabriel makes two plates, then puts covers on the pans on the stove. He joins me on the couch and turns the TV on, pulling up an on-demand soccer game. When I catch sight of an all too familiar logo, I decide it's time to leave.

"I should go." I pull my shoes on and grab my purse.

"You don't have to. We want you to be comfortable here."

They do? Still, it's late and all I want to do is go home and go to bed. "I have to feed my cat. He missed dinner."

"Then I'll walk you out."

I'm disturbing his dinner. It seems like he's home from a long shift. "I'll be fine."

He stands, ignoring me. "Liam will kill me if I don't walk you out. Please, you'd be doing me a favor." His smile is easy and natural. Long dark lashes frame big brown eyes. His slight accent makes his speech interesting.

"Fine." It's easier and quicker to let him walk me down a flight of stairs than argue. I grab my phone and follow him out, down the stairs and through the crowded bar. He walks me all the way outside to my car.

"Wait, Kat! Dammit, excuse me," Liam says, peeling off from the cops parked out front. He runs over to us, and he shares a silent look with Gabriel.

"It was a pleasure to meet you, Kat," Gabriel says, pulling me in for a hug. He releases me quickly while I'm still stunned, then heads inside.

"We didn't get to talk," Liam says.

"You're busy. It's fine. We can talk another day." My keys jingle while I fiddle with them.

"I wanted to ask you if we could start over."

"Start over?"

He takes a deep breath and lets it out slowly. "What if we pretend the clinic never happened? Say it was a date instead? You don't have a pack, right? I do. Let us court you."

Hope blossoms, only to be squashed by reality a moment later. If it weren't for the baby, would they be interested in me? "I'm not joining your pack out of pity."

"It's not out of pity. I meant it when I said I like you. You're cute and funny. You fuck like a wildcat. You smell like a plate of Christmas cookies I want to take a bite out of. And you're carrying my baby. I'm begging you. All I'm asking is for you to give us a chance. And if it doesn't work out, then we tried. We'll settle for friends and co-parents. Please."

I chew my lip and hesitate. The truth is, I'm scared. I don't know what to do. Single parenthood was something I chose out of necessity. Being packless wasn't my choice. Maybe he's right. There's nothing to lose by seeing if we click. If I'd bumped into him at the bookstore and we'd hit it off, I wouldn't have had any qualms about being courted by his pack. They're my age with stable employment and their own place.

The pregnancy complicates everything, but does it need to? My due date is seven months away. That's plenty of time to decide whether this is going to work. Besides, it's not like I have a better idea.

"Okay," I sigh.

"Really?" His eyes widen.

"I'm not making any guarantees," I warn him.

"You won't regret this, I promise. We're gonna be so good to you." Liam cradles my face in his hands and bends down, kissing me.

I'm so surprised by it that my lips part. Liam takes advantage, deepening it. His lips move against mine, kissing me until I'm dizzy. He crowds me against my car and curls over me. My lips part wider and he pushes a little more. Darts his tongue inside and twists it around mine.

Someone wolf whistles from the sidewalk and I blush, but he doesn't stop. His hand gropes around to my backside, and he cups a handful of ass. Pulls me up onto my toes and deeper into the kiss.

By the time we surface for air, my pussy is slick and he has a very visible bulge in his jeans. He wasn't faking his attraction to me or my scent. He really likes me, and the feeling's definitely mutual.

Liam pinches my chin between his thumb and fingers. "Text me back when I text you so I don't worry," he says with a bit of a command. Not quite a bark, though. Alpha commands make the omega in me want to rush to obey and placate. "Please," he adds to soften the order.

"Okay."

"Good." He lets me go and steps back. "Drive safe. Let me know you made it home."

In a daze, I unlock my car and get inside. I make the familiar drive home. When I get there, I ignore his order for a bit, but the command fizzles underneath my skin. It feels naughty. I've always been pretty submissive in bed outside of a heat. Heats make me a bit feral, but ignoring direct orders goes against my nature.

After Waffles gets a belated dinner with some treats to make up for waiting for so long, I can't put the task off any longer. I strip out of my clothes and throw them into the hamper. Then I send him a text telling him that I'm home and going to bed.

Good, he answers. *You need at least eight hours of sleep. Good night, Kitty Kat. Sleep well.*

For the first time in a while, I do.

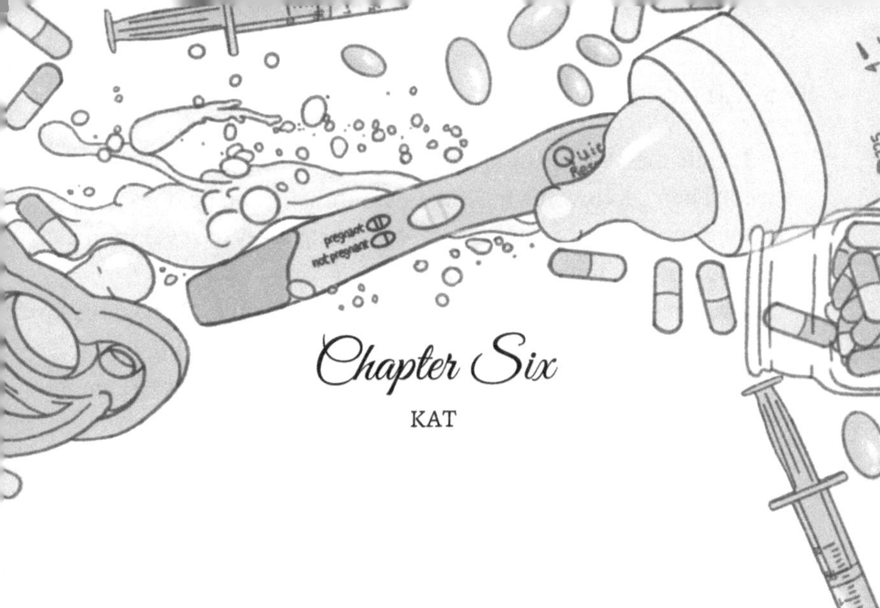

Chapter Six

KAT

I WAKE UP DAMP BETWEEN MY LEGS AND MY FIRST THOUGHT IS panic that it's happened again. I shove a hand down the waistband of my sleep shorts. They come out covered in clear arousal, not blood.

Now that I'm more awake, I'm aware of my pussy being swollen. My clit throbs. I haven't masturbated since the six-week scan when I found out about everything. I was too upset and anxious.

My body makes its needs known. Maybe I'll feel better if I satisfy this need before I get up and get on with my day. I should take advantage of this morning's lack of nausea while I can.

I pull my vibrator from the nightstand drawer and slot it between my thighs. It rumbles to life and I use it to rub my clit, my hips flexing with the urge to grind.

Repositioning it, I tease my entrance and pull up a private browser on my phone. Breeding, pulsating creampie compilations have always been my favorite. I find a good one, a video with lots of male moaning, and watch.

I grab the vibrator and work it in, building up to a faster speed. Then I follow his movements. I thrust when he does. Dig the vibrator in deep on my g-spot when he pauses to revel in the sensation of his partner's pussy.

The man in the porn clip orgasms repeatedly. Cum spills from the woman's swollen pink cunt. She flexes, pushing it out, to show the audience his volume. He comes a lot. Like Liam. But this man's a beta. He doesn't have a knot.

The recent memories of Liam's perfect cock push me over the edge. My orgasm swells, tension pulling taut. My nipples tighten. Breathing shallow, I chase the sensation. Drive the vibrator and its tingling clit tickler in deeper.

The beta in the clip comes again with a guttural moan. His perineum pulses, his balls pulled up tight. I come with him, and then he pulls out. The proof of his pleasure is evident. Cum drips from her, and my pelvis tightens like a hard ball. There's a sense of pressure deep within me. It's something they don't warn you about. That orgasms are different when your uterus isn't empty.

After a minute, the cramp fades. And there's only slick on the vibrator when I pull it out. I close out the browser tab and lie there while the aftershocks settle.

Then I take full advantage of how good I feel today. I go through my morning routine and make myself a breakfast of hash browns and an omelet stuffed with veggies. I still don't have an appetite for meat right now.

My phone chirps, and I check my messages. It's Liam saying good morning and asking how I am. If I'm eating right. Offering to drop off groceries if there's anything I need.

It's sweet. He really wants this baby. It's a relief in a way. My old pack was so burnt out from trying and failing to conceive. Toward the end I wasn't allowed to talk about it. Whenever I did, all we did was fight. If I'm honest with myself,

I can admit that we probably weren't a great match. Our scent match wasn't enough to overcome our different lifestyle plans. A part of me never thought he'd really make it to the pro level in soccer. Although I never would've admitted it.

I send Liam a photo of my breakfast so he'll stop worrying. He sends me back a selfie of him and his packmates in bed. They're shirtless and tangled in the sheets. Liam is packed with alpha muscle and Gabriel clearly spends a lot of time at the gym, but Matthew has more of a wiry build. They're all so different, but they look good together.

Three men. It makes me wonder why he matched with a female omega.

KAT

You didn't want a male omega?

LIAM

Gender doesn't matter to us

Gabriel and I are bi

Matthew is demi and pan

We've all been with women before

When can we go on a date?

What did you have in mind?

Bubble tea

Really?

You don't like it?

I hear the girls talk about it at the bar

Do you even know what it is?

Carbonated tea?

Okay we're definitely getting bubble tea now

Are you busy today?

My schedule is flexible

What time?

The lunch rush dies down around 3

I'll pick you up

What's your address?

After a brief hesitation, I give him my address. Once I'm done with breakfast, I get a bit of work done. And when my phone alarm goes off, I close my manuscript and get ready.

First date butterflies flutter in my stomach. Even though we're doing things backward. This seems more intimate. Probably because we'll be talking. Sex is easy. Especially during a heat. Making a real connection takes work.

My hair is impossible. I haven't done anything with it for three years except throw it up in a ponytail or leave it down. My days of a full face of carefully perfect makeup and blown out hair and push up bras are behind me. I'm not even sure if my makeup is still any good. It's probably all expired.

I video call Jen and prop my phone up while I fuss with my hair. She answers from her spot lying on her living room floor surrounded by brightly colored toys.

"Why are you on the floor?" I ask her while brushing my hair out.

"I stepped on a toy. I'm waiting for the agony to fade. Are you getting ready for your big date?"

"Yeah but I don't know what to do with my hair. I'm so out of practice. I haven't done this in forever."

"Three years isn't forever. But you do need a haircut.

There's nothing wrong with a sleek ponytail. Besides, alphas go crazy about seeing an omega's neck."

My hand goes to my old faded bite marks on instinct. The pack bond has faded, but I'll carry the scar forever. "I can put my hair to the side."

Jen frowns and moves her phone to a different angle. "Might be better to rip that bandage off early."

I know it's something I'll have to tell them about if we're really going to try and make this work. But not today. I want today to be nice.

Her toddler cries in the background, and Jen sits up. "My boss is calling. I want to hear everything when you're done. I'm living vicariously through you right now."

We hang up and I focus on my hair, pulling it all to the side in a low pony. I curl the ends so it looks fancier, then use whatever makeup is salvageable. I keep it light and natural, then change into a floral sundress and brown sandals.

The doorbell rings after a bit. Waffles meows and races to the door. When I answer it, Liam is standing there holding a bouquet of wildflowers.

"Oh! They're beautiful. You didn't have to." I take the flowers from him then realize I have to invite him in now. I picked up a bit so he wouldn't see a mess when I opened the door but I can't remember when I last vacuumed. Embarrassment makes me blush. "Let me put these in some water. Come on in."

He follows me in while I head to the kitchen to find a vase. Liam shoves his hands into his pockets and looks around, studying the art prints on the wall.

"Your place is nice," he says. "How long have you lived here?"

"Thank you. I moved in three years ago." Waffles follows

him and loudly begs for treats. "That's Waffles. Don't let him convince you that he's starving. He lies."

Liam laughs and crouches, reaching a hand out for Waffles to sniff. Waffles rubs his face on Liam's shoes while purring and his tail wiggles with excitement. He meows, trying his best to convince Liam that he hasn't eaten in days.

"Sorry, kitty. Mommy says you're cut off."

My body flushes with warmth after he calls me Mommy. I like the sound of the word on his lips.

I snip the ends off the flowers and put them in water, taking a moment to arrange the blooms. They're a pretty mix of different flowers in shades of purple, pink, and blue. "All done."

Liam strolls over to admire them. "Gorgeous." He puts his hand around my waist and pulls me closer, then bends down. "The flowers are pretty too."

He dips his head most of the way but pauses. Waiting. He wants a kiss, but he's letting me decide.

I stretch up and close the distance between us. The kiss is sweet. A gentle brushing of lips with a promise of more to come later.

We pull apart and his hand slides to my hip before dropping away. "I'll drive?"

"Okay." My heart is fluttering with excitement as I grab my purse and follow him out.

The bubble tea shop isn't far. Liam studies the menu with a frown, squinting at the myriad of options. There's a column for tea bases, then flavors, then pearls.

When it's our turn to order I get a classic brown sugar tea with tapioca pearls. The girl asks him what he wants, and Liam flounders. I take pity on him and order him a strawberry milk tea with strawberry pops.

"Thanks," he says, scratching the back of his head. "I didn't realize tea could be complicated."

I smile. "They do give you a lot of options."

We grab our teas and big straws from the counter and find a table by the front window.

Liam watches me shake my drink and stab the pointed straw through the top film. He does the same and takes a tentative sip.

"It's not carbonated at all," he says, staring at the drink. "Why do they call it bubble tea?"

"Because of the pearls."

"Then why don't they call it pearl tea?"

I shrug and sip my drink. "I don't know. That's just what they call it."

"What do I do with them? They keep getting in my straw." The skin between his eyebrows creases with worry.

I suppress a grin. "You suck them up. They're edible."

"I have to suck the balls?"

A couple of people look at us, and I blush with amused embarrassment. He's ridiculous. I can't tell if he's acting clueless on purpose to make me less nervous. "Yeah, you suck the balls."

On his second sip, he grins. But on his third, he finally gets one of the pops. I can tell the moment it explodes in his mouth because his eyes widen.

"What was that?" he asks, staring at his drink with suspicion.

I suppress a laugh. "Some of the pearls burst."

"You did that on purpose. Yours are different from mine. This tea was sabotaged. Let me try yours."

I put my drink down between us. "Okay, but some people don't like the tapioca pearls because they're chewy."

"Hmm. I'd better play it safe then." Instead of taking a sip of my drink, he leans forward over the table and kisses me. His tongue darts between my lips for a quick taste, and then he pulls away. "Very sweet."

The PDA is shameless and I blush all the way to the tops of my ears. "You're bad."

He grins, his cheek dimpling. "Only if you like it."

"Well, is it everything you thought it'd be?" I ask, trying to get us back on track. This is a bubble tea shop in the middle of the day, not a dark booth in the back of a crowded bar.

His eyes roam over me. "It's better than I ever could have expected. So did you write any more naughty books I'm not cool enough to read?"

I tuck a loose strand behind my ear and play with my hair. "No. I'm working on edits right now. I busted my ass and banked some manuscripts last year because I knew my schedule was going to be crazy with all of this. That way I can still have new releases without having the pressure to write."

"Smart. I never thought about how all of that planning and scheduling works."

"Have you always worked at the bar?" I ask.

He lounges back in his seat, getting comfortable. "I grew up in it. Started out by rolling napkins and helping in the kitchen. Doing easy stuff like making dressing cups. Once I got to high school I started working there part time. I've done everything. Back of the house, front of the house. My dad is a firm believer that a good manager knows how to fill in any gaps to keep things moving. I took over ownership about five years ago when my parents decided to retire. They moved to Florida to get away from the cold and snow. What about you? Does your family live around here?"

"I have an older brother, but he lives in Chicago so I don't get to see him very often. My parents still live here in my child-hood home."

"Have you told them about…"

I shake my head. "No. It's early and I didn't want to get their hopes up. My best friend Jen is the only one who knows." A new thought occurs to me. "Have you told anyone?"

"Uh…" He scratches his chin stubble. "We told everyone. They're really excited."

I grimace. "You aren't supposed to tell anyone for a while. At least until the second trimester."

"Yeah, I'm realizing that now. I'm sorry. I didn't know. They knew we were on a waitlist for adoption, but it's so competitive for a baby. That's why we decided on the co-parent route. It was more affordable than surrogacy."

I wish he hadn't told anyone, just in case. But there's no way to unspill the milk. And if things don't work out, I won't be the one calling everyone with the bad news. I guess it's fine.

"How are you?" he asks.

I play with the straw in my drink, using it to stir the tapioca pearls. "Better. Today's a good day. I'm excited for the second trimester. The nausea should hopefully be gone by then."

"Really? I thought it lasted the whole time."

"It can for some, but not usually. Have you read any books about what to expect?" I ask.

His eyes light up. "No. Do you want to go with me? You can tell me which ones are good."

"Right now?"

When he nods, I agree. He slides out of his seat and we go to his truck. I finish my bubble tea on the ride and toss it out when we get to the store. The bookstore smells like paper, ink, and happiness. It's my favorite place other than home.

I show him where the family planning and parenting section is. The traditional favorites are there, plus some new ones that look interesting. I pick up a book with a pretty cover and flip through it.

"This is a good one, right?" He shows me the tried and true book that pretty much every new parent buys or gets as a gift.

"Yeah, that's a good choice. Some of the advice might be old, though. I think it was originally written in the eighties."

"I like the one you picked. The diagrams are nice." He stands behind me, a hand going to my hip as Liam reads over my shoulder. He's so tall and warm against my back.

"You should get it then." I hand it to him and he palms it along with the other one.

"Anything else?" he asks. "What about that one? That doctor has a TV show. I've seen it play on the TV above the bar."

His thumb draws circles on my hip. I try to follow what he's saying as he reads the synopsis on the back page to me. His deep voice is distracting. I could listen to him read the classified pages and never get bored.

"Yeah?" he asks.

I have no idea what he asked me. "Yeah."

Liam adds it to our growing stack and sets them down on a shelf. Then he stretches over me, his front rubbing against my back, to grab one from the top shelf.

He cracks a book open with one hand and drags his other hand around to my front. His palm covers my still flat belly. Cupping our tiny speck of a baby. Liam shows me an illustrated book he likes. All I can think of is how much I like being dwarfed by him.

His scent wraps around me, and I lean against him. His presence is steady, the rubbing of his hand sweet.

I feel… safe. Almost cherished.

My biology wants me to give in. To surrender to the strong, virile alpha who got me pregnant. We're a scent match. I'm carrying his baby. My instincts don't understand why I'm not already bitten and claimed and building my nest.

But life is more complicated now than it used to be in our caveman days. We've evolved.

My panties grow damp from his close proximity. The heat from his palm. The way he touches me. The horniness is because of the pregnancy. All that extra blood flow my body shunts toward my uterus. My nipples tighten into hard points that rub against my bra.

Liam adds the book to our stack and leans over me. He groans in my ear. "If you keep smelling this fucking good, I'm not going to be held responsible if I get us banned from the property for lewd behavior."

"Then you should probably stop touching me. I can't help it."

"Neither can I, kitten. You were made for petting." He sniffs my hair, then withdraws and neatens his stack of baby books. "Is there anything else you want? My treat."

"Really?" Those are dangerous words to say to a bookworm in a bookstore. No matter how many books I own, the answer to that question will always be *yes*.

"Anything," he promises. "As many as you want."

I drag him to the romance section. He watches, amused, as I pore over the shelves with serious determination. There's a lot of historical and paranormal romance among the contemporary, but not much else. Nothing too taboo or fun like you can find online. But that's fine because I read a mix of genres.

While I'm debating between two books, a dark romance and a popular romantasy book, he peruses the aisle. I read their blurbs, then read the first page or two to see if I like the author's style. The romantasy is written in a tense I don't prefer so I put it back and find another option. A werewolf pack romance. I love the pack romances the most.

"This is wild," Liam says, flipping the pages of a book.

"Are all of these like this? I had no idea. I thought romance books were sweet."

His question pulls my focus out of the book I'm skimming. "Which one is that?"

"There's more of these sitting out on a table. Something about viral books. There's one about a girl and her priest, a minotaur getting handjobs, and a blue alien. This one's about the Irish mob."

My eyes snap to the book he's holding, to see its cover. But I can't see it from this angle. The color drains from my face. It can't be. "What's it called?" The words squeak out of me.

He glances at me, confused, then tips the book up.

My stomach drops.

It's mine. I knew its sales were doing well, and I'd been tagged in a lot of review posts on my socials, but I didn't know it was in bookstores. I don't pay much attention to reviews and social media or it makes me self conscious when I write.

Liam squints, studying me. "Have you read this one?"

I pretend to study the shelves. "Mmm." God, I'm such a bad liar.

"Wait… Is this your book? That's not your name on the cover."

Looking around, I make sure nobody is paying attention to us. "Will you keep your voice down? Give me that." I reach for the book, but he pulls it away at the last second. Scowling, I reach again.

He puts it over my head like this is a game of keep away. "No way. I'm gonna read this so I know exactly what my girl likes."

"It's fantasy, not reality. I'm not into everything I write about." I go on my tip toes and stretch up to reach it.

Why is he so fucking tall?

Liam holds the book infuriatingly one inch out of reach.

"Then you won't mind me reading it. Apparently I could use the pointers because this mafia boss has mad dirty talk game."

"Give me the book, Liam. I'm not kidding." He can't read it. I'll die of embarrassment.

Instead of doing what I say, Liam maneuvers the book open one-handed. He starts reading it right there in the store while he fends off my grabby hands. It's infuriating how easily he thwarts my efforts to grab the book from him. His other hand slides down to palm my ass and give it a squeeze.

I stiffen in surprise. "Stop that," I croak.

He uses his pinky to turn the page. He's surprisingly dextrous. "Hold on, kitten. They're doing it on the table while the old boss bleeds out on the floor and the lieutenants all watch. Wow, this is graphic."

With a pained groan, I close my eyes. He's never going to let this go or pretend this didn't happen. When the hand on my ass starts to knead, my eyes pop open.

"What are you doing?"

His hand slides over, tracing the cleft of my buttocks. Dipping lower, to tease my pussy through layers of fabric. My clit throbs and I glance around to see if anyone's watching. This section of the store is empty. It's early on a weekday and most people are at work.

"What are you doing?" I ask again. Whispering, trying not to draw attention to us.

"You like it when I'm assertive. And I can smell how wet you are." He flips to another section of the book and keeps reading. "Your safeword is waffles. Do you understand?"

He's right. I've always liked the thrill of potentially getting caught. Josh always had to be careful about his image with the press. And he never understood why I liked it. I can't explain it. There's something electrifying about having a naughty secret. About doing something you're not supposed to. About getting off when you shouldn't be. Where you shouldn't be.

"Can you remember your safeword for me, kitten?"

"Yes." Are we really doing this?

He flips a page with one hand and hikes the back of my dress up with the other. His fingertips trace over the curve of my ass. Skims the elastic waistband of my panties.

"There are cameras," I point out.

He turns the next page. "There's no way they have someone monitoring them live."

"There are people in here."

"Then you'll want to be quiet."

When he touches my damp slit through my panties, I want to moan. But I can't. He rubs me up and down, soaking the fabric in my arousal. My clit throbs and my pussy plumps as he teases me. I watch the aisle like a hawk, using his larger frame to shield me. The back of this aisle leads to a dead end with self help books and travel guides. It's not exactly crowded.

There's only the sound of him turning pages and the low din of people on the other side of the store. The beeps of the cash register. People talking and the grinder whirring in the coffee shop.

He gets bolder, working his hand down my panties. My thighs spread as I fidget, hanging onto him for support.

When he touches my clit without the fabric to dampen it, I have to bite back my moan. I'm soaking wet. We shouldn't be doing this. I'm going to cry when I get banned from my favorite bookstore.

But when he leans down and curls two fingers inside of me, I don't stop him.

They pump, in and out, my pussy making a wet sucking sound. It has to be loud. Surely everyone can hear this. But nobody comes running to point and shout. I swallow my breathy sounds and twist my fingers in his shirt.

His hard cock presses against my thigh. Reaching down, I rub him through his jeans. Turnabout is fair play. He sucks in a breath, but doesn't stop. Neither do I.

He fingers me, alternating between plunging two fingers inside me and rubbing my mound. My clit. Through his jeans, I trace the outline of his cock. Rub along his flared head. Stroke over his shaft. He dresses to the left.

An older woman walks past our aisle and I freeze, but Liam doesn't stop. He can't see her. I'm not sure if he'd care if he could. She heads to the section with the bibles and Liam rubs me faster. Impossibly fast. The last time I was fingered this well was by a guitarist.

Pressure builds. I'm going to come. In a bookstore in broad daylight. My breathing gets heavy and I bite my lip to stay quiet. I lean into him, using his rock solid frame for balance.

I can smell him. His arousal. Everyone in this store can likely scent us too, even if they don't know where it's coming from. My hips rock with him, building to a rhythm. Chasing a forbidden pleasure.

When I come, I can't hold back my moan. It comes out low and throaty. All I can do is hope that I was quiet enough that the entire store didn't hear me. I squeeze his cock through his jeans and enjoy his grunt in response. Being that hard in jeans has got to be uncomfortable.

Liam pulls his hand out of my drenched panties and lets my dress settle over my thighs. He brings his soaked hand to his mouth and licks it clean, his chest rumbling with a subtle purr.

Panting, I come back down to Earth. I can't believe we did that. It was scary. Exhilarating. I want to do it again.

"We should go," he says. Liam reaches down and adjusts his

erection in his pants so it's slightly less noticeable. It doesn't do all that much. He's big. "Grab all of your books, kitten."

After that stunt, I grab the boxed collector's set of the romantasy series I've been eying for months. I already own all of the books, but I love them. And the special edition books are illustrated inside with painted edges and gold foiling. It costs an obscene amount of money.

He doesn't bat an eye as the cashier rings us up. He pays for them, then slings an arm possessively around my hip and carries the heavy bags to his truck. I go to my side, but he beats me to it, reaching around to open the door for me.

I slide into his truck and he puts the bags in the backseat of the cab, then shuts my door and goes around to his side. After we buckle our seatbelts and he pulls out onto the road, I twist in my seat to stare at him.

He watches the road, but flicks his eyes to me every once in a while. "Yeah, Kitty Kat? You okay?"

My thoughts are jumbled. I vacillate between telling him to never do something so dangerous again and begging him to do it again right now. It was better than I'd always imagined. "Did you like that?"

Liam reaches over and takes my hand. He strokes his thumb along the back of it, then pulls it over the seat divider and sets it on his erection. "You know I did. I like watching your face when you come. Smelling what arousal does to your scent. Hearing your breathy little pants when you try to keep it together, but can't. If I thought we'd get away with it, I'd have pulled your panties down and bent you over right there."

I'm still wet, still throbbing, and his nostrils flare as he drags in a deep breath. Scenting me. The vein in his neck bulges, Throbbing. His erection swells against my hand.

He's really fucking into this. Into me. This attraction isn't pity at all. And I like what I've seen of him too. He's sweet, caring, goes after what he wants, and knows when to be pushy and when to back off.

He can play the alphahole. But can he take it too?

I take my hand off his trapped cock and reach for the button of his jeans. It's hard to work the stiff material open one-handed, but eventually I get it. Carefully I slide the zipper down, making sure not to catch him. Liam isn't wearing underwear.

The steering wheel creaks under his hands as I take his thick, heavy cock out and stroke him. My fingers make a ring around his base, teasing the extra skin that will form his knot. I drag my hand up, fanning them over his flared head. Tracing the uneven edge of his corona. Dip the edge of my thumb into his slit where fluid starts to bead.

His scent bursts into the cab as pre-cum pearls. Thick, heavy, woodsy musk.

"Do you like this?" I ask him, stroking him.

"I'd like anything you wanted to do to me." His cock twitches in my hand. At a red light, he brakes and drags his eyes over me. "I wanna see your pretty tits."

My heartbeat kicks up. My butterflies flutter faster. With my other hand, I pull the neckline of my sundress down. The top of this one is so tight now from pregnancy that I skipped wearing a bra today. My breasts are swollen and tender. I work the tight fabric down until my areolas and then my nipples are visible.

He groans like a wounded animal, then pulls his attention back to the road as the light turns green and traffic resumes. "That's good." His hips twitch, bucking his cock deeper into the jerking ring of my hand. "You're so good at that, kitten."

I like his praise. I like the way it makes me feel inside. Golden and warm. With one hand I work him, and with the other I play with my breast. Gently squeezing it. Stroking my nipple into a firm peak, then pinching it. My clit throbs. My pussy clenches like they're connected. My breasts have never been this sensitive before. I think I could orgasm from having them played with.

"Almost there," he groans. I don't know if he means that we're almost at my house or he's about to come. Maybe both. "Show me your perfect pussy. Take your panties off."

I let go of him to follow his order. I drag the flared skirt of my sundress up and hook my thumbs in my panties, then pull them down and lift off the seat to get them over my butt. They twist around my thighs. I get them over my knees, then slip my legs out one by one. Once they're off, I drop them on the floorboard.

He puts on his signal, then turns left, glancing down at me when he's straightened out on the mostly empty street. I spread my thighs, hitching one leg up by putting my foot on the seat and spreading myself open.

"Oh, fuck. That's a good girl. Play with your pussy. Make yourself feel good."

I take him back in one hand and spread my folds with my other one. I touch him while I touch myself. Slicking my fingers through my cleft. Rubbing my clit and spreading my arousal around. Finding a steady rhythm as I jerk him too.

Pre-cum drips down my knuckles, and I use the fluid to make him slick. He pulls into my driveway and parks, blowing out a breath. A glance out the windows shows me that none of my neighbors are out tending their gardens or walking their dogs. They're inside, out of this heat, or at work still.

"Come for me," he demands. "I want to hear your pretty cries."

He touches me. Slides his rough hand over my shoulder and the tiny strap of my dress. Palms my breast and touches it reverently. Toys with my nipple. I fidget in my seat, gripping his cock tightly so I can focus on myself. It's too much to manage all at once.

My hips grind my clit against my hand as I rub myself furiously. It'll take a lot to come again so soon. I'm not in heat, and I've already come twice today. I whine as I chase the elusive high of another orgasm.

"That's it, kitten."

The pressure builds in my pelvis. Swells, pulling taut. I look down at my lewd, public display. The knowledge that at any moment the mailman could walk by and see this tips me over the edge. I come, walls spasming, core empty. I bite my lip, moaning. My cunt pulses, throbbing. Slick leaves me wet between the thighs.

"So fucking perfect." Liam unbuckles my seatbelt, then threads his fingers in my hair and drags me closer. He pulls my face to his, crashing his mouth to mine. The kiss is possessive. Fierce.

His other hand drops down to cup mine, wrapped loosely around his cock, and he makes me stroke him. Our hands slide up and down his shaft while his tongue forces its way past my lips. He tastes every inch of me while he fucks my hand, hips rising to thrust into the tight ring of my fingers.

My hair loosens, my side ponytail falling, as he manhandles me. I like it. I enjoy knowing how desperate I've made him.

He moans into my mouth—and that does it for me. I love it when men moan. When they're loud and whining.

I push at his shoulder and Liam pulls off me, his eyes unfocused as he looks at me, concerned. I twist on my seat, getting onto my knee. Angling over his lap. Getting settled. With my ass in the air, I bring the head of his cock to my lips.

Liam groans and lets go. Lets me take over as I feed his cock into my mouth. His hand drops to my head and my sagging ponytail. Fingers card through my hair, petting me.

He's salty and musky at first, and then I taste his pheromones. Sweet pine. It shouldn't be this good. Crisp. Spiky. Sweet. A little perfumey. The herbal taste settles my stomach, and I suck, cheeks hollowing, searching for more.

I've heard that an alpha's cum is good for a breeding omega. But I always chalked it up to a myth told by horny alphas trying to get laid.

I want more. Need it. I squeeze his base, pulling. Milking him for more. The drops of pre-cum aren't enough. His cum will be so much better. Richer, thicker with pheromones.

"Fuck, Kat. You're good at sucking cock," he groans. His fingers tighten in my hair, pulling lightly as he pulls and pushes my head down, setting the rhythm. "Don't stop, kitten. I'm close."

I can't pull his balls out because of his tight jeans, so I play with them through the fabric instead. Massaging over them. Cupping their heavy weight. I keep my lips tight around his flared head and lave him with my tongue, dipping it into his slit. Fluttering it over the sensitive skin underneath where it connects to his shaft.

His knot swells, bumping against my lips and nose. I fist it, my fingers tight, and bob faster. My jaw aches. My hair falls completely as he fists his hand at the base of my nape. Squeezing until it aches, dull and delicious.

Liam groans, his hips lifting to drive his cock in and out of my wet mouth. "Kat," he moans.

It's my only warning before he comes. His cock jerks in my hand. Pulses. A lash of semen strikes across my tongue with every involuntary movement.

"Don't swallow yet," he orders.

I whine, annoyed, but obey. Let him empty into my mouth. Collect every drop. I fist his knot, squeezing out another spurt. Once he's spent, I pop off his cock and sit up.

Liam grabs my face, and I go still. Freezing like prey caught by a predator. It's an instinctive response.

His grip is firm but not bruising as he palms my jaw in one big hand. "Open."

My mouth falls open, showing him the wad of cum gathered on my tongue. It starts to drip from the corner of my mouth. He grunts. "Swallow."

I close my mouth and swallow. My throat bobs as I drink his pine tinged cum down. It rolls down my throat, coating my stomach. He grins, showing off one canine. Sharp alpha teeth. The sight makes me shiver, but not with fear.

"That's my good girl." His thumb slides across my slick mouth.

Liam tugs me forward and grazes my lips with his. He kisses me, no hesitation that my mouth still tastes like him.

"When can I see you again?" he asks after we pull apart.

I tug the top of my dress up so my breasts are covered and settle on my seat. His pub is probably busiest on the weekends and I set my own schedule. "Monday?" That's four days from now.

"Monday," he agrees, nodding. "Come over for dinner. Matthew is a wonderful cook, and I want you to meet my pack properly."

Nervous, I nod. Family dinner with the pack is a big leap up from first date fun. But I'm pregnant with his baby. None of this is normal. We're doing everything out of order.

"I'll walk you to your door, just give me a second." He lifts his ass up and shoves his cock and swollen knot down the leg of his jeans. Once he's tucked away, he grabs the bag with my books from the backseat and gets out, coming around to open my door.

Such a gentleman. Except when he's fingering me in public. Not that I'm complaining.

He walks me to my door, and once I've unlocked it, he pulls me back in for one last kiss. A long, passionate one. The kind that steals my breath and makes me rise up on my toes to make it deeper. I've missed kissing, and he does it well.

We break apart, and he watches me go inside where Waffles is already meowing and telling me he needs food in his bowl.

"No," I tell my needy cat. "You're getting fat again." I play with him instead, pulling out my phone to call Jen and tell her everything.

"Shut up," she says when I tell her that he fingered me in the bookstore then bought me all the books I wanted. "So when are you mating him? Because a guy who fingers you and buys you books is one hundred percent mate material."

I toss Waffle's jingle ball across the room and watch him fetch it while I grin. "I still have to meet his pack. They might hate me."

"They're not going to hate you. But I will if you don't send me photos. I want to see these men. Are they handsome?"

"They're all pretty different, but yeah." All three of them are handsome in their own way. Liam's energy straddles feral and sweet, making his guy-next-door look deceiving. Gabriel is tall, athletic, and seems easy going. It's Matthew I don't know anything about other than his photo. And I've never seen how the three of them interact with one another.

"I can't remember the last time one of the guys fingered me," she says, distracted.

"Really?" Waffles meows, annoyed that I've stopped playing. I toss the jingling ball again.

"When we try to stay up late to have some adult fun after the kids go to bed, we usually end up falling asleep on the couch."

I drop Waffle's ball and switch to the feathers attached to a pole. He rolls onto his back and bats at them half-heartedly.

"You could leave the kids with one of their grandmothers and go spend a weekend away somewhere."

She makes a thoughtful sound. "We should. We haven't had a mini vacation alone since the baby was born. Ooh, Brian just got home. I'm gonna go ask him what he thinks. Call me on Monday."

"Bye." I hang up and focus on Waffles, playing with him until he grows bored. I put his toys away in his basket, then unpack my books from the store. It takes me an hour to decide how I want to rearrange my shelves to display the pretty books in their fancy slipcase.

When I'm done, my mind drifts back to our date. I can't help but smile.

I wonder if he's found my little present yet...

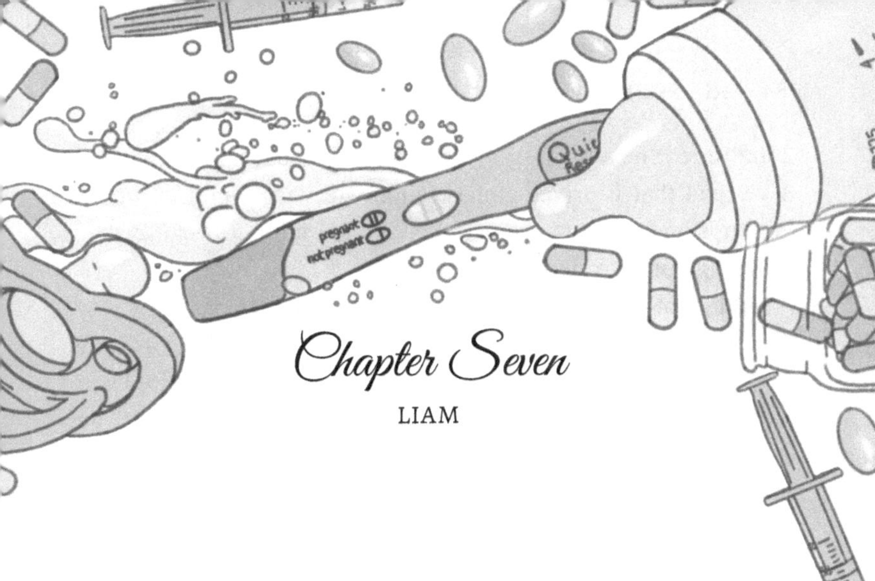

Chapter Seven

LIAM

"How'd it go?" Gabriel asks.

I shut the door and drop the baby books onto our kitchen table. "It went great. I think she's perfect for us." Then I pull the balled-up perfumed underwear from my pocket and toss them at him.

He catches them out of the air. "Nice. These are cute."

"She's coming over for dinner on Monday. Is Matthew home?" I glance around the apartment, but don't see or hear him.

"No. He's stuck at the bank. They're short a manager so he's covering another branch."

"Hmm." I turn my attention back to the pink underwear that smells like her. "What do you think?"

Gabriel shrugs. "You know my sense of smell isn't as good as yours. If you think she's a good fit, then I believe you."

I pull Gabriel against me, rubbing his back. "I want you two to like her too or else it's not going to work. You know you both get a say."

He smiles, amused. "Of course we do. I never thought we wouldn't. You know, I haven't seen you this worked up in a long time. She's really got you going. Because she's pregnant? I've read that it drives alphas wild." He wraps an arm around my hips and tugs me against him. "Is that it? Is it because she's carrying our baby?"

"It's not just that. She's pretty. Funny, in a sly, sarcastic way. Her scent drives me nuts. And pregnancy is making her tits huge." I can't wait for her milk to come in. For her nipples to drip with it and her belly to swell. "The books said she'll get hornier in a few weeks. All the blood flow to her pelvis." I waggle my brows at him.

"And you're going to help her with that little problem?" Gabriel grins.

"I hope we all will."

"Matthew may need some time," he says. "But I'm happy to help our omega with her urges. Show me these books."

I dump the books out of the bag. Gabriel looks through them, then picks up the dirty novel. Her book. "What's this?" he asks.

"She wrote it. She's an author."

"Really?" He cracks it open to a random page, his eyebrows rising. "Oh." He grins and flips to another section. "This is raunchy."

"She let me finger her in the store," I tell him, my cock jerking at the memory. Of her breathy little noises. How hard she tried to stay quiet. How much she soaked my hand. How her thighs trembled and she leaned on me for support. Trusting me to catch her. Protect her while I made her feel good.

Gabriel laughs and puts the book down. "It's always the quiet, bookish girls who are the filthiest in bed. Is that how you got the panties?"

"No. I got those in the car. She blew me while I drove her home."

"*Caralho*," he says, chuckling. "I can't wait to really meet this girl. You can't have all the fun, you know?"

"Have I been neglecting you?" I ask, mostly teasing but also slightly concerned. I have a one-track mind at times. I don't want my packmates to feel neglected.

Gabriel gives me a sly look, like he knows what I'm doing. "Maybe a bit," he pouts. "You've been so distracted by the baby."

"Can't have that," I say, sliding my hand down his toned stomach. I reach around and cup his ass, then drop a kiss on the side of his neck. "Not when I have *meu benzinho* right here." I smack him on his nice, round ass. "Go prep, and I'll show you how much I still love you."

"I've been *very* neglected," Gabriel says as he walks backward toward our bedroom. "Do you have enough energy left to handle all of this?" He gestures up and down his body. He's been putting in a lot of time at the gym and it shows.

I grin. "I think I can rise to the occasion."

He shoots finger guns at me. "I'm going to hold you to that."

Gabriel disappears into our bedroom, and a moment later I hear our shower run. While he's getting clean, I put the baby books away on our bookshelf and leave the novel on my nightstand. I want to read it first before Monday. Learn what our girl likes. Her secret fantasies.

I put her panties in my nightstand drawer. My alpha instincts won't let me toss them into our dirty hamper. I'll keep them until the scent fades, then steal another pair. Until she's in our nest for real, it'll have to do.

I undress and toss my dirty clothes into the hamper, then lie down on the bed. Gabriel's shower is brief. He comes out, steam billowing through the open door, with only a towel wrapped around his waist. The water makes his brown hair darker against his golden brown skin.

He joins me on the bed, and I pull him close, going on my side. I slot my leg between his thighs and claim his mouth, kissing him until he's moaning. His cock thickens, and I rub mine against him. Run my hands down his arms. His chest. His back. He's put on a lot more muscle.

Grabbing him, I flip us, pulling him on top of me. The towel slips and I shove it down his round ass. Still kissing him. He moans into my mouth as I get a nice grip and spread his cheeks wide. His cock slides against mine as he grinds while straddling me.

I finger his asshole and test it. Nice and clean, and already lubed. Pushing past the tight ring of muscle, I work a finger in and out of him. Add a second. Rub his prostate until pre-cum drips on my stomach. He tips his head back, breaking our kiss to suck in a breath.

Lifting him off my lap a bit, I fist my cock and notch it between his cheeks. Rub my cockhead along the cleft of his ass, teasing his hole. On the third teasing pass, he pops his ass out and my head catches on his rim. It dips inside. He sighs and stretches, using his palms on my chest for leverage as he seats himself on my cock. He takes the first inch, stretching wide. Slow, measured thrusts open him up for me.

"You feel so good," I tell him, knowing how much he craves the praise. They all do. "So hot and tight for me. Can you take all of me?" It's been a while since we practiced him taking my knot. Sometimes it's too much effort. Some days all we want is a quick, easy fuck.

Gabriel drops his head, and we lock eyes. "I want all of it. All of *you*."

I put my hand over his chest, finding his heartbeat with my palm. My hips flex, my cock going deeper. Still slow.

Controlled. I spread the lube he prepped with deeper until he takes me all the way to the root. His eyes flutter once his ass claps against me.

"*Papai*," he groans. His body moves with me, fucking himself on my cock. "Harder."

Bending my knees and digging my heels in the bed, I fuck up into him. Slam my cock home.

"Harder," he begs, eyes closed and mouth soft. Lost in the pleasure.

I fuck him harder, bouncing him, only stopping when my cock pops free. He whines in annoyance as I growl in frustration. "On your knees."

Gabriel climbs off me and gets on his knees in the middle of the bed. I go behind him, taking a moment to appreciate the beautiful sight he makes. Ass up in the air, face down. I check to make sure there's still enough lube, then set my cock to his puffy hole and push in. With this angle, I can go deeper.

"Mmm, fuck, that's good," he moans.

If he can talk then I'm not doing my job right. I use my leg to move his higher, knocking him off balance. I lean over him, covering him. Pushing his body into the mattress as I make him take my weight. My teeth nip at his shoulder. His neck. My cock drives deep, balls slapping against his ass. He takes all of me now.

My pelvis tightens before I'm ready to come. I slow my pace, ignoring his whining. Wrap a hand around his neck and pull him up and back. Bring his face in range so I can make him twist back. Kiss him.

"*Cachorro*," he whines. Calling me a naughty dog in Portuguese.

I shove two fingers in his mouth and hook him like a fish. Make him look at me with his wide, surprised eyes. I chuckle. He knows I don't tolerate brats. And he can't talk shit if his mouth is full. He whines, annoyed, and his tongue slides along my fingers. As if that's going to gross me out. His tongue has licked worse places than my fingers. A string of drool drips from the corner of his mouth.

"Bad boys get their mouths stuffed."

He groans, his throat bobbing to swallow his pooling saliva while I fuck him like this. He doesn't fight me. No matter how strong he gets, how many hours he spends lifting weights, we both know who will come out the winner if we grapple. I'm an alpha, and he's my beta bitch. He's fucking *mine*.

Does he need a reminder?

"You're mine," I tell him as I fuck his ass harder so he knows who's in charge in this bed. "Do you get that?"

He nods, my fingers still in his mouth. The primal urge I have to lay claim and conquer simmers down.

The front door opens and Matthew calls out that he's home. *Perfect timing.*

"In here!" I yell. "I need you, babe."

"What do you need?" he asks, his voice getting louder as he gets closer. He stands in the open doorway, one hand loosening the tie around his neck.

God, he looks good in a suit. "I need you to plug Gabriel's filthy mouth with your cock."

"Again?" Matthew laughs and tosses his tie onto the dresser. He undoes the buttons on his wrists and throat, then pulls his dress shirt off. "That's twice this week."

"He doesn't learn," I say. "Or he likes it but he's too shy to ask."

Gabriel makes unintelligible noises as he tries to talk around my fingers, and Matthew looks at the both of us like we're incorrigible.

But he does as ordered. I watch Matthew undress.

Matthew doesn't make a show of it, but the sight of him

getting bare is still erotic. He slips out of his dress shoes and socks, then shucks off his pants, underwear, and undershirt. Underneath his tailored suit, he's trim and lean. Freckles dot the pale skin of his shoulders. His cock is soft, but as he stands there watching us fuck, it gets harder.

Matthew likes to watch. My little voyeur. He strokes his cock until it's erect and bobbing, and then he does as he's been told. He gets on the bed, and once he's in position, I let Gabriel go. Gabriel falls on Matthew's cock like a good boy. He knows that the only way I'll let him come is if he gives up on being naughty.

"That's nice," I say as I watch them together from my vantage point.

I love this. Love spit roasting one of my boys with the other. Will Kat let me do this to her? From what I've read of her dirty book, I think she will. I think she'll love having all of her sweet little holes stuffed full. Three holes and three cocks. The math works out. I wonder if she's ever taken a cock up her ass, or if we'll be the first.

How the fuck did I get so lucky?

Thoughts of the day when all four of us are piled into one nest together makes my groin tighten with the need to spread my seed. My fingers dig into Gabriel's firm ass and I tug him back, using his hips to control him. I pull him down to meet every hard thrust. Plunge my cock deep inside his belly.

My knot swells, stretching his hole wide with every push and pull. Unlike a pussy, there's no front pubic bone to lock my knot inside. I pop my swollen knot free of his ass, then slowly force it back in. Gabriel sucks Matthew's cock, moaning loudly around his mouthful.

The sight of his swollen pink asshole sucking my knot in deeper pushes me closer to that edge. My fingertips make divots in his skin. Matthew's needy, breathy sounds he makes while he fucks Gabriel's mouth tips me over. I come, shooting my load deep inside until my ballsack is empty.

My breathing is ragged as I come back down to Earth. God, he's so perfect. So hot and tight. I rock, tugging on our tie. Enjoying the way his ass tightens down on me. Squeezing. My cock pulses with one more shot of cum.

While Gabriel finishes Matthew, I reach around to stroke Gabriel's cock. He bucks, fucking himself into my hand, his ass pulling on my knot. Then he whimpers.

"Shh." I lean my weight over him, pinning him in place. Trapping him under me. He's so hard his cock is almost flush with his belly. My poor tortured baby. I stroke him, squeezing his shaft and using his skin for sliding. "That's it. Be a good boy and come for me. Just like this."

I nip his shoulder and tug him harder. Faster. My grip is punishing over his sensitive head. Exactly how he likes it. He keeps a firm grip when he strokes himself.

Matthew drops his chin to his chest to watch the slide of his cock in Gabriel's mouth. "Fuck, that's good. I'm gonna come." Matthew fucks Gabriel's face, chasing his pleasure. Forcing the other beta to take it. To breathe when it's over. Then he cries out, his thrusts slowing. He empties into Gabriel's mouth, and neither of us have to tell the beta to swallow. He does it without question.

Gabriel pops off Matthew's softening cock to arch his back and babble a string of nonsense in Portuguese. His legs tremble while I stroke him. Work him up into a frenzy.

He comes without warning, his cock pulsing in my hand. I jerk him slower, milking the cum from his cock until he's empty and pliant. Gabriel collapses on the bed, his cheek resting on Matthew's thigh.

I stroke Gabriel's back, telling him he's perfect. That they both did such a good job. Matthew gives me a loopy smile.

"Not that I'm complaining, but this wasn't what I expected to come home to tonight."

"It's her fucking panties," Gabriel says. "She's got him wound up tight like he's in his twenties again."

"Hey." I nip Gabriel's neck in warning, but all the mouthy brat does is laugh. "I don't need omega slick to fuck you stupid." To prove my point, I twist my hips and tug on the knot still swollen in his ass.

Gabriel groans and twists his upper body to the side. "Beast. Do you see what she does to him?"

"Really?" Matthew asks. "When do I get to meet her?"

"Monday," I tell him. "She's coming over for dinner."

Matthew makes a thoughtful hum. "I'll try not to get stuck late at work. What kind of food does she like?"

I frown. "I'm not sure, but I can ask her."

"I could make my *avó's churrasco*," Gabriel offers.

"Or something less spiced," Matthew says. "Something bland and easy on the stomach. Baked mac and cheese? Carbs are probably easier for her. You said she's been nauseous."

"I'll ask her, but I think that sounds good." One of the books I bought today might have a chapter for recipes.

Since the swelling in my knot has gone down, I pop myself free. Gabriel grunts and I watch my cum make a mess of his thighs before I find his discarded towel and clean him up. Spent, we collapse in the bed in a tangle of limbs. It creaks under our combined weight as we settle and get more comfortable.

"This was nice," I say. I've missed this. The old days when the three of us were obsessed with one another. Before infatuation gave way to love and then comfort. We've been together a long time, through all the ups and downs. Life is good. It's about to get better.

"It was," Matthew says, spooning Gabriel. "I'll try to not be so late all the time. It's hard while the bank's short staffed."

"I know." I reach over Gabriel and rub Matthew's shoulder. "But they'll give you time off for the baby once it's born, right?"

"She's not an official packmate and I'm not the father," he says. "HR said I can use my vacation, but I don't get twelve weeks of parental leave."

"That's bullshit," Gabriel says.

It is.

And it's all the more reason to make Kat a part of our pack. I can't imagine bringing our baby home without Matthew or Gabriel being there.

Now I have even more reason to convince her that we're perfect for her.

"I'll fix this," I promise them.

Chapter Eight

MATTHEW

I PULL THE OVEN OPEN FOR THE EIGHTH TIME IN TWENTY minutes to make sure the cheese is melting properly. As if it's possible that cheese won't melt in a hot oven. I'm nervous. I want this dinner to go well.

This woman is carrying my baby, and while Liam says he's reasonably sure it's all a done deal, I'm not so convinced. Seven months is a long time. Long enough for her to change her mind. And while my dad says we have a good legal leg to stand on thanks to Liam's smooth-brained rutting alpha idiocy, this is our baby. I don't want to spend months or years locked in a legal custody battle.

When the lust and pheromones fade, will she resent us? Regret this? This woman will be in our lives for the next eighteen years at a minimum. What if we're not the pack she always dreamed of? I read that alphas and omegas form attachment through touch and sex and the exchange of fluids. Some evolutionary heat-rut byproduct from the ancient days when they bonded before they knew one another. But I don't think I could force myself to fuck her if I don't like her. That's not how I'm wired.

"You're letting the heat out," Gabriel says with a knowing glance. "It'll cook faster if you close the door."

I close the oven and make myself busy with the broccolini. I blanched it in advance, and now I'm drying it off so it'll get a nice char. "I want everything to be perfect."

"It will, *meu amor*." Gabriel bends down and kisses my cheek. "She'll love dinner. And she'll love you."

"That's easy for you to say. You're… you." I wave a hand up and down his torso.

"What does that mean?" Gabriel puts his palm on his chest like he's actually confused.

I sigh with exasperation. "You understand exactly what I'm talking about. You're tall, fit, good looking, and you're exaggerating your accent on purpose because you know people love that shit. You immigrated here when you were five. You don't have an accent when you speak English unless you want to."

"I have no idea what you're talking about." Gabriel pulls a bottle of white wine from the rack. "What wine should we pair with macaroni and cheese?"

I snatch the wine from his hands and put it back. "She's pregnant, remember? She can't have wine."

He looks offended. "A small taste is okay. It's not like I'd encourage her to get drunk."

I shake my head and check on the mac and cheese again. It's bubbling nicely. When it's done, I'll broil a cracker topping with some butter. "Didn't you read any of the books Liam bought?"

Gabriel pours himself a glass of water instead. "I did. It was very dirty. I loved it."

"What? No. Not *that* book. The pregnancy ones. Didn't you do an OB rotation in school?"

He leans against the counter, drinking his water. He shudders. "I try not to remember that rotation." Gabriel grabs me by my shirt, wrinkling it as he tugs me against him. He kisses me, then stares into my eyes. "She'll love you. Like I do. Just be yourself."

That's what I'm worried about. I'm not flirty like Liam and Gabriel are. I have to spend a lot of time with someone and like them before I grow those sort of feelings or interest. That's never bothered me until now. Because we're in a time crunch. She's already ten weeks pregnant.

What if platonic isn't good enough? Omegas and alphas usually have high sex drives. That's why more often than not, they end up in packs. Gabriel is happy to help out, but me? I don't know. I don't know *her*. I've never even seen her.

There's a knock on the door, and Gabriel goes to answer it while I panic and hide in the kitchen.

"Come in. Dinner's almost ready," Gabriel says, playing host. "Would you like something to drink?"

"Water is fine," she says.

Gabriel comes into the kitchen to get her a glass of ice water, and Kat follows him, looking around. She spots me and gives me an awkward smile.

I knew it. I told them this was weird. I said we should have gone to a restaurant. Somewhere neutral.

"Hi," she says, pulling her long hair to one side. "I'm Kat. You must be Matthew."

"I am. It's nice to meet you." I try to shake her hand, but realize that I left my oven mitt on. Embarrassed, I pull it off and try again. "Oh, sorry. I was cooking."

"Well, it smells great, so thank you." She shakes my hand once and lets it drop.

"Thank you. I was happy for the excuse to try a new recipe."

Her smile becomes more genuine and some of my worry eases. They were right. She's nice.

"It still needs about twenty minutes before it's ready," I tell her.

"Is there anything I can do to help?" she asks.

I don't particularly want her in my kitchen. It's small. But I can't say no. "Want to help me cook the broccolini? I blanched them, but they still have to cook in the cast iron pan."

She steps up beside me and watches my movements. I put our heavy cast iron skillet onto a burner, then turn it up on high and heat up some grapeseed oil. Once it's hot, I add the broccolini and give her a spatula. "Spread them out so they're not clumped together. Let them get a good sear until they blacken. I'll grab the salt and pepper for you."

Kat uses the spatula to move the broccolini around while I set the salt and pepper grinder out for her to season them. "Liam said you were a good cook."

He did? I wonder what else he's told her about us. "I like it so long as someone else does the dishes."

"Do you do most of the cooking?" she asks.

"Don't let him lie to you," Gabriel says, coming back to the kitchen. "I cook too. You have to try my *pão de queijo*."

"What's that?" she asks.

Gabriel joins us in the kitchen and leans against the sink, out of the way. "A chewy Brazilian bread made from tapioca flour and cheese."

"That sounds really good," she agrees.

"I told you she would like Brazilian food." Gabriel looks her up and down, then winks. "I had a feeling she had good taste."

A light blush stains her cheeks and she focuses on turning the broccolini over to sear the other side. "I can't stomach anything but carbs right now," she says. "Eating every couple of hours helps. Big meals make me sick. But I can't complain too much. The nausea is a good sign, and it'll get better soon in the second trimester."

"Do you like wine?" Gabriel asks. He ignores my subtle expression telling him to *stop*.

"Normally, yeah," she answers. "Every once in a while."

"What sort of wine would you pair with mac and cheese?" Gabriel asks.

"I guess it would depend on the cheese?" She looks to me for help.

"There are six," I answer. "Sharp and mild cheddar, monterey jack, shaved provolone, parmesan, and cubes of gouda." The cheese alone was a hundred dollars from the bougie grocer down the street. But I like shopping locally when I can. And it was too short notice to go to a farmer's market. Also, if I'm honest, I wanted to impress her.

"Maybe a chardonnay," she says.

"Excellent." Gabriel finds a bottle of chardonnay from our rack and searches through the junk drawer for our bottle opener.

The oven beeps and I ask her to step aside for a moment so I can pull the mac and cheese out to do the topping. I crushed the cracker and herb mixture in advance. While the butter melts, I sprinkle the topping on. When that's done, I pour the melted butter all over and put it under the broiler to crisp. I glance at the broccolini and decide it's cooked enough to start the plating.

"That looks done to me. Let's get it off the heat," I tell her.

"Okay." She reaches for the handle, and I realize too late that she doesn't expect it to be hot. She must be used to nonstick pans where the handles don't heat up. "Fuck! Oww."

"Are you okay?" I grab her wrist to look at her hand. There's a red mark, but it's not bad. Not yet. "We should put some ice on that."

"Not ice," Gabriel says, intervening to peer at her burn. "It'll make it blister. Let's stick your hand under cool water."

He brings her over to the sink and puts her hand under the cool tap.

"I'm ruining dinner. I'm sorry," she says while I take over the food prep and Gabriel tends to her injury.

"This little thing?" he says, pulling her hand out of the cool water to inspect it. "Hmm. No, you're right. We might have to amputate," he deadpans.

I glance over my shoulder at him, horrified, but she laughs. "You're kind of ridiculous."

"See?" Gabriel says, putting her hand back under the water. "You get us so well already." He winks at her. "I'll set the table."

He grabs a stack of plates from the cabinet and goes to set the dining table. We cleared it off and I put a tablecloth and fresh flowers on it this morning before work.

The front door closes and Liam calls out that he's home. "In here," I answer.

He comes into the kitchen. "Well, this is a pretty sight. And that's a lovely smell. Hello, handsome," he says, prowling toward me and pulling me in for a kiss. "Hello, beautiful." He does the same to Kat.

After he pulls away and says he's going to change out of his work clothes for dinner, she glances at me shyly. As if checking to make sure that everything's okay. I like that.

I smile at her and nod to the drawer to her left. "The silverware is in there if you don't mind taking it to the dining room."

"Of course." She turns the tap off, dries her hand, then gathers up four sets of knives, forks, and spoons. Kat takes them to the dining table, and I hear her and Gabriel talk in low voices.

I take the macaroni and cheese out of the oven, turn it off, and transfer the broccolini to a nicer dish. Carefully I take both out to the table and set them on two wooden trivets next to a basket of fresh sliced bread. I got it from the bakery down the street. I get the crock of butter from the fridge and put that next to the bread.

"Are you sure?" Gabriel asks, holding the bottle of wine and a wine glass up.

Kat waves him away from her seat. "No, I'm fine with water. But don't let me stop you."

I like that too. She's easygoing.

More at ease now, I slide into my seat and give into Gabriel's insistence that he pours me a glass. He sets down filled wine glasses for him and Liam too. Liam joins us. He's changed into slacks and a black button-up with the sleeves rolled up. He takes his position at the head, then takes the first scoop of dinner, loading up his plate.

"How was work?" he asks me.

I tell him about the new person they hired at the bank. They start next week for training. Gabriel catches us up on some of the latest drama at the hospital. One of the overnight staff got caught sleeping in a supply closet.

Liam passes the serving spoon to Gabriel. We all take turns filling our plates. Once we've all been served, Kat looks between us. "Did you want to say grace?" she asks.

"Hmm?" Liam looks up from his forkful of mac and cheese. "Do you want to?"

"Didn't you say you're Catholic?" she asks.

Gabriel snorts and raises his glass of wine to his lips. "He goes to church twice a year. On Easter and Christmas."

Liam gives him an unamused expression. "And weddings and funerals. I don't have to kneel in a church to believe in God."

"He's a lapsed Catholic," I explain, seeing her confusion. "His parents were very religious. We don't see them very often.

They moved far away and… well, they had a hard time with the *mated to men* thing."

"Oh." Her brow furrows. "I'm sorry."

Liam shrugs it off and chews his food. "It took time for them to come around, but they're fine now. Especially with…"

With the baby on the way.

The mood in the room shifts a little as Liam puts his foot in his mouth.

"Mmm." Kat stabs her fork into her mac and cheese and takes a bite, chewing slowly. "This is amazing."

I give her a smile and hand her the bread basket. "I'm glad you like it. Thank you for helping."

She pushes her broccolini around on her plate. "I'm not sure I helped much, but thanks for letting me. I like to bake more than cook."

"Oh?" I arch a brow in interest and lean toward her. "What do you like to make?"

"We've lost them," Gabriel says to Liam, trying to steal the attention. "They'll be talking about yeast for hours."

"Ignore him," I say. "He's jealous because he burns everything that's not breakfast or Brazilian food his mom taught him to make."

"That shepherd's pie was delicious, thank you," he says, acting offended.

I rise to the bait. This is a familiar old squabble. "There were eggshells in it. There aren't even supposed to be any eggs in shepherd's pie."

"The egg yolk in the mashed potatoes makes it brown better," he argues.

"Ignore him," I tell her. "Just talk over him. It's the only way you get a word in sometimes."

"Normal things, I guess," she says. "Cookies, cakes, brownies, that sort of thing. Although I did go through a bad spell and got really into making bread after my… after I went through a tough time. I even tried to make my own sourdough starter, but it's a lot harder than it seems."

"See?" Gabriel says, talking to Liam. "Yeast."

"Shh. I want to hear this," Liam says.

"Bread is really difficult to get right," I say. "There's a lot of chemistry and science involved. Cooking is generally easier than baking," I agree with her.

We spend the rest of the dinner chatting and eating. Once we're done, Liam suggests a movie. It's a tactical move we talked about in advance. Our couch is big enough for three people, but not as comfortable for four. That means we'll get to touch her. He says that's really important for omegas who like small, enclosed spaces and pack piles.

"What kind of movies do you like?" he asks, bringing up one of our streaming services.

"I'm not picky," she says. "I'll watch almost anything."

"How about this one?" Liam pulls up a thriller. It's the psychological kind, not the gory chainsaw kind. "I heard the reviews were good and it's new."

"Sure."

We sit on the couch. Liam takes an end seat, putting her between him and Gabriel. He knows I don't always like to be touched by people I don't know well. I take the chaise portion, settling myself against Gabriel's leg.

Ten minutes into the movie, Liam's omega seduction plan falls apart. Kat falls asleep, her head on his shoulder and her sock-covered feet tucked under Gabriel's thigh. It's cute. And then Kat begins to softly snore. The cuteness factor drops a smidge.

We sit through the movie anyway, scared to move or turn the movie off and wake her. The pregnancy must make her tired. I read that fatigue is really common in the beginning.

The movie is good, but I predict the twist about halfway through and lose interest. Instead, I turn on my side and study her. The mother of my child. She's pretty. Liam's gorgeous. Our baby is going to be adorable.

Liam plays with her hair, moving it out of her face. It's an excuse to touch her, really. He's already feeling possessive.

And because I'm staring up at her, I see what they don't.

Old healed pack marks bitten into the side of her neck.

Our omega's been claimed before.

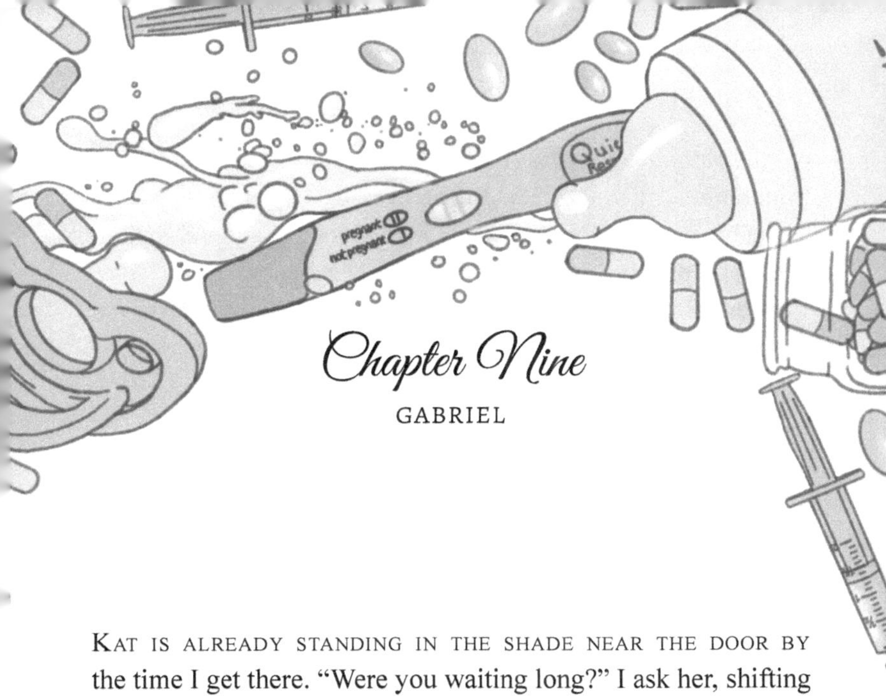

Chapter Nine

GABRIEL

Kat is already standing in the shade near the door by the time I get there. "Were you waiting long?" I ask her, shifting my duffle bag higher on my shoulder.

"No. Only a few minutes," she says. "Jen dropped me off. My car's in the shop."

"I'll give you a ride home when we're done."

She flashes me a smile. "Thanks."

She looks good. Tight spandex hugs her curves. Her pregnancy isn't showing yet even though she's twelve weeks along now. She's wearing light blue yoga pants and an extra-long strappy sports bra to match. Kat looks good enough to eat.

I put a hand on the small of her back and get the door. "Let's go sign in."

The worker checking everyone into the gym smiles at us. I hold my card to the reader, then sign her in as my guest and pay for her day pass with my phone.

"Oh, I could have gotten it," she says.

As if there was any chance I'd let her pay for our first date. "Don't be silly. I'm the one who asked you to join me. Come on, the classes are on the fourth floor." I grab two rolled towels from the stack and lead her to the elevators.

"This gym is insane," she says, looking around before getting on the elevator. "I heard it's really expensive."

Normally it is. "I get a huge discount because I work for the hospital. We send patients here for rehab and PT."

The elevator beeps and the doors open.

"What do you do at the hospital?" she asks.

"I'm a physician's assistant."

"I didn't know that was a job. Do you like it?"

"I do," I answer. "I like working thirty-six hours a week and helping the trauma team and surgeons."

Kat shivers. "Writing about blood and gore is one thing. I don't think I could handle seeing it in real life."

Kat's adorable. I'm beginning to see why Liam was so drawn to her, even without the scent match driving him wild. There's something about her that drives up the protective instincts. The elevator jostles to a stop before I can think of a response.

We get out on our floor and find the right studio for our yoga class. It's a prenatal yoga class, and getting into it is difficult because it's popular. I had to sweet talk the instructor into squeezing us in.

We take our shoes and socks off and store them in a cubby outside, then walk in barefoot. There are mats for the students to use. I get her one and a resistance band and blocks, then help her set up her station. Folding chairs have already been set out to mark the spots for students, and about half of them have already arrived.

We sit together, mimicking the others. She sits cross-legged while I sit behind her, giving her support. I take the opportunity to study her while the both of us wait.

With her hair up in a ponytail, I can see the old mating

marks that Matthew swears he saw the other night. It's true. She's been mated before.

Kat looks over her shoulder at me. "I don't think I'm showing enough for this class," she whispers.

The pregnant women and male omegas here are further along than she is. Their partners touch and cradle their big bellies. I reach around and do the same. "This class is hard to get into. It's good to start early."

She lets me hold her, stiff at first, then leaning against me for back support. I rub her belly where our tiny bean is nestled safely in her womb and growing. It's flat for now. Only a hint of softness that says she's healthy and fertile. But soon she'll start to show. I can't wait.

"When's your next scan?" I ask her.

"Twenty weeks, so a while. I'm only twelve weeks along right now."

"We'd all like to be there, if that's okay with you." Matthew and I weren't allowed to attend the first one to confirm the heartbeat and due date. The clinic wouldn't let us since we weren't involved with the breeding. I don't want to miss all of our baby's milestones.

"Of course," she answers.

The instructor comes in and starts giving instructions, explaining how this works for the new people in the class. Kat sits upright and listens intently. I'm a bit more distracted. From my vantage spot behind her, I can see right down her sports bra. It's a bit too tight for her. Her breasts are already getting bigger.

The instructor dims the light and turns on gentle new age music. "And now for the partners, your job is to provide support. Pregnancy affects a person's center of gravity and balance as the baby develops. Let's start with some breathing exercises to develop nice, healthy lungs before we move into tree pose."

Kat is right. The class is slightly awkward with her flat stomach. But I don't mind the excuse to spend time with her. Or touch her. I want her to be connected to all of us, not just Liam. Whether that's strictly friendship or something more is up to her, but it's important she knows I'm here for her. However she wants me. We all are.

When she moves into tree pose and tries to stand on one leg, she wobbles. I catch her before she topples over. Kat hangs onto me as I get her upright again, providing support while her ankle wobbles again. "Shit, this is hard," she whispers.

"You'll get stronger," I promise her. It's a weekly class, and I've worked it out with the other PAs on my team to always have Tuesdays off.

When it's time for floor work, she doesn't need me as much. That means I get to stare at her shapely ass while she arches and scoops her back in the cat-cow pose.

"Don't enjoy this too much," she mumbles.

Grinning, I splay my hand across her lower back and make her dip lower, pushing her ass up higher. "What do you mean?"

She twists and gives me a knowing look while I smile.

"Now lay your chest down and twist, bringing one arm through. This is called threading the needle. If it's not comfortable to be that low, you can use a block. This is prenatal yoga so we're focusing on opening up that pelvis. Making a nice, healthy core to help with the baby's birth."

Kat watches the instructor, then moves into the pose. I stroke her back, brushing lightly over her ass, then drag my hand back up to her ribs.

For the warrior and goddess poses, I actually have to do more than tease her. Her balance is shit. It's a good thing we're starting this early. I don't want her falling once her belly's bigger.

"Now we'll end in a nice, easy seated pose. Bring your

hands together, and if you'd like to set an intention for the day, do so now." The instructor pauses, giving people time to meditate. "Om," everyone says, dragging the sound out until they run out of breath.

"I feel taller," she says after I've helped her stand. "That was harder than I thought it would be."

I'm glad she liked it. Matthew hates the gym and Liam barely has to do more than think about weight lifting to bulk up. It'll be nice to have a workout buddy. "Stretching is good for you. And it'll help with the aches later. Do you want to see the rest of the gym? There's a pool."

"A pool?" she asks, excited. "Absolutely."

I make a mental note to sign us both up for a water aerobics class sometime. I look good in a swimsuit. She definitely won't be able to resist me then.

"And there's a hot tub, but you can't use that until after you have the baby. There are steam rooms and a dry sauna in each locker room." I take her around the gym, showing her the running track that circles the room of weight machines. There's a smaller room filled with free weights, and there are eight studios for yoga, pilates, and aerobics. The pool and hot tub take up the entire bottom level, and there are indoor courts for various sports as well as a tennis, basketball, and pickleball court outside. A juice bar with small alcoves for people to rest or get some work done on the wi-fi takes up half of the second floor. Physical therapy and outpatient rehab spaces occupy the other half.

"It's a beautiful fitness center," she says. "Did you want to work out? I know you're not just here for the mommy-baby yoga." She eyes me before looking away as if she's self-conscious.

Has she been looking? The thought gives me hope. I trust Liam's nose. If he says she's pack, then I believe him. Besides, it's nice to not be the newest packmate. Matthew and Liam have known each other for so long that sometimes it's hard to not feel slightly intimidated by the depth of their history.

I bring her back to the weight room and show her how to use the machines, resetting the weight down to the lowest setting, slowly adding more until I see what she can handle. Once she's set, I find another machine and move the pin down.

Building muscle as a beta is hard work. Alphas seem to pack on muscle simply by thinking about exercise. For everyone else, it takes determination and perseverance. After ten machines, I've sweated through my shirt. I move around to the chin up bar and whip my shirt off, tucking it in the waistband of my shorts. I grab the bar and start doing pull ups.

While I'm working, I look for her among the machines. Kat's sitting on the bicep curl, staring at me, while a middle-aged man hovers nearby for his turn, annoyed. I wink at her as I pull myself up again and she turns pink.

She's not the only woman sneaking glances. I tighten my abs while pulling myself up, then shift to the side to work my obliques. Women linger near the stretching station by the pull-up bar. It's nice to be admired. To have all of my hard work appreciated. As a beta, I've always had to work harder to be fit. Kat can admire me as much as she wants. I like knowing that she's interested in me too and not just our alpha.

But how interested is she? I'm itching to test that. To see if she wants me, too.

When Kat's done with her workout, she comes to join me. I drop from the pull-up bar and put my hand on her back. "Let's find a quiet corner."

I bring her to a classroom that's not being used today and lay a mat down on the floor. She eyes it warily. "What's this for?"

"You need to stretch or you'll be sore. I'll help you."

"Uh-huh," Kat says skeptically. But she sits down on the mat and starts working on her leg muscles. When she twists into a hip crossover, I push her leg a little further and assess her hip bones to make sure she's opening up her pelvis properly.

"You just want another excuse to touch my ass," she says, eying me.

"It's a nice ass." I grin and stare at her cute butt. "Does it bother you?"

She thinks for a moment. "No."

I push a smidge harder, using my other hand as a counter-pressure. Her hip joint cracks, releasing tension.

"Oh, shit. That was amazing." Kat's groan of relief gives me dirty thoughts. It makes me wonder if that's what she'll sound like when I'm buried deep inside her and making her feel good.

"Can you do the other side?" she asks innocently.

I pop her other hip, then notice the damp spot on her light yoga pants. Is that sweat or arousal? I drag my hand down between her legs, rubbing over her pussy. Her yoga pants have the diamond shape at the crotch instead of the flat seam. It's a perfect target.

"How about here? Is there tension here?" I ask.

Her eyelids flutter while I massage her pussy, rubbing up and down. "Yes."

"Do you want me to relieve it?" I ask, pressing her yoga pants into her cleft while I rub. *Say yes. Meu Deus, please say yes. Please say you want me, too.*

She glances around the empty classroom, then nods. I grab her under her hips and tug her onto her back. Spread her thighs so her legs are bent on either side of me while I kneel between them. Once she's settled, I zero in on her pussy again.

I rub her diamond-shaped seam, pressing my thumb into her slit. Is she wearing panties under them? A thong? I didn't see a panty line during yoga. God knows I was staring at her ass enough to tell.

Liam says pregnant omegas are insatiable and needy. God, I hope that's true. I'm gonna make her fall in love with me one orgasm at a time until the thought of walking away from us is unbearable. Because I think she could be perfect for us. She could be exactly what our pack needed.

Her cheeks flush a pretty shade of pink and her breath catches. Her breasts push together making a pretty Y shape at the top of her bra. Her tits are natural. A perfect handful. I reach my other hand up and palm one, squeezing it.

She flinches and I could kick myself. She's pregnant. They're probably sensitive. I settle for teasing her nipple instead. Circling the ring of her areola as it puffs up, swelling from her arousal. Her nipple hardens into a firm peak that tents the fabric of her sports bra.

"Does that feel good, *meu docinho*?"

"What does that mean?" she asks instead of answering me. Her hips flex. She grinds her pussy harder against my hand.

"Hmm… It means you're sweet. My sweetie."

"I like that," she sighs, her hips rolling with the movement of my hand. Making a rhythm.

The damp spot spreads on her fitted yoga pants. I dig them into her, soaking more of it. Watching it darken. I rub her firmer. Faster. She moans and her hands fidget on the yoga mat. Her breathing gets louder and faster.

The door of the studio opens, and I twist to look over my shoulder. There are two middle-aged women standing there, looking confused. "Is this the aerobics class with Marie?"

Kat chokes on a moan, but I don't stop rubbing her. They can't see anything really while I'm blocking their view of her. I stroke my thumb up and down her wet slit, going over where I know her clit must be. Again. And again.

"No, it's not," I tell them. "I think that's down the hall in studio one."

"Oh. What are you doing in here?" one of the ladies asks.

I think fast, coming up with an excuse. "Crunches. She's taking a quick break."

"I can hear her panting. You're really working her hard. Are you a new personal trainer?" one asks.

"I could use a trainer," the other woman adds.

I flash them a smile, and keep rubbing Kat's pussy. "No. I'm her boyfriend." I love the way that sounds. It makes me want to say it again.

The other woman says something like *lucky* and the door closes as they go searching for their class.

"Fuck," Kat whines once they're gone. She bites her lip and lets out a filthy moan.

If she was wearing a tennis skirt, I would. But I'm not as ballsy as Liam. And I really don't want to get banned from my gym. "Later," I promise her.

Kat groans, her nipples rock hard and her hips grinding. I rub her faster until she stiffens. Until her breath catches and her muscles tense. She's about to come and her body won't let her move. All she can do is lie there and take it, then fall to pieces against my hand.

Her head arches back and she comes, slick soaking the crotch of her leggings. It stains her leggings with an obvious dark spot.

Oops. We're gonna have a hard time hiding that.

She pants and lies there, spent, her legs falling wider apart as she recovers. I give her pussy one last fond rub, then take one of her legs and bend it toward her chest.

"What are you doing?" she asks, frowning.

"Stretching you."

"I didn't think you were serious about that." With a grunt, she lets me do it.

"I'm always serious when it comes to health and fitness." I put her through a series of gentle stretches so she won't get sore. I do the same while she watches, then pull her up from the floor.

I hand her my shirt.

"What's this for?" she asks.

"To cover you." I point to her crotch where her arousal has soaked through the light material and made it darker.

"Ah, fuck."

"We should probably get you some darker workout clothes." And a tennis skirt. Several of them.

She puts my shirt on and it dwarfs her, the hem going halfway down her thighs. It's cute. Like it's oversized on purpose. And the blend of our pheromones plus her arousal is going to drive Liam insane. I can't wait.

"Let's go, *meu docinho*. You've earned a smoothie."

Kat makes a face and follows me out, down to the floor with the snack bar. "Can they make toast?"

"They serve sandwiches and wraps, so probably." I know it's hard, but I wish she'd eat more than carbs. What brand of prenatal vitamins is she taking? Some brands are better than others.

I get her toast and a strawberry banana yogurt smoothie, then order one with coconut, pineapple, and their energized protein powder for myself. We eat at the tables and people-watch. All sorts of folk come to this gym since it has medical services too. I think they even do medical massages somewhere.

"Done?" I ask when she's drunk half her smoothie and there's nothing but crumbs left on her plate.

"Yeah." I throw our trash out and lead her out to the front. We drop our used towels off in the enormous laundry basket.

I unlock my car and open the door for her, then close it once she's in and go around. With the windows cracked and the AC pumping, it cools down quickly as I drive her back home. Once I'm on the main road, I reach over and take her hand, holding it. She squeezes it and turns in her seat to look at me.

"I still don't know much about you guys," she says. "Doing things backward like this is… It's been odd."

How we met was unconventional, but that doesn't mean it's bad. I like to think that everything happens for a reason even if we don't know what that reason is at the moment. It's easy to expect the worst of life. Especially when you've seen the trauma and misery that I've seen because of my job. It's harder to have faith. But isn't that what faith is? Belief in spite of the way things seem.

"You want to know more about me?" I ask her.

"Yeah."

I think about what to tell her while I navigate traffic. "I was born in Brazil, but I barely remember it. My parents immigrated here when I was a child. I was held back in school for a year while I learned enough English to attend regular classes. My parents decided that it was best to speak only English at home so we'd assimilate faster. By the time I learned enough English to be in regular classes, I was a year older and bigger than the other kids. That made it harder for me to make friends at first."

Kat makes a sympathetic noise and squeezes my hand for support. She's empathetic and kind. I like that about her.

"A few kids made fun of the food I brought from home, so I asked my parents for lunch money instead. I wanted to fit in. To hurry up and become American. I learned how to be what people expected. At the time, I didn't realize that I was giving up parts of myself and my heritage that I'd one day struggle to get back. The truth is, that being a son of immigrants made me feel like I never truly belonged to either world. I wasn't American enough for Americans and I wasn't Brazilian enough for Brazilians. Like I had one foot in each country but didn't belong in either. It took me a long time to figure out who I am and decide that I'm the one who gets to choose where I want to belong. Finding my pack helped ground me."

"I can't imagine what that was like," she says after a moment of silence. "It must have been so hard."

I like that she hears me, but doesn't try to erase the pain of my childhood. That she doesn't offer empty platitudes. Instead, she listens.

"It was hard, but it was worth it. I like to think that things work out the way they should if we let them. That all the bad and hurt is worth the good. Because in the end, it led me to my pack. And I wouldn't trade them for anything. It took a long time, but I finally found my home."

"That sounds nice," she says wistfully. A peek at her shows me that she's looking out the window.

Should I push? My heart rate picks up at the thought. I don't want to blow it. But I don't want to sit on the sidelines either while Liam gets to enjoy our new packmate all to himself either.

"I hope you'll find your home with us too," I tell her.

Kat ducks her head and makes a noncommittal noise, but her tiny wistful smile tells me she likes the idea. It's okay if she's not ready to admit it to herself yet. I don't know what her old pack did to her, but I'm looking forward to erasing every single doubt from her head. Liam said that omegas need constant touch and sex while they're settling into their pack. I'm more than happy to take one for the team and reassure her about how badly we want her.

"It's okay if you need time, sweetheart," I say. "I'll believe it for both of us until then." At the next red light, I bring our clasped hands to my lips and press a kiss to her knuckles. Her skin is so damn soft and underneath her sweat and faint pheromones I smell her body wash and shampoo. It makes me hard.

"What about you?" she asks.

"Hmm?"

"Aren't you… You didn't come. Don't you want to?" She eyes my lap where my semi tents my workout shorts.

Liam wasn't exaggerating about her love of car sex, I guess. I was going to wait until we got back to her place, then suggest we take a shower together. But if she doesn't want to wait then I'm not going to complain.

"Good idea, *meu docinho.*" There's a spot not far from here that might work. I turn off at the next intersection, then go a ways down the road until I pick up a backroad.

"Where are we going?" she asks, looking out the window.

"There's a trail I used to jog on that nobody really uses."

I tug my hand free and work it down the waistband of her yoga pants. A thong. This girl's gonna fucking kill me. I slip under her thong. Her pussy's still wet. Perfectly slick and ready for me and what I've got in mind.

"Take my shirt off," I order. I want to see her breasts.

She does it, wiggling out of the shirt under her seatbelt and tossing it into the backseat. Spreads her legs wider for me too. I work two fingers between her lips, find her clit, and rub until she's panting and fidgeting again.

By the time she starts to grind, we pull up on our destination. A seldom-used hiking trail with a tiny parking lot off an old country road. I found this place once by accident. The trail's okay. No spectacular views. I think that's why nobody really comes here.

I pull my hand out of her panties and slide my seat back, making room. Then I take my seatbelt off and push my shorts down. My cock springs free, aching and ready. I pat my thigh. "Come ride me."

"I don't know if I'm flexible enough for this," she says.

"We'll work on this every Tuesday too."

She snorts and undoes her seatbelt. "Like a standing dick appointment? Sexercise?"

"Exactly." I pat my lap and wait expectantly.

Kat creeps awkwardly across the car. I help her climb onto my lap, pulling her pants down in the process. The round globes of her sweet ass on my thighs are heaven. I pull her thong to the side. It's light pink. So cute and sexy. This girl's definitely gonna be the end of me.

"The angle's weird," she complains while hovering and using the steering wheel for balance.

There's nothing wrong with the angle. I brush my cock against her wet slit, soaking it in her juices. And then I notch it at her entrance and thrust inside, pulling her onto my lap so she's sitting on me.

She moans as I bottom out inside her.

"Angle seems fine to me," I tell her, using her hips to lift her up and down on my cock. God, her pussy is so damn good. Tight, wet, and ready. There's no need to prep. No careful planning or skipping dinner. Just pull her panties to the side and sink all the way in. A soaking wet hole ready for cock. So fucking easy.

"You feel so damn good," I tell her. "Such a good girl. Your pussy's so wet for me."

"Oh, God," she moans, abandoning the steering wheel to lean on the dash instead. "Don't stop."

The only downside to this position is I can't watch her pretty breasts bounce while I fuck her. *Next time.* Next time I'll make her straddle my lap so I can suck on her nipples while we fuck.

Her ass and thighs jiggle with every thrust. I watch it in amazement, addicted to seeing how hard she's taking my cock. She's delightfully squishy in all the right places.

"Gabriel," she moans.

I love the sound of my name on her lips. Love her breathy pants. Her stifled moans. Watching her lose control, making her need me. Making her crave me and how good I can make her feel. Who needs a knot? I can make her come without one.

I'm really looking forward to our weekly gym sessions.

Our body heat fogs the windows despite the AC's attempts to cool it down while idling.

With one hand wrapped around to stroke her clit, I fuck her hard. Fast. Thank God she's short or her head might hit the car's ceiling. I thrust with my hips, summoning every ounce of strength in my legs to fuck her raw. Thank God it wasn't leg day today.

Her thighs quiver. Shake. Her soft, rounded skin ripples. Each breath of hers comes out more ragged. More desperate.

"That's it, *meu docinho*." I strum her clit, no mercy. "Come on my cock."

As if she's obeying my command, or she was waiting for permission, Kat comes. She cries out, her walls clamping down. Fluttering on my cock. It's too much. Too tight and perfect.

My balls pull tight against my body. I spread my thighs wider and thrust deeper, slower. I come, cock pulsing. Balls emptying. My cock jerks inside her, and my thrusts turn languid. I pump cum into her, driving it in deep with each milking thrust.

We sit there, recovering, while birds chirp outside and the wind blows through the trees.

Next time I'll take her into the woods, strip us both naked, and fuck her up against a tree. Exactly as nature intended. I'll rut her raw and fill her till her pussy's dripping.

"Fuck, *meu docinho*." I pet her, my fingers making circles on her exposed skin. "That was good."

"Mmm."

She's languid in my arms. Sweet and pliable. I cradle her, letting her calm down. Watch her breathing return to normal. I kiss her temple, taking a moment to enjoy whatever shampoo she uses. Girls always have the best-smelling hair. That's probably my favorite thing about them.

She leans back against me and I rub her, enjoying the feel of her in my arms. All mine for the moment. But I won't mind sharing her. In fact I can't wait for the day when Liam and I split her between us. It's someone else's turn to be the spit roast, and Matthew always seems to weasel out of it.

"That was so good," I say, rubbing her arms. Her belly. Cradling her, because she's precious.

"Best workout ever," she sighs.

I huff out a laugh. "Cardio is good for the baby."

"Oh yeah? Is that doctor's orders?"

"Yes. At least thirty minutes a day three times a week."

"Only three?" she asks, teasing me.

"Minimum." I grin and grind her pussy down on my softening cock. "More is better."

"Mmhmm. I'll bet it is."

"You liked it," I goad her. "You like being naughty. Nearly getting caught."

After a brief pause, she admits it. "I do."

I squeeze her round thighs. "So do we."

"Even Matthew?" she asks.

Ah. "Matthew takes more time to get to know someone before he thinks of them like that. But don't let that fool you. He's the most perverted one of all."

"Liam said he's demisexual. I want you all to know I won't push him."

She's sweet. Sweet enough to eat. I nip her shoulder, then smooth the sting with a kiss. "He likes you."

"He does?" Her tone is surprised.

"Mmhmm. But he's banned you from his kitchen. It's for your own safety."

She laughs, and my softening cock nearly dislodges from her wet pussy. "Don't threaten me with a good time. I don't mind at all if he wants to do all of the cooking."

"He loves to feed us. That's how he says he cares. Why do you think I spend so much time at the gym?"

I wait for her to move when she's ready. Once she's recovered, I reach back and grab my shirt from the backseat and hand it to her. "Clean up with this."

Kat rises, my softening cock sliding free. She rubs the T-shirt between her thighs, then fixes her panties and pants. I help her collapse into her seat, then use the dirty shirt to wipe my cock. I tuck my cock away and fix my seat and mirrors.

The car sex was messy, but I'm glad she's already pregnant. That means I don't have to worry about condoms. Liam is the one who wanted to be the biological father. I don't care much either way. This means a lot more impromptu fun for me.

"We could use a shower, hmm?" I ask her. Maybe my plan for shower sex doesn't need to be postponed. Why not? In fifteen minutes I can be ready to go again.

"I got sweatier than I thought I would."

Once we're both situated and buckled in, I pull back onto the road and head toward her place.

She's quiet for a stretch. "You know what I realized?"

"Hmm?" I ask, concentrating on the road now that there's more traffic.

"We fucked and you came inside me, but we haven't kissed yet."

She's right. A fact I'm happy to rectify immediately as we pull up at a red light. "How thoughtless of me."

"It is," she agrees. *Cheeky girl.*

I reach over the console and thread my hand through her sagging ponytail, using it as a grip to pull her forward. I claim her mouth, kissing her slow and sweet. Tasting every inch of her. Her lips part for me like a good girl.

A car honks behind us, and I realize the light's turned green.

Hitting the accelerator, I head toward her home and, more importantly, her shower. I owe her a makeout session. Nobody said we couldn't be naked and wet too.

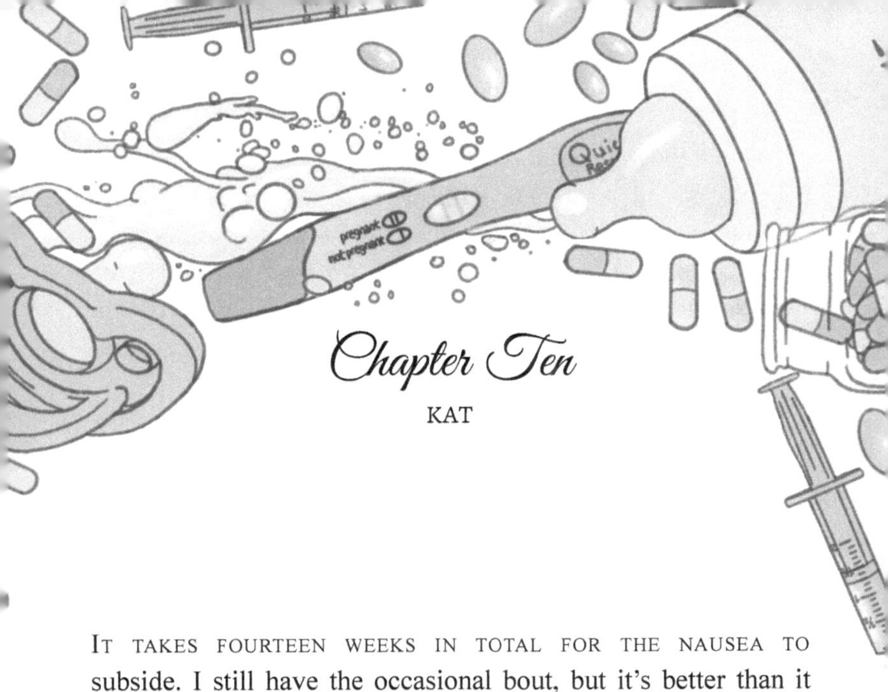

Chapter Ten

KAT

It takes fourteen weeks in total for the nausea to subside. I still have the occasional bout, but it's better than it was. My appetite's rebounded with a vengeance.

So has my appetite for other things. The constant pumping of blood to my pelvis makes me nearly as horny as a preheat. It would be unbearable if I didn't have two men happy to provide on-demand dick at a moment's notice.

I spend so much time at their place above the pub. If it wasn't for Waffles, I'd probably move in out of sheer convenience.

Concerns for the future worry me, though. Their place is too small for four adults and a cat, and a baby and all of a baby's stuff. And so is mine. My tiny house is perfect for me, Waffles and a baby. But all of us in a thousand square feet… We would be tripping all over each other.

We're going to need a bigger place, but I'm scared to pull that trigger and bring the topic up. That's a big commitment. And I've seen how quickly commitments can fall apart. Even ones that were supposed to be forever.

Things have been good. Better than good. But nothing is ever guaranteed. A lot could still change in six months.

I decide to hold off on that conversation. I can start looking, see what's on the market, and bring it up once we're past the twenty-four-week mark. There might not be anything good in this area right now anyway. I haven't house hunted in a few years.

But that's easy to fix. I find a real estate app and wait for it to download.

Liam texts me, breaking me out of my anxious planning for the future with a welcome distraction.

LIAM

Good morning kitten

How'd you sleep?

KAT

Good

I have energy again

Probably the first night I've slept less than 12 hours

You need the rest

You're growing a human

Are you coming over today?

I was supposed to meet up with Jen but she canceled

The baby is sick

So I get to see your pretty face today?

You've seen my pretty face four times this week

Are you sure you're not getting sick of me hanging around?

Never

Besides I have something for you

?

Dick? lol

You naughty girl

We got a good deal on eggplants this morning

Eggplant fries are the day's special side item

How could I possibly say no to that?

And I'll give you as much dick as you want too

How selfless of you

Right?

I'm practically a saint

And Gabriel says it's basically doctor's orders

Gotta keep that uterus happy with daddy's pheromones

It's carrying precious cargo

And I love when you say my name as you come

Even more when you scream it

I have a surprise for you too

What is it?

You'll have to wait to see it

I'll come by after I get some work done

See you soon

See you soon kitten

Don't keep daddy waiting too long

It's hard to focus on my work, but I make myself go through my ARC reader's feedback. I fix typos they've found and make mental notes of what they liked, what they didn't, and what needs to be adjusted. A few hours later, I set the edited manuscript aside for formatting later.

Standing, I stretch my stiff body, then play with Waffles a bit. "Sorry I've been gone so much." He meows and flips his belly into the sunbeam, blinking lazy eyes at me. It's too hard to resist the temptation. I pet his fluffy belly until he gets annoyed. Then I scatter some treats around the house for him to find while I'm gone and grab my stuff.

The pub is packed for a Thursday night. I see why once I

step inside. There's a sports game playing on half the TVs mounted around the room.

Liam sees me almost instantly, his face splitting into a big smile. I don't think I'll ever get tired of him looking at me that way. He's wiping a beer glass dry. The moment he gets a full look at me, he nearly drops the glass. Fumbling, he catches it before it can shatter on the floor.

I dug a fitted pink dress out of my closet today because it's tight. It shows off how big my breasts have gotten and the definite roundness of my belly that now looks like something more than bloat. I'm finally showing.

"Move over to a booth, Sal," he says to an old regular.

"What for?" Sal protests. "I haven't finished my pretzels."

"Don't you know you're supposed to stand for pregnant women? Here. Take a beer on the house and your pretzels with you. You can watch the game over there." He pulls a beer and sets it in front of Sal.

"Hmm?" Sal seems more interested in moving now that he has an incentive. He slides off his stool and gives me a onceover. "Oh. Well, aren't you a pretty little thing? If I were forty years younger…" He smiles wistfully, then takes his beer and pretzels and shuffles off.

I take Sal's seat and wait for my ginger ale. It's become our tradition. This time he puts a little cherry syrup and some bright red cherries in it to spice it up.

"Well, my surprise doesn't seem nearly as cool now," he says, setting the drink down on a napkin in front of me. He leans on the bar.

I grin and accept the drink. "I don't know… It sounds really good. I'm starving now no matter how much I eat."

"That's good. Means things are going right." He taps an order into the screen, then gets pulled away by a group of college guys. I think it's a little crazy that the pub's owner is acting like a bartender. But he said he misses it and that tending bar was always his favorite job. So he does a few hours here and there and fills in when someone's out sick.

I watch him work while sipping on my cherry ginger ale. He chats with regulars, clears off dirty glasses, and pours fresh drinks. He's right. It's mostly a beer and food place. They have more kegs on tap than bottles of liquor. Although no Irish pub is complete without a proper selection of whiskey.

One of the waitresses brings out my food from the kitchen. "Hey, Amanda."

"Hey, Kat. Oh my God! You're finally showing."

How many people did they tell? I rub my tiny belly and smile. Now that we're past the worst of the risk, I'm less nervous about people knowing. "I am. My app says the baby's the size of a kiwi."

"Congratulations," she says, moving the plate of eggplant fries and garlic aioli to where I can reach it. "I have one at home. Enjoy this time and sleep as much as you can. It goes by fast."

"I will."

She disappears to check on her tables and I eat my food. It's good. Liam gets me a refill of my drink while he's making his rounds. By the time I'm done eating, the real bartender—a beta named Eric—shows up.

"Took forever for the tow truck to come. I'm sorry," he apologizes.

"Don't worry about it," Liam says, clapping a hand on Eric's shoulder. "Accidents happen. That's why they're called accidents." He gives Eric a run down of who has what tab started.

When they're done and Liam turns to me, my body tightens with anticipation. He leans across the bar again. "If you're done with your eggplant, I've got another one to show you."

"Oh, do you? Is it in the back?" I tease him.

He winks at me. "It's upstairs."

I slide off my stool and follow him to the back, to the roped-off hidden stairs that lead up to the apartment. He lets me go first. Probably so he can watch my ass.

The minute we're inside, he pounces on me. The door hits my back as he crowds me against it. His hands wander all over my body. Tracing the flare of my hip. Ghosting over my small baby bump. Grabbing a handful of tits. They're less sore now than they were.

My nipples tighten, aching, and rub against my bra. And while he's groping me, he's kissing me until I'm breathless. We're both ravenous, but not for food.

We break for air, and he slides his nose down my jaw. My neck. His tongue licks my skin, tasting my pheromones where they're strongest at my scent gland.

"Sorry for the garlic breath," I apologize. Maybe I should have gone lighter on that aioli. It was so good, though.

"You've got me so hungry for you, kitten. I couldn't care less." He grabs my thigh and lifts it, holding me upright as he pins me against the wall. My tight skirt rides up, exposing my panties. His hips flex and his cock rubs my core through our layers of clothing. "You're so pretty with your baby bump. It makes me want to put another baby in this sweet little pussy."

My laugh turns into a moan with his grinding. The rub of his cock against my slit makes my brain short circuit. "That makes zero sense."

"What doesn't make sense is the fact that you're not naked right now."

He lifts me, his hands going under my ass, and my legs wrap around his hips. Liam carries me deeper into the apart-ment. Lays me down on their bed that smells like them. Like

Liam's evergreens and Matthew's icy snow woods and Gabriel's crackling fire. Like safety and pack.

"Am I crushing you?" he asks, trying to keep his weight off me as he keeps me under him.

"I like it." I slip my hands under his T-shirt and work it up, feeling all of the muscles of his back. He's so strong. A perfect alpha. I love the sense of safety his large frame gives me. The instinctive need I have to be covered by him. Hidden. Protected.

Liam sits up and grabs the edge of his shirt, pulling it off. He tosses it aside.

I run my hands over his chest and stomach. Trace the lines of his abdominals. The dip and bump of muscles. The breadth of his chest and his hair. A few strands are gray. I love it. It makes him so masculine and the hair traps his pheromones, making his smell stronger.

His hands cup my belly. Squeeze my inner thighs, spreading me wider. He brushes a light touch over my mound before moving higher, to palm my breasts. He's obsessed with my bigger breasts.

He traces the round shape of my areolas until they're puffy and pinches my nipples until they're rock hard and aching. I grind my hips, rubbing my pussy over his cock. Impatient. He strains against his jeans.

"Liam," I whine.

"Yeah, kitten?"

"I need you to fuck me."

Liam grins and pulls away, his hands reaching for his belt buckle. "Then get naked, kitten. I want to see that baby bump and those tits in all their glory."

I twist and try to get the zipper of my dress down. It's harder to get out of it than it was to get into it. He's already naked, his ruddy cock jutting into the air. And I haven't gotten very far at all.

"I think the zipper's stuck."

"Let me help." He puts a knee on the bed and climbs back in, then taps my hip.

I roll over onto my front.

"Let me see." Liam reaches for the zipper and tugs on it. It proves difficult even for him. He jerks the tab down, but it catches. It won't unzip.

"Is it stuck?" I ask.

"It's stuck." He gropes my ass, massaging it and spreading my cheeks apart.

"That's not my zipper," I tell him, glancing over my shoulder.

"It's not my fault your ass is perfectly spankable."

"Is it?" I ask, lifting my ass up high. God, it's been so long since I was spanked. "Are you sure about that? Maybe you should test it and find out."

He makes a rough sound in the back of his throat and gives my ass a light slap. It's barely a spank.

"You can do better than that," I goad him.

"Do you remember your safe word?" he asks, rubbing circles with his thumbs.

"Waffles."

He slaps me harder, but the blow doesn't leave a sting behind. His touch is light over my dress. It leaves me aching for more. It's good. Like my body is my own again. I feel more like myself again.

"I can take more," I tell him.

"I have another idea. Do you trust me?"

I barely pause before answering. They've all been nothing but great to me in this weird situation we've found ourselves in. Kind, patient, funny, and sexy as hell. Gabriel makes sure I get enough exercise. Matthew makes sure I'm eating healthier. And

Liam makes sure my sex drive stays manageable. In their own way, all of them take care of me.

"I do."

"How much do you love this dress?" he asks.

I wore it twice before I got pregnant, and in a week or two it probably won't fit at all. The zipper barely went up today as it is. I doubt I'll want to wear the tight bodycon dress after giving birth. "I don't care about it."

"Stay there. Whatever you do, don't move."

His ominous warning makes my pulse race. He leaves the room and comes back a moment later. I look over my shoulder, my breath hitching when I see what he's holding.

A knife.

The expression on his face is one of eager anticipation. Like a kid in a candy store. *Did he get to that scene in my new book?* The one where the mob boss cuts her tights and underwear off and fucks her over a table during a meeting while his under-bosses watch.

The front door opens and Matthew calls out that he's home. Is it already after six?

"In here!" Liam yells, grinning. He spins the knife in his hand. "Perfect timing. I need you."

"What do you need?" Matthew asks, coming closer. He stands in the doorway, head tilted. "Oh. What are we doing with that?"

"I need an audience. Want to watch?" Liam asks.

"I love it when you get creative," Matthew says. He drags the chair from the corner to the opposite side of the bed. Then he sits, his hands going to the buttons on his collar. He undoes them, loosening his shirt at the throat. His shirt cuffs are next.

The casual, confident way he sits with one ankle resting on his other knee is hot. When Matthew rolls his sleeves up his forearms and stops them halfway, I have to wonder if he's doing it on purpose. His expression is inscrutable. He's harder to read than the others.

The cool slide of the knife against my thigh jerks me out of my thoughts. The metal is smooth. Dangerous. Liam runs the flat of the blade across my thigh. Works his way toward the inside. He slaps my inner thigh with it.

"Wider."

I spread my thighs wider, opening up my core and straining the fabric of my tight dress. His warm hand sneaks under the skirt, stroking me over my panties.

"Is this making your pussy wet?" Liam asks while the blunt edge of the knife drags down my buttock.

"Yes." My eyes slide shut and I fist the sheets.

His hand rubs over my mound. Checking if it's true. He strokes me with his hand and the knife until my panties cling to me. To the damp spot sticking them to me. My pussy throbs.

He slips his hands from between my legs, then grabs the hem of the skirt. The sound of his knife puncturing and cutting through the fabric is loud. The tight fabric gives as he cuts a slit in it, then puts the knife down to rip it wide.

Fuck, that's even hotter than I dreamed it could be.

Liam takes his time with my dress. Making small cuts and ripping them wider. Sticking his fingers through the holes he's made. Teasing me all over while he slowly carves me out of my dress.

He tugs my panties to the side and slicks his thumb between my lips. Smearing my wetness. Spreading the proof of my arousal. He rubs my slick over me, then presses a finger inside.

"So wet for me. What a good pussy."

"How wet is she?" Matthew asks.

"Soaking."

Any sassy comeback I have is lost when he pumps. He adds

another finger. They move against my front wall and my pelvis tightens.

When he pulls free, my pending orgasm stuttering out, I moan with annoyance. Liam has the nerve to chuckle.

He finishes off my dress, cutting through the seam at the top and ripping it apart. Once the dress is a tattered mess that's falling off me, he goes for my panties next. The knife cuts clean through one side before I can protest. They sag, the fabric covering my pussy shifting.

"I liked those," I pout.

"I'll buy you more." He cuts the other side.

"Not my bra."

He yanks the tattered dress and panties out from under me, then lays the knife down at the edge of the bed.

Matthew reaches over and takes it, setting the point on the chair's arm and twirling it. His stare is dark and unreadable as he watches us.

Liam unhooks my bra and pulls it out from under me, tossing it to Matthew. The pink bra lands in his lap, but Matthew never lets go of the knife he's toying with. His eyes never leave us. We've been careful not to fuck in front of him before. *Is this really okay?*

Clothes rustle and the bed dips. Then the blunt head of Liam's cock probes at my slick entrance. My eyes flutter shut as he seats his dick inside me. All I can do is groan and twist my fingers in the sheets.

He fucks me deep and slow. Until the awful need I have for him is quenched. Pleasure builds as he dicks me down into the mattress. This was exactly what I needed.

"Harder," I beg him.

Liam pulls back out and slams home. My ass claps against his thighs. I moan and he tugs me up by my hips. Pulls me properly onto my knees, my face still pressed into the bed. It's not a proper nest, but it smells like them. All three of them. They had sex last night after I left. I wish they'd invited me to watch.

He fucks me from behind, doggy style. Fast. Needy. A hand between my shoulder blades pins my front to the bed. He tugs my hips up higher. Ass up as high as it'll go. Puts me where he wants me. Until the angle of his rapid thrusts is perfect and my toes curl.

"God, she's so fucking wet," he tells Matthew.

"How good is her pussy?" Matthew asks.

"It's fucking perfect."

"Pull her hair," Matthew orders.

Liam does it. He threads his fingers into my hair at the nape and makes a fist.

My breath rushes out of me with a low, throaty moan. I squeeze my eyes shut.

"Harder," Matthew orders. "She likes it."

Liam fucks me harder. Pulls my hair with one hand and squeezes my ass cheek with the other. The rapid, deep thrusts overwhelm me. My scalp burns with a dull, delicious ache. And Matthew watches all of it. Our depravity. Directs it.

I don't know if it's the audience or the position, but Liam's wild. It's like my heat all over again. When the sight of my upturned ass made him nearly feral to mount me.

My thighs tremble with the force of his thrusts and my orgasm swells. It tightens in my core, pulsing. Consuming.

"I'm gonna come," I moan.

"Come on my dick, kitten."

He barely gets the pet name out before the tension snaps. As if I were waiting for permission. My body goes still for an agonizingly long second, and then my pussy spasms.

"Oh, fuck," he groans. "That's it."

"Describe it," Matthew orders.

"She's milking my cock. I can't... I can't hold back any longer. God, I love this pussy. Your pussy's so damn good, kitten."

His pace slows, thrusts becoming deep and languid. He comes with a groan. Cock pulsing. Breathing hard. Cum filling me to bursting. His knot swells. Plugging me tight. Stoppering all those healthy pheromones in deep where I need them. Where I crave them. He's got me addicted to his dick. To his purr and pheromones, and to his kindness. He makes me feel safe again. Desired and cherished. I haven't felt that way in a long time. Longer than before my old pack split up.

Liam lets go of my hair and strokes me fondly. He uses my aftershocks and flutters to milk his knot. Collapses on top of me, his weight and scent a comforting blanket of alpha. I'm protected.

His thumbs rub circles in my skin and he purrs for me. Slowly our breathing returns to normal. Once we're somewhat recovered, Liam shifts us so we're on our sides. He spoons me, his bigger body covering me from head to toe. A purr rattles in my chest too. All we need is a big fluffy blanket and this would be perfect.

Matthew sets the knife aside and drapes a fuzzy blanket over us like he's some sort of mind reader. It's pale blue with a delicate floral pattern. I don't remember this blanket being here. *Did they buy this? For me?*

Matthew climbs into bed with us, settling on his side too, but facing us.

"Kat, I'd like to ask you something," Matthew says.

My gut reaction is to ask if something's wrong. If we went too far with him in the room before he's ready. "What is it?"

"Can I touch your baby bump?"

The request is so sweet. Tentative, compared to the stern

persona he had in that chair. I move my arm to give him access to my stomach and smile. "Of course."

He pushes the blanket aside, exposing me, and reaches for my belly. His palm is warm and his touch is gentle. It's also in the wrong spot.

I cup his hand with mine and move it lower. To where our baby is. I push his fingertips down harder. His eyes widen with surprise when he finds it. The firm ball of my full uterus.

"That's our baby?" he asks, his voice full of wonder.

"Yes."

"They're not moving."

I laugh softly. "It's too early for that. The baby has to get bigger first."

He studies me quietly, his attention focused. It's slightly awkward. He's the only pack mate I haven't been with. I'm not quite sure what to expect.

"You were right. Her breasts are a lot bigger," he says.

His comment takes me completely by surprise. I blush and Liam chuckles. Liam reaches around and cups one, gently squeezing. Pinching my nipple. My pussy throbs around his knot like they're connected.

"More sensitive too," Liam says. "But less sore."

"Can I?" Matthew asks.

Confused, I nod.

Matthew palms my other breast. Testing the weight. Judging the firmness. My nipple's responsiveness.

"When do they get milk?" he asks.

"Not…" My clit throbs like he's touching it instead of my nipple. "Not until closer to the end."

"Do you need to come again, kitten?" Liam asks. "You're squirming."

"Y-yes," I pant. Is this okay with Matthew on the bed? I don't know what the rules are, and I'm too nervous to ask.

Being added into an existing pack is so different from forming one as you go.

"Did I do that to her?" Matthew asks Liam.

Liam nips my earlobe, then licks out the sting. He curls a hand around my hips and finds my clit. "Does your pretty pussy need petting?"

"Yes." My nipples are so hard they hurt. Matthew touches them, seemingly fascinated, while Liam strokes me between my legs.

Liam groans when I squeeze his knot. Grinding my ass against him, tugging at that swollen base of his cock. He breathes hard in my ear. Thrusts shallowly.

He strums my clit. Rapid circles that make my stuffed pussy clench. I clamp down, squeezing him.

"Oh, fuck," Liam groans. His cock pulses, spraying my walls with a lash of cum.

"What?" Matthew asks.

"Her pussy sucks the cum right out of me."

"Really?" Matthew's interest is piqued. "I want to try. Can I, Kat?"

"O-okay." I don't care who makes me come as long as one of them does. Fast.

Matthew takes over and I groan in disappointment as the tension in my pelvis fades while they switch over. It starts again when Matthew strokes me. Gentle, slow movements that are good but won't make me come.

But he gains confidence as he goes. Exploring my folds. Finding my clit. Pulling the hood back to touch more of it. He rubs light circles over me.

"How is that?" He asks.

"It's good," I answer.

Liam says, "Faster."

Matthew speeds up, going from slow and explorative to

rapid strokes that make my eyes want to roll into the back of my head. I grind into his hand, adding pressure. Tugging on the knot stretching my slick-covered hole wide. My moan is strangled into a needy whine.

My breathing hitches. "Oh, God."

"That's it, kitten," Liam says. "Ride my knot. Fuck yourself on Mattie's hand. Come for us. That's our good girl."

I'm not going to last long. Not with Liam's dirty praise in my ear and Matthew's beautiful, dexterous fingers. How is he so good at this? We lock eyes and share the moment together.

I come, gasping, and something sparks in Matthew's eyes. He strokes me through my orgasm, keeping our connection as I clench down tightly on Liam's knot.

Liam's cock kicks, earning me another spurt of cum. The pressure in my pelvis is intense. I can't take anymore. Not another drop.

"Let me clean you," Liam says to Matthew.

Matthew holds his slick-coated fingers up for Liam to swipe at with his tongue. Liam purrs while he licks the beta clean. And then he turns his attention to me, hugging me against him and covering me with the fuzzy blanket again. Tucking me in so I don't get cold.

Matthew settles down with his head propped up on one arm. "Thank you."

"Anytime." I mean it. Anytime he wants to finger me like that, all he has to do is crook a finger. The guy is blessed with a natural gift.

When Liam's knot softens, he slips out in a mess of cum and slick. Thank goodness for stain-guarded bedding. We lie there, recovering slowly.

"Can I ask you another question?" Matthew asks.

I nod, too tired for words.

"I noticed it a while ago, but we decided to wait for you to bring it up. But you never did. What happened to your old pack?"

The question is so out of left field that my brain takes a moment to process it. I blink rapidly. "What?"

"You have an old mating bite on your neck," he says. "That's what it is, right?"

My teeth clench. It's a fair question. Something I should have brought up by now, but couldn't. I still get a lump in my throat when I think about it too much. It's been three years. I thought I'd be over it by now. But I'm not sure you ever really forget about your first love.

"We were high school sweethearts," I say. "Josh and me. We thought it was so lucky for us to get into the same college. I studied some of everything. I hadn't decided what I wanted to do yet, and he was there on a sports scholarship."

I play with a corner of the blanket and refuse to look at either of them while I tell them the story. "During one of my heats, we slipped up with our birth control. I got pregnant. So we got mated. And then he was recruited. I quit school to follow him and the team. What else was I supposed to do? When I lost that pregnancy, it was sad. But I think both of us were relieved too. We were so young. I wanted kids, but living in a new town, away from my family and my friends, with nothing to do all day while he was busy training... I was depressed. It didn't seem like the right time."

Liam hooks me around my ribs, dragging me flush against him. He purrs, a low sound that makes my breathing come more easily. It's comforting and sweet.

"Josh hit it off with one of his teammates and I became interested in one of the journalists we saw a lot. We met at one of the big social events. Things were better for a bit. He was happier, so that took pressure off me.

"A few years later we tried to get pregnant on purpose. We

struggled. I thought I was being punished for being relieved that the first pregnancy didn't take. I got depressed again. Stopped going to events that weren't really optional. Barely wanted to leave my nest. Everything was such a chore and I had zero energy for any of it.

"And then he had a great string of games. He got recruited again. Transferred to a better league. He was so happy. But I hated the surge in media coverage. The constant need to be *on*. Hair done, makeup perfect, squeezed into compression underwear, feet pinched into high heels. Looking effortlessly beautiful. Because someone was always watching. Filming. Taking photos.

"I never really clicked with the other players' spouses. I had a few I was friendly with but nobody I was really close to. I stopped enjoying the parties and events again.

"I wanted to keep trying after our losses. Thought it was the only thing that would make me happy again. They were ready to give up. After a while, it was clear we wanted different lives. They moved on."

Without me. I don't have to say the last part out loud. It hangs in the air unsaid between us.

Matthew takes my hand and squeezes it. "I'm sorry."

My smile is bittersweet. All of that hurt at the time. So badly that sometimes I thought it might kill me. But it didn't. And now I'm on the cusp of maybe getting everything I've ever wanted. It's terrifying. Because I want it so badly. My stomach is sick with bouts of anxiety that come and go.

"They abandoned you?" Liam growls.

His anger is validating. I was so angry too, once the heartbreak faded a bit. Now I'm mostly numb after three years.

"It wasn't their fault. Sometimes bad things happen. And we weren't a perfect match to begin with. It was young love. Puppy love. If we'd gone to different colleges, our lives probably would have turned out totally different. I doubt we would have stayed together."

Part of me wishes I'd picked a different school. That we'd lived in another neighborhood and I never met Josh. That I'd listened to my parents and chosen a career over a boy. But I thought I was in love. That we were fated to be together.

"Still," Liam grumbles.

"I'm sorry you went through that, but I'm glad you're here," Matthew says. "You know, I was worried about the co-parenting thing in the beginning."

"You were?" Liam asks, sitting upright to look over me.

"Giving our baby up to a stranger for half the week? No, I wasn't thrilled with it. But a lot of omegas like to make their packs instead of joining one that's already formed. What choice did we have? It was co-parenting, surrogacy, or adoption. Both of those other options are a lot harder and more expensive to do."

"I wish you'd told me this," Liam said. "We could have talked about it."

Matthew shakes his head. "You would have told us to forget about it. You'd have done the alpha thing and put your pack's needs above yourself. Because that's who you are. And I love you for that. But I want this baby too."

I squeeze Matthew's hand, and he gives me a small smile.

"Gabriel and I weren't allowed to meet you," Matthew says to me. "We had to trust this guy's nose. That's hard for us betas. We don't have the sense of smell for pheromone compatibility that alphas and omegas have. So I'm grateful that his nose was right. And that Liam fucked up and didn't ask questions when they threw him into a heat room with zero instructions."

"Hey," Liam says, pretending to be offended.

"He's an idiot sometimes, but he's our idiot." Matthew

looks at Liam fondly. "And that was one thing he did right. We like you a lot. I can't believe we got so lucky."

I'm speechless and happy and completely overwhelmed. My eyes get damp, and Matthew notices. He plants a kiss on my forehead, then cuddles closer.

Liam wraps a muscular arm around all of us. He kisses my neck over my old scars, and for the first time in three years I don't mind them being touched.

In the middle of our cuddle pile, I find peace. Talking about my old pack helped. It wasn't as scary as I thought it would be. Sometimes the fears in our head become worse than the reality.

I doze off in the safety and comfort of their arms until Gabriel comes home. He leans against the doorway, a smile on his face. "Did I miss all the fun?"

"Come here, but be good," Liam says while Gabriel undresses.

"I'm always good." Gabriel tosses his scrub top onto the floor.

Liam snorts.

Gabriel shoves his scrub pants down. "And you like it when I'm bad."

"Not tonight," Liam says.

"Is something wrong?" Gabriel throws his scrubs into the hamper and climbs onto the bed.

"No," I answer, reaching for him. "It's cuddle time."

Gabriel smiles and lies down on Matthew's empty side. "I like cuddles. But if we're all going to puppy pile, we should consider getting a bigger bed."

Liam makes swirls along my arm and back while Gabriel and Matthew get comfortable.

I don't tell them that I'm looking at bigger houses. Not yet. As sweet and lovable as they all are, I'm not ready for that yet.

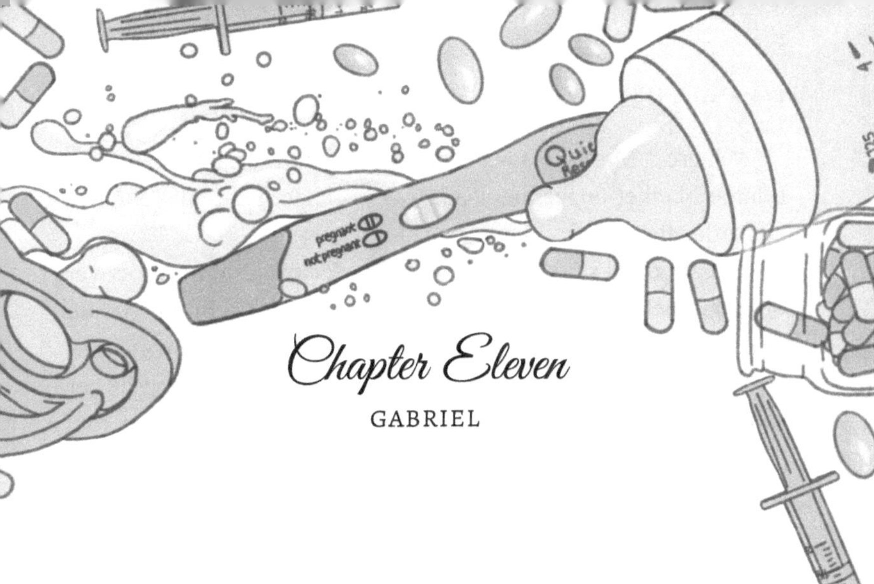

Chapter Eleven

GABRIEL

"Wow, it's crowded." Matthew surveys the lake's beach where hundreds of sun tents and umbrellas make colorful dots along the sand.

"Where should we set up?" I ask them while Liam grabs our stuff from the back of the truck and loads up the wagon.

"Close to the bathrooms," Kat says. "I pee every hour."

She's exaggerating, but it's somewhat true. I grab Kat and haul her against my side, rubbing my hand over her baby bump. She's visibly pregnant now that she's sixteen weeks. "Sounds good."

"By the bathrooms then." Liam points. "They're over by the concession stand that way."

We traverse the hot sidewalk and then even hotter sand until we find a spot. Liam and I put up the sun tent, burying the poles to hold it in place. It's not too windy. The beach is artificial, trucked in around the lake to make a shoreline. It's not as good as the clear turquoise waters of Brazil, but it's better than nothing during this heatwave. Everyone else had the same thought, it seems. This is the last hurrah of summer. In a few days, the temperature drops.

"There," Matthew says as he positions the beach chairs and a large blanket under the shade we've made. He grabs our bag and rifles through it. "Sunscreen?"

"Yeah, thanks," Kat says, reaching for the hem of her cover up. She peels it off, revealing her swimsuit. It's a bikini. White with crocheted lace and cute string ties that make bows at her hips and back. Her pregnant belly sticks out over the top of her triangle bottoms and her full breasts strain the cups of her top. "I can't reach some places anymore."

"I'll rub you down." I take the sunscreen out of Matthew's hand before he can protest. He quirks one eyebrow, then smiles and shakes his head.

Liam grabs his wallet from the bag. "I'm going to see if I can buy us more ice. I don't think we packed enough to last us for the day."

"Come here, *meu docinho*." I squirt sunscreen into my palm and rub them together, then rub it into her skin. She's so damn soft.

"I can do my front," she says.

"Nonsense." I ignore her protests and take my task seriously, rubbing sunscreen over her from head to toe. Applying it carefully to her pretty face, making sure I get her neck and ears. She holds her hair up for me. I move around to her back, making sure to work the sunscreen along her nape and underneath the edges of her suit.

For her legs, I kneel on the blanket and run my hands up and down each one. When I get to her ass, I have fun groping and teasing her while I make sure that area's protected from the sun, too. I work my hands under her bikini bottom.

Kat gives me a knowing look. "I don't think my ass is at risk of getting burned."

"You can never be too careful," I tell her, moving to the other buttock. "Skin cancer is no joke, and you're pale."

Once she's fully coated, I pull my shirt over my head and slip out of my sandals and shorts. Kat's eyes travel immediately down my body. "Wow," she says. "Those are tiny. And tight."

"Do you like what you see?" I tense my abdomen, showing off the extra work I've been putting in at the gym lately. Matthew tosses me the bronzing oil and I spray it on my chest and abs, rubbing it in. I make sure to dip my coated hand below the edge of my tight red Sunga shorts. I started wearing them after my first trip to Brazil to meet my extended family. Getting your first pair is like a right of passage for the boys there as they turn into men.

Kat rips her eyes away from my cock and the way it strains my swim trunks. She sees the oil I'm rubbing all over myself. "You're not worried about skin cancer for yourself?"

"No." By the end of the day, my skin will be nice and dark. I tan quickly, and my base tan from jogging shirtless has already gotten me halfway there. Kat, on the other hand, is blessed with none of my melanin. I don't want her creamy skin to burn and peel. Matthew either. He turns as red as a lobster, then bursts into freckles. "Sunscreen?" I ask him.

Matthew nods, and I wipe the tanning oil off my palms with a towel, then grab the higher spf sunscreen for him. I rub him down, coating him thoroughly. I get under his suit, using the excuse to knead his ass and bump my cock against his. His shorts are loose and dark blue. They hide his thickening cock better than mine.

"They were sold out of ice," Liam says, coming back empty-handed. He shoves his wallet into the bottom of our bag to hide it.

"Sunscreen?" Kat asks him.

"Thanks, kitten. Wanna rub me down?" Liam stands there and lets Kat tend to him, coating him in white sunscreen and working it into his skin. When she copies us by groping him underneath his loose patterned swim trunks, I can't help but grin. She's a fast learner.

Liam grunts, but holds still for her until all of us are coated. She clicks the top closed and tosses it into our beach bag. "All done?" Liam asks.

"Yeah."

"Good." He scoops her up, and Kat shrieks, alarmed, as he carries her through the crowd toward the water. "Because I'm gonna need the cold water after *that*."

Matthew and I follow them to the water.

"Don't toss me in!" She wraps her arms around his neck and clings to him.

"Of course I won't." Liam seems offended that she thinks he'd do such a thing. "But I'm not letting you walk. The sand is hot. You'll burn your feet."

"You're ridiculous." Kat rolls her eyes, but smiles. But the smile drops from her face when she gets her first taste of the water's temperature. "Crap! That's cold."

"It's better to get it over fast," Liam says, wading in without stopping.

Fuck, it's freezing. She wasn't kidding.

Kat struggles in his grip, gasping as cold lake water splashes her legs and ass. "Oh my God! Wait... wait! I'm not used to it yet!"

Liam ignores her complaints and carries her in deeper until the water laps at her neck. "See? It's better if you get it over with quickly."

She clings onto him like a baby koala. "Don't you dare drop me."

"Never." The look Liam gives her is obsessive. When rowdy kids next to us splash around, he turns them so the cold droplets hit his back. Ever the gentleman.

"Hey, Mattie," I say, giving Matthew a side eye. "Were you ever baptized?"

Matthew looks up from the stray water plant he's picking off his back. "No, I'm not religious. Why? Wait… No." His eyes go wide with fear.

Before he can splash away, I grab him and crush him to me. "Deep breath, *meu amor*." Then I bend my knees and take him with me as I dunk us both below the water. Liam is right—it's better to get acclimated fast. Like ripping off a bandage.

We surface and I shake my head, droplets spraying everywhere.

"Let's see how you like it," Matthew says. He grabs my shoulders and, grinning, I let him shove me under. I skim my hands over his body as I float back up. Get a good handful and squeeze his ass.

Breaking the surface, I release my breath and suck in air and shake my head to send droplets splashing at him. I grin. "I liked that a lot. Let's do it again."

A whistle blows and a lifeguard shouts through their megaphone. "No roughhousing!"

Oops.

Kat shakes her head at us, but smiles. "You're gonna get us kicked out and we just got here."

I pull Matthew to me, my hand on his ass to keep him from floating away. "I'll behave."

"I'm not sure you know how," Matthew says with a grin.

"Put me down," Kat says, fidgeting. Liam lets her feet drop but he stays close. As if the murky lake full of people and lifeguards and park rangers is full of unseen dangers. She paddles around, treading water and keeping cool. "Oh!" she yelps, pulling up short.

"What is it?" Liam's muscles tense. Like he's prepared to scoop her up and haul her out at a moment's notice.

"I think I smacked a fish with my foot." Kat reaches for him. "I changed my mind, pick me up. I hate when I can't see the bottom."

Liam scoops her into his arms and moves them further out where fewer fish swim around. They seem to be thicker in the shallows where the lake is warmer and the bugs hover.

"Hey," I say to Mattie, tugging him against my chest. I drop my voice so it's husky. "Want to go to the bathroom?"

"I went before we left."

"No." I dip my hand beneath the edge of his suit and skim and palm his entire ass cheek. "Want to *go to the bathroom?*"

"Really? Here?" He glances around.

"Why not?" I ask him. "They'll keep each other entertained."

It's not Liam's fault that he's been a bit distracted lately. His alpha instincts drive him to be preoccupied with his omega while she's pregnant. Vulnerable. The dynamic specialist whose brain I picked at work told me what to expect while we're expecting. Besides, all it does is give me and Mattie some extra time together. I don't mind that at all.

"Okay," he agrees, his voice husky.

We slip away, dripping all over the hot sand as we trek up to the concession stand. There are multiple bathrooms here. It's a big state park. There's even a mixed gender family bathroom that's private.

Perfect.

I steer him inside and shut the door, locking it. And then I'm on him. His body melts against mine, slippery and wet with sunscreen and water. I pick him up, my hands under his ass, and lift him onto the sink.

His thighs spread for me. A perfect invitation. I step between them, grinding our clothed cocks together while I kiss him senseless. We need to be quick. Quiet.

He writhes against me, kissing me harder. His frenzy feeds mine. Nails rake down my back and our cocks harden. The sound of people outside the flimsy door makes it hotter. I do my best to make him moan as I tug his dick free of his loose swim trunks.

The ruddy tip of his cock leaks, pre-cum making a sticky mess of my hand. I squeeze, jerking him, while my tongue thrusts past his lips. Fuck his mouth in time with the movement of my hand.

I'm so hard. My cock aches inside my tight swim briefs.

It's a fast and dirty public fucking. Matthew's hips thrust his cock into the ring of my hand and I jerk him faster. Squeeze harder. Until he comes for me. I swallow down his moans, enjoying the way Matthew hums with pleasure. Enjoying the way his warm cum splatters on the both of us. It drips down his cock and my fingers, but some of it's splashed across my abs.

"My turn," he says once he's caught his breath.

Matthew slips off his perch and gets to his knees. I fist his wet hair while he tugs my swim briefs down. Takes my cock in his hand and licks the tip. Swallows the bead of pre-cum pearling there. His mouth is hot and wet as he takes me all the way back. Deep throats me like a fucking champion.

"*Oh querido Deus,*" I groan, shoving my briefs down more to watch him take me to the root. He swallows, his throat constricting around my head and shaft.

Matthew pulls back, leaving only the tip in his mouth and laving it with his tongue. He fists my shaft and tugs while he sucks me. I pump into his hand. His mouth. Grip the counter when my knees nearly buckle. His cheeks hollow like he's trying to suck my soul out through my cock.

My balls pull up tight, that dull ache forming in my pelvis. The pressure that says *soon*.

His eyes meet mine. We keep eye contact while he swirls

his tongue around my cockhead, bobbing his head. I brush the back of his throat again. And again.

"Fuck." My eyes flutter shut as he swallows me down again. Lets me fuck his throat. I hold him in place. "That's good."

His eyes light up, enjoying the praise, and tears gather at the corners, making them glassy. His face flushes pink. But still he doesn't tap out. I pull back and let him breathe. He pops off my cock to stick his tongue out to tease me. My cock taps against his lips, a mix of his saliva and my pre-cum connecting us with a thread that grows heavy, then breaks. He sucks in a lungful of air and coughs. Once his color's better, I fist my cock and put it back to his lips.

"I'll tell you when I'm close," I tell him.

He nods and opens his mouth wide, sucking me down. Bobbing. Fondling my heavy balls until they pull up tight against my body. My pelvis aches again. A dull, steady thrum. Closer. Closer. *There.*

"Now."

Matthew's nostrils flare wide, and I thrust deep. Fucking down his open throat. Watching the way he struggles for air. When his face gets pink again, I can't hold back. I give into the sensation tingling through me. Feel my entire pelvis tighten, then jerk. I come, splashing down his tight throat. Shoot my cum straight down to his belly.

When the worst of the pulsations are over, I pull out and check on him. Matthew coughs and catches his breath, wiping the smear of cum and spit from the corner of his mouth onto the back of his hand. His hair is mussed. His cheeks are pink. His lips are swollen. He looks like a perfect mess.

I help him up, then kiss him. We cuddle as much as we can, standing in a public bathroom. It's like the good old days. Like cruising in the park as an awkward nineteen year old desperate to find another man like me. Now there are apps. Back then, it was dangerous. Part of me misses it. The thrill of spreading your legs in a stall and tapping your foot against someone else's. Seeing them reciprocate. The little flutter your heart made with the match. Anonymous, brief encounters. Perfect in their simplicity. An itch scratched.

Here, with Matthew kneeling half-nude on a dirty bathroom floor, it feels a little like that again. Nostalgic in a way that straight people don't understand.

"I love you," I tell him, stroking his back.

His nose rubs against my jaw as he straightens up. "I love you too. We should head back."

"I have a better idea."

"We don't have lube," Matthew warns.

"Not that kind of idea." We separate and fix our suits. He wets a paper towel and cleans us both up.

A quick run back to our stuff then a half-hour of standing in line later, Matthew agrees that my ideas are always the best. We return to our sun shade and blanket with handfuls of dripping ice cream cones.

Kat sees us first, looking up from her chair. She puts her book face down on the arm to keep her place. "Ice cream? I fucking love you." She takes her double cone of mint chocolate chip and vanilla from me and licks the dribble of melting ice cream already dripping down her hand.

The rest of us go still for a beat.

"Which one's mine?" Liam asks, distracting us from her slip up. She probably doesn't realize what she's said. Everyone loves ice cream. Even people who can't eat it suffer through the consequences.

"The double cookie dough one," I tell him, ending up with my waffle cone of pistachio and vanilla.

Matthew plops down on the big blanket and licks his chocolate and strawberry ice cream. Even sitting in the shade, it's hot. Half our ice cream ends up dripping into the sand, and we sacrifice some of our water and paper towels to clean ourselves up. Then I join Matthew on the blanket to get some sun.

Kat goes back to her book, and Liam hovers over all of us like a fussing mother hen. He offers us water bottles from the cooler, then reminds them to reapply sunscreen. There are sandwiches and fresh fruit too, he explains. He's packed enough food to keep us fed for days instead of hours.

Rolling onto my stomach on the blanket, I wrap my hand around Kat's sandy ankle and stroke her with my thumb. She glances at me and smiles, then goes back to reading her book.

Maybe she didn't mean it yet. Maybe it was only a slip of the tongue. But I'd like to think it's the beginning of something more. And I'm excited to see where that goes.

Chapter Twelve

KAT

Liam, Matthew, and Gabriel are already waiting at the doctor's office by the time I arrive. I'm fifteen minutes early. So what time did they get here?

Liam stands when I enter, shoving his hands into his pockets and taking them out, then wiping them on his pants. He's nervous.

"Sit," I tell him. "I'll go check in."

He sits back down, his leg jiggling. Gabriel and Matthew try to distract him with a magazine.

"Hi," I tell the receptionist. "I'm Kathleen. I have an appointment at one o'clock for my twenty week scan."

"Got you," the beta says, looking at her screen. "And I see you've been here before. Any changes to your insurance or address since your last appointment?"

"No." I take the short form she hands me. It's for acute symptoms or issues that the staff need to be made aware of for today's appointment.

"Fill that out and bring it up when you're done." She cranes her neck to look beyond her screen and smiles. "Is that your pack? First baby, huh?"

I glance at them and smile. "Yeah. He's more nervous than I am." And I'm anxious as hell. This is the scan that says if our baby is developing normally or not. I've never made it this far before. All of this is uncharted territory.

The receptionist chuckles. "The new parents always are."

I take the forms with me and join them, sitting to fill out the front and back. Matthew takes it up for me so I don't need to haul myself out of my chair. I'm only halfway through this pregnancy, but I already feel huge. I've had to buy completely new clothes and shoes. My socks are the only things that still fit me. I didn't realize pregnancy made your feet grow.

After a while, a nurse in powder blue scrubs stands at the door to the back, a chart in her hand. "Kathleen," she reads from it.

They don't react to the name until I stand, then they follow me with shared looks between them. The woman takes me to the phlebotomy station where they draw blood for genetic screening, then shows us to a room. "You don't need to change, just expose your belly once the tech comes in."

"Thanks." I sit on the exam chair while they settle on the plastic chairs around the room.

Gabriel picks up an anatomical model of a pregnant uterus. The plastic baby pops out, and he scrambles to catch it before it hits the floor. "Shit."

"Put that down before you get us kicked out," Matthew hisses through his teeth.

"I didn't realize it was two pieces," Gabriel says, defending himself. He puts the model down, but the baby pops out again. It clatters onto the counter.

"Did you break it?" Matthew asks, horrified. "They're never gonna let us come with her again."

"Haven't you seen these models before?" Liam asks, his brow pinched.

Matthew takes the plastic baby from Gabriel and pops it into the model, then holds his palms up and backs away from it slowly.

"I don't work in obstetrics," Gabriel says. "If the ambulance brings me a trauma patient who's pregnant, I'm having a horrible day."

Their antics distract me from my anxiety. We don't wait long for the ultrasound tech to come in and turn down the lights. "This may be cold," she warns me before squeezing a generous amount of gel onto my bared stomach.

The ultrasound probe is a firm pressure that she moves around my belly, taking measurements and photos as she goes. She talks as she works, telling us what she's looking at. Counting limbs, fingers, and toes. Measuring the spine, heart, and brain. Making sure everything is developing normally. The scan takes longer than I thought. She works for an hour, some of her work frustrated by the baby's lack of cooperation. The baby wants to stay curled in a ball, napping. To all of our disappointments, she can't get any pictures of the face.

"I'll get what I can but if I can't get everything you may need to come back," the tech says. "Try changing position. Sometimes that makes a stubborn baby move."

I shift onto my side while she switches her focus to the placenta, which she says is nice and high. Liam reaches forward, rubbing his hand across my gel-covered belly.

"Hey," he says to our baby. "Be good for your daddies. We all want to meet you today."

There's a flutter inside me. Like a flopping fish. A quick swipe that's been driving me nuts for the last week. Is it the baby or gas? I've never been able to tell. My rounded stomach doesn't move. It's still too early for that. Maybe now I can finally get my answer. "Did the baby move?" I ask the tech.

She drags the probe over and presses, searching. And then we see it. Our baby's face. The baby is sucking on their thumb.

"There we are," the tech says, freezing the recording and taking pictures. "Good job, Daddy. Talking to them is so important. They learn your voices before they're even born."

"We should get some baby books and read to them," Matthew suggests.

"Good idea," Gabriel says. "And music. I read it's good for their brain."

She takes a lot of photos of the baby's face and head. The baby stops sucking their thumb and yawns. My heart melts and my eyes get damp. Liam wipes ultrasound gel off his palm with a tissue and takes my hand, squeezing it.

We did it. That's our baby, right there. Healthy and happy.

"Do you want to learn the sex?" the tech asks.

Do we? I glance at my pack. We haven't discussed it yet. "Is that okay?"

Liam glances at the others, who all nod. "Yes."

The tech smiles and sets the ultrasound probe in its hook. "I'm all done. I'll go get the doctor to go over everything."

The ten minutes it takes the Maternal Fetal Medicine doctor to come feels like a lifetime. He spends a few minutes reviewing the photos and measurements the tech took. "Everything looks good. You're developing on track. You have an anterior placenta that's nice and high. Baby looks nice and active. I just want to listen to their heart real quick."

He adjusts the ultrasound machine and has me lie on my back while he gets the probe where he wants it. A rapid whooshing fills the exam room as he studies the baby's heart. "That's a nice, fast heartbeat. Your blood work will take about a week to run. We'll call you with the results and make a follow-up appointment if you need one, but from what I can see now everything looks good. Lisa said you want to know the baby's sex?"

"Yes," I answer for us all.

The doctor moves the probe again, pulling back so we can see our curled-up baby. "It's a girl."

"A girl…" I swallow past the sudden lump in my throat. We're having a daughter. After all these years, all of the heartache and failed cycles and loss, I'm going to have a little girl. My eyes grow hot and my vision blurs with unshed tears.

And it's all thanks to a paperwork mix-up. I've never been so grateful for a clerical error in my life. Because it brought me here, to this moment. To this pack who accepts me as I am. Who's as happy to go out to eat as they are to watch reruns on the couch. To the beta who tries new cookie recipes with me. And the beta who makes me work off those cookies and get stronger. To the alpha who finally put a baby in me.

Liam squeezes my hand and brings it to his face, pressing a kiss to my knuckles. His eyes are bright and shiny, too. "A girl," he says with wonder. "We made a little girl."

"Have you chosen where you want to give birth yet?" the doctor asks. When we say no, he pulls brochures from an organizer on the wall and hands them to Gabriel. "Most hospitals do tours once or twice a month for prospective parents. Birthing facilities do them more often, but they don't take as many patients and their slots fill up fast. I'd pick your facility out sooner rather than later."

"Thank you, doctor," Gabriel says, looking through them.

The doctor leaves, and Matthew brings me the tissue box so I can clean my belly and fix my clothes. It's real. This is really happening. Part of me didn't want to get my hopes up. Get too excited. Was convinced this was a dream I'd wake up from. Told myself that I was getting too attached to them, which would only lead to being disappointed again like I have so many times before. What pack wants another pack's leftovers?

But the point of viability is only a month away. It's time for us to pick a birthing center. Everything suddenly just got very real. We're having a baby, and I don't have a proper nest. My house is too small. They live above a bar.

We're not ready.

My bliss turns to quiet anxiety. I follow them out to the lobby in a bit of a daze. My mind churns over an increasingly long list of things to do in the next twenty weeks.

"I've heard this one sucks," Gabriel says, weeding through the brochures. "No, absolutely not. This one's too far from a hospital with a NICU." He pulls three from the stack and tosses them into a trash can.

"I'll call and get us on their lists for a tour," Matthew says. He takes the rest of the brochures from Gabriel to look them over while we head out to our cars.

Liam squeezes me against him. "Is everything okay?"

"Hmm?" I say. His question pulls me from my distracted thoughts. "Yes. My brain's spinning with planning. There's a lot to get ready for."

Liam pulls me against him and rubs his hand up and down my back. He kisses my forehead. "We're here for you. For anything you or the baby needs. Are you coming over? Please say yes."

"Later," I tell him, distracted. "There's an errand I need to run first, then I should go spend time with Waffles. I'll come over for dinner?"

He sniffs the top of my head deeply and squeezes me. "It's getting harder and harder to watch you walk away from us. My instincts hate it. Don't be gone too long. I don't think I can stand it."

I sense it too. The urge to stay buried in a soft, cozy nest of their familiar scents. To swaddle myself in a mountain of blankets and pillows that smell like them. Their bed isn't big enough for a growing pack. Neither is mine. We need a bigger place, and fast. This baby is going to come before we know it.

"Did you mean it?" I ask, needing to hear if what he said once in passing was true. Or if it was only something he said in the moment. "When you said you'd want to have more kids."

Liam lets me go so he can cup my face, his thumbs stroking over my jaw. "Kat, we'll give you as many babies as you want us to put in you. How many do you want? Four? Five?"

"Five!" My eyes widen. Five is excessive. "I was thinking of three." I'm thirty-five. We'd need to have them pretty fast. Omegas stay fertile longer than betas, but still.

"Three?" He drops a hand to cup my rounded belly. "Three is easy."

That's easy for him to say before the babies get here. "You might change your mind when we're buying three different sizes of diapers. And not sleeping for the next five to ten years."

"Good thing there are four of us," Matthew says. "We can take turns. Packs make it easier. I don't see how beta pairs get through it."

"And don't forget my mother is dying to get her hands on her first grandbaby," Gabriel says. "She's offered to come stay with us and help."

We still need to do the whole meet each other's families thing. But first things first, there's something I want to see. I plant a kiss on Liam's scruffy cheek. He shaved this morning but he's already got stubble growing. It's all that extra testosterone from being an alpha. "We can talk about it over dinner."

"Don't be long." Liam sees me into my car, shutting the door for me.

I tap an address into my phone, then wave at them as I pull out. The GPS tells me which way to turn. Across town where business centers and restaurants get left behind for subdivisions. Where all of the houses look almost the same.

I pass those too, going out to a country road where the houses get older. Grand Victorians and turn of the century Edwardian houses. The original owners were wealthier and could afford to live farther out of town. They splurged for the upgrades on their kit homes.

They also had large families. This one has five bedrooms, four if we want an office. In the late eighteen hundreds it belonged to a doctor. He saw his patients on the first floor, and the family lived above it. His first-floor office has been converted into the main bedroom. A modern bathroom was added, tied into the kitchen plumbing on the other side of the wall. An octagonal room on the first and second floor makes a turret that the covered wraparound porch attaches to. The attic that used to house the servants is tall enough it could be converted into a family living room and play space.

Overall, the house is over three thousand square feet. It's only been on the market for two weeks. The plumbing and electrical were all updated, but the roof is original. It probably needs replacing soon. A roof like that could cost thirty or forty thousand to replace. The septic system and well need investigating too.

Practicality tells me not to get too excited. But this house… It's a dream come true.

It's been painted sage green with plum and cream gingerbread. The gilded accents are worn and need redoing. But the house looks almost exactly like the realtor's photos. A blessing, compared to some of the other houses I've seen. Those had creative angles or straight up photo editing to make them look better than they really are.

Not this house. This house is gorgeous. It's my dream house. The house is surrounded with flowers. Whoever lives here now loves to garden. There's an oak tree in the front with a red swing hanging from it on chains. I can imagine sitting there, a child in my lap. Reading to them, and watching their siblings play on the lawn.

Trees ring the property, old and established. There's a small creek out back in the woods behind the property. I never saw myself as the sort to live outside of the city. To give up convenience for quiet. But there's a peacefulness here that I like.

I think about our children, older and playing in that creek. Catching fireflies in a jar and fishing. Walking barefoot in the grass. Planting seeds in the garden with them. Writing my books in that sunny round tower nook while they're in school. Helping Matthew bake pies from the blueberry bushes we'll plant in the back. The basement is large. Big enough to turn it into a fitness center for Gabriel. With a small section held aside for Liam to make beer. He mentioned wanting to try it once, but they don't have the space for the equipment that would take.

In this house, there'd be no shortage of space. A family of seven would fit it nicely. And the schools are good. I play with the GPS, learning how far away it really is. Forty-five minutes to Matthew's bank. A half hour to Gabriel's hospital. The same for the bar. And I can work anywhere as long as there's electricity and wi-fi.

I snap a photo and text it to Jen.

JEN

Gorgeous!

What do they think?

KAT

I haven't told them yet

Girl...

I know

I'll tell them tonight

How'd the appointment go?

Good

It's a girl

Bitch why didn't you fucking lead with that?

OMG!

I want this house so bad

But I can't tell if it's a good idea or nesting instincts driven by hormones

Is this crazy?

I can't tell anymore

It's not crazy

But play it smart

I know

I will

I draft an email to my lawyer while sitting in the driveway of my dream house. A month ago I asked her to write up a pre-pack agreement. But then I couldn't pull the trigger. It was hard to deny the urge to wait until the third trimester. But now… I've felt her move. Seen her face. This baby is real, and this house might not be on the market by then. I'll regret it if I don't try to get this house.

Part of me can't believe I'm doing this again. Potentially getting mated. Signing up to get brought into an already formed pack. One that doesn't need me to survive, only to be their breeder. But those thoughts are my fears whispering dark thoughts to me. Old insecurities rearing their head. Because I was easy to discard once.

But I want to have their babies. I want the future they're offering me. A big house full of love and life. Snuggling my children in our nest. Reading them bedtime stories and kissing their scraped knees. Dressing the entire family up in matching costumes for Halloween. Seeing their faces light up on Christmas morning. Showing them all of the amazing things in the world.

But this time it's going to be different. I'm not a young, naive omega anymore. I'm going into it with a clear head and legal protection. Because I refuse to spend weeks in mediation, arguing over *stuff*. Vacation properties and furniture and cars. Having to sit opposite the pack that didn't want me anymore while our lawyers fought on how best to split up assets and what to liquidate so I could be bought out. *Rejected.* It was humiliating.

I have more to protect now. A carefully mended broken heart. A daughter on the way. And the experience to know I never want to repeat that awful separation process ever again.

Once the email whooshes, I know I'll get the paperwork overnighted to me in the mail in a day or two. I take a deep breath and put my car into reverse. It's time for dinner. And time to lay all my cards down on the table.

If they're not all in, I'd rather learn it now.

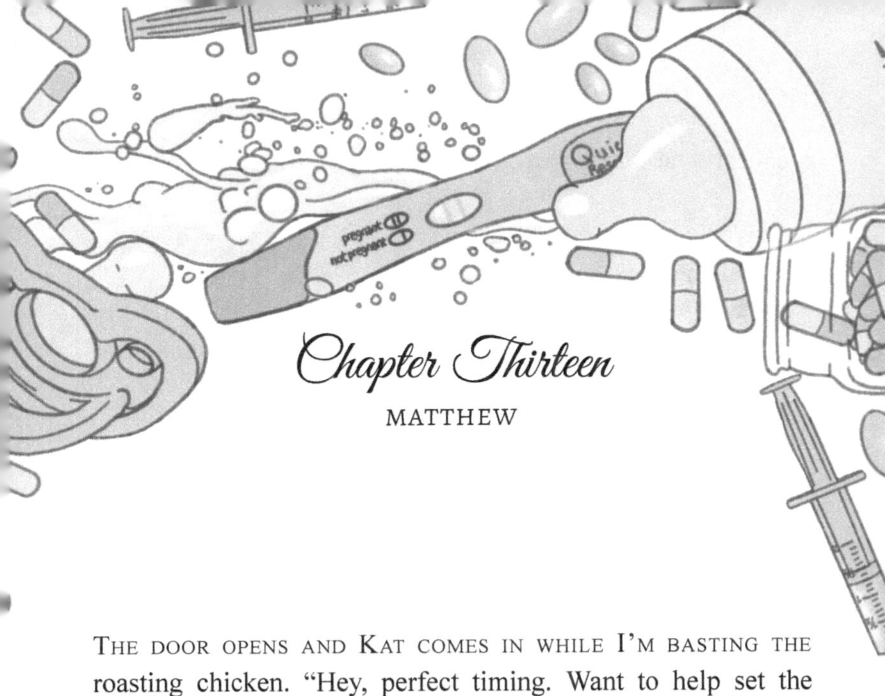

Chapter Thirteen

MATTHEW

THE DOOR OPENS AND KAT COMES IN WHILE I'M BASTING THE roasting chicken. "Hey, perfect timing. Want to help set the table?" I ask. "Gabriel and Liam are dealing with a beer delivery."

"Sure." She tucks her long hair behind her ear. Her nervous tick. "I actually wanted to talk to you."

"Oh?" *That doesn't sound good.*

I shut the oven and put the baster down on the spoon rest, then take off my oven mitt. Is this because she and I haven't… I've tried to show her in other ways that I care. Cooking her favorite dishes. Watching the movies she likes with her. Has it not been enough? Is being her friend not enough for the sake of our pack?

"Some of your family are lawyers, right?"

My stomach flip flops with nerves, and my thoughts veer in a totally different direction. "That sounds serious. Is everything okay?" She's not changing her mind, right?

"Yeah, everything's fine, but… what kind of lawyers are they?"

Is she in trouble? "My uncle is an estate lawyer. And I have a cousin who does family law and another who does criminal law."

"Would your cousin be able to look something over for you?" she asks.

I busy myself with turning over the vegetables I have browning in the cast iron. "I'm sure they would if I asked them to. What's going on? Can we help?"

"I'd rather tell everyone all at once."

"Okay." Inside, I'm panicking. On the outside, I try to hide it by staying busy. I pull the serving dishes down from the cabinet. "Why don't you set the table? Dinner is almost done. They should be up soon."

Kat grabs the stack of dishes from the cabinet and carries them out to the dinner table. I plate our food. Gabriel and Liam come upstairs with perfect timing. They see Kat and both greet her with a kiss.

Once we're all seated, I can't bring myself to eat. Neither can Kat. She moves her food around on her plate. Liam watches, paying attention to those small details like he always does. Typical alpha, perfectly in tune with the dynamics of his pack. He sees the strain, and gives me a questioning look. I shrug in response, stabbing my fork into a roasted carrot. I don't know what the problem is or how to fix it. When she doesn't really listen to Gabriel's funny story from work, Gabriel finally notices something is amiss.

Kat puts her fork down and the room gets quiet. "This is awkward and I don't know how to bring it up so I'm just going to say it."

Shit. She doesn't want to do this anymore.

The thought terrifies me. And not just because she's carrying our baby. But because I like her. I never thought our pack needed an omega until I saw how perfectly she slotted into place. I like that her presence gives me an excuse to cook more.

To try new recipes. I like watching movies with her. Picking out a new book for us to buddy read. Hearing her laugh at Gabriel's stories. Watching the three of them play together.

"I found a house," she says. "It's a little more of a commute for you guys, and it's old but it's been updated. It's on septic and well water, that's something I've never dealt with before, and the roof needs to be looked at, but the kitchen is amazing. You'd love it, Matthew. The basement has lots of room for hobbies and storage. It has five bedrooms, two baths, and there's a tree with a swing out front. I think it would be perfect for us."

I blink, too surprised to really understand what she's saying. "You found us a house?" Were we house shopping? I glance at the others who are also as surprised as I am. I guess we weren't house shopping.

Her eyes flick between us, gauging our reactions. "I know we're not an official pack yet, but I worry about how long it'll last on the market. I want to show it to you guys and make an offer."

Liam puts his fork down and frowns. "You want to buy a house?"

"Yeah. We'll need the room for all those kids." She pulls out her phone and taps on it, then hands it to him.

"Does that mean we can get a dog?" Gabriel asks.

Liam flips through the photos of the house. "It's a beautiful house," Liam says. "But we can't afford it."

Liam hands the phone to me. My eyebrows rise at the price. He's not kidding. It's on the market for almost a million dollars. Even if we put up the bar and her house as collateral, we wouldn't be able to get a mortgage. Not without raiding our retirement funds. It really is a beautiful house, though. I can see why she likes it. And the kitchen makes my heart ache to walk away from it. It's enormous with an industrial size fridge and a double oven that would make holidays a breeze.

I pass the phone to Gabriel, who looks at the listing and nods. "It's very nice."

"So here's the thing…" she says, fidgeting with her hair. "I can."

"You can what?" Gabriel asks, handing her phone back to her.

"I can afford it," she says. "But I asked my lawyer to draft a pre-pack agreement first. I don't want to make an offer without that."

"You can afford it," Liam repeats to her, his eyebrows drawn together.

"Yes. My settlement from my pack dissolution was generous. The money made me sick. I bought my house and let the rest sit in the bank. Never looked at it again. My books do well and they make enough for me to live off. So it's all sat collecting interest."

So that's why she wants me to reach out to my cousin. The one who does *family* law. Relief hits me. "I can ask Ryan to look it over. And I can ask my uncle about the real estate deal. If he can't help us, I'm sure he can recommend someone who can."

"Thank you," she says, smiling once more.

"So I can pick out a dog, right?" Gabriel asks. "I'd like one to go running with."

We all look at Liam, who's still processing. "We haven't even seen this house yet."

"I drove by today," she says. "The outside looks exactly like the photos. I can find a real estate agent and get us an appointment so we can see the inside. If that's… what you want." She stabs a carrot with her fork and fiddles with it. "Is that what you want?"

"Why wouldn't it be?" Liam asks, frowning.

Kat shrugs. "I don't know. I wasn't part of your original plan. You might not want to move, or..."

"No, you weren't part of our plan."

Kat deflates, her shoulders rounding. She sets the carrot down on her plate and wipes her fingertips on her napkin. Then she stares at her plate. "Right."

Liam reaches over and takes her hand from her lap, squeezing it. "You're so much better than any plan I could have come up with, kitten."

She perks up. "Really?"

"The way you fit so perfectly between us. It's like you were meant for us. I never bought into that woo-woo nonsense about fate, but maybe my nana was right. Because the first day you stepped over that threshold, I knew you were coming home to us. Knew you were ours."

Kat takes a deep breath. "If I hadn't gotten pregnant though..."

Liam shrugs and rubs his thumb across her knuckles. "Then I would have had to try harder on your next heat. Because there is no way in hell I was going to let any other alpha do it. And for the record, kitten, your old pack was full of selfish idiots. But I'm glad for that, because now we get to show you how a real pack supports one another through good times and bad. For better or worse. Because when you truly love someone, you don't walk away from them when life gets hard. You cling to them harder, because the dark is cold and lonely and it's the pack that keeps you warm."

A lone tear rolls down Kat's cheek and she brushes it away, then lets out a nervous giggle. "How long were you saving that one?" she asks, her cheeks pink. But she's smiling.

Liam grins. "A while. It's Mattie's fault. He's making me read your books with him."

"Oh my God," she says, rubbing the rest of the tears from her eyes. "Please tell me you didn't read my first one. I didn't know what I was doing then."

Fuck, her old pack really did a number on her self-esteem. "Of course I did," I tell her. "I like seeing how your writing's evolved over the years. It's definitely gotten kinkier." I wink at her, and she groans with embarrassment.

"So where did we land on this dog thing?" Gabriel asks, stabbing a cluster of vegetables onto his fork. "Because I was serious."

"I like dogs," I say.

"Me too, but maybe not a puppy," Kat says. "We could adopt an adult."

After a minute of silence, Liam agrees. "Okay. We'll look at the house. And dogs. And I'll sign whatever agreement Mattie's cousin says is good. But I want my mating bite on your throat before we go buying a pack house and moving. And I want our pack name on the baby's birth certificate."

Oh, shit. He's been so careful to tiptoe around the subject of mating. She gets cagey whenever he ever so slightly brings it up. Gabriel and I both glance between them.

Kat nods, agreeing, and Liam growls. Low and subtle. The hair on the back of my neck stands up at the sound. I've never heard him make it before now. He's only ever growled when there was a particularly nasty incident at the pub.

"Mattie," Liam says, his voice deep and jagged. "You'd better clear the table of whatever you want to save in the next thirty seconds."

My eyes widen when I realize he's serious. Gabriel helps me save my grandmother's porcelain and the cut crystal salt cellar we got as a pack present. We get the most precious things shoved to the other end of the table and blow the candles out by the time Liam gets out of his chair and pulls Kat out of hers.

"You can't bite me now!" she says. "We have to wait for the paperwork."

"Fine." Liam spins her around and bends her over the dining table. He pulls her dress up and tugs her panties down. I can tell the exact moment his fingers connect with her pussy because her eyes flutter and her hips rock against the table, making the place setting clink.

"I'm not going to bite you," Liam growls. "But I'm sure as hell going to mark you today." He leans over her, moving her hair to the side. Exposing her throat. Licking her. "Let the whole world know you're ours."

"Liam," she sighs, adjusting her stance. Spreading her legs wider. Giving him easier access.

"How long have you been looking at houses?" he asks her.

"A… a while," she admits.

"Did you daydream about it? Living with your pack?" He rucks her dress up higher, exposing the curve of her bare ass.

"Yes."

"I've been dreaming of it too," he admits. "Of waking up to your pretty face instead of a cold spot where you should be. I don't like it when you leave."

"I spend more time here than at my own house," she says, fidgeting under him.

"It's not enough," Liam growls. "It's never enough. I want all of you. I want you in our nest. I want my bite mark on your neck. Our babies in your belly. Once I have you, Kitten, I'm never letting you go. Is that what you'd like? Do you want to be ours? Forever? Because I won't settle for anything less than an eternity of you."

"Yes," she agrees.

The wet sound of his fingers plunging in and out of her competes with the low rumble of his growl. The rough sounds turn into a purr as she submits. Hangs her head, exposing her throat for him.

It's fascinating to see. The change in them both. He's always had a dominant, rough streak.

Gabriel tugs at the top of her dress until her breasts spill out. Her pink nipples are visible through the sheer lace of her low-cut bra. Gabriel tugs her breasts free and pinches her nipple until it's hard.

Liam stops fingering her so he can work his pants open, his thick cock filling his hand. It's already huge, the beginning of his knot evident. Kat's so small compared to him. How does she take it? But her body's designed to complement his. To take an alpha's cock, a knot, to be the gentle cushion for all that pent up aggression.

"Tell me you want it," Liam says while he fists his cock and rubs it up and down her slit.

Kat bends forward more, pushing her ass out. Putting her breast more into Gabriel's hand. "I want you. All of you."

The way she glances between Gabriel and me tells me she means our pack. That we're not some consolation prize she puts up with for alpha cock. Beyond her body's urges, she likes us.

"Tell me you want my mark on your throat," he demands.

"I want it."

His hips thrust, burying himself inside her, and his lips wrap around her throat. He sucks, his cheeks hollowing, while he's buried deep. Bruising her skin. Making a temporary claim where his teeth will one day cut. Where they'll carve the bond of our pack into her.

I reach a hand up and play it over my own neck underneath the collar of my shirt. Where my tiny scent gland lies, a firm knot under the skin. Unblemished, unclaimed. Do I want that, too? I've never thought about it before. Not all alphas claim their betas. It's not technically necessary. We don't have the overactive scent gland that signals our availability to others. But what would that be like?

She moans, and the dishes clatter as Liam ruts her on the dining table. A spoon near the edge slides off and hits the floor. I'm too busy staring at their spectacle and caressing my own neck to think of catching it.

Liam lets her scent gland go with a wet pop, leaving a dark purple mark behind. He nips her, hard enough to bruise without cutting skin. "Five bedrooms?" he asks, leaning back to deepen his angle while they fuck. A firm grip on her shoulder keeps her in place.

Kat's hands slide against the tablecloth, bunching it. "Yes."

"That means four babies." His hips smack against her ass. Liam shoves her dress up so we can all watch how her soft skin ripples with the force of their fucking.

"Three and an office," she counters.

"Or four and we'll build you a detached office. Your own private space in the back." The slaps of their skin grow louder. Rapid.

Kat's head drops forward, and I move the roasted vegetables before her hair gets into them. She moans. "You agreed to three."

"That was before I realized how much room we'd have to expand. I want to renegotiate."

"While you're balls deep inside me?" she asks, incredulous.

"Yes," he agrees, completely shameless. "Is it working?" He grins.

"We said three."

"I want to try for a boy next. And Gabriel and Matthew, if they want. That's four. Four is a perfect number, don't you think?" he asks us.

The thought of having a baby that looks like Gabriel and one like me is enough to make me agree with him. And I remember how lonely I was as an only child. How often I wish I'd had a sibling to play with. A big family would be nice. Gabriel and Liam both came from big families. "Yes."

"Yes," Gabriel agrees while he plays with her breast. He's worked a hand underneath her bra until he's touching skin.

I lean over to slip a hand between her legs. She's so wet that she's dripping. Does the thought of bearing all our children really make such a needy mess of her? Slick drenches her inner thighs and then my fingers. I stroke her puffy lips and work in between them. Find her clit and add pressure, rubbing it while he fucks her.

"Oh, fuck. That's not fair, Matthew." Her hands tighten into fists, shifting the table cloth underneath her. A water glass topples over. It rolls off the table and hits the carpet without breaking. She looks at me, her face scrunched with strain. It's cute. Like she's confused that he can make her feel so good. That we all can. That I'm rubbing her clit.

"Four babies," Liam promises between grunts. "We're keeping you pregnant."

Her clit is swollen. A firm little bud. It throbs under my fingers. Her cunt pulls taut, clenching tight around Liam's cock. I rub her clit faster. Touch her how she likes it.

Gabriel wraps a hand around her throat and tips her head up. Surges out of his seat to kiss her, swallowing down her moans. He buries his hands in her hair to keep her from pulling away. From arguing against what we all know she really wants. After all, she hasn't said *no*.

We keep her busy. Distracted. It's Liam's cock she'll come on, but it's my fingers that will tip her over the edge. Gabriel's kisses that keep her pussy clenching. She needs me and Gabriel, too. We're pack.

I don't have to fuck her to show her how she fits between

us. How much she completes us. How much we want her here, between the three of us.

"You're so wet for me, kitten. That's our good girl," Liam says. "Fuck, I need to have you deeper."

Liam stops and pulls out to reposition her, ignoring her muffled cries of protest against Gabriel's lips. He grabs her leg and lifts it, setting her knee on the dining table. Her panties twist around her leg, riding up her thigh. "This is in my fucking way," he growls, grabbing the carving knife. "Don't move, kitten."

He pulls the panties away from her body, slips the knife underneath, and saws upward. The fabric frays, then falls apart. They sag down her leg.

Kat breaks her kiss with Gabriel to look at what Liam's done. "I liked those," she says. "You need to stop cutting my underwear off me."

Liam shoves the torn panties aside until he has full access to her pussy. He tosses the knife aside and grabs her buttocks, spreading them apart to see her completely. "If you don't want me to cut them off, then stop wearing underwear around me."

Her complaints disappear when his cock nudges at her entrance again. He pushes inside her and sets a relentless rhythm. I work a hand between her thighs again. Pull her cut panties aside and find her clit. "Oh, fuck. Oh my God."

"We're gonna put so many babies in you," Liam says, groaning as he buries himself deep.

"Four is too many," Kat says.

"How? If you can do three you can do four."

"It's too many, Liam. I'm too old."

His response is a slap on her ass. "No, you aren't. But if you want to have them fast, I'll have you pregnant again with your next heat."

"Oh, fuck," Kat says, arching back to meet his thrusts.

"Don't stop." She reaches back to grab his thigh. To hold onto him.

His hands roam over her body, fingers sinking into plush skin and making divots as he holds her firmly pinned against the table. One leg propped up for easy fucking.

"It's what you were made for," Liam says. "What your body wants. My baby in your belly. My knot in your pretty cunt. My teeth in your smooth white throat."

Gabriel kisses her throat. Her shoulder. He works the thin strap of her summer dress down her arm and pushes her bra down with it until her tits bounce free. They're full and heavy. The nipples hard, aching points. He plays with them. Cups her breast and brings it to his mouth. Licks and sucks, then gently bites. Her pussy spasms against my fingers.

"We'll give you a nest full of chubby, round-cheeked babies," Liam continues. "You can protest all you want, but I feel the way your pussy clenches around my cock. How it's begging for my knot. My cum. Your body tells me everything I need to know. That it wants this. So be honest, Kat. Do you not want it, or are you afraid you can't have it? Because we're going to make all your deep desires come true once I mark your pretty throat. All you have to do is say *please*."

"I want it," she admits. "But you might feel differently later."

"I won't." He fists her hair and drags her head back. Exposes the throat he's bruised. Our pack's temporary mark. A promise for more to come. "I hope our babies have your eyes."

The table creaks from their antics. It's a miracle it holds at all from the way he pounds into her.

He's relentless. I had no idea his breeding urge ran so deep. That it made him so insatiable. He's been stuck in a near permanent state of rut since the day he met her.

"Liam," she moans.

He nips her ear. "I hope we have a boy next."

Gabriel toys with her peaked nipple while I tease her clit. She's there on the edge again a moment later. Her face flushes red. Her mouth rounds with a wordless moan.

"That's it, kitten," Liam purrs. "Come for us."

We hold her there. Balanced on that precipice. Her breathing grows uneven. And then she comes, loud and devastated. Her head drops back onto his shoulder in full surrender while her body pulses. While she submits to her alpha. To her pack.

"You're taking me so well," Liam praises her. "Here's your knot, pretty kitty. Here's your cream."

He sucks in a breath with his final thrusts before his knot swells and locks them tight. Liam turns her head. Exposes more of her bruised throat. Her pale skin is already turning colors. Round purple marks cover old faded scars. He nips her, ignoring her whine, hips jerking and slowing as he comes.

We pet her while she catches her breath. Let her settle on his bulbous knot. Gabriel and Liam run their hands over her chest and arms, smoothing her hair from her face. I pet their tie. Stroke them where they're stuck together.

And then because I can, because it makes me feel involved, I make her come again. I play with her clit until she shudders on Liam's knot, her pussy milking him. He grunts and eyes me, his gaze catching mine. He purrs with approval.

Liam kisses Kat's cheek and strokes his thumb over the bruise on her neck. "Four?" he asks.

Breathless, she nods. She leans against him for support while they wait for his knot to shrink.

"Four," she says. "But if you change your mind after the third, I'm going to say I told you so."

Liam kisses her forehead. "I won't. I can't imagine a baby this pack makes that I wouldn't love."

They stare at each other while the word love hangs in the air. Until Kat's stomach growl interrupts the tender moment.

"You're hungry. You need to eat," Liam says. He pulls free and gently puts her propped leg down on the ground. He rubs a hand over her pregnant belly and kisses her temple.

Kat fixes her clothes as much as she can. The wrecked panties are a lost cause. I grab her a new pair from the bedroom while she uses her old ones to wipe herself dry.

"Thank you," she tells me.

"You're welcome. I can re-warm dinner while you two wash up." I gather the food, and Gabriel helps me bring it all into the kitchen.

Liam and Kat disappear into the bathroom to get cleaned up. I put the food in the oven to reheat while Gabriel fixes the table. Until it's once again pristine and beautiful. Like the impromptu fucking never happened. Although I can smell the sex. The blend of their musk and pheromones. If it's this strong for me, a beta, it has to be hell on Liam and Kat. No wonder they're constantly horny. Our tiny apartment traps in all the pack scents. Like a den. I hope the new house, as big as it is, feels as much like home as our apartment above the pub has been. I close the oven and turn on a timer.

"One of the other PAs bought a house, I'll ask them who they used," Gabriel says. He leans against the counter and taps on his phone.

"I can talk to my cousin," I say, pulling out my phone to send Ryan a text about the contract we'll be sending his way soon. "He'll make sure the paperwork is in order." Not that I think she's trying to pull a fast one on us. Kat isn't the type. And I guess she's loaded. That was a surprise.

"Did you have any idea about all of this?" Gabriel asks.

I blow out a breath and pull my oven mitts off their hook. "Not a damn clue." She doesn't dress flashy. No designer purses or expensive brands. She drives an older car. Her home is modest. I never would have guessed she had *buy a million-dollar house* money. As far as surprises go, though, I can think of worse ones to get hit with. A bigger place is high on our needs list. This baby will be here before we know it.

"What kind of dog should we get?" Gabriel swipes through his phone.

I glance at his screen and see that he's browsing an animal rescue app. "One that's good with cats."

Gabriel makes a thoughtful sound. When the oven beeps, I take the food out and re-plate it. I hope the inside of the house is as nice as it looks in the photos. Because I can't wait to get my hands on that kitchen.

Chapter Fourteen

KAT

THE REAL ESTATE AGENT UNLOCKS THE FRONT DOOR BY punching a code into the lock box. She has dark brown skin, and her thick curls wave around her shoulders with a curly bang that frames her pretty face. Vibrant pink lipstick brings personality to the modest gray pantsuit that hugs her figure.

"This house was built in 1882, and it's a Queen Anne-style Victorian," she tells us. "The house has been tastefully upgraded over the century. A lot of the original trim has been restored, and the stained glass windows over the stairs are original too."

The entryway takes my breath away. Dark, gleaming wood makes up a grand carpeted stair. The entrance has room for a wide hall tree for hats and coats and winter boots. The front room used to be the parlor, and the octagonal turret has been fitted with benches for reading. A Victorian fireplace with cast iron and porcelain tiles makes up the focus of the room.

"Are those operational?" I ask.

"They were retired in place for safety." The agent shows us through the house, highlighting the amenities. "The first floor has the living room, the dining room, the kitchen, and the study was renovated into a main bedroom with a modern bathroom added. The upstairs has four bedrooms, a full bath, and a sitting area that you could use as a playroom. Or the attic can be converted into a living space as your pack grows."

The baby makes herself known, and I rub my hand over her. She's been more active since lunch.

"What does the house use for heat?" Liam asks.

"Oil and forced air," the agent answers. "The furnace is in the basement. You'll see small holes in the floors where the radiators were removed. They sell wood-colored plugs that you can insert to fill the gaps if they bother you. There's no cooling system installed, but the ductwork is present if you plan to add central air."

"This is the bedroom?" Gabriel asks.

The main bedroom is a good size, and the ceilings on the first floor are tall. Crown molding and a picture rail interrupt the patterned wallpaper.

Matthew runs his hand along the carved wooden door trim. "It's like a dollhouse," he says.

We tour the first floor bedroom and note the lack of good closet space. But the clawfoot garden tub in the bathroom more than makes up for it. We move onto the kitchen.

"Oh. My. God," Matthew says, rubbing his hands over the smooth, marble countertops. "This kitchen is huge. And the island has a range? With outlets! Wait, is that a pantry?"

He moves about the kitchen, checking out the enormous fridge and double ovens. I stand at the farmhouse style double kitchen sink. You can see the side yard where a prime patch of level grass calls to me. The perfect spot for a vegetable and herb garden. I imagine washing dishes while the children play with the family dog. My heart clenches tight in my chest with yearning and bridled excitement.

"I'd like to see the oil tank and furnace," Liam says,

keeping us on track with the important things like utilities and safety.

The agent opens the door to the basement and flicks on the light. It's not a bad basement. A bit too damp to finish without waterproofing. And the beams need a sweeping to get rid of spiderwebs. But the basement will be good enough for storage and a workout machine and Liam's brewing equipment.

"Your laundry machines go here," she says.

"What's that?" Gabriel asks, pointing at the silver thing sticking out of the ceiling.

"A chute," she answers. "A pipe that runs from the second floor to the basement. Your laundry collects in the basket you place underneath."

That's going to come in handy with four kids and all the dirty clothes they make.

"Want to see the upstairs?" she asks.

We follow her up the two flights of stairs to the second landing. It's slightly less grand, the rooms smaller and the ceilings lower. The family quarters weren't for visitors to see, so less money was put into the trim.

The bedroom with the octagonal turret will be an amazing princess room. Perfect for our baby girl. All of the children's bedrooms share one bathroom, but the tub makes up for that. It's deep with claw feet. A shower curtain on a ring is suspended from the ceiling.

"The attic stairs are here," she says, pointing out a door I didn't notice. They're fixed stairs rather than a pull-down ladder. "The servants lived here," she says. "The doctor who built this house kept a cook and a maid. The ceilings are tall enough that this space could be finished but it would need to be connected to your heating system first."

I don't know how they withstood the heat in the summer. It's boiling hot. But the view of the woods from the large front window is stunning. It's hard to believe that the edge of town is only a twenty-minute drive away. Out here, this house feels like we're in our own little world. "This view is spectacular."

"You should see the back," the agent says. "Let me show you the porch and backyard."

When we step outside, Liam wraps his arms around me from behind and squeezes me. We hang back while Matthew and Gabriel pepper the real estate agent with questions. Gabriel wants to know how far back the property line goes and how much fences cost while Matthew asks about the school system.

"Do you like the house?" I ask Liam, my heart catching in my throat.

"No."

My stomach sinks. What's wrong with it? Is it too far away? Too remote? Too old?

"I love the house."

I let out my held breath and his hand drops lower, rubbing over my belly. I'm not far enough along yet for him to sense the baby moving but that doesn't stop him from trying. I cup his hand with mine. "I love it too."

"Are you sure about this? This is the first house we've looked at."

It's not the first house I've looked at. I've looked at twenty-seven houses. But it is the first one I've shown them. And that's because I fell in love with this house the minute I saw it. This house and the life it represents is my dream come true. It makes me feel like a fairy tale princess. Like all the hardships I went through were necessary because they brought me here. To this moment right now. To this pack. And I want it all so badly it hurts.

"It's your money so it's your choice," he says. "We'd be happy anywhere that we're together."

"Really?" I ask him, needing to be sure. Are we really going to make an offer today? This is a big choice. An enormous commitment. Under normal circumstances, I wouldn't consider buying a house and moving in with someone after only a few months of knowing them. I knew Josh nearly my entire life before we decided to court. But nothing about my courtship with Liam and his pack has been normal. We've done everything backward.

Liam's large callused hand rubs over my belly. "Pack isn't a place or a home or a nest. It's the people you love." His voice is deep and rumbly in my ear. He kisses me on the temple. "Buy the house if you want to, Kat. We'll follow you anywhere. You're worth chasing after."

My eyes mist with unshed tears, and I try to stop it but I can't. Damn pregnancy hormones. The smallest things make me cry. I can't watch a sad movie or an animal rescue commercial without bawling. I sniff, trying to pull back the tears, but it's too late. I can't stop them. They roll down my cheeks.

"Hey, shh, come here." Liam turns me, tucking my head into his chest. He rubs his hands up and down my arms. "What's wrong?"

"I'm… I'm so happy," I choke out. Crying like this is frustrating. I hate the lack of control over my emotions.

"Aww, kitten." Liam smiles, then bends down and kisses my tear-tracked cheeks. "Don't cry. Want to go get ice cream after this?"

I'm pregnant and it's ninety degrees outside. Of course I want ice cream. I'm growing a human. I've earned it. Besides, Gabriel's gonna make me sweat it off tomorrow in the mommy-baby yoga class anyway. My thoughts are distracted long enough for the worst of the crying impulse to fade. I sniff and rub my sensitive eyes. "Yes."

"Everything okay?" Matthew asks from across the yard, a hand raised to shield his eyes from the sun.

"Yeah!" Liam waves. "Put in the offer. Pending inspection, we'll take the house."

A half-hour later while I lick my melting ice cream, my mood is completely changed. Satisfied. This has been a whirlwind of a day. Anxious worrying. Elated house touring. The rush of putting in a bid on my dream house. Happy weeping. And now ice cream.

Gabriel and Matthew take turns sampling each other's flavors. Liam steals a bite of mine when I'm not looking.

"Hey!" I jerk my ice cream away, careful not to lose the top scoop. "Didn't anyone tell you not to steal ice cream from a pregnant woman?"

"I must have missed that day in health class." Liam makes exaggerated movements like he's going to steal another bite.

I twist, keeping my cone out of his reach. Ice cream melts down my hand, making a sticky mess of me. The powder-coated lattice metal seat sticks to my thighs where my dress rode up when I sat, keeping me from getting far.

"Is he bullying you?" Gabriel asks.

"He is!" I shout.

"It's melting," Liam says. "I was helping her finish."

"Here." Matthew hands me a stack of napkins to wipe the trails of chocolate off my hand before it can drip all over my dress.

"Thank you. See?" I give Liam a pointed look. "That's how a gentleman behaves."

Liam reaches behind me, grabs a handful of ass, and squeezes. "Must have missed that day of health class too."

That one ass squeeze is enough to trip my mind from ice cream into dirty thoughts. It doesn't take much to get me excited these days. And Liam likes to take advantage of that every time he can.

I glance around to see if anyone is watching. Most of the

people crowded around the ice cream shop are hanging out on the shaded porch where you order. It was more crowded when we first got here. But the group of kids in baseball uniforms are gone now.

We ended up at the only table that was open, the one at the end of the gravel courtyard by the fenced-off trash. It doesn't smell the greatest, which is probably why nobody else wants to sit back here.

Liam drops his hand onto my thigh, then drags it inward. He nudges, insistent. His fingers dig into my skin.

"Spread," he orders.

My nipples tighten and I stiffen. "Here? Really?" Despite my protests, a wet spot forms in my panties.

Liam gets up and sits down sideways on the bench seat. His body cages me in, and his hand goes back to my thigh. Shoves his hand in between them, even though they're clenched together. His thumb rubs my skin where my dress rides up my thighs.

He leans down close to my ear and makes a hungry sound. "I finished my ice cream and now I'm in the mood for a different kind of sweet treat. I've always liked cookies better anyway."

I swallow. The wet spot in my panties gets bigger. "There are people here."

"There are," he agrees. "But they're not paying attention to us. You'll want to be quiet then. And fast. Can you do that for me, kitten?"

After a moment of hesitation, I give in. "I guess that depends on you."

His grin shows a hint of alpha fang. "Is that a challenge?"

"It might be."

I let my knees fall apart. He runs his fingers up my inner thighs. Ghosts them over my panties. Rubbing lightly. Then firmer. Tracing the seam of my sex through the thin excuse of fabric. My pussy's wet and they stick to me, a damp spot growing until they're slick. The way he rubs my mound leaves me aching.

"I'm always up for a challenge," he says, stroking my clit again. "Let's see how fast you can come and how quiet you can be."

My ice cream melts, forgotten. He hooks my panties aside and touches me, finally. Skin to skin. I'm so wet. There's no resistance as he presses the tip of his finger between my lips and strokes my clit.

"Mmm." I bite off my moan and mash my lips together. It's nearly impossible to stifle the sounds I want to make when he rubs my clit like that. With practiced, firm circles.

"What was that?" Liam asks, taunting me. "Did you say something?"

Matthew and Gabriel chuckle softly, still licking their ice cream while they watch and keep an eye on our surroundings. I glare at Liam, but all he does is smile with amusement and stroke my clit faster. Firmer. Adds another finger for wider coverage.

My breath comes out as a pant and my pussy throbs. I'm always close these days. Because of all the blood flow and pressure in my pelvis. I've never had such easy orgasms before. Pregnancy agrees with me.

Liam dips two fingers into my hole. Teasing me. Gathering up slick and spreading it over my clit. "Do you still have issues with my behavior?" he asks.

My hips itch to rock against his hand. I stifle the impulse. Stay still and quiet so we don't get caught. The round metal picnic table isn't opaque. There's nothing to hide that his hand is under my dress if someone walks by and looks. "No." He needs to hurry up and let me come. Before we get banned from my favorite ice cream shop or arrested for lewd behavior.

Gabriel and Matthew watch with amusement while they trade ice creams and Liam fingers me underneath the picnic table. There are people oblivious to what we're doing fifty feet away. But they won't be for long if I don't stop moaning. I bite my lower lip to stifle the unruly sounds he finger fucks out of me. I can't help it. He knows exactly how to touch me. How to work me up. How to make me come. And how to keep me on that edge, balanced without toppling over. Edging me.

"Liam," I whine, trying so hard to be good. To be still and quiet. The need to come is unbearable. My fears of getting caught are gone. I don't care who sees so long as he doesn't stop. If he stops, I might die.

"That's a good girl making all that sweet slick for me," he says, his voice low.

The pressure building in my pelvis tightens. *Close. Nearly there. Stay quiet.*

He rubs me faster, making firm circles around my clit. Working quickly. Dipping his fingers down to curl them inside me. My soaked pussy makes sloppy wet sounds.

"Say please," he orders.

My obedience is instantaneous. I would get on all fours with my ass in the air right now and let him mount me if he told me to. "Please." The word comes out breathy. A slutty word moaned with desire.

He stops fingering my hole and focuses on my clit again. I'm so close.

My toes curl in my sandals and my thighs tense with the restrained urge to fuck myself on his hand. I can't. We'll get caught. People murmur, their conversations faint background noise as they move about. Talking and laughing. Car doors open and shut as more park. Oblivious to what Liam's doing under-neath my skirt around the corner.

"Are you gonna be good for your alpha and come?" he asks.

I nod. A whimper escapes me, and everything pulls tight. There's a second of nothing. Of sheer torture. The calm before the storm. And then an orgasm rips through me. My cunt pulses against his hand, spasming on nothing. Empty and hungry for more. Always needy.

My hand tightens and the waffle cone crunches while I ride through the waves of aftershock. Cold ice cream smears down my hand, drips down my arm. The cone breaks completely, my ice cream dropping onto the picnic table. It's nothing compared to the small river of slick coating his hand and my inner thighs. Soaking into the back of my dress. Dripping onto the bench.

I abandon my ruined waffle cone and curl my fingers through the metal lattice table while I ride his hand and the aftershocks of my orgasm, oblivious to our surroundings. All I care about are the pulses and tingles rippling through me. About my alpha's hand wedged between my thighs and the pleasure he gives me.

Once I'm settled and panting, Liam pulls his hand free, scooping up as much slick as he can. He shoves his fingers past his lips and hums around his mouthful. "So sweet." He purrs while he licks himself clean.

I press my knees together and fidget in damp panties on my seat. By the time my breathing is back under control, Matthew has my spilled ice cream cleaned up.

"Damn. I really wanted that," I say.

"I'll get you another one," Gabriel says, getting out of his seat.

"In a cup," Matthew suggests.

"Are you happy now?" I ask Liam. Grumpy now over my ruined ice cream.

Liam grins. "I'm not sorry that cookies are my favorite dessert. Wait until you try Matthew's Christmas cookies. It's a family recipe. They're almost as good as your pussy."

I MULL OVER HIS COMMENT THE ENTIRE CAR RIDE HOME WHILE I eat my ice cream in thoughtful silence. The pub is busy, and I say hi to the regulars who've come to know me. Liam pauses to answer someone's question while we head upstairs. I clean up and change into fresh underwear. I go through them at an alarming rate around these men. Matthew pulls out his laptop to check his emails while Gabriel changes into his workout clothes.

"Going to the gym?" I ask him.

"I'm gonna get a run in before dinner. Work off that ice cream." Gabriel leans over me on the couch and kisses me, then Matthew. He grabs his earbuds and heads out.

I drag a knitted throw over my legs and get cozy, then turn the TV on and flip channels, but nothing catches my attention. I'm still stuck on what Liam said.

Christmas... It's only August. But December isn't that far away now. Only a few months. The baby's due mid-January. It hits me that this is my last Christmas before my life completely changes. Before all of ours do.

"What are we doing for Christmas?" I ask Matthew. With my old pack, we rotated whose family we spent the holidays with.

"Hmm? Oh. We usually rent a big ski chalet up in the mountains. Everyone comes, although Gabriel's family don't fly in from Brazil every single year. They're saving their airfare for after the baby's born. What about you? What does your family do?"

I turn down the volume on the TV while a home improvement show plays in the background. "They'd probably like a ski chalet, although I don't think they'd actually want to go skiing. We always did a small dinner the night before, then presents in the morning, then a big family dinner with the rest of the family. Josh's parents live next door to my parents so I got to see them half the time when the pack wasn't visiting the other families."

Matthew looks up from his typing. "Josh was your old alpha?"

"Yeah. We grew up next door to each other." He was my first kiss. My first everything. And then he threw away all of our history when things got hard. My inability to move on was holding the pack back. Keeping them from moving on.

And he was right.

After I left, Josh had his best string of games. For the first time ever, I don't have an emotional reaction when I remember it. No anger or hurt or resentment. Only the facts. It didn't work out. That happens sometimes. Scent matches aren't a guarantee you'll live happily ever after.

The baby moves. As if reminding me that I have more important things to fixate on than old regrets. Tiny repeated pokes make a pattern on my right hip from the inside. It's a strange sensation. *What is she doing in there?* I rub the spot.

"Is it the baby?" Matthew asks, looking at where I'm rubbing. "Can I feel?"

"Of course."

Matthew puts his laptop aside and slides across the couch. I grab his hand and bring it to my belly. His touch is tentative and light. I push his hand down harder, right over the spot where she was moving.

"It might be too early still," I warn him. The baby app on my phone says our baby girl is the size of a carrot.

The baby goes still, as if she's shy. "Try talking to her," I suggest.

"I could read a book to her. I downloaded some."

The suggestion makes me smile. He looked up baby books? That's so sweet. "Okay. Let's get comfortable." I put a pillow behind my head and slouch down, reclining. Matthew sprawls out between my legs, his head propped on my belly. He pulls out his phone and opens his reading app while I turn the subtitles on for the TV show I'm barely watching.

"Alice was beginning to get very tired of sitting by her sister on the bank, and of having nothing to do," Matthew reads. "Once or twice she had peeped into the book her sister was reading, but it had no pictures or conversations in it, and *what is the use of a book,* thought Alice *without pictures or conversations?*"

"Are you reading *Alice in Wonderland*?" I ask, surprised.

"Yeah." He tips his face up to look at me. "It's my favorite book."

I chuckle, my belly bouncing and his face along with it. "I thought you meant a baby book."

Matthew frowns. "It is a kid's book."

"It took me by surprise, that's all."

He's so earnest. It's cute. I brush a curl out of his eyes. His hair's getting long. He usually gets it trimmed by now. But we've been rather busy lately. He doesn't seem to mind my affectionate petting. It's the omega in me. I crave the exchange of scents. His weak beta scent gland in his neck has the highest concentration, but there are pheromones in our hair too.

"Okay," I tell him. "I'm sorry I interrupted. Carry on."

After a brief pause, he does. He reads the whole first chapter to our baby so she can learn his voice. And I half-watch the home design show. It's a nest makeover show. When I notice that Matthew is glancing at it too, his attention to his book waning, I turn the volume up.

"Are you ready to see your dream nest?" the host asks the anxious blindfolded omega.

"Yes. I'm ready," the omega answers.

"Then take your blindfold off in three... two... one!"

"Oh! Wow. How did you do that?" the omega says, excited.

They show a montage of the before and after. Before, the room was beige and bland. With big box store furniture that has to be put together with an allen wrench. Now it's a mermaid lagoon.

Someone painted a mural on the walls and ceiling to make it look like an ocean at sunset. The carpet's been pulled up and hardwood floors installed. The nest is half of a pirate ship, made to look like it's been broken and drifted into a lagoon. It takes up nearly the entire bedroom. Mountains of soft, cozy blankets and jeweled pillows make the surface soft. Fake flowers and pillows that look like moss covered stones decorate the base of the ship nest. Netting decorates one of the walls. Seashells and a starfish are stuck in it haphazardly.

"Wow," Matthew says. "That's... something."

"Horrible?" I suggest.

"Yeah, it's bad. It's like a teenage girl's mood board threw up on a room."

"I don't know why anyone still goes on these shows. Their makeovers are obviously rage bait."

"What kind of nest do *you* want?" he asks.

I blush. Because I have a mood board dream nest. I've made several over the years as my tastes change. But once I saw the house, I knew exactly what I wanted it to look like.

"I'll show you." I pull out my phone, somewhat nervous. What if they hate it? I haven't had to share a space with someone and compromise on decor in years. Their house is traditional and cozy. My dream nest is… well, different.

I pull up the mood board I made and hand it to him so he can scroll. My heart thumps in my chest while I wait for his verdict.

"Wow. That's not what I expected."

"Too much?" I ask. It's my nest, but I still want them to be comfortable in it.

"It's darker than I assumed it would be. I like it."

He hands the phone back to me, and I scroll through my saved images again. The mood board is full of dark, gleaming wood. Deep green or teal or sometimes black walls. Dark floral wallpapers. Big beds draped in rich velvets and satin, with four posters and a canopy to enclose it and make it cozy. Gallery walls covered in gilded framed paintings and one wall that's nothing but shelves covered in books. Dark oriental rugs cover hardwood floors. When I saw our house's dark wood trim and red chestnut-stained hardwood floors, I knew I wanted to high-light those. It would be criminal to paint all that gorgeous trim white.

"You don't think the nest will be too dark?" he asks.

"The ceiling's so tall and there are a lot of windows. And we'll add accent lamps, of course. Maybe some fairy lights. Do you think they'll like it?"

"It's surprisingly not too feminine."

The tension coiled in my body relaxes. "What, you expected a pink and glitter unicorn dreamland nest?"

His cheeks blush pink. "Something like that. I like it," he adds. "You did a good job."

His praise is nice. And I'm glad he likes my ideas. That eases some of my worries.

"We should go to Nested," Matthew offers. "We can pick out most of our furniture somewhere else, but Nested has the best nests from what I read. They'll probably have something like this."

I raise my eyebrows. "We should probably close on the house first before picking out furniture."

Matthew shrugs. "You're paying cash so unless the inspection comes back with big red flags, you won't have problems closing. Besides, there might be back orders."

That's a good point. And I'm excited to start furnishing our house. There's going to be so much to do. Paint, hang up curtains, buy furniture, pack and then unpack, then set up a nursery. Moving is so much work. I'm already exhausted simply by planning it. And I'm grateful that this time I'll have a pack to help.

Moving into my single omega house was bitter sweet. Moving into my dream pack house is already completely different. Exciting. Like the future is full of wonderful surprises.

Matthew sucks in a breath. His hand skims over my baby bump. "I think I felt her."

"Really?"

The baby kicks again, and his eyes light up with wonder. He moves his hand around my belly, keeping track of her.

"Hi, baby," he says, talking to my belly. "I can't wait to tell Liam I was the first to feel you. He's gonna be sooooo jealous."

I smile and pet his curls while he talks to our baby, then goes back to reading to her from his book. Trying to get her to move again. We lie there like that, with me half-watching the nest makeover show, half-watching Matthew. It's comfortable and intimate.

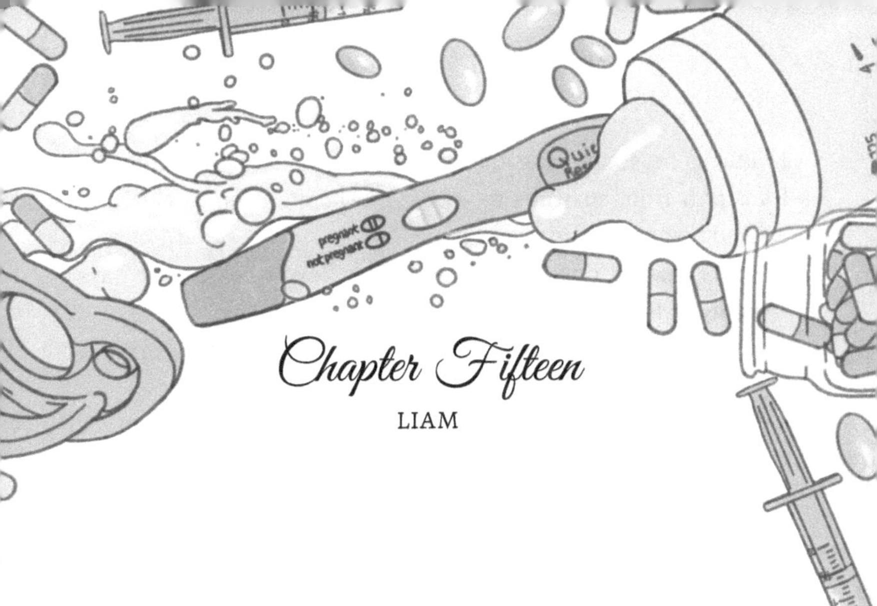

Chapter Fifteen

LIAM

"ONE PUMPKIN SPICE DECAF LATTE WITH AN EXTRA PUMP OF caramel syrup and whipped cream with a cinnamon sugar sprinkle," I say. I hand Kat her tall white cup of coffee that's more like a dessert.

Kat takes a long sip, then makes a sinfully throaty sound that makes all of us twitch. Then she sighs and smiles. "I know people think it's basic, but there's nothing better than the first pumpkin spice latte of the season. Even if it's kind of hot for apple and pumpkin-picking today."

Matthew pulls up the orchard's website on his phone. "They have hayrides too. And a bakery."

"And beer," Gabriel adds, excited. "I want to try their pumpkin ale."

I pull out onto the road and follow the GPS, my hand gravitating to Kat's thigh. She's so cute today. She's wearing jeans and a loose plaid button up left open over a tight white shirt. Her hair is up in some sort of messy bun with lots of loose strands that frame her pretty face. She's wearing glossy pink lip stuff that makes me want to kiss it off her. Muss her up.

"Ooh, look. They do haunted stuff soon in October,"

Matthew says, showing the others the photos of the orchard's transition from seasonal to spooky. "There's even a real headless horseman. On an actual horse."

"We should come back for it in a few weeks," she says, twisting in her seat to see the pictures on his phone.

My hand slips to her inner thigh and I give her a squeeze, my eyes never leaving the road. "Is that safe?"

"Why wouldn't it be?" she asks. "I love haunted houses. So long as they don't touch me. They don't touch you, right?"

"They shouldn't," Matthew says.

"Your blood pressure's been good, right?" Gabriel asks.

"Yeah. The doctor says everything is fine." She takes another sip of her coffee, muttering the rest into her drink, "But if he calls this a geriatric pregnancy one more time…"

"I think it would be fine," Gabriel says.

I still have my concerns. "Maybe we should call the doctor to make sure."

"There's less scary stuff for families," Matthew adds. "The haunted house is an extra charge. There's a spooky corn maze and a haunted graveyard. There's also a photo booth where you can dress up like witches or vampires and get a sepia print so it looks old-timey."

"Oh! Can we go? Pleaseeeeee," Kat begs. "I haven't done any of this stuff since I was a teenager."

She covers my hand with hers, squeezing it, and I melt. It's crazy how much I hate saying no to her. How she wraps me around her pinky finger. Makes me eager to please her. To see her lips curl in a smile or her eyes lose their focus with lust. There's something about her presence that's simply natural. Right. Like she's been a part of us all along, but we didn't know it. Like a limb that's fallen asleep, but regains feeling a bit at a time before exploding back to your awareness. I fucking love this girl.

"Please?" Gabriel and Matthew echo in unison.

I cave. "Fine." Their squeals of delight make me smile. "But nothing too scary."

They spend the rest of the drive planning what they want to do today. Once we get closer, the traffic gets thicker. We fall into line and follow the parking attendant's pointing, then park in the open dirt lot. It's a short walk to the gate where I pay an astronomical fee for entrance which comes with a small paper bag for the apples. At least they don't charge for the wagon I grab for our pumpkins and mums.

The orchard is crowded. Families, packs, and couples meander, some heading over to the orchards and others making use of their bakery, shop, and brewery.

"Apples first?" I ask.

"Apples," Kat agrees. "The map says the Honeycrisps are over there. Oh, look. There's a guide for which kinds are for baking and which are for eating. I've never heard of some of these varieties."

"I could make a pie," Matthew offers. "Or a crisp? Want to help me, Kat? You like baking."

"Sure. That sounds like fun." They debate which kind of baking apple would be best.

My mouth salivates from thinking about it. And the thought of Matthew and Kat huddled together in the kitchen in matching aprons with smudges of flour on both their faces makes me rock fucking hard. Makes me want to bend them over the counter and rut them.

I shift our empty apple sack to hide my hard on. There are families here. A small horde of children race each other toward the line for the tractor pulling the hay ride wagon behind it.

"Honeycrisp!" Gabriel points out, checking the tree's colored ribbon against the map. They use a complicated sorting system of colors and stripes to mark each variety.

A lot of the trees in the front have been picked over. Discarded, mushy apples scatter the ground. A few apples dot the very tops of the short trees where nobody can reach. We head further back in the row until the pickings get less sparse.

"This one looks good." Kat twists an apple off the tree and buffs it on her shirt. She takes a bite. "It's good. Definitely a honeycrisp."

"Are you illegally eating an apple we haven't paid for yet?" I ask, equally surprised and amused. We've been a bad influence on her. It's all the semi-public sex. She's been deliciously corrupted by us.

"The baby was hungry," she says, shrugging. Kat holds the apple out to me. "Want to try it?"

"I do want a taste." I tug her closer and bend down, capturing her lips. Her lip gloss is strawberry flavored and her mouth tastes like sweet, juicy apples.

Underneath that, the warm autumn day has made her sweat. Her pheromones perfume the air. Sweet, dirty cookies. The sort covered in colorful sugar crystals. Her thick, fertile scent tempts me to drizzle her cookies in my icing. I grind against her, enjoying the way she squishes under my grabbing hands.

"There are families here," Gabriel reminds us.

We separate and she swipes a thumb over my mouth with a giggle. She wipes off the smear of lip gloss that transferred from her mouth to mine. "Be good," she warns.

"Oh, I can be very good," I promise, my voice low. "Exceptional, really."

"How many of this kind do you want?" Matthew asks.

"Three or four," she answers, helping them pick out the best ones. "Let's go find the baking apples next."

We fill the bag until it's nearly bursting at the seams. The tiny paper sack holds more apples than I thought it would. I'm glad we didn't get the bushel. Once we have our apples and pumpkins and mums picked out, we take a break in their covered eating area.

Gabriel sips on his pumpkin ale while Matthew and I split the fried sampler. It's bursting with fries, onion rings, loaded potato bites, and fried pickles, and I wash it all down with an ice cold cider. Kat gets cinnamon sugar crystals all over her face while she eats her apple cider donut.

When she sneaks a fried pickle, adding it to her next bite of donut, I can't help but watch in amazement. Is this her first pregnancy craving? I hate that there's so much of her life that we miss. That she's not always with us. But whenever I gently bring up mattress shopping or offer to clear out a drawer for her, she gets cagey.

She's not ready yet. Part of me worries she might never be. That she's still not sure about us even though we're nearly halfway through this pregnancy. I don't mind taking things slow, but we are on a deadline. I want her to wear my mating bite and put our pack name on the birth certificate. More than that, I want *her*. We all do. Because she's perfect for us. In the depths of my soul, I recognize her as mine.

I turn the plate so the pickles are closer to her and pretend not to watch as she demolishes them. I'm glad her appetite is back. I didn't like it when she couldn't eat much. It made my instincts to protect and provide crazy whenever she turned down food.

The hayride slowly rolls back through its loop. "Want to take a hayride?" I ask everyone.

Kat licks the sugar crystals from her fingers and my cock strains my jeans. "Sure," she says, wiping her face clean with a napkin.

Gabriel finishes his beer and tosses out our trash, and we get in line. Nobody will bother our stuff where I parked it in the shade. A wagon full of people bundle out, and then we all climb up and get settled. Once the wagon's full, the driver takes off.

We bump along, swaying from the dirt road full of rocks and pits. A gentle breeze cools the sweat on our skin. I put an arm around both her and Matthew, rubbing his back while I pull her closer into my side.

The farm is bigger than it looked from the gates. The visitor area is a fraction of their apple orchards. The other trees are cordoned off, a cherry picker left in between rows while farmhands take a break. On the other end of the you-pick visitor section, there's the corn maze, a sunflower field, and a huge playground with a bounce house for kids.

"Look, they have something called apple cannons," Matthew says, pointing.

"What's an apple cannon?" Gabriel asks, craning his head to look.

A minute later, we have our answer. Compressed air makes a loud *thunk* as someone shoots an apple hundreds of feet away near the treeline. It explodes on impact, missing its target.

"I want to do that," Matthew says.

"We're doing that next," Gabriel talks over them.

"Man, that's so cool," Kat agrees.

I let out a huff of laughter. Three against one. I'm outnumbered. "Fine."

The man driving the tractor stops, letting people off. About half the wagonload departs, splitting off toward different activities. Others climb on, eager to be taken to the front of the orchard.

I follow my pack toward the apple cannons and pay the bored teenager for all four of their compressed air powered cannons. She gives each of us six bruised apples. Targets have been set up across the field. There's an old car, a dilapidated school bus, bales of hay with a bullseye spray painted on them, and big steel barrels staggered about.

"Ready? Go!" the teenager yells.

I load an apple from my basket into the cannon, aim, and launch it. It misses my target, but hits the ground and explodes anyways. Matthew's hits the school bus, bursting apart. Gabriel knocks a milk can off a hay bale and Kat's apple shoots all the way toward the tree line where it disappears from view.

"Good shots," I tell them both.

"Oops," she says. "These things are hard to aim."

Abandoning my cannon, I go to her section to help her. "The gun's heavy. Let me help. What do you want to hit?"

"The school bus."

I help her load and aim the heavy cannon, letting her do the fine adjustments while I keep it roughly aimed in the right direction. Her ass is pressed against my front. I don't actually need to stand this close, but I'll be damned if I don't take advantage of the excuse to rub my pheromones all over her. My cock is at half mast. It hasn't gone down since I saw her lick sugar off her thumb.

Once she's satisfied with the angle, she pulls the trigger. The cannon *thunks* and her apple hits the bus, exploding into vaporized bits of apple.

"Yeah!" She does a fist pump that makes me grin. "Let's try that big milk can next."

Gabriel and Matthew finish before we do and join us to watch as Kat shoots apple after apple until they're all gone.

"Why is that so satisfying?" she asks.

The sun is setting and the crowds have thinned by the time we finish. The families with young kids are mostly gone or leaving. Only a few couples and packs remain. My eyes travel across the field. I spot the corn maze and grin. "Want to do the maze?"

"Hell yeah," she agrees easily.

Gabriel and Matthew give me knowing looks. They're remembering the last time we came to a fall-themed orchard. When they got on their knees and took turns sucking me off in a dead end.

I buy the map from another teenager and fold it up, putting it in my back pocket. We disappear inside, swallowed quickly by the tall green stalks. The maze is huge. There's a small one by the kid area for the young ones. This is the big one they'll fill with costumed actors next month.

Solar powered lamps flick on as the corn maze grows darker. Spookier. Now that the sun has set, it's getting cooler. Kat still smells like dirty cookies that are begging to be covered in cream. We let her lead, following her navigation blindly. Solving the maze doesn't matter. That's not why we came in here.

"We've passed that scarecrow before," she says, looking around. Kat leaves the scarecrow and comes up to me. "That's three dead ends this way. Do you have the map?"

The maze is harder in the twilight. It's also perfect for our needs. "I do. But we don't need to hurry." I palm her ass, squeezing it through her jeans. Fucking jeans. I wish she'd worn one of her cute sundresses. But it doesn't matter. I can still pull them down and fuck her.

"We don't?" she asks, stiffening for a second before melting against me.

"They don't close till nine." I thank my lucky stars for their brewery. Some people travel far to get here for their famous hard ciders and themed ales. I squeeze her other ass cheek through her pants, then switch to her front. She shifts her feet apart in the dirt and I push my hand between her legs. Trace the seam of her jeans.

Her hips tilt, rubbing her clothed pussy harder against my hand. "How much time do we have?" she asks.

I move to the button on her jeans and tug it open. Slide the zipper down. They're stretchier than I thought, with triangles of expanding fabric by the side seam. I push them down her hips and wiggle her panties down with them.

"Enough for this."

When I cup her pussy, she's already slick for me. My finger slips between her labia, gliding through her wetness. She loves it. The thrill of us taking her in public. The risk of getting caught.

This omega's gonna be the death of me. Or the reason I end up in jail. Her sweetness inspires me to do lewd things with her.

"You like that, kitten?" I ask, working a finger up inside her. She's soaked. I add another finger, pumping until she squelches. Her pussy swells in my hand. Plump with arousal, her clit swollen and begging for petting.

"Yes," she whispers.

A group of people chatter not too far from us. All that separates us is a few rows of corn. With all the twists and turns, we won't see someone coming before they're on us. I need to listen for them instead.

"Can you be a good girl and stay quiet, or do you need Gabriel to keep your mouth busy?"

Kat whimpers and rides my hand, gripping onto my shirt for stability. "I need him."

I pull my hand free, ignoring her frustrated whimper. "Then get on your knees."

She gets down on her knees so fast that all the blood rushes to my cock and my head spins. It's a beautiful sight. My pregnant omega kneeling at my feet.

Gabriel kneels before her, his hands working on his belt. Kat helps him, pulls his cock free, then leans down and swallows his cock. I circle around behind her, kneeling in the dirt. Grab the rolled edge of her pants and twisted panties and work them down her thighs until her beautiful ass and pussy are exposed.

I wish the light wasn't so dim. That the corn maze wasn't so dark. The tall stalks of closely-sown corn make the shadows long. It's eerie.

While I can still see, I dig my thumbs into her pussy and spread her wide. Watch her pink hole tighten when she clenches. Her asshole puckers. One day we'll fill that hole. Has she ever had a cock up there before? Or do we get to take that cute little hole's virginity?

Her wet pink pussy glistens. Beckoning me. Her pheromones are thicker here. Sweet arousal pumps into the air, filling my sinuses and making me lose all reason. Like a siren's call, I'm desperate to answer. I can smell that she's pregnant. That the baby's mine. And it satisfies some deep, primal desire in me that I've never had the likes of before. This need I have for her isn't as simple as desire. It's a craving. And I'm addicted.

"Are you joining or keeping watch?" I ask Matthew.

"Watching, of course."

My filthy voyeur. He's always watching. Waiting. Patient. More patient than me. But no less depraved once his engine's been revved. I can't wait until the day she stokes his flame so all four of us can burn together.

The wet sucking sounds that her mouth makes has my cock dripping. I undo my belt buckle and jeans, and hook my thumbs in my boxers, shoving it all down. My dick springs free, thick and ready. It points toward her pussy, defying gravity, as if it already knows where to go.

I fist the base of it and line us up. Notch my dripping head between her slick lips. Sink into her wet heat. Her back arches, pushing herself down on my cock. Taking me deeper. Over these last few weeks, she's learned how to move with me. How to take me. Her pussy's well trained now.

I sink all the way into her and let out a low, satisfied rumble. Gabriel meets my eyes from across her other end and I share the moment with him. Thrusting into her. Watching the way she bounces on his cock. Seeing the effect it has on him. The way his eyes flutter shut and his hands smooth over her. Gathering up the stray bits of hair that have fallen out of her messy bun so he can watch her suck his cock.

Matthew watches, his attention split between the sight we make, sprawled out fucking on the ground like animals, and the corn maze. Watching for trespassers. Protecting our impromptu nest, like a good beta should.

A purr breaks free from the tight reins of my control and I swallow it with an inhale of air. I tug Kat's hips back to meet my thrust, fucking into her harder. Pushing her to take more of Gabriel's perfect cock.

God, she undoes me. Makes me borderline feral. I want to hunt her in the woods one day. After she's had our baby. When she's near her heat, her body begging me for another. Chase her by sound and scent. Find her. Wrestle her to the ground. Rip her clothes off and rut her into the dirt. Fill her pussy with cum. Put another baby in her.

That primal, savage instinct wants to keep her like this. Fertile. Her body round and supple. Breasts swollen with milk. I can't wait till she starts lactating. Can't wait to lick droplets of sweet milk from her nipples while Gabriel licks her pussy and Matthew fucks her ass.

Her pussy clenches around my cock as if it hears my thoughts and answers. Hungry. Needy. Desperate for alpha pheromones. For a pussy full of cum. I'm going to seed her deep, then tug her panties back up. Let our mess soak her panties and jeans, so she knows she's ours with every squelching step Kat takes.

"Fuck," Gabriel mutters softly, sucking in a breath. His grip in her hair tightens.

He has my sympathies. I know exactly what he's feeling. Our omega's good at sucking cock.

"Did we turn this way before?" a stranger asks.

"I don't think so," someone else answers. "Shine your light on the map again."

Her pussy clenches tight on my cock. I fuck her faster, my balls slapping against her cunt. I don't care who stumbles upon us right now. There's no way in hell I'm stopping before I've drained my balls inside her.

The corn rustles and a footstep scrapes against a rock, sending it skittering. My heart flutters with fear. Anticipation. Arousal.

"That way's all dead ends," Matthew tells them.

"Oh, thanks," the woman answers. "Babe, I want to go," the woman complains. "This is boring. Get us out of here."

"Let's just walk through the rows of corn," her boyfriend answers. "I want a beer before the beer tent closes."

The corn rustles again. Our interlopers walk on, oblivious to our misdeeds. Her pussy flutters, squeezing my cock. Milking my balls. She comes, her moans a whimper around the cock in her mouth. Gabriel groans, low and throaty.

I can't hold back anymore. Not with the filthy noises they make as they try to be quiet and fail.

My groin tightens and my knot swells. I pull her hips down and grind my cock inside her.

Kat pops off of Gabriel's cock and twists to look over her shoulder. "Don't knot me."

It's too late. I couldn't stop it even if I wanted to. And I don't. There's nothing better in this world than an ass or pussy squeezing an alpha's knot.

My cock pulses, jets of cum filling her tight channel. My knot swells, keeping all those pheromones locked in tight. Protecting her sweet, perfect pussy from any competitors. My breathing is hard and a soundless purr stutters in my chest. My teeth ache with the suppressed urge to bite her soft skin.

"Oops," I say. My remorse is a lie. My instincts demand this. Her pussy full of my cum. Her belly round with my baby. Her neck scarred from my bite. I'll settle for two out of three. For now.

"You have to pop it free," she orders. "What if the orchard closes?"

"I'm not going to risk hurting you. Stop wiggling if you want my knot to go down." I purr for her, trying to get her to settle.

Kat goes boneless, her cheek pressed to Gabriel's thigh. "S'not fair," she mumbles, her words slurred and slow.

The effect of an alpha's purr on an omega is inescapable. A bygone biological effect from the days when alphas hunted for their bride from a rival tribe. Stole them away in the night. It's hard for them to resist us when we purr. And I have a great purr, though I've never had to use it before. There's something satisfying about giving into all these alpha urges I've suppressed all my civilized life.

"Shh." I grind my knot against her tight entrance, enjoying the squeeze. Prolonging my pleasure. And I purr while Gabriel gathers her hair from her face. Strokes her fondly, his lap her pillow. My purr revs until she's boneless while I rock against her, and reach around and find her clit.

Her pussy tightens around me. Squeezes. Quivers, tight and willing. "That's so good, my sweet little kitten. You can take some more, can't you? Just one more, then we'll go."

I'm a greedy bastard. It's her pussy's fault, really. If she didn't want me to get addicted, she shouldn't have been so sweet.

Kat whimpers, trying to be quiet while I stroke her clit. She fails. Anyone left in the corn maze with us is getting an earful.

My balls ache and my groin tightens. I rub her faster, choking out a final orgasm from her. One last spurt of cum from me.

"How did Gabriel taste, kitten?" I ask her. I'm curious if she likes his flavor.

"Good. He tastes smoky like whiskey."

Whiskey, hmm? Maybe that's why I was drawn to him when we met at that soccer game.

We stay like that for a while, and I purr while my knot slowly shrinks. By the time it pops free, we only have twenty minutes to make it back to the front entrance of the orchard.

Gabriel and I help her stand and I fix her clothes while she leans against him, then me, sleepy and satisfied. It's time to put our omega to bed. If only she had a proper nest at our place. Maybe then she wouldn't want to leave.

My heart pinches with the worry of being a bad alpha. Of not giving her everything she needs. Deserves, really.

She yawns, and I scoop her into my arms. "Come on, kitten. It's been a long day. Let's put you to bed."

"But Waffles needs dinner," she protests, but she's already burying her face in my neck. I can't hear her faint omega purr, but I can feel it. It thrums from her throat and right into my heart.

"I'll feed him," Matthew offers.

"He needs to be cuddled and played with too," she adds.

"I'll play with him and pet him," Matthew reassures her.

"See? It's all taken care of," I tell her. "We've got you. And Waffles."

Gabriel takes the map from my back pocket and uses his phone as a flashlight, directing us through the maze.

"You know, it might be easier if we all lived in one place," I say, hesitant to bring this up again and ruin a perfect evening. But I'm not gonna stop trying to convince her of what I know is right. One day I'll say the exact thing that makes her realize we're her pack. That she's ours. That all we need is a bite mark to make real what our instincts already know. "With Waffles. So he wouldn't be alone so often." It's manipulative. I'm beyond caring at this point. I'd say anything to make this official.

All she says is a sleepy, "Hmm."

I carry her all the way to the hayride pick-up area and we ride it to the front, grabbing our wagon of stuff that's miraculously still there. We're one of the last groups to leave. The parking lot is mostly empty.

Gabriel loads our stuff into the cargo box built into the back of the truck while I work on getting her in and safely buckled. She's asleep instantly when we hit the road. We stop at her place for half an hour for Matthew to feed and play with Waffles as promised, then we steal her away to the bar.

The noise and crowd wakes her long enough for her to climb the stairs, use the bathroom, and collapse into bed. It was a long day for a pregnant woman.

We peel her out of her clothes and settle her in the middle of the bed, covering her in soft blankets. She has more energy now than she did, but she still gets tired early and needs a lot of sleep.

Gabriel and Matthew go through their nighttime routines. And I sit on the edge of the bed and contemplate how to convince a stubborn omega that we're the right pack for her.

Chapter Sixteen

KAT

Nested is an omega's wet dream, including their air. Their pheromone filtration system is state of the art, and I swear the calm, sweet vanilla scent they pipe in has extra ozone in it or something. When the glass doors slide open, I'm giddy with excitement.

"Oh, wow. This store is enormous," Matthew says.

"You've never been in one?" I ask. Not even to buy a gift or something for someone? Nested is a huge chain and this store is a Plus version. It doubles as a warehouse hub for their distribution network. I like that it caters exclusively to omegas. It's omega owned and omega staffed.

"No," Matthew says. "My parents are betas."

Liam grabs us a cart while Gabriel picks up a store map from the acrylic display stand. Whatever's not on the floor can be ordered and shipped to your door within two days if it's in stock. Efficiency is important when you're dealing with heats.

"Divide and conquer?" Liam asks with a frown, looking around at the huge store. The showroom has displays and inspiration set ups designed to mimic real nests, but the back is the warehouse which contains every item they sell.

Matthew and I already made a list of what we're looking for today complete with SKU numbers and prices. A few omegas who are checking out a display of cute, shaped pillows give Liam sideways glances, their nostrils subtly flaring. Trying to scent him. They practically eye fuck him as they search for a claiming mark on him first, then me. A side pony covers my old claiming bite. They glance at Liam's temporary mark that's fading on my throat, then my pregnant belly. I can practically hear their silent judgment from across the display racks.

Good enough to breed. Not good enough to claim for real.

A low growl vibrates in my chest, and I glare daggers at them. I should have fucked him in the car and rubbed my slick all over him. Let them know he's taken even if neither of us is wearing the other one's bite. At least not yet. The lawyers are still working on the paperwork, going back and forth over small details.

"No way," I tell him. There's zero chance in hell that I'm letting him wander off so that half the store can undress my alpha with their eyes. He's handsome as fuck. A successful business owner. Genuinely kind. Good to his betas. And phenomenal in bed. I'm going to cling to him in this store like a baby monkey till I've got his ass locked down with a mating bite. "This store is big. Let's stick together."

I take one of Liam's hands, holding it, and think really hard at the other omegas to *fuck off*. Too bad telepathy isn't real. I try anyway. Just in case. *You never know.* A growl slips out of me by accident.

Liam glances at me with curiosity. "You okay?"

I dodge his questioning gaze and glare at the omegas who can't take a fucking hint. "Yeah. But if they don't stop undressing you with their eyes they won't be."

"Who?" Liam looks around to see who I'm glaring at.

"What's wrong?" Matthew asks.

"I think our omega's feeling a bit territorial," Gabriel says with a grin. His expression is delighted. As if I've paid them the highest compliment. He tugs me closer and slips his hand down to squeeze my hip.

"What," Liam says, "them?" He looks at the omegas who are suddenly busy studying whatever display they're in front of. "I didn't notice."

"You didn't?" I ask him.

"No." Liam grabs the end of my hair and plays with it. "Why would I when the best omega's right here with us?"

My heart flutters and embarrassment makes my cheeks heat with a blush. I clear my throat, but I can't keep the tiny smile from my face. "I guess we should get started. You grabbed a map?"

"Oh, wow," Gabriel says, looking up from the map he's reading. "Did you see there's a food court?"

"Really? What do they sell?" Matthew asks, looking at the map.

"International food. There are three dishes from every country where they have a store. Look, they have *pastel* from Brazil." He hands me the map. One of the segments of the unfolded brochure has flags from around the world and the food items they sell listed next to each flag. "It's a hand pie with beef and spices. You'll like it."

"Sounds good, but let's furniture shop first," I tell them. We follow the map's complicated directions to the nest furniture area. The building is a maze—someone could get lost in for hours if they aren't careful.

When we find it, I'm impressed by their selection and variety. They have all the various decor styles from Swedish modern minimalist to white fairytale princess canopy beds to mid-century modern. They also have round, oval, and a heart-shaped nest for omegas who want something different. I'm drawn to the more traditional rectangular one with four posters. It comes with optional bed curtain rails and four wood stains to choose from.

"What do you think?" I ask them, running a hand along the poster's ornate spiral carving. Wooden rosettes decorate the corner where each curtain rail meets another. The curtains go on the inside, leaving the decorated wood on display. "Oak? Or the walnut color is nice."

"Walnut," they agree, then debate the sizing. Matthew pulls up the house's listing and finds the architectural drawing that was done when it was renovated in the nineties. They study the dimensions of the main room and discuss furniture layouts.

Once they've determined what size we need, Matthew takes the paperwork from its plastic sign and we move onto mattresses. It takes an hour of testing and debating to find one we all agree on.

"I think these go with the bed," Gabriel says, holding up a white package. "It's like mosquito netting."

I glance at the bed curtains he found. "They are, but I don't want white."

"What color do you want?" he asks, confused.

They have twenty options for bed curtains but none of them are right. They're all solid colors. "Not those." I grab Gabriel's hand and lead him to the regular curtains where they have patterned ones. "These."

I hand him the curtains that I haven't been able to stop thinking about since I saw them. They're a bluish-green and muted with a cream, gold, and green floral motif embroidered on them. They're also expensive and you only get one panel a package instead of a set. We'll need eight for the bed. It's hard to justify spending a grand on bed curtains. But they're perfect.

My omega instincts won't let me walk away now that I've seen them in person. They're prettier than they were online. The gold threading is metallic. It gives them a subtle glimmer in the light.

I *need* them.

It's probably the pregnancy, but my nesting urges have been off the charts lately. I've rearranged my bedroom three times and stolen dirty clothing from each of them to hide underneath my pillows. A workout shirt from Gabriel. An undershirt from Matthew. And a pair of Liam's boxers that he sleeps in. Soon I won't have to rely on stolen garments with fading scents. I'll have their pheromones direct from the source in my nest. I wish we were ready to close on the house. The wait is killing me.

"Pretty," Gabriel says, tossing the curtain into our cart.

I count out the rest and grab seven more, adding them. A bedding set in the distance catches my eye and I'm off on the hunt. They exchange amused looks while I test the bedding's texture swatch against my cheek. If I'm going to be ass up for them for every heat then I want something that's soft against my face.

"Did you realize there were so many options?" Liam asks the others.

I don't pay attention to their quiet conversation about thread counts and ply. I'm too busy touching swatches and rubbing sheets together to hear if they squeak.

Not smooth enough. I don't like their microfiber. *Flannel would be too hot.* Their jersey knit is awful with the way it almost tries to stick to my skin when I pet it. *Too stretchy.* I brush my fingers against my jeans to get rid of the memory of its texture. Their high thread-count cotton is nice, but once I find the satin, I'm done for. I pick a creamy color that's a shade lighter than the lightest tone in the curtains. Then I balance out the silkiness of the sheets with a textured cotton duvet cover in a muted leaf green hue.

It's the throw blankets that get me while I'm trying to pick out pillows. There's a velvet tasseled throw with a leaf pattern that's been burned into it. The price of it is nuts. It's a throw blanket. It won't keep us warm. It's purely decorative. Decadently, vainly decorative. I try to put it back, but my fingers refuse to unclench and drop it.

"Do you want that?" Matthew asks quietly.

I can afford it. I live modestly. My books do well. And the interest I've earned on my settlement money goes up every month without my lifting a finger. I deserve a pretty throw blanket I can afford. But it seems kind of selfish to want it. We're going to have a baby very soon. Kids are expensive. We'll need to save for college one day.

But it's so damn pretty.

"Kat," Liam says, distracting me from my spinning thoughts.

"Hmm?" I say, distracted. He cuts me off by grabbing my chin and turning my face to him.

It's such a small, innocuous gesture. A dominant act he probably doesn't think twice about. Then he smiles. A slow, sexy grin that makes me pulse between my legs. *Oh, he knows. Has he been reading more of my books?*

"Put the blanket in the fucking cart, kitten," he says, his voice husky.

Slick makes a damp spot in my panties, and his nostrils flare, scenting me. My arousal. I blush. "It's stupidly expensive."

His eyes darken as my scent overpowers my nullifying wash. "But you like it, so we're buying it. God, you're so fucking cute. I love seeing you shop like this. It's terrifying. Put the blanket in before I spank you for being naughty. For not listening to your alpha when he gives you an order."

Oh, God. That's the worst thing he could say to me while I'm working to get my pussy under control.

"Fine." I can talk him into that spanking later. I let Gabriel take the blanket from me and add it to the cart. "But if any of you get cum on that I'll cry. I don't think it can be laundered."

"Buy two," Liam says to Matthew. "In case they discontinue it."

Matthew takes another one from the stack and adds it to our rapidly filling cart.

I make a dismayed sound, but Liam distracts me with a swat on my ass. The blow is dampened by my clothes and doesn't sting, but it makes my damp spot grow. My blush deepens. After so much semi-public fingering and fucking, I didn't realize I could still be embarrassed by getting turned on in public.

"Remember those days?" An older alpha and omega couple nearby chuckle, and I know it's us they find amusing.

"Pillows," I tell Liam, trying to distract my pack.

It works. He drops his hand away and tugs me against his side, walking us over to the section with pillows. I pick them in a daze, too distracted by Liam. His hand wanders while I study the row of them. He makes circles with his thumb over my waist. Caresses the flare of my hip. Occasionally slips down to fondle my ass through my jeans. The fact that I didn't wear a dress or skirt is probably the only thing saving us from getting banned from Nested for life.

When he tugs my back against his front, his thumb grazing the underside of my breast while he rubs my rounded belly, I can't take it anymore. My eyelids blink slowly and my next breath comes out as a pant. "Liam, I can't think when you do that."

Instead of letting me go, he tucks a loose strand of hair behind my ear and kisses my temporary claiming mark. "Good. You don't need to think."

His hips press into me, his half-mast erection noticeable

against my backside. I'm not the only one affected by his shenanigans. I stare at Matthew and Gabriel for help, but neither looks ready to jump in and intervene with our terminally horny alpha.

"Our nest is gonna be crazy," I warn him.

"It's going to be perfect. Do you know why?"

He nips my bruise, a fresh waft of pheromones thickening the air between us. My nipples tighten and my damp spot grows. If he keeps this up I'm going to soak through my jeans.

"Why?" I ask, my voice soft and breathy. It's taking all of my willpower to not grind my ass against his thickening cock.

"Because you're the one making it for us."

Oh, fuck. I can't handle it when he says nice things to me in that growly voice. How far away are the bathrooms in this maze of a building, and will they notice if we slip into the family one? I scan the ceiling where their black dome cameras watch the floor. A steady red light says it's real and probably monitored.

"Can I help you guys find something?" a shop attendant asks from behind us.

I startle, my body stiffening. I didn't hear or smell the omega worker approach us.

"Pillows," Liam says.

"This is the pillow section. All of the pillows you saw in the floor displays can also be found here. Is there one in particular you're looking for?" the shop attendant asks.

I grab the nearest pillow I can reach. It's one of their fun shaped ones. This one is a margarita, and the salt on the rim is textured cottony fluff. "Found it. Thanks."

"Let me know if you need help with anything else," he says brightly, taking up a post nearby. He neatens rows of fun and cutesy pillows that don't need straightening. It's clear he's hovering to keep us in line.

My blush makes my ears hot. Liam chuckles and I slap the margarita pillow against his chest, then pull myself out of his orbit. I really don't want to get banned from Nested. They have the cutest baby stuff.

"Should we find the nursery sets?" Matthew asks when we come across that section.

"This is cute," Gabriel says, looking at a white sleigh crib.

"It is," I agree. It's pretty and traditional, but too modern-looking for our new house. "Do you see anything more vintage?"

"Here." Matthew motions us over to a display room.

We join him and my heart skips a beat. It's perfect. The fake walls have been wallpapered with a soft green paper covered with bunnies in different poses. They're realistic, like Beatrix Potter's watercolors more so than cartoonish. The crib has thin slats with a solid curved headboard. The wooden frame along the bottom is carved and it sits on clawed feet. The sign says it converts into a toddler bed and then a twin. I can almost see our little girl growing up with this set in her princess tower room.

"It's perfect." I run my hand over the crib's carvings. "I want all of it. Including that wallpaper."

"I'm not sure if they sell that," Gabriel says. He finds the set's acrylic sign and slides out a paper with the information on it.

Matthew looks up from his phone. "They do. I found the SKU number."

I spin around and find Liam. He's leaning against the fake wall, his arms crossed and a satisfied smile on his face. "I want this set."

"Okay," he agrees. Liam kicks off from the wall and pulls me into a hug, kissing my forehead. "If you want it, then you've got it, kitten. Do we need anything else?"

My feet are killing me. My bladder is going to burst if I

don't find the bathroom soon. And I'm starving. How long have we been here? There aren't many windows in this section of the store. The fluorescent lighting means it could be two in the afternoon or morning and you'd never be able to tell.

I rack my brain but can't come up with anything we're missing. We've already planned to go living and dining room shopping another day. "No."

"Good. I could eat a horse," Liam says.

"I read that they don't sell those anymore," Matthew says. "The meatballs are all beef now."

"What?" I ask, horrified.

"Thank God," Gabriel says, equally horrified.

The food court is appropriately positioned near the checkout line. A cashier rings us up, double checking our furniture requests. It takes six oversized bags to fit all of the bedding and decorations we're buying. The rest has to be scheduled for delivery. Thankfully there aren't any significant back orders and a lot of the items we picked are in stock at this location. We set a delivery date for two months out. That gives us plenty of time to close and pack and paint.

The total price on her register makes me sweat. Outside of buying my car and house, I've never made such a big purchase before. Before I can dig my wallet out of my purse, Liam's grabbed his from his pants pocket. He hands the cashier his card.

She's too quick for me to stop her. She slides his card and hands it back, then tears off the receipt. "I thought…"

Liam squeezes my hip where he's holding me. "I don't have million-dollar house money, but we're far from broke." He kisses the top of my head. "And we like spoiling you."

They brought me here to take care of me, I realize. When was the last time someone took care of me? All three of them split up the bags, taking two each. I follow them to the food court, and they find us a table.

Gabriel gets all three Brazilian dishes while the rest of us pick and choose a variety from the menu. The Canadian *poutine* ends up being my favorite. Crispy fries covered in gravy and cheese curds? It's heaven. I take a bite of Gabriel's *pastel* and moan around my mouthful.

"That's so good," I say, taking another bite before handing it back. My stomach gets so full it's becoming uncomfortable. The bigger my belly gets, the less I can eat in one sitting. And the more I have to pee.

"Wait until we go to Brazil," he says. "The food in Belo Horizonte is the best. But all the tourists want to go to Rio de Janeiro. They don't know what they're missing."

"I can't wait," I tell him. "I've been to Brazil before, but I didn't get to see much of it."

"You have?" Gabriel asks. "When? Where did you go?"

The last thing I want to do is spoil today with talk of my old pack. Of Josh. Today has been perfect. "It was a work trip to Rio years ago. I have to pee again. Be right back."

I find the bathroom and pee, then take a few minutes to clean my panties as best I can with nothing but toilet paper. I'm gonna need to start wearing heat panties every day if Liam's going to keep this up.

By the time I'm done, they've cleared our table and they're shouldering our bags.

"All done?" Liam asks.

I fall into step beside them. "All done. I've got everything I need."

Liam and Gabriel secure the bags in the bed of his truck, and then we all get in. It's not a bad drive back into town. Liam's hand on my thigh is a heavy, comforting weight. I trace the veins on the back of his hand and caress his calluses while he drives. It's a good hand. Strong. The hand of a hard worker. There's a faded scar on one knuckle. I wonder if he got it from breaking up a bar fight.

He turns our hands over and captures mine, threading our fingers together. Gentle. Always so gentle with me. And thoughtful.

Gabriel and Matthew talk in the backseat. Discussing which home improvement store has the best brand of paint. A perfectly boring, domestic conversation that makes me warm and fuzzy inside.

Emotion bubbles up in me. Unable to be contained any longer. "I love you guys."

Liam squeezes my hand and glances at me, not taking his eyes off the road for too long. "I love you too."

"*Eu te amo*," Gabriel says, reaching over my seat to play with my hair. He strokes a section between his fingers. "*Meu docinho.*"

"We love you," Matthew says. "And I have to say… I'm really grateful the clinic fucked up the paperwork. I can't imagine doing this with anyone else."

"Me too," Gabriel agrees.

"Me most of all." Liam drags our threaded hands to his mouth and kisses my knuckles.

My eyes mist with unshed tears, but I refuse to cry. I don't want to spoil this moment with tears, even if they're happy ones. Liam drops our hands to his thigh while he navigates on the highway, his attention focused on keeping us safe.

"Your place or ours?" Liam asks once we reach the edge of town.

"Mine." I need to feed and hang out with Waffles, and I can stuff our shopping bags in a corner of my office. There's no room in their apartment above the pub.

Waffles runs up screaming with a meow, his tail twitching,

as I unlock the door. He sees Matthew and runs straight past me to rub his cheek against the beta's leg.

"Traitor," I say to my wayward furry son. "You haven't been feeding him treats, have you? The vet said he's overweight. He needs to lose two pounds."

"Of course not," Matthew says, picking Waffles up and tipping him on his back. He pets my cat's fluffy belly while Waffles purrs.

I stare, shocked. Waffles never lets anyone but me touch his belly. "What magic spell have you put on my cat?"

Matthew shrugs. "We hang out when I come over to feed him." He carries my surprisingly docile cat into the living room while Liam and Gabriel bring the bags in.

"You can put those in my office," I tell them, pointing down the hall. While they're doing that, I open my fridge to see what's in there. There's spoiled milk and ancient Chinese takeout and a bag of slimy rotting salad mix. I spend more time at their place now than mine. Water is fine, I decide, pulling out four glasses and filling them with ice and water from the fridge door.

I bring all four glasses over and set them down. Matthew is holding Waffles to his face and whispering something to him. Sitting down next to him, I give him an amused look. "What are you telling him?"

"That he has a sister coming and he has to be nice to her."

Waffles purrs, unperturbed. When he's had enough, he wiggles until Matthew sets him down, then walks over to his food dish and loudly meows.

"No," I tell him. "It's not time for dinner yet."

"Is Mommy being mean?" Matthew chuckles and gets up to grab the laser pointer.

Being called mommy puts butterflies in my stomach. I rub my belly. She's finally settled down after that big meal.

Liam and Gabriel come back, Liam holding something in his hand. "Is this your new book? I didn't think it was out yet."

"What?" I stare at what he's holding. "Oh, that's my proof copy. It's not live yet."

"November first, right?" Liam asks. "That's soon."

"You remembered that?" I think I mentioned it in passing but that was weeks ago.

"He signed up for all of your socials," Gabriel says, flopping down onto the couch.

"And your newsletter," Matthew adds.

I glance between them. "Seriously?"

"Of course." Liam sits and flips through the book. "I want to be involved in anything that's a big part of your life."

My heart swells in my chest. That's so sweet.

Liam flips faster, his thumb making the pages fly by. "Whatever sex scene it lands on, we're doing."

My eyes widen with panic. "What?"

"You write a lot of sex scenes," Liam says. "It'll land on one. And whatever they're doing, we're gonna do."

Oh no. This isn't a good book for that game. "The readers like spice. But I told you I'm not into every single thing I write. It needs variety, you know?"

"Hmm," he says, like he doesn't believe me. His thumb stops and he cracks the book open, his eyes skimming across the page. His eyebrows rise, and then he grins.

"What... what chapter are you on?" I'm afraid to ask. Because he means it. Unless I want to use my safeword, we're doing whatever spicy scene he lands on. That book is one of my dirtiest. It's a polyamory mafia romance where the heroine, an omega of course, is abducted by a rival mafia pack who want to get back at her father, the Don, for a business deal gone wrong. Of course they all fall in love by the end of the book. But it doesn't come easy and they aren't always gentle or understanding at first.

"Gabriel, we're gonna need you for this one too," Liam says, passing the book over.

I'm sweating in my seat while Gabriel reads the passage. The scene he landed on is over halfway through the book, so that's not too bad. At least it won't be the scene with the gun.

Gabriel flips the page and lets out an ominous chuckle. "Dirty girl, *meu docinho*." He grins. "I like your thinking."

"What is it?" Matthew asks.

Gabriel hands him the book. I try to intercept it but their arms are longer. They jerk it out of reach. "You guys are jerks," I say without any heat to my words.

Matthew reads the passage. "With the baby, is that safe?"

"As long as we're clean and she's not having any pregnancy-related issues down there," Gabriel answers. "Are you joining?" he asks Matthew.

We all wait for Matthew's answer. He's never initiated anything with me and I haven't pushed it. He turns the page and skims more of the scene. "Well... it wouldn't be a gang bang if there were a hole left empty."

Shit. It's that *scene.*

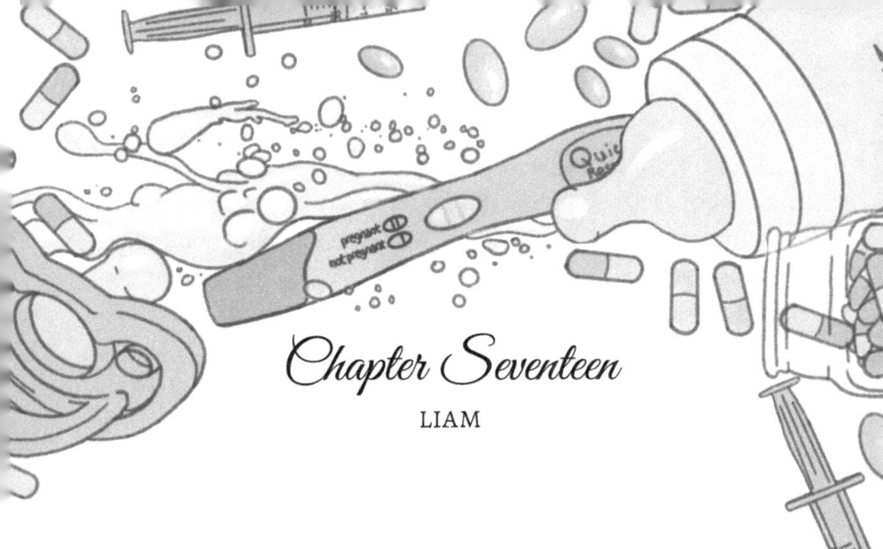

Chapter Seventeen

LIAM

"Okay, so… I have to tell you guys something," she says, capturing our combined interest. Her next words are hesitant, like she's confessing some dark sin. "I've never actually done anal."

"You haven't?" I ask, confused. Because she writes about it often. "It's in a lot of your books."

"It's a popular taboo that's not too risky. Wait, how many of my books have you read?"

I shrug. "All of them."

"All of them?" she squeaks. "That's like twenty books."

"Twenty-three," Matthew says. He flaps her latest one, the new release that's not out yet. "Soon to be twenty-four. Can we borrow this?"

She slaps her hands to her face and drags them down slowly. "Oh my God. Even the…"

"The one with the stepbrother?" I ask. "Yeah. That was Matthew's favorite."

"I liked their banter," Matthew chimes in. "They were funny."

She groans louder, like she's pained.

That's enough of that. Our omega has nothing to be ashamed of. There's no desire, no fantasy we'd ever shame her for. I love her filthy mind. She's given me so many good ideas. I stand up, the couch creaking from the loss of my weight, and extend a hand to her. She has trouble getting off the couch sometimes but she's too proud to ask for help.

"Come on, kitten. We'll go home and Gabriel will check you to make sure it's safe and walk you through it."

"It's not that bad," Gabriel says. "Matthew and I do it all the time."

Kat hugs Waffles to her chest and squeezes him in a hug, then sets him down and takes my hand. She lets me pull her off the couch and into my arms. "Okay."

See how quickly she gave in? Hardly a protest at all. There's no shame in finding all the different ways to please yourself or your lovers. But I am curious about one thing. "Your old pack never…"

She shakes her head. "Christian, the other athlete, only liked men. He only took a supportive role during my heats. Cooked, did laundry, helped me bathe, that sort of thing. I only had sex with Josh and Isaac."

"Hmm." I keep my comments about her lackluster old pack to myself as I lead her out to the truck. Gabriel and Matthew follow, locking up behind them.

She's quiet and fidgety in her seat, so I turn the volume up and play one of the artists she likes. I saw the name in her music app when she fell asleep with it open one day.

Kat's still nervous when we get to the pub, but she appears less like a startled rabbit about to bolt once we're inside the apartment, surrounded by the scent of pack.

Gabriel takes over, talking to her softly as he leads her to the bathroom to get examined and then get ready. If he says it's not safe, we'll detour and come back to it later. I'm a patient man.

Matthew and I both start undressing while we hurry up and wait for them. "Are you okay with this?" I ask him, checking in.

He sits on the chair to take off his shoes and socks. "Yeah. I'll take her mouth. Gabriel is slimmer."

He'll be easier for her ass to take, he means. In her virgin hole. *Fuuuck.* The possessive alpha in me wants to claim that cherry for myself. But my cock isn't fit for an anal virgin. She'd never trust us back there again.

I grunt my approval. "Sounds good."

"Well, this isn't what I thought we'd be doing today," Matthew quips with a smile.

I shake my head and laugh. "Me either."

That's something I love about her. Our life hasn't been dull since the moment she stumbled into it. Part of me can't believe it's been a few months since we were accidentally matched. Other times it seems like we've known her for years. I had lost hope that we'd bring an omega into our pack. When I didn't find one by my thirties, I thought I never would. That it wasn't in the cards. And I made peace with that. Matthew and Gabriel were enough. They are enough. But now, with her, we have even more.

My shoes and clothes thump to the floor in a messy pile as I shrug out of everything and stand there nude. Half-hard, my cock is ready.

The bathroom door opens and Kat stands there fidgeting with Gabriel behind her. Like she doesn't know what to do with her hands. Her swollen belly is round with that dark stripe up the middle. Her full breasts are already pointed, her nipples firm and pink. As pink as her cheeks. She's embarrassed. But there's nothing to be embarrassed of. Not with us.

I thought we'd never add a scent-matched omega to our happy little pack. But I'm so damn glad to be proven wrong.

"She's prepped," Gabriel says, rubbing her shoulder. "Everything looks good."

"Are you ready, kitten?" I ask her, holding out a hand.

Her eyes flick down to my hardening cock and she swallows. Gabriel prods her forward into the room before she can balk. We sandwich her between us. Trapping her. So she can't scamper off like a frightened bunny. She has to know we'd never hurt her. This is stage fright, nothing more. She'll adjust.

"Think of it as research," I tell her, brushing her hair back. Smoothing it out of her pretty face. I lean down and place gentle kisses along her forehead. Her cheek, and lips. Her neck. I suck her scent gland into my mouth and graze it with my teeth.

"Research?" she echoes, her voice breathy.

My mouth pops off with a wet sound. "For your books." I hold her against me, my hands roaming over her back and buttocks, and suck her scent gland back into my mouth. Licking it. Nipping her with teeth. Until she's moaning and pliant in my arms. She sways, and I steady her.

That's better.

"Do that again," she begs. "Please."

I love it when she begs. I nip her scent gland harder. Teasing both of us. My teeth ache to bite her, but I won't. I promised her I wouldn't. Not yet. No matter how desperate I am to make her mine. Ours. Until the paperwork is finished, we have to be patient.

I'm so fucking tired of being patient.

But not for this, for today. Not for being the first to introduce her to one of life's greatest pleasures. Teaching her to enjoy it, and us, completely. All three of us. Matthew watches, his stare heavy, while Gabriel and I get to work.

Gabriel plasters himself to her backside, feeling her up and kissing the nape of her neck. Carding her hair to one side to get to her nape. My hands skim his while the both of us caress her until she's relaxed.

Her body radiates heat as we get her ready. Get her nice and turned on and wet. It's a slow seduction. Thorough. I kiss every inch of her. Her shoulder, the freckle on her forearm. One palm, and then the other. I set her hand on my pecs, my abs tightening when she rubs it over my nipple. Moves lower, over the muscles, to my groin.

Gabriel plays with her breasts, pinching her nipples, then soothing them. Rubbing her pregnant belly and fondling her ass. Her thighs. I reach between her legs to see how ready she is. Ghost over her wet slit, then inch farther back. A metal plug is in her ass, stretching her virgin hole open. Easing the shock of having something in there for the first time ever.

When I push on it, teasing her, she moans into our kiss.

"Pull her hair," Matthew suggests, directing us.

He's usually right about these things. I bury my other hand in her hair, grabbing her by the roots at the nape, and tug her head to the side. She gasps as our kiss breaks, and I study her face. Her lips are swollen and pink from being kissed. Her eyes are dark and dilated. The vein in her neck juts out, calling to me. A siren's lure that makes my sharp canines ache.

"You're going to take all of us tonight," I tell her.

She nods. A small bobbing of her head that pulls against my hand. With my grip in her hair, she's not going anywhere. The time for scared bunnies to run from their pack is over.

While gripping her, I walk us backward and drag her with me. I sit, urging her to straddle my lap. Help her get settled. Her round belly rubs against my abs. Soon we'll have to get more creative with positions. When she's more pregnant than now.

"Lift up," I order.

Kat sits up higher and I let go of her hair and reach down between us, grabbing my cock and dragging it along her wet slit. Rubbing my precum over her, letting our pheromones merge. She's hot and swollen. Ready. Her sugar crystal cookie scent is thick with sex and desire. Kat's eyes flutter when I drag my cockhead up and down her. Rub it along her slit. Let it dip into her hole and tease her. A prelude for what's to come.

I set my tip against her pussy, and work it in. Just the tip. Her pussy is heaven. A tight, wet grip. Like a homecoming. The first thrust is always the best. When I sheathe myself in her.

"Sit," I order.

Kat bites her lower lip and sits, impaling herself on my cock. Her walls stretch, accommodating. She goes slowly over my girth. Over the widest part of my shaft. Slower than I would go. It takes all of my will power to stay still and let her fuck herself onto me. Taking me one slow, torturous inch at a time. My fingers make divots in her ass while I hold steady and let her do it. Watch her face as she adjusts to taking me in her cunt while her ass is stuffed with a pretty toy. It rubs against me through her inner wall. The fullness inside her makes her extra tight.

My God, what's it going to be like when we're both fucking her? My groin tightens and my cock throbs with anticipation.

Once she's fully seated, both holes stuffed, I let her take a moment to recover. We'll take this slowly. "That's my good girl."

I cup her jaw and pull her face to mine for a kiss that's more tender than the way I hold her. She likes the rough handling. Of being reminded that she's mine. Ours.

"How is it having both holes filled?" I ask her.

Her hips cant, rocking. Grinding her clit down on my pubic bone. I grope between her ass cheeks and manipulate her plug. Her pussy grips me tight in response. Clenches around me. She moans. "It's so good."

"How does it *feel*?" I ask her again, wanting more.

Naughty? Wary? Is she loving it? Disgusted? Her answer will tell us how to proceed.

"Full. I've never been so full before."

She's about to be even fuller. I glance over her head and nod for Gabriel to stop stroking his dick and join us. His cock is slick and shiny with lube.

Lying back, I make us comfortable. Get her into position. Keep her steady on my cock while Gabriel spreads her ass cheeks apart. He teases her first, plucking at her butt plug. Pulling on it only to push it back in until she's wiggling and moaning while she's trapped between us.

"Oh, fuck. That's so good. Why is that so *fucking* good?" she asks, her breaths getting harder. Faster. Her pussy clenches tight on my cock as he toys with her. Gets her hole used to stretching.

"Of course it's good," I tell her, fisting her by the hair again and dragging her lips to mine for a rough and claiming kiss. "We'll always make you feel good. We're gonna drown you in pleasure. Tell me right away if anything hurts, kitten."

Her hips move, grinding her clit against me. Pushing her ass back into Gabriel's hands. He plucks the butt plug free, and she cries out, her cunt throbbing.

Before her hole can tighten again, he lines the head of his cock up and sinks inside. My eyes damn near roll back in my head as he works the tip in. His flared cockhead rubs against my dick through her inner walls. He stretches her, taking it slow.

It's agony. It's fucking wonderful. I could die right now and be happy for it.

She's as much of a panting, sweating mess as I am by the time he's worked his cock all the way inside her. I hold still, my thick cock buried in her pussy, while he works in and out of her ass. And she takes him beautifully. Takes us both so well. Like she was made for us.

"That's our good girl," I tell her, grabbing her face. Making her look at me.

Her brow is pinched, as if she can't fathom how much she likes it as Gabriel starts to thrust. Slow, gentle rockings. Getting her used to the slide and movement of his cock in her tight little ass. Her mouth drops open, rounding, in a soundless moan. Her tits jiggle as he thrusts harder. Faster. While I stay still. Torturously still. I grit my teeth and fight the urge to move. His cock rubs against mine, through her. I've never known something so obscenely perfect before.

When I can't take the stillness anymore, I don't. I grab her hips like they're handles and lift her off my cock. He plunges deep in her ass, and on his outswing, I fuck up into her.

"Oh my God," she whimpers, her eyes squeezing tight. Savoring it. As if shutting out one sense makes all the others sharper.

We both fuck her, finding a rhythm. Slick and lube and the pulsing of her perfect cunt make it easy. She's so damn easy to fuck. To love. So delightfully adventurous and curious about exactly how good we can make it for her. And I intend for us to keep finding new ways to surprise and delight one another for a very long time.

"Look at you," I tell her, marveling at how good she is. How perfect she is for our pack. "Being such a good girl. Taking two of us. Can you take one more?"

She nods, and I lean back without pulling out of her. I take her with me so she's laid out on top of me with Gabriel standing behind her. Matthew joins us. He steps up, his hand working his cock. Pre-cum drips from his tip and runs down his knuckles as he jerks himself, keeping his cock ready. For her. For exactly this perfect moment when all of us will finally have her. He climbs on the bed, getting into position on his knees.

"Normally I'd take it easy on you," Matthew says, looking

down at her. He grabs her by the back of her head and holds her still. Rubs his cock against her face, dragging it across her cheek and angling it toward her mouth. Smearing a line of precum in its wake. "But that's not what you want, is it? That's not what you wrote."

She looks up at him with her doe eyes as he leans over her. "No," she admits.

"Open," Matthew says. "Stick out your tongue."

Kat does it. She's quick to obey. Perfectly submissive and pliant to our whims. To the pleasure we bring her. Matthew sets his cock on her tongue, rubbing himself along it. Measured thrusts push his cockhead inside her before he pulls back, using her tongue to slick himself in the warmth of her mouth. "Tap me three times if you need me to stop. Do you understand?"

She makes a muffled noise that sounds like agreement, and Matthew surges inside. Holds her head in position as he fucks her mouth. Using her to stroke his cock.

Her pussy clamps down on me and Gabriel, and we both groan. We fuck her harder. Faster. Filling all three of her holes and abandoning restraint. The urge to rut overtakes me. Clouds my thoughts. Until all I can think of is the perfect way her body bends for us. Takes our cocks and begs for more. Her pussy is a dripping, slicked-up mess, and her tight ass clenches on Gabriel's cock while Matthew fucks her face and sighs as he grinds her nose against his groin.

My lips peel back over my teeth and I clamp them together, holding back the base urge to bite her. To mark her. Claim her for good as ours. It's unnatural to have the urge so strongly outside of a heat. Maybe that's why I've been so lost in the rut ever since I first came in her sweet, fertile pussy. Because my alpha instincts don't understand why we haven't marked her before someone else can. Breeding her is only half the equation. My instincts demand that I lock her down. Stuff her with my knot, my cum, cover her in my pheromones, and bite her until she's bloody and every competitor knows she's claimed. That they've lost.

She comes, her walls clamping down, and her sounds are muffled on Matthew's cock. Her pussy tightens, strangling me, and I can't hold back. My groin tightens. My balls pull up tight. My knot begins to swell. Instinct demands that I put it in her. Keep her fertile womb locked up tight. I'm too lost in it to remember that it's not the best idea.

Heat lashes through me and the swelling tissue pops. Lodges behind her pubic bone and locks us together while my cock kicks. Spurts thick ropes of cum. Drenches her walls and fills her with pheromones and seed. Keeps her cervix and full uterus nice and happy.

Gabriel lets out a strangled sound, his chest heaving as he pants above her. His cock rocks deep inside her, dragging over my bulbous knot. The rub makes my groin tighten, my cock pulse. Another spurt of seed. Again. He fucks her ass faster. Using her body for his own pleasure, now that she's found hers. She comes again, her thighs shaking with the strain of it. Kat says she's never had multiple orgasms before us, and the urge to see how many we can wring from her one day makes me giddy.

Kat's pussy flutters with aftershocks, milking my knot. Squeezing down, asking for more, even if she thinks she can't take it. She can. I slap her on the ass, enjoying the way her soft flesh jiggles under my hard palm. This is what she's fucking made for.

Her groans and moans and whimpers are stifled around Matthew's cock as she blows him. While he fucks her face, her pink lips stretched obscenely wide around his girth. Saliva dripping down her chin as he makes a mess of her.

"*Meu Deus*," Gabriel groans, slamming home and staying there. His hips stutter, his rhythm slowing. I know when his cock pulses with each lash of semen from where I'm buried deep inside her. He stops, his dick lodged deep, his flared head caught where it is from the girth of my knot in her cunt.

"Did she come?" Matthew asks through gritted teeth.

"Twice," I answer, really fucking proud of us.

"Thank God. I can't hold myself back anymore." His thrusts turn slower. Deeper. "She's so good at sucking cock." He pulls halfway back and fists his base, jerking himself. Using her mouth to keep his tip nice and wet until he comes.

"Fuck, I'm gonna fucking come," he warns her. With his other hand, he grabs her face. Holds her still. "Don't you dare swallow. I want to see it."

Her cheeks hollow as she sucks on his cockhead while he jerks himself. Matthew comes with a grunt, his groin pulsing as he empties his load on her tongue. He makes a tight ring around his base with his thumb and middle finger, stroking himself until there's nothing left.

When his balls are done emptying his load in her mouth, he pulls out with a wet pop. "Open."

Her swollen lips part.

"Show me your tongue."

Kat sticks out her tongue, cum and saliva dripping from the tip where she's collected his spunk.

"That's a good girl," he says, practically purring. "Now you can swallow."

She pulls her tongue back in and swallows, her throat working to drink him all down. Her eyes are so dark, her pupils blown wide. He grunts and lets her go, his hand dropping away. His thumb strokes her cheek, a sweet gesture after such a rough face fucking.

Kat surprises us all by latching onto his cock again. Laving him clean until he's shuddering from oversensitivity. She purrs.

I sense the vibrations all the way down to her pussy where my knot is softening.

Once it's deflated, Gabriel pulls free and I lift her off me, setting her back down after it flops onto my stomach.

God, that was fucking good. I'm not sure we'll ever top that. She's still purring, although her eyes stay closed more than they open. She settles on my chest, her head tucked under my chin. Gabriel grabs a throw blanket and drapes it over her, rubbing her shoulders and back through the soft fabric.

My own purr rumbles through me as I draw lazy circles on her skin. Winding her down now that we're done winding her up. The mess we made of her drips onto my groin and thighs, soaking into the bedding. I'm beyond caring. We need to do laundry anyway.

"I love you guys," she murmurs, yawning and sleepy.

I crane my neck and kiss the top of her head. Balls empty, instincts satisfied, surrounded by my pack, I've never been happier. "We love you too."

"Love you," Matthew says.

"*Eu te amo, meu docinho,*" Gabriel says. They rub her down, petting and stroking her.

"Rest," I tell her.

"Does anything hurt?" Gabriel asks.

"No." She snuggles closer, and I motion for Gabriel and Matthew to join us. They settle on either side of me, tucking close. Pulling the blanket over all of us. I'm boiling and sweaty after that workout, but I don't want her to get cold. So I endure it, as any proper alpha should.

It takes a while to recover. I'm getting old, and my body's making that known, but I'll be damned if Kat doesn't make me feel like a teenager again some days. She was exactly what we needed to knock us from our routine.

Before she can fall asleep for real, I jostle her awake by

grabbing her under the ass and sitting us up. "Time to go wash up, hellcat."

Matthew pulls the blanket off. She makes a sigh that's sleepy and content and tightens her arms around my neck as I hoist us out of bed and carry her to the bath.

Gabriel starts the shower and makes it warm. Not too hot. Once it's ready, I set her down and make sure her legs aren't wobbly. I step in behind her. The shower's too small for it, but that doesn't stop me. I help her get her hair wet and lather shampoo through it, rinsing the fragrant suds free to circle down the drain.

I take special care to soap up her body, cleaning her thoroughly while she runs conditioner through her hair and rinses that out too. I'm gentle between her thighs in case she's chafed. Her pussy is still swollen and throbbing when I clean her there, ignoring the way her hips rock against my hand. I wash the cum and slick and lube off her.

Matthew bundles her into a fluffy towel and helps her dry her hair while I shower quickly. We take turns, the hot water running out before all of us are done. We'll need a better water heater once we're in the house. With all the kids we're gonna have, I wonder if a tankless style would be better.

At the sink, we take turns brushing our teeth in the narrow bathroom. It's all elbows bashing into one another, but the domesticity of it makes my instincts happy. I don't mind the small, tight spaces. It's den-like. Easier to protect the pack if we're all shoved together.

We climb into our too small bed, naked and wedged together in a puppy pile underneath the blankets. Kat falls asleep nearly instantly, and I lie awake a bit, looking between my packmates. Gabriel gives me an easy smile from across her. I tug Matthew closer to me and pull his leg over mine as he spoons me sideways. He tucks his head up against my neck, his breath warm against my throat.

The room smells like sex and musk and pheromones. Like a plate of Christmas cookies sitting on the windowsill of a house in a snowy, winter landscape. A fire in the hearth roaring, making smoke as the logs crackle and pop while snow covers the woods in a blanket of gentle white peace.

It smells like pack, and it's perfect.

Chapter Eighteen

MATTHEW

The mailbox squeals as I open its metal lid and find a thick packet of letters inside. The return label is my cousin's office address. *It's here.* Our copy of the papers from the lawyers. We signed them yesterday, and they overnighted us copies for our records.

Liam's gonna lose his mind. He's been planning this night for weeks, before Kat dropped the house bomb on us and sped up his timeline.

I slip past the crowd and stop short. The pub is way too packed for a weekday when there's no game on. Gabriel spots me from his place at the bar where he and Kat are sitting while Liam covers someone's absence.

He works too hard. Does too much. He can afford to hire more staff, but to be honest, I think he likes it. Likes feeling needed. As if O'Donnell's wouldn't feel as homey and friendly without an O'Donnell behind the bar. Maybe he's right. I don't understand much about family legacies. I threw a wrench in my parent's plans when I decided not to go to law school. But I like my job at the bank. The hours are good. I get weekends and holidays off. It's a solid career.

"Hey. How was work?" Kat asks me.

"Same as always," I answer.

"I have to pee again. Save my seat." Kat pulls herself off her bar stool and walks to the bathroom.

"Want a beer?" Gabriel asks, signaling to the bartender for service.

"Yeah." I take Kat's seat to keep it warm for her and to prevent someone else from snagging it. "What's going on? Why's it so crowded?"

"Word leaked that some famous athlete is in town," Gabriel says, looking around. "I guess he comes here from time to time. I think everyone's hoping to catch a glimpse."

"I got this. Go serve those guys," Liam says to his bartender. "Hey. I've got a new coffee ale in. Want to try it?"

"Sure." I watch the pub while Liam pulls a beer for me and sets it down.

The crowd thickens, voices rising as they congregate around someone who just arrived. The gossip makes its way back to us. It's the athlete. Napkins get thrust at him for signing, and a few people ask for selfies. I watch it all in amusement, wondering if we're going to need to put someone on the door to fight overcrowding and keep the fire marshall happy.

Eventually the athlete makes his way over to the bar, pausing to chat with people. I recognize him vaguely, but can't place his name. I've never been as into sports as Liam and Gabriel are.

"Oh, shit," Gabriel says. "That's Fischer. He's a football star. His team made it to the World Cup last year."

After a bit of schmoozing, the athlete finally makes his way to the bar. Someone gives up their seat for him in exchange for an autograph on their damp coaster.

"Hey, man. Can I get your…" His eyes scan the weekly beer

menu chalk painted on a blackboard. "I'll try your chocolate stout."

"Sure." Liam pours the athlete's beer into a snifter. "Here you are. Need a menu?"

"Nah. I'm having dinner with the family in a bit. Wanted to pop in for a pint and cool off. It's hot out there. I used to come here whenever I was visiting my family on break from college. It sure hasn't changed, huh? Still looks the same as it used to."

"Yeah," Liam says, cleaning glasses in the sink under the bar. "Nothing's changed except the owner, but it's family-owned."

"I like that," the athlete says, glancing around at the decor above the bar. Vintage framed photos and memorabilia decorate the original wooden bar above the racks of barely used liquor bottles. "I'd rather come to places like this than corporate chains, you know?"

"That line was crazy long," Kat says, fighting her way through the crowd.

The athlete twists in his seat. "Kit Kat?"

Kat freezes like a deer in the headlights. "What are you doing here?"

My shoulders stiffen as he drags his eyes over her from head to toe and back up again. His gaze lingers over her belly the most.

"You're pregnant," he says.

Her hand lands on the top of her stomach. "Yeah. I am. Why are you *here*, Josh?"

"My mom's birthday," he says. "I'm only in town for a few days."

She shakes her head and blinks, as if clearing her thoughts. "Right."

Oh no. Josh. I put the pieces together quickly. Liam does too. He squares up, his muscles bunching. Gabriel appears pained. As if the shock of learning that Kat's shitty ex is one of his favorite athletes has rocked his world in a way he'll never recover from.

"You look… good," Josh says, cradling his stout in his palm. "I didn't realize you got mated again."

Kat gives him a questioning glance. "Why would you?"

Josh ignores her tone and frostiness and presses on. "When are you due?"

A few of the patrons watch, interested, while Liam bristles. It's the final straw. I'm surprised he's held it together this long. He throws the wooden divider that closes the bar off from the patrons up and goes to Kat's side, pulling her against his broad chest.

He gives Josh a smile with too much teeth to be completely friendly. "You've met my omega?"

"You're with the bartender?" Josh asks, looking back at Kat for confirmation.

Liam sticks his hand out, using the movement to angle Kat slightly behind him. "Liam O'Donnell. I'm the owner."

Unperturbed, Josh shakes his hand. Their knuckles blanch white as they squeeze each other as hard as they can to see who gives in first. It drags on until it's supremely awkward. I roll my eyes at their macho alpha pissing match.

"Joseph Fischer," Josh says. "I play for the—"

"Nice to finally put a face to a name," Liam says, interrupting him. He pumps their handshake.

"Same."

"Thought you didn't know she found her new pack?" Liam asks, sniping at him.

"This is the rest of my pack," Kat says, interrupting them before someone can break a hand. She pinches Liam's side through his shirt, then hides the gesture with a few quick pats to his abs.

"Matthew," I say, waving awkwardly.

"And I'm Gabriel," Gabriel says. His normally faint accent is thick like it gets right after he spends a lot of time in Brazil with his family. "I saw your World Cup Qualifier game." He clicks his tongue against his teeth. "That was a nasty kick you took."

Oh, holy shit. I stare at Gabriel like I've never met the man before. It's such a subtle, petty insult. He's bringing up Josh's personal worst game, the one that had him rolling on the ground, crying dramatically. His team won despite his theatrics, but still. It was embarrassing. I don't get why soccer players sometimes pretend that minor injuries are so terrible.

Josh's jaw ticks. "Thank you. I'm fine now, and it's always nice to meet my fans. Do you guys want me to sign anything? I don't mind."

My eyes widen at his complete inability to read the room. I choke on my sip of beer and end up having a coughing fit. Gabriel squeezes my thigh under the bar counter. As if I'm choking on purpose.

Kat's phone rings, and she pulls it out of her pocket. "That's Jen. I have to go. I promised I'd meet up with her and grab dinner. We haven't had a girls' night out in forever." She goes up on her tiptoes and tugs Liam down so she can kiss his cheek. "I'll see you after?"

"Of course. Have fun with your friend," Liam says. "Come over whenever."

She hits the button to answer her call and holds her phone up to her ear. "Hey, one sec." Kat glances at Josh. "Say hi and happy birthday to your mom for me." Then she tugs on her coat and spins to leave while talking on the phone with her friend. The crowd swallows her and her conversation up.

"Hey, Kat, wait," Josh says, chasing after her.

Liam steps into his path, blocking him. His face is thunderous, a warning that only an idiot would ignore. "I don't think so."

Josh holds up his hands in surrender. "Hey, man. I'm not trying to edge in on your claim. I have my own pack. I only want to talk with her. I don't like how things ended. I was hurting too. I didn't handle it well. Let me apologize to her. Please."

Liam looks slightly less murderous, but no less wary. I slide off my stool and go to his side, putting a hand on his arm. "Don't throw first," I whisper, low enough so that only he can hear it. This asshole's rich and famous. We don't need problems. I don't want to have to make an embarrassing phone call to my uncle.

Liam's frame vibrates with tension. One bad move from the ex-alpha, and Josh's gonna be on his ass on the floor. And not a damn person in this bar will say they saw anything. They know Liam. That he's level-headed and fair. So if he kicks someone's ass, it's because they asked for it. Still, in this modern day of cell phone recordings you can't ever be too careful. The last thing we need is a lawsuit.

Gabriel drains his ale and sets the glass down, then joins us. He crosses his arms over his chest, the movement making his tight black shirt strain over his hard won muscles. He's been putting in a lot of hours at the gym. He's nearly as beefy as some alphas. And Liam's got about four inches in height on Josh. I don't want the trouble, but my pack could grind him into the dirt if we had to.

"Let me go and apologize to her," Josh says, holding his palms up in a placating gesture.

Liam leans in. His voice dips low in a tone so deep it's nearly a growl. "If you make her cry, I don't care how rich or famous or loved by the public you are. I'll break your fucking legs and you'll never kick a soccer ball again."

Josh's eyes widen. He sizes Liam up for one second before he must decide that he's completely outmatched and disadvantaged. Even with the crowd of witnesses around us. Liam's not the bluffing sort. His great-grandpa kept pace with the Irish mob after prohibition. Big balls run in the family.

"Yeah, I got it," Josh says. "No tears. I'm just gonna…" Carefully he slips around us. We turn, tracking his movements. I grab Liam's shirt sleeve to keep him from tromping after the alpha.

"Let me follow him," I say.

Liam and Gabriel let me go. I'm the least intimidating and the most level-headed of the three of us. I can watch the alpha without escalating things.

The crowd parts for me, their gazes lingering with questions, as I make my way outside to the parking lot. Josh is there already, talking to Kat beside her car. Her arms are crossed and she's frowning, but she doesn't seem distressed.

She sees me from across the parking lot, but nothing in her posture or expression changes. I raise my eyebrows dramatically, silently asking if she's okay. Kat flicks her fingers at me in greeting, then turns her attention back to her ex.

I can't hear all their conversation from back here. Only fragments. He asks how she is, making awkward small talk. When she doesn't bite, he finally apologizes.

Slowly I inch closer. If he does something stupid like touch her…

"I hate that I lost so much," she says. "You were such a big part of my life for so long. I can't look at old photos because you're in nearly all of them. I couldn't talk to old friends about it because they were your friends too. It took a year for people to stop asking me about you. It was so damn alienating. And I can't talk about any of it."

My heart twists in my chest. Does she think she can't talk

about her old pack with us? It's not a fun subject, sure, but we'd never tell her to stop. Not if she needed it.

"I'm sorry," he says. "I'm so damn sorry for it all, Kit Kat."

Her expression turns thunderous. "Don't call me that. You lost that right when you told me to pack up and go."

"I'm so sorry. I was hurting and I didn't know what to do. I couldn't handle it."

"Like I could?" she spits out, throwing her hands wide.

"They were my babies too," Josh says, his tone broken. Full of emotion. "I couldn't lose another baby, Kat."

Kat's face twists from one expression to another. Anger to shock, then something like pity. She collapses in on herself, and the muscles in my body tense, ready to spring forward if she needs me.

"I know," Kat says softly. I barely catch the words from this distance. "I get that."

"I couldn't lose another one. I'm sorry, Kat. But I didn't have it in me to keep trying. I didn't want it as badly as you did. Didn't understand how it was worth all the grief and pain to you. The fucking heartache. I needed to move on or I'd never get over it. But I'm sorry that I wasn't there for you enough. With practice and my games and all the missed doctors' appointments. As hard as it was for me, it was worse for you. And I wasn't what you needed me to be. I'm not asking you to forgive me. But… I guess I just wanted you to know I'm sorry. I wish I'd been kinder to you."

She's silent for a moment. All of us stand there, waiting. Undecided if I should intervene now, I hesitate. My body thrums with the urge to rush in and scoop her up. Save her from this asshole. But my feet are rooted to the spot. She deserves the chance to handle this however she wants. So I wait for a signal, a sign that she wants my help.

Kat folds her arms again, but appears less angry. "Me too. I was so angry that I couldn't do the one thing I'd always wanted. The thing that was supposed to be as easy as breathing because of my dynamic. I felt like a bad omega. And then when it kept happening, you didn't want me anymore."

Josh reaches out and touches her upper arms, rubbing them soothingly. For a moment I see red. But Kat doesn't shove him away from her or back up out of reach. My anger turns to fear.

What if she wants to go back to her original pack? He's famous and rich. A world renowned athlete. What can we really offer her that he couldn't? She's proven she can get pregnant now. What if he decides he wants a second chance? What'll happen to us? Our baby? Panic grips me. I don't want her to go. And not because she's carrying our child. Because I love her. And I think I'm starting to want more than friendship from her.

"We had other issues, Kat."

She closes her eyes and sighs, then opens them again. "I know."

"You aren't broken or bad. Clearly. I mean… Look at you. You're huge."

Now Kat shoves his hands off her. "Oh my God! You're such a dick sometimes."

"Yeah but it made you less sad," he says. "I mean it, though, Kat. You're not broken. You're not a bad omega. And you're gonna be a great mom. I'm glad you moved on and found a new pack. Although your new alpha might be a bit of a dick. You might want to watch out for that one."

"Liam?" She clocks her head. "He's been nothing but sweet to me."

"He threatened to break my legs."

She perks up. "He did?"

"If he ever hurts you, tell me. I can help you get out. It's the least I can do."

I bristle at his implication. That Liam is a bullying alphahole who'd ever lay a finger on one of us in anger. He would never.

Kat waves his offer away. "I'm fine. But… thank you for caring. Tell your mom I said hi."

He takes a step back and shoves his hands into his pockets. "Do I get to hear when you're due now?"

Kat rubs a hand over her pregnant belly. "January. I'm twenty-six weeks. It's a girl."

"A girl." Josh smiles wistfully. "I hope she looks exactly like you. You were really cute in pigtails."

"Thanks. I hope she has her daddy's eyes."

Josh backs up and pulls his car keys from his pocket. He clicks a button that makes a sporty red luxury coupe beep. "I should go. Before your alpha comes out with a baseball bat."

Kat and I watch him drive off. I close the distance between us before she can leave too. I need to see how she is. What she's thinking and feeling and if she's okay.

"Did Liam really threaten to break his legs?" she asks.

"Yeah. That guy was lucky I was there to talk Liam down."

Her face is unreadable, and then she breaks out into a smile that makes my body unclench. "I wish I'd seen it."

Her grin is infectious. I smile and close the small gap between us, pulling her into a hug. "He growled too."

"Really?" She tips her head up and rests her chin on my chest. "Think he'd reenact it for me tonight?" Kat waggles her eyebrows.

Absolutely. Liam's being delicate with her because of her state. But he can be a caveman when his rut is riding him hard. "I think he could be persuaded. But if you really want to get him going, you should try edging him. Liam hates how much he loves it."

Her eyes sparkle with amusement, and she squeezes me before letting me go. "Good idea." She zips around me.

"Where are you going?" I call out, chasing after her. "Aren't you gonna be late for your friend?"

I follow her into the pub and the crowd watches us as we find Liam. Liam doesn't have a chance to ask if she's okay before Kat grabs him by the shirt and pulls him down. She forces him to either bend or rip the collar of his shirt.

He bends down for her.

Kat smashes her lips to his in a scorching and awkwardly long kiss that's full of tongue and groping. A few of the regulars at the bar hoot and cheer. When they come up for air, Liam looks at her with a dazed expression.

"Not that I'm complaining, but what was that for?" Liam asks.

Kat grabs his dick through his pants and gives him a squeeze. The hollering gets louder. "You'll find out tonight." Then she spins on her heels and heads toward the door.

Liam rearranges the erection straining his jeans. "You're gonna leave? Right now? After *that*?"

Kat pushes the door open but pauses in the doorway and looks back over her shoulder. "It's girls' night. I have a date with my best friend and some virgin margaritas." She gives him a sunny smile and a jaunty wave. "See you later!"

I laugh, then laugh harder when Liam gives me a confused and slightly pained expression. *Poor guy.*

Gabriel throws an arm over my shoulder and pulls me against his side. "What happened?"

I cover my mouth with my hand and rub my jaw. "Nothing much. All they did was talk. But our girl's a fast learner."

Chapter Nineteen

KAT

WALKING UP TO MY PARENTS' DOOR AND KNOCKING IS THE hardest thing I've done in a long time. Since I first came home, packless and depressed, three years ago. I told my mom to be prepared for a big surprise, but I didn't tell her what it was. It didn't seem right to tell them over the phone.

I hesitate, then take a deep breath and knock. It doesn't take her long to answer the door. "Good timing, Kathleen, I was just… Oh." Her gaze shoots down to my belly, then up to my neck, her expression closing off into something unreadable.

I put a hand on my bump. "Hey, Mom."

She recovers quickly and ushers me inside. "Come in and sit so we can talk. I just took the coffee cake out of the oven, but I suppose you won't want the coffee to go with it now, huh?"

My mom makes the best coffee. There's no way I'm missing out. "A small cup is fine."

She busies herself cutting into the coffee cake, plating two slices for us and moving them to the kitchen table, then going to the coffee maker. My childhood home smells exactly like I remember. Like sweet treats and the coffee she brews nearly all day long. She pours us both cups then sets down the small carton of creamer on the table. I hang my coat on the back of the chair and sit.

"So…" my mother says, sitting down too. "Do you know who the father is?"

I mix sugar and creamer into my coffee and palm the cup, soaking up its warmth. The familiar smell is comforting. "Of course I do. His name is Liam."

"Do we get to meet him?"

"Yes. And the rest of his pack. Matthew and Gabriel. I didn't want to tell anyone and get their hopes up before I knew it would stick this time."

Her expression turns pained. "So you've been going through this alone? Baby, you could have told me. There's nothing you can't tell me or your fathers, you know."

A lump forms in my throat. "Jen knows. And my pack. We haven't made things official yet, but we will. So I haven't been alone. But I didn't want to say anything until things looked good."

"And they do?" she asks, leaning forward in her seat. "When are you due?"

I rub my belly idly. "January. Everything looks great. We're having a girl. What are you doing for Christmas?"

"Christmas?" Her eyebrows raise toward her hairline. "I haven't thought that far ahead, but I suppose the usual. Why?"

I stuff myself with her coffee cake, still warm from the oven, while I tell her about my new pack. Their family tradition of getting together at a ski chalet. I leave out the details she doesn't need to know, like how Liam and I met. She doesn't pry.

"We'll need to plan your baby shower," she says, turning serious. "And soon. Have you decided where you want to have it yet? And I'll need a guest list and head count for the catering."

"I'd like to have it in our new house," I tell her, dropping another bombshell on her lap. "We sign the paperwork and get the keys next week."

My mother takes it all in stride. I suppose finding out I'm buying a house is nothing compared to learning she has a granddaughter on the way. "I'm excited to see it. Does it have enough room?"

I think of our house and it's three thousand square feet. "Plenty. I'll send you the address once we have it painted and we're settled in. We can do housewarming and a baby shower all in one. Where are Dad and Papa?"

She pours herself another cup of coffee and wraps up the rest of the coffee cake to save it for later. "They're looking at fishing boats. I tried to talk them out of it, but they're taking retirement hard. They don't know how to not be busy all day."

I smile wistfully at the family photos hung up on the wall. My parents' mating ceremony photo is next to my high school graduation portrait. Family vacation photos fill the gaps. There's a new one I haven't seen before. My two fathers are standing on a shore, holding up a massive fish with grins on their faces.

"I have to go," I say, getting up and putting on my coat. "There's a lot to do right now. You'll tell them I stopped by? Give them my love?" And tell them that I'm pregnant and getting mated. I don't need to ask her the last part. There aren't any secrets within a pack.

"I will." She shows me to the door and gives me a big hug on the porch. "I love you, baby. And send me a sonogram photo so I can put it on my fridge. I can't wait to tell my scrapbooking ladies about my first grandbaby on the way. Sharon won't shut up about her son's big Wall Street job. Maybe this'll give the group something new to talk about."

She hugs me tighter, and I squeeze her harder in return. Then we pull apart. "I will."

Once I'm back in my car and driving home, I can finally relax. Ripping that bandage off was hard, but I'm glad it's over. I didn't like keeping this a secret from them, but I couldn't handle the pity from another lost pregnancy.

Our baby girl kicks my bladder, as if she's proving she's in there. When I get home, there's a package on my porch. Not the brown-boxed shipping kind. The hand-delivered white box tied with a big red velvet ribbon sort.

Despite its size, it's not heavy when I pick it up. I tuck it under one arm and get my key in the lock with the other. The minute I'm inside, Waffles races to the door, his tail quivering and his mouth open in a hungry, cackling meow.

"I'll feed you in a second, but I really have to pee," I tell him. I set the box down and run to the bathroom. I can't go an hour without peeing now. Coffee was probably a mistake, but it was so good. It was worth it.

After, I put food in Waffles' bowl, an early dinner since I probably won't be coming back tonight. I give him fresh water, and check that his robot litter box is fine. It was ridiculously expensive, but worth every penny. Especially while I'm pregnant and can't scoop it.

I forget about the box until it catches my eye. There's no note. "What are you?" I ask it while I cut the red ribbon off and rub my thumb along its nap. It's real velvet. Its contents are wrapped in crisp, scented tissue paper. There's an embossed sticker with the name of a clothing boutique holding the two edges together. I break the seal and start pulling garments out.

There's a white dress inside. It's formal and made of thick white satin. Long sleeves flare out like a bell before they gather at the wrist again. The neckline is an off-the-shoulder sweetheart cut with pleated fabric that cups over the breasts. The dress is fitted to stretch over my baby bump, then flare out at the hips in a wide circle of skirt. The wide neckline is sexy for an omega. It'll show off my neck and nape.

Underneath the dress, there's lingerie. A strapless bra and matching panties in the softest shade of pink. The panties are smooth in the front, but an open cage of straps in the back. Inside the big box are three smaller ones. Nude pumps with a modest heel take up the larger box. In the smaller one is a sex toy. A black silicone wearable that's shaped like a butterfly with a rounded protrusion that curls inside. In the tiniest box is jewelry. Silver drop earrings with starbursts at the ends and a matching bracelet.

Only Liam would think to give me a gorgeous, sexy dress and jewelry and then send it along with a sex toy. I pull out my phone and load our group chat.

KAT

What's all this stuff for?

LIAM

7 pm

GABRIEL

We'll pick you up

MATTHEW

Stay home, there's another surprise coming

???

A knock on my door pulls me away from my phone. On my porch there's a young black man with a buzzed head and gold eyeshadow. He's holding a big rolling silver suitcase. "Are you my lucky lady?" he asks with a grin.

"I guess so."

He looks over my shoulder into my house. "Where can I set up? I need an outlet."

"What are you here for?" I ask, pulling the door open for him.

"Your hair and makeup, honey. Your beaus ordered you the deluxe glam package. Cute cat." He stoops to pet Waffles.

"Is the kitchen okay?" I ask him, showing him where it is.

"It's perfect." He puts his suitcase on my table and unfolds it like an accordion. The top comes up and the sides butterfly open. Drawers swivel out revealing rows upon rows of cosmetics. He pulls curling irons of various sizes out of the big bottom section and plugs them in.

"Can I see your dress?" he asks. "So I know how to do your hair."

I pull the dress from the box and hide the other stuff in the tissue paper.

He whistles. "Oh, honey, that's nice. Is that your wedding dress?"

My heart trips in my chest. Because what else can it be? I stroke the gown's fabric and lay it out on a chair so it doesn't get wrinkled. "I think so." What are they planning? And how did they manage to keep it a secret?

He pulls various things from his drawers, comparing colors until he decides what he wants. "Let's do a side-swept look. Show off those collarbones and that neck. Now go wash your face and do your skincare, then change into something easy to slip out of so your shirt doesn't mess up your hair."

Following his instructions, I wash my face and run a brush through my hair, then change into a robe. He chats with me the entire time he's working. He starts with my hair, curling and spraying it and pinning it up to cool. Once it's all curled, he moves onto makeup while my hair sets.

"I'm thinking soft glam," he says. "Pinks and champagne. Unless you want something more dramatic?"

"That sounds good." I watch him study five different shades

of nude pink lipsticks before settling on a color. He pokes and prods me, turning my face this way and that as he applies foundation and concealer. Then he sets it all with a shit ton of powder, and lets it do something called baking. He moves onto my eyes while my face sets.

Holding still when he does my mascara and eyeliner is difficult. He pulls out a package of new false eyelashes and trims them to size, then applies a coat of glue and waits for it to get tacky.

"Pout for me, pretty," he says when he gets to my lips. He even does my nails. Shaping them and painting them a pretty ballet slipper pink until they're glossy. I play the role of his doll until he's done. He uses a fan-like brush to wipe the extra powder off my face, then sprays me down with a setting spray. "Now your hair."

I lay a hand over my old mating bite. "Cover this side, please."

He does it without asking any questions.

I tell him about my pack while he works. He pins my hair up, the pins digging into my scalp before slotting into place. He weaves the curls he made and braids it all to the side in a complicated half-up, half-down style that pulls to the side. He gently pulls the dangling curls apart to add volume, then sprays it all down with hair spray until it barely moves.

"There. Gorgeous." He holds a mirror up so I can see.

He's done an amazing job. I look like my old self. Like the hopeful, happy girl I was when Josh took me to his first awards banquet. When I dressed up in a designer dress they loaned me to match his gifted suit and dozens of photographers wanted photos of us on the event's red carpet. I don't miss those days. The shine wore off that penny a long time ago when event appearance became compulsory no matter how I felt about attending. But I still like feeling beautiful.

"It's perfect. Thank you," I tell him.

He packs up his stuff and gives Waffles one more scritch on his chin, then goes. I glance at the clock and see that it's six. Plenty of time to finish getting ready. I put music on while I shave my legs and put lotion on. I skip the scent nullifying stuff and go for the one with the faint vanilla scent that blends in perfectly with my own pheromones.

The lingerie is silky smooth, and I recognize the brand. It's from a specialty shop in London. I have to wonder how long they've been planning this without me knowing or getting suspicious. The underwear covers almost nothing of my ass. The back is all crisscrossing straps with a wisp of fabric that turns into the wide gusset.

The strapless bra fits me perfectly, and the silicone grips—and my belly—keep it from sliding down due to my pregnancy heavy breasts. I put my jewelry on and study my reflection. I'm sexy as hell. They're going to lose their minds when they see me like this.

I smile, thinking of ways to make Liam feral. I want him to growl for me again.

At six-forty, I wiggle into my dress and figure out how to get the zipper up without help. The dress skims my curves, enhancing what pregnancy's already accentuated. My ass and thighs are fuller than they used to be. My belly thick and rounded. My breasts heavy and, thanks to the expensive bra, pressed together deliciously. The off-the-shoulder neckline and side-swept hair means my entire, unblemished neck and scent gland are on display. My long earring tickles against my shoulder when I turn my head.

I don't need lube to insert the toy they bought me. I hike the hem of my dress up, pull my panties aside, and push it in. It nestles into place inside my already slick pussy. The butterfly's curved wings and the tight panties hold it in place. I practice sitting and walking with it in. It's strange, but not painful. A knock at my door interrupts me.

Waffles runs to it, meowing, and stretches his body up to paw at the door. I shoo him aside by scattering treats on the ground and open it. The sight of all three of them standing there on my porch in tailored suits takes my breath away.

They're equally speechless. Their eyes roam over me, lingering on my breasts and my baby bump. Liam holds out a hand and turns to the side. Behind him, I see a short limo instead of his truck.

"Are you ready?" he asks.

He's not asking about dinner. But for what comes after. When he bites his claim into my neck and brands me as his. Their omega.

I pull the door shut and lock it and put my hand in his. "I am." I've never wanted anything more than this moment. A pack that loves me. A family on the way. My girlhood dreams come true. In his black tux and pinned corsage, he looks every inch the groom. They all do.

They lead me to the limo, and a driver gets out and comes around to open the door. Liam hands me inside and lets me get settled on the seat, and then they follow me in. The driver slides into the front seat and pulls away from the curb.

"Where are we going?" I ask them.

"First things first." Liam reaches into his jacket pocket.

The sex toy buzzes to life and I jolt in surprise.

Liam's smile is slow and full of sinful promises. "Good girl."

He doesn't stop the buzzing after his test to see if I'm wearing it. It stays at a dull, low buzz. Once I get used to it, it's easier to ignore. Sort of.

I fidget in my seat and bite my lower lip. "In a white dress, everyone's gonna see a damp spot," I warn him.

"You're wearing slick panties. You'll be okay, kitten."

"Really?" There was hardly any fabric to them.

"Trust me."

I do. I trust him. But that doesn't mean turnabout isn't fair play. I put my hand on his thigh and stroke him, drawing circles on his leg. "Thank you for my presents, Daddy," I say in a husky voice.

Matthew lets out a laugh and reaches for the buttons that control the limo. A privacy screen rolls up, separating us from the driver. Gabriel lounges, undoing the button of his coat and letting it splay open. He grabs the bottle of amber liquor from the bar rack and pours himself a glass.

"This is going to be fun," Gabriel says with a smile, taking a sip.

I drag my hand higher up Liam's inner thigh until my pinky grazes his clothed cock. His dick twitches. "You look *really* good in a suit. You all do."

They've put effort into getting ready. Shaving, slicking their hair back with pomade, and putting on silver cufflinks and tie pins. Did they buy the suits or rent them? I hope they bought them. Otherwise the shop's gonna be pissed when they get the shirts back with no buttons. I want to rip their clothes off them while I ride them. The pregnancy hormones have been driving me nuts ever since I opened the box. And the toy nestled against my pussy isn't helping. It's only stoking that fire into an inferno.

Liam grabs my hand and lifts it to his mouth, kissing my knuckles. He uses the movement to hide his reach for the toy's remote. The toy hums faster. The butterfly's wings make my entire pussy vibrate. I forget that I'm teasing him as he teases me back mercilessly.

He turns my wrist over and kisses the inside where the

skin's thinner and more delicate. "Be good, kitten. Or we'll never make it to the restaurant."

That doesn't sound like a bad idea. "I'm not that hungry." I squirm, grinding on the toy. Trying to drive those buzzing sensations deeper. Fuck, I want to come. And he hasn't even touched me yet.

Liam taps the remote again. The vibrations switch from a constant buzz to a stuttered pulsing. It's impossible to use it to come. The vibrations are too irregular. I let out an annoyed whine, but all my alpha does is grin.

"You're beautiful, kitten," he says.

"I want to ride your cock."

He nips the palm of my hand and settles it back on my lap. "No."

It's payback for teasing and edging him the other day in the pub. It's got to be. I groan and settle in my seat while the driver takes us across town. We pull up to the nicest restaurant in town. The one you need to make reservations for several months in advance to get a table unless you want to go on a weekday.

"How'd you get us a reservation here?" I ask, frowning.

"Made it a while ago," Liam answers.

"You've been planning this all this time?"

"Of course," he says. "I knew you were ours from the minute you walked into my pub."

My heart seems three sizes too big for my chest as the driver pulls up to their valet parking and gets out to open our doors. Matthew and Gabriel get out first and extend a hand to help me. I hold the fabric of my dress out of the way and let them help me out. Liam is at my back a moment later, urging me forward with a hand resting on the small of my back.

I'm finally ready to be theirs. Forever.

The restaurant is gorgeous. It's tiny, hence the long reservation list. The lighting is low and ambient. Low music plays over hidden speakers, and large well-tended plants decorate the gleaming, luxurious space. It's all leather and marble, dark stained wood and polished brass. A well-stocked bar makes up one wall and booths line the other with tables scattered in the middle. People eat, the clink of their cutlery mixing with their conversations. The food smells amazing and my stomach grumbles in eager anticipation.

"O'Donnell pack," Liam tells the *maître d'*. "We have a reservation for four at seven-thirty."

"Your table is ready. Follow me." The *maître d'* takes four leather bound menus and shows us to our table. Leather and wood chairs ring the tablecloth covered table. There's a small vase with a red rose in the center. She lights the tea light candles, then leaves.

The minute we're seated and settled, Liam changes the setting on the toy. It's a different pattern of interrupted buzzing. I bite my lip and fidget in my seat. Attempting to read the menu. My eyes won't focus. My mind won't pay attention. I read the same few lines over and over again.

"Welcome to Le Chat Noir," a server says, greeting us. He's a beta. "Here's our wine menu. What can I get you to drink?"

Liam orders for us. "Three glasses of your McCallan twenty-five on the rocks and a raspberry mojito mocktail for the lady."

A food runner brings us a basket of thin, crispy breadsticks and the server leaves to put our drink order in while we study the menu. Gabriel and Matthew debate the steak versus the lamb. I'm too wound up to decide what I want. All I can think about is dick.

"Liam," I whine, trying hard not to fidget too much in my seat. "Please." I don't know what I'm asking for. For him to stop. To let me come. Or to fuck me and put me out of this misery. He can take his pick. I'm up for any of them.

The buzzing changes back to the low, steady thrum and I sigh in relief.

The waiter comes back with our drinks balanced on a small bartender's tray. He sets them all down in front of us and sticks the tray under his arm. "Are we ready to order, or do you need a few more minutes to decide?"

Liam and Gabriel both get the steak while Matthew orders the lamb. The waiter looks at me expectantly. I frown and glance at the menu again. Shit. I never figured out what I wanted.

"She'll have the coq au vin," Liam tells him, taking my menu from me.

The waiter leaves with our menus to put our order in. I take a sip of my drink and have to stop myself from guzzling it down. It's so fucking yummy. Gabriel digs into the bread and offers me half his breadstick. They're long and thin. Handmade and crispy like a pretzel.

"Are we doing anything after dinner?" I ask them.

Liam sips his scotch, the large spherical ice clinking against the glass. "What do you think we're doing after?"

Dicking me down into the mattress, I hope. But there's more than that. We all know it. "You're claiming me."

His eyes drift down from my face to the exposed skin between my shoulder and neck. My scent gland. He reaches over and cups his hand around the nape of my neck, his thumb stroking over it. "I am."

He looks at me for confirmation. I nod.

The toy buzzes rapidly, making me jump in my seat. "Good girl."

Fuck. Fuckfuckfuck. His thumb presses into my scent gland, my perfume scenting the air as he rubs my pheromones into his skin. Scent marking himself. Claiming himself as mine. My hips rock before I can stop them, the chair creaking.

His other hand is under the table. Hiding the remote that controls my toy. He hits its button again, making it faster. Staring at me and rubbing my scent gland as he torments me in public in this lovely restaurant I'll never be able to eat in again without blushing. My breathing gets faster as I fight the urge to moan. To give up all pretense of decorum and rock my way to an orgasm. The vibrator teases my clit, and stimulates me inside. Leaves my pussy dripping. I hope he's right about the panties. Otherwise, when I stand, the entire restaurant is getting a show of exactly how wet I am.

His eyes darken in the already dim light. His pupils expand to swallow up the sight of me as I quietly fall apart beside him.

Before I can get too close to coming, he hits the button again and the vibrations go back to pulsing. My orgasm stalls out. I groan, the forgotten breadstick snapping in my hand as my fist tightens.

"Rude," I tell him, annoyed. He either needs to stop teasing me all together or let me come. Why did I agree to play this horrible game?

The vibrations change their pattern. A long, swelling buzz followed by short, rapid bursts of pulses. "What's rude, kitten?"

I drop my breadstick on the table and make a fist, bunching up the tablecloth. "You are."

"Let our poor omega eat," Matthew chides him.

Liam leans back in his seat, and the buzzing slows to the low thrum that makes my pussy drip but doesn't drive me delirious. "I suppose I can be generous and let you enjoy our dinner. If you say please."

I'm beyond shame at this point. If he demanded that I get under the table, pull his cock out, and blow him as the price of coming, I would. "Please."

Liam hides his smile with his drink.

"Here," Gabriel says, handing me another breadstick.

I bite and chew, eating it quickly in case Liam decides to toy with me some more. The waiter brings our food out, and my attention is quickly diverted. My stew is a fragrant shallow bowl of spiced chicken, mushrooms, and other vegetables in a red wine reduction. We eat, talking about nothing important. My conversation with my mother. The pub's next order of seasonal beer. Matthew's day at work. The pickle ball class that Gabriel wants to take.

The waiter clears our plates and brings us dessert menus. "I don't know if I can eat anymore," I tell them, full even though I only ate half my dinner.

"We'll split a piece of the strawberries and mascarpone mille-feuille," Liam says to the waiter. "I heard it's the best thing on their menu," he tells me.

I suppose there's always some room for dessert.

Liam clicks the remote controlling my toy up. It buzzes to life with a vengeance. I squirm in my seat, attempting to stay quiet as they talk quietly without me. It cycles through functions and speeds, never settling for long. Keeping me guessing as I subtly rock, maneuvering the silicone butterfly's wings into the perfect spot.

My breath hitches and I rock, no longer caring if anyone is watching. If I don't come right now, I'll never forgive them. I'll never play their sex games again. The waiter brings out our plate of dessert and new forks.

I worry that Liam's going to shut the toy off again, but he doesn't. Instead, he racks it up. Dials up the intensity and makes it faster. My walls clench down on the toy, and I let out a low moan I can't stifle.

Liam stabs a fork into the dessert and holds it up to me. "Open."

My lips part, and he sticks the forkful inside. I close my lips around the fork and taste the first decadent bite. The buttered puff pastry is flaky, the mascarpone cheese is salty and tastes of vanilla, and the strawberries have been lightly roasted to make them sweeter, then covered in strawberry syrup. I chew and swallow, using the dessert as an excuse to moan as he plays with the remote.

They all take turns eating forkfuls of our dessert while Liam drives me to the brink of orgasm inside this fancy restaurant. They save the last few bites for me. Feeding me small forkfuls and letting me lick their utensils clean, all while Liam sets the toy nestled in my pussy to a merciless rhythm.

I'm going to come. I rock in my seat, trying to drive that toy in deeper. It's small compared to their cocks. Barely more than a tease inside me. But if I angle it right, it hits a spot of nerves inside me that make my toes curl in my heels. My pussy throbs against the vibrating toy. Slick soaks into my pretty panties. It seems like I'm flooding them. Like I've never been wetter in my life.

"Liam," I moan, squeezing the edge of my seat. Fidgeting. Clenching my trembling thighs.

"Open." He feeds me the last bite of dessert and hits the button on the remote.

I can't take it anymore. I chew, distracted. Salty and sweet flavors burst along my tongue and the tension pulls taught between my thighs. He clicks it again and I shatter, moaning loudly. My walls clamp down on the silicone toy and waves wash over me. They make my pussy spasm and clench. Leave me dripping. And then I'm oversensitive. It's too much. Far too much.

"Swallow," he orders. So I do. The toy buzzes faster. Impossibly so. My reward. My orgasm hurdles forward. Into the swell of another. A bigger, deeper one that promises to wreck me in its aftermath.

"One more. You can do it," he says, scooping up the dregs of our dessert. The final bite. But that's not what he means.

He wants another orgasm. And my body is eager to obey, even if mentally I balk. I can't. It's too much. I won't be able to hold my noises back. Already people are looking at us. Curious. Confused. I notice the heavy weight of their stares. See the alphas flare their nostrils, scenting me.

He slides the dripping syrup-covered strawberries past my lips. Deposits them on my tongue. I clamp down, scraping the fork clean as he pulls it out. Liam grabs me by the back of my neck and squeezes gently. "Good girl. Now finish."

I swallow my mouthful of dessert and squeeze my thighs together. Increasing the pressure building there. Shoving me over that edge into orgasm. It hits me like a truck. Runs me over with pleasure and leaves me moaning and breathing hard as I try to stay quiet and fail. I shiver, far beyond oversensitized.

He clicks the toy off and the absence of buzzing is jarring, but welcome. Aftershocks zip through me, leaving me breathless.

"I'll have whatever she's eating," someone tells their waitress.

My face burns with a blush. Liam leans in, brushes his lips against my ear, his voice deep and husky. "That's our good girl. You're so beautiful when you come for us."

Our waiter comes over to take the empty dessert plate and forks away and I can't look at him. I drop my eyes and lean against Liam's shoulder.

"Will you be having anything else?" the waiter asks.

"The check," Gabriel says, taking over. The waiter brings the bill in a leather book and they pay while I recover. While I remember how to breathe.

I'm dazed, satisfied and full, as they help me out of my seat. My ankles wobble as I stand on my unfamiliar heels. Liam tugs me against him and wraps his arm around me, taking some of my weight and keeping me from falling.

"Come again," the *maître d'* says as we pass her station at the front.

"Oh, we plan to." Liam chuckles and walks me out.

The cool evening air wakes me up a bit as we wait for the valet to let our chauffeur know to pull around. "Is anything else planned?" I ask.

"You'll see."

His promise both delights and frightens me.

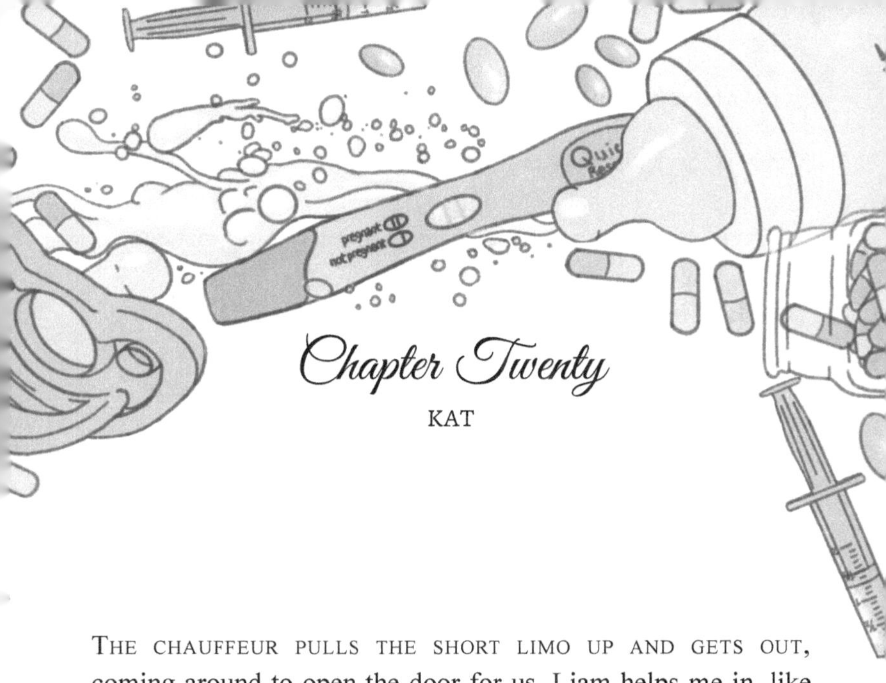

Chapter Twenty

KAT

THE CHAUFFEUR PULLS THE SHORT LIMO UP AND GETS OUT, coming around to open the door for us. Liam helps me in, like before, and Gabriel and Matthew climb in after us. The driver takes off once we're settled.

"I found a nonalcoholic champagne," Matthew says, pulling the bottle from an ice bucket hidden in the alcohol cabinet. He wraps the cork in his handkerchief and works it off with a loud pop, then pours us all glasses.

I tip my glass up to my lips to drink it, then notice something inside. It's not ice. I stare at it closer, but the limo's lighting is dim. I hold it up to the window and turn it and it sparkles from a passing streetlight. "Is that a ring?"

Matthew smiles. "It was my idea."

"And I picked the ring out," Gabriel says.

I take careful sips of champagne to empty the flute, then tip it so I can pull it out. The ring is beautiful. It's a white gold setting with an oval center diamond and a ring of tiny stones paved around it and the band. "It's beautiful."

"I know that alphas and omegas don't usually do rings,"

Matthew says, "but it's a beta tradition. It didn't seem right to skip it."

Tears swell in my eyes and threaten to ruin my makeup. "I love it. Which finger does it go on again?"

"Here, let me." Gabriel slides out of his seat and gets on his knees before me. He takes the ring from me and reaches for my left hand. It slides onto my left fourth finger. The fit is perfect.

"How did you know my size?" I ask, holding my hand up to the light and moving it to watch the stones glitter.

"I measured your finger with a piece of string while you were sleeping," Matthew says.

So much planning and thought went into this. I'm speechless. "Thank you." I press my hand to my heart. "I love it."

"While I'm down here," Gabriel says, grabbing my dress hem and inching it up. The fabric pools in my lap. He palms my knees and spreads them wide, then drops a kiss to my inner thigh. Gabriel hooks his thumbs in the sides of my panties and tugs at them.

I lift my hips, letting him slide them down. He lifts one leg at a time, pulling my feet free, careful not to catch the panty's straps on my heels.

"Look at you," Gabriel says, rubbing his thumb over the black silicone nestled between my folds. "Soaking wet. Did you like being teased in the restaurant, you dirty girl?"

"Yes." I spread my legs wider for him.

Gabriel pulls the toy free with a wet sucking sound. He sticks the knobby protrusion into his mouth like a pacifier and licks it clean, then pulls it out with a wet pop. "So sweet. And I hardly got any dessert. But that's okay. You can be my dessert."

He dips his head between my thighs and cleans me with his tongue. Licking up my slick and sucking my arousal-plumped lips into his mouth. I moan and get more comfortable on the seat, leaning back to enjoy his feasting between my thighs.

Gabriel sucks my clit in his mouth, making circles with his tongue. Then fucks it into me, teasing my sensitive hole. My thighs clench and unclench around his head.

He shifts my leg so he can angle deeper. Penetrate further. Lap up more of my cream. My back arches and my heel digs into his back, but he doesn't seem to care as he eats my pussy like he's starving.

"Gabriel," I moan, tangling my hand in Gabriel's hair. Urging him deeper. My hips twitch against his face as he licks me and suckles my clit. "Oh, fuck. You're so good at that." My fingers tighten in his slicked-back hair, mussing it. "You're so good at eating pussy."

Matthew slips onto the bench seat beside me. Trapping me between him and Liam. He grabs my face and pulls me toward him. Presses his lips to mine in a surprising kiss. Our first. I moan into his mouth.

He joins us in sex occasionally. But not always. Sometimes he only watches. The nights he participates, when he fills my mouth, are always my favorite. Ever since they taught me what having multiple holes stuffed at once is like, I've become addicted. Addicted to *them*. To their cocks. Their delicious scents and cum.

The way they stare at me, like I'm precious. Their constant devotion. The way they hold and rub my belly. How Matthew's already building a library of baby books even though we haven't moved into the house yet. How Liam sends me photos of various fruits and vegetables, tracking the size of our growing baby. How Gabriel grabs me, randomly, spinning me into a dance and singing songs that sound amazing in Portuguese. I love them so much it nearly hurts. It almost seems like a wonderful dream I'll wake up from at any minute.

Matthew's tongue pushes past my lips and dances with mine

while Gabriel laps me up, relentless and determined to make me gush slick right into his mouth.

I moan and wrap an arm around Matthew, dragging him closer against me. He angles his head and deepens the kiss, shoving a hand down my dress into the cup of my bra. He grabs a breast and squeezes. Finds my nipple and pinches it lightly.

I let out a cry, and he swallows my sounds down and pinches harder. Twists the tight, firm bud as his tongue fucks my mouth and Gabriel sucks on my clit. My nipples are sensitive. He swears that I'll be able to come from nipple stimulation alone with enough practice. I'm so glad the uncomfortable soreness I had at first has gone away.

Gabriel's tongue flicks at my clit in rapid bursts and he pushes two fingers inside me, pumping deep. Curling them to stroke along my inner wall. My groin tightens and my back arches. My shoes dig into him, urging him on. His fingers pump faster. Harder. Curl more. And his tongue never stops. Slick makes wet, vulgar sounds as he fingers me.

I come hard, my thighs trembling. A gush of slick bursts from me as my walls clamp down on his fingers. The relief is enormous. A release of pressure that makes me sigh. Gabriel moans against my pussy and licks me until my walls stop fluttering.

"*Meu Deus*," Gabriel says. "I think she squirted."

I pull away from Matthew to check. Gabriel's front is drenched. His tux is probably ruined. I sit up, shocked. "Did I pee on you?"

Gabriel lifts his suit jacket to his nose and sniffs. His tongue darts out to lick it. "No. It's slick. I think you squirted."

I'm still horrified. "Oh my God. Your suit's ruined." And probably my dress. And maybe the limo. They're never getting their cleaning deposit back.

Gabriel rips at his suit, pulling his shirt free and unzipping, then shoving his pants down while Liam calmly watches. Gabriel's cock is hard and dripping. A bead of pre-cum pearls at his ruddy tip. "It's fucking hot. Spread your legs for me, *meu docinho*. I need to fuck you. Right now."

He reaches around to grab me by the ass and pull me forward on my seat. I lean back so I don't topple off it. Gabriel shoves my legs apart and gets into position between them. He strokes his cock, then lines his head up with my slick opening.

"Do you have any idea how badly I wanted to sneak off to the bathroom with you so we could fuck?" he asks as his cock slides home.

I'm so wet that he slides in easily, bottoming out in a single thrust. His hips snap, setting a relentless rhythm. My body yields to him easily. It's like I've known him forever.

"I'd have let you," I say, teasing him. Because I know how much he likes almost getting caught.

"Fuck, you're so wet." He stares at me, keeping eye contact as he takes me hard and fast. Desperate. "Show me those big, pretty tits, *meu docinho*."

Matthew tugs my dress and the strapless bra down. Since the dress is off the shoulder, there's nothing to stop it from sliding down until it reaches my baby bump. My nipples grow painfully tight in the air conditioned limo.

Gabriel fists a breast, his fingers sinking into my softness. He curls down and lifts it up, bringing the nipple to his lips. He sucks my nipple into his mouth, nipping me with his teeth while he squeezes and fucks me.

"Gabriel," I moan, arching into it. I lift my legs and wrap them around him, my heels digging into his ass.

He groans and fucks me deeper. His tight adonis belt strikes my poor, sensitive clit with every thrust. Each sucking pull on my nipple zings straight to my clit.

Gabriel pops off my breast and switches to the other one.

"I'm next," he says, squeezing me. Confusing me. "I'm breeding you next."

Liam doesn't say no, which only makes Gabriel more confident as he palms my swollen tits and tweaks the nipple.

"You want my baby, don't you?" he asks.

"Yes." My legs tighten around his hips and my clit throbs with every smacking thrust. "I want to have your baby."

Gabriel's eyes screw closed and he grits his teeth like he's trying to do it right now. Like I'm not already five months pregnant. His pace slows, turning languid. He fucks me deep, his cock pulsating inside me. Pumping me with cum with every jerking thrust.

Once his balls are emptied, he catches his breath. Fucks his cock back into me slowly, pushing his leaking cum back in. When he's too soft, he pulls out and bends my legs back as far as they'll go.

Cum and slick drip from my pussy. Down the crack of my ass. Gabriel scoops up a trickle and presses it back in, then slaps my pussy. I jolt and let out a surprised yelp. He moves back, taking his seat and fixing his pants.

"How are you?" Matthew asks. He reaches down to stroke me between my legs. Scoops up more of Gabriel's trickling cum and feeds it back into me. Testing the walls of my pussy and pressing in deep. His prodding is gentle and thorough.

"Phenomenal," I answer. I wait to see what he does. See who's next in their turn with me.

Satisfied with my answer, Matthew shifts from clinical to sensual. He strokes my clit. Drags his fingers through slick and cum until my pussy's squelching. Scissors those fingers open and stretches my hole. Gets me ready. But for whom? I don't want to ask, though, and ruin things. Don't want to push if he's not ready. He's never fucked my pussy before. Only my hands and my mouth.

"Are you ready for the rest?" Matthew asks.

I lock eyes with him and nod. Whatever he wants to give me, I'll happily take.

Matthew slides off his seat. My breath catches as he unbuttons his jacket and pulls it open. Flicks open his belt. Undoes his pants' button and slides his zipper down. He shoves his briefs down and his thick, swollen cock flops free.

We lock eyes as he fists his cock and tugs. Jerking his cock harder until he's fully engorged. His dick is thicker mid-shaft. It curves slightly upward. His ruddy head is perfectly shaped and scalloped. Matthew stares at me as he jerks himself. My pussy throbs, slick cooling against the air.

"Do you trust me?" Matthew asks, his voice calm.

I don't have to think before I answer. "I do."

"Are your breasts sore today?"

I shake my head. The soreness only lasted a few weeks. When it faded, I thought the worst might happen, but the baby's fine. I cried happy tears of relief when the blood work came back good afterward.

"I read your latest book," he warns me. "Front to back. It's fucking filthy."

I swallow, remembering what I wrote. The kinks I sprinkled in. "Did you like it?"

He nods. "This part was my favorite." He lifts his hand from his cock and brings it down on my breast. Right on my nipple. The crack of his hand against my skin is loud. The pain is instant and it's delicious. Warmth blooms and my delicate skin turns pink. My clit throbs, another trickle of cum and slick escaping as my channel tightens around nothing. I'm so empty and aching.

"Mattie," Liam barks.

"She likes it," Matthew says, his eyes never wavering from mine. "Don't you? Our sweet girl has such dirty fantasies." He slaps my breast again. A third time. Until my nipple stings and my clit pulses like they're connected by a string. "I asked you a question. Answer me."

"Yes," I whimper.

Matthew switches, slapping the other one. Three, to make them even. My nipples have never been harder. They're tight, aching points. He raises both hands and brings them down together. Slapping both breasts at once.

I cry out, and pant. He grabs my nipples and pinches them. My cunt spasms, desperate for filling. "I like it," I admit.

"Of course you do," Mattie says, his voice calm. He tips his head to study me. "Because you're our perfect, filthy little slut."

I moan and wiggle under him. He pinches harder, twisting my nipples until my hips buck, trying to fuck myself on a cock that's not in me. I'm seconds away from doing what I said I never would and begging him to fuck me. I bite my lips to stifle the impulse. I'll take only what he offers.

"Look at you," Matthew says, letting my nipples go to drag a hand up my chest. My collarbones. My throat. He wraps a loose hand around it, making a necklace of his fingers. "Panting like our precious whore. Leaking slick and cum all over the pretty dress we bought you. Ruining it. Your cunt begging for more cock. In that slutty hole that can't be satisfied no matter how much we fuck it. That's what you desire, isn't it? For me to fuck you?"

I tremble underneath him. "Yes."

His fingers squeeze ever so slightly. A purr rattles through my chest. An instinctual response to a threat. Designed by evolution to soothe a rough rutting alpha. Matthew's eyes light up like it's Christmas morning and I'm his present.

He squeezes harder. Not enough to obstruct airflow. Only enough for me to feel the throb of my heartbeat against his hand. The way my pulse batters at his thumb and fingers. It's the same pulse making my pussy throb.

"Careful with her," Liam growls.

"I know what I'm doing. I know exactly how much she can take. Does your slutty hole want my cock, omega?" Matthew asks.

"Yes," I whimper, my throat bobbing against his hand.

Without letting me go, Matthew gets into position. He's shorter than Gabriel. He has to put a knee between my legs and balance on the seat to line us up. When his cockhead rubs against my mound, I whimper again.

Matthew takes his time. He drags his cock up and down me. Covers my pussy in his scent. He's not as fragrant as an alpha. His scent is muted. But Liam and I can still smell him on me. His cockhead slips over my swollen, tender clit and I don't know if it's Gabriel's cum or my slick or Matthew's pre-cum that wets his way.

He pushes inside me, slow and controlled. Opening my channel. My mouth drops open and I moan as he feeds his cock into me, inch by inch. Slow and measured. It's a torment. It's bliss.

His grip on my throat slackens once he's bottomed out inside me. But it doesn't slide away. It goes around, cupping my neck from the back. Pulling my face closer to his so he can stare deeper into my eyes while he takes me for the first time.

"Your pussy is so fucking good," he moans. "You're so wet for me, Kat."

"Your cock is amazing," I tell him. Encouraging him. Holy fuck. My eyes nearly cross as he fucks me slow and deep. He's so big. As big as some alphas, but without the knot. If I was blindfolded, I'm not sure if I could tell him and Liam apart until he came.

"Are you going to be my good little slut and come on it?" Matthew asks.

Nodding, I agree. I wish I could see it, see the way his cock thrusts in and out of me. But my baby bump is in the way. Instead, I feel everything. Every slide of him in and out. The way his flared head catches on my entrance. Hear everything. The wet sucking sound of my needy pussy as he picks up speed. Fucks me faster. The smack of our skin coming together in the back of this limo.

Matthew groans, a ragged sound that makes me clench around his dick. His knee slides on the leather seat, spreading me wider. Stretching my groin to its limits. He shifts, adjusting. Angling deeper. Grinding himself against me once he's all the way in. Rubbing against my clit.

I throw my head back against the seat and close my eyes, my fingers tightening on the leather car seat. "Fuck."

"You like that, baby?" he asks, doing it again. Again. Another. Slow, deep thrusts with a grind at the end that make my channel clench his dick and my clit pulse.

"Yes. Oh, God." Something takes over me. A rush of need. I need this orgasm. Need to have Matthew empty inside me. Need to get him addicted to my pussy so he fucks me with his thick cock again.

I wrap my arms around his neck and pull him tight against me. Wrap my legs around him too. Dig my heels into his ass so he has to risk impalement if he doesn't make me cum right fucking now.

Matthew grabs my throat again, pressing lightly. Making my pulse pound in my head. Leaving me a bit dizzy. I'm throbbing, impossibly ready to come again. I've never come so much in one night before outside of a heat. Didn't know it was possible. Wish I'd known it sooner. We could have been having so much fun this entire time.

"Feels. So. Fucking. Good," he says, punctuating each word with a thrust and a grind. "Come for me, baby. Come on my cock. I hear omega pussy's the best. Show me."

Maybe it's the fact that he's grinding the hell out of my clit or that it's Matthew inside me, but I come. Like my body is obeying his orders. Like he's an alpha, using his bark to make me compliant.

I come, heat washing over me as my pussy spasms on him and my lungs drag in air. My head pounds and I'm dizzy as I come down slowly. Matthew waits for my aftershocks to settle, then drops his head and starts pounding into me. His lips press against my throat. Suck my skin between them. He grazes his blunt beta teeth across my scent gland.

"I'm gonna come in this pussy," he warns me. "But before I do, you know that means it's mine. That I'm marking this territory with my cum. And I'll take it whenever I want. And you wouldn't ever think of saying no to me, would you?"

"No," I pant. My leg muscles quiver with tension, but the rest of me has been fucked till I'm docile. The craving for a cozy nest to curl up in hits me hard.

"That's good," he says, thrusting faster. "Because you're ours. And we're gonna make sure you and your pussy never forget it."

Matthew comes with a groan, using my spent body to milk his cock. He pumps me full, cock kicking deep inside me. Then he stills. Breathing hard and sweating, he drops his head against my chest and lingers. His frame jerks with a shudder before finally going still.

My legs slip to the floor and I drop my hands to his back to hold Matthew to me. I tuck his head under my chin and make swirls across his back while his hips flex. While he works his cum in deep. Fills me with his faint pheromones and marks me as claimed in his own way.

Happy tears threaten my eye makeup so I sniff them back. "Thank you," I whisper as the moment becomes tender. As we become lovers as well as partners.

Matthew presses his lips to my scent gland and kisses it, then nuzzles me. He rubs my scent over his face, marking himself. He takes a moment to gather himself, then slips out of me. A fresh rush of slick and cum drip down my ass.

Matthew pulls away and settles on his original seat, his cock soft and wet against his thigh.

"Holy. Fuck," Gabriel says, staring at Matthew like he's never seen the beta before.

"Are you okay?" Liam asks, rubbing my knee.

I'm too spent for more words right now. I need a minute to recover. Or a thousand. I give him a thumbs up instead, which makes him chuckle.

"You ready for me, Kat?" Liam asks.

I groan and fidget on my seat. Only noticing at this moment that the limo has stopped. I guess we've been loud enough that the driver knew to leave us alone. I'm sure we aren't the first pack to fuck back here.

"Yes," I finally manage to say. "But I don't think we're getting your deposit back."

Liam chuckles and undoes his jacket, spreading it open. He gets his pants undone and shoves them down to his knees, palming his cock and stroking. Not that it needs it. After our show, he's as hard as rock. He pats his bare thigh.

"Come sit on my lap, kitten, and purr for me."

I shift my legs, trying to move, then make a face. "I'm not sure I can. My legs are jelly."

"You don't need to do anything but come over here and sit," he promises.

I kick my heels off and take it slow. The moment I shift off my seat, gravity takes over. Our fluids drip down my leg.

They've made a cold and sticky mess between my legs. I gather my dress up to my waist, aware that my breasts are still on full display. They're pink from Matthew's tit spanking.

Liam helps me onto his lap, lining his cock up with my wet slit. He slides inside to the hilt with no resistance. Our betas have done a good job getting me ready for my alpha. "That's it, kitten. Lean back. Let me do the work. All you have to do is purr for me."

I lay my head on his shoulder and lean against him. Liam sniffs the top of my head. The side of my throat. He licks at my neck, lapping my scent gland clean. Preparing me for the moment I've been waiting for my entire life. He rucks my dress up higher and grips my hips in his large hands, lifting me up and down on his thick cock. Doing all the work, like he promised.

"Such a good girl, taking all of us," he praises me.

His hands roam over me. Soothing my breasts. Splaying possessively over my collarbone. Rubbing my throat, as if he's reassuring himself that I'm fine after the light choking.

I'm more than fine. I'm fucking flying.

My thoughts are slow and faint. Background noise. All I can think about is pleasure. His. Mine. Our pack's. I'm in subspace, I realize. He could do nearly anything to me right now and I'd take it happily.

"Do you know why I let our betas go first?" he asks.

"Hmm?" It's all I can manage. Words are too difficult right now.

"So that my knot locks all three of our scents in this sweet, fertile pussy. So that when I bite my claim into your throat, you know that it's for all of us. That's what you want, isn't it, kitten? To be ours?"

"Mmhmm." The slide of his thick alpha cock in and out of me is delicious. It's so wet with cum and slick. So stretched and ready. My mind tries to latch onto what he said, but I keep getting distracted by the way his big balls slap against my mound when he tugs me down on his cock. He fucks me faster. Lifts me up and drops me down. Grinds us together. Lifts me again. My rounded thighs slap against his firm ones. A *plap, plap, plap* sound that's unmistakable for anyone walking by our parked limo.

His pace picks up. Like he's carving a home for himself inside me with his dick. One increasingly hard thrust at a time, turning brutal and relentless. My pussy surrenders to him. Gets slick with arousal. An omega's natural defense for a blindly rutting alpha. The rougher they are, the more our bodies make us love it.

And I do. He stretches me wide and plugs me deep until the hole inside me is filled once more. I forgot how much I missed having a pack. How much I crave it and the safety and comfort of numbers.

Liam grabs me by my hair and tugs my head back, angling me. Exposing even more of my throat. He presses the side of his face against it and growls, deep and rumbling. "Answer my question, omega."

My pussy tightens on him and a purr stutters through my chest. I don't remember what he asked. I whine, distressed. I can't disappoint my alpha. I need to pay attention. Need to think beyond the tightening need in my pelvis. The all-consuming urge to come on a knot. My focus is spotty like it gets during a heat. "What?"

His fingers dig tight into my hips and ass. His hips lift off the seat. Thighs bouncing me. Only his tight grip on me keeps me firmly planted. My cunt sheathes his cock perfectly. It's what my body was made for.

Liam groans, like he's in pain. He growls again, his fingers tightening in my hair. Pinning me in place. His knot swells against my entrance. It tugs at my pubic bone. Pulling free with force and effort. I whimper as he shoves it back in.

"Do you want to be our omega? Answer me now, Kat," he asks again. "Right now." His patience is gossamer thin.

"Yes!"

Liam's mouth slots over my scent gland. Sucks it into his mouth. His tongue licks over me. Savors my pheromones. My pussy tightens when he sucks the sensitive gland into his mouth.

His swelling knot rubs over the front of my walls. Pops free. Pushes in. Until it's nearly too swollen to budge.

Liam opens his jaw wider, angling his head. His sharp canines graze my skin. Nicking me with every bouncing thrust.

"Bite me," I beg, my pussy clenching on his cock. Squeezing his growing knot. I fist my hand in his jacket. "Please."

His teeth clamp down, cutting skin. His mouth is warm and sharp. He scissors his jaw, working his teeth in deeper. Penetrating me. Lighting up nerves as he marks me. He growls as he bites me deeper until the bond snaps into place between us hard and fast.

It's an overload of sensation. Foreign whispers of thoughts and feelings. Pleasure. His. Mine. I can't tell the difference. It doesn't matter anymore. Satisfaction washes over me through the bond. Thoughts that aren't mine. Of conquest and pride. Of claiming. Breeding. Marking. Victory, and I'm the cherished prize.

He forces me down onto his swollen knot and pushes it in. Forces my pussy to stretch around it and take it. It pops inside, lodging behind my pubic bone, and swells shut. Locks all of their cum inside me. Ties us together.

Liam reaches between my legs and rubs my aching clit as he gnaws his mating bite even deeper into my throat. I scream with the force of my orgasm. Whimper. I come so hard, my belly tightens. Rippling contractions roll down my abdomen in waves. Something cold and wet trickles down my chest. My breast. Drips off my nipple. How much am I bleeding?

Purring, Liam eases his jaw apart. The pain is dull and achy. He licks it, making it throb. I pant, settled on his lap, knotted and bred, as he laps at his claiming bite. The longer he keeps it open the higher the chance it'll scar. The better the bond.

I don't have any concerns about the mark fading. He bit me so deep that I think he hit muscle. My shoulder is too sore to lift, and I'm too spent to care about moving. Especially while he purrs like that for me.

"Did you know it was this brutal?" Matthew asks Gabriel.

"Mmm. Her dress is ruined."

Good. Omegas like to preserve their mating garments in special keepsake boxes. The bloodier the better. The deeper the mating bite, the tighter the bond. And the less likely an alpha has to repeat it. My focus is fuzzy as I sit on his lap, impaled on his cock and knotted into place, while he tends to my mating bite. Licking it to keep it clean and help it scar.

Liam's presence is there inside me. A happy whisper of a thought. I curl up in that presence, satisfied. He's strong. Fit. Kind. A good breeder. My instincts are satisfied. I chose him and this pack well.

We stay like that for what seems like forever. Once his knot softens and releases us, I'm awake and aware enough to use the fabric of my gown to wipe the blood and saliva off my chest. Liam pulls me off his softening cock and turns me sideways so I'm across his lap. I tuck my head under his chin and enjoy being held like this. Like I'm precious.

Something nags at me, and finally I parse it out. There aren't any other echoes. "You didn't bite them," I say.

"You can tell?" he asks. "I thought that was a myth."

"No." With my old pack, I could sense the echoes of the

others through Josh's connection. It's like tossing two stones into a pond and watching the ripples overtake one another. "You can tell if you listen closely. I want you to bite them. So I can have them with me too."

"Okay," Gabriel agrees.

"Do we get a say in this?" Matthew asks.

"Are you afraid of a little love bite?" Gabriel asks, amused.

"That shit looks like it hurt," Matthew says. "I like giving pain more than taking it."

"Don't you want to be completely in the pack?" Gabriel asks.

"I won't force you," Liam says, interrupting their arguing. "It's your choice."

I like that. That he cares enough to ask, to offer, instead of demanding. He's gonna be a good dad.

Liam bursts into a purr as he hears the echoed pride I have when I think of him.

"What is happening?" Matthew says, looking between us.

"They're mated," Gabriel says. "They're linked now so they have more awareness of each other. Thoughts, moods, feelings."

"Like… psychically?" Matthew asks.

"Not like words," I tell him. "More like… impressions. They're stronger when you're closer. Fainter when you're apart. And if you're too far apart for too long, it fades unless it's renewed." The day my connection faded completely, I didn't get out of bed. It's a terrible thing to lose your bond. But I'm happy it brought me to this moment right now. I wouldn't go back and trade this for anything.

Gabriel gives Matthew a curious glance. "How did you not know this?"

"My parents are betas, remember?" Matthew says.

"Didn't you pay attention in health class?" Liam asks.

Matthew shrugs. "What… what does it *feel* like?"

"Like being really in tune with your partner," I tell him. "Knowing if they're happy or sad or angry. Echoes of thoughts or feelings, but not actual words. It's kind of like they're always with you in a way."

"Oh." His expression softens, turning thoughtful. "That sounds nice."

"It can be." It can also be agony. My depression messed with Josh's head. It made it hard for him to focus on his games. And I've heard a few horror stories from other omegas. Ones with abusive alphas. But I won't have to worry about that. I picked a good one. Maybe the best.

Liam squeezes me like he heard the train of my thoughts and kisses my temple. I smile and cuddle closer to him.

Gabriel shucks his jacket off, rips his tie off, and starts on the buttons of his shirt. He peels it away and moves to the seat next to us. "Do it."

Liam shifts me, settling me beside him. He pulls Gabriel closer on the other side. They stare into one another's eyes. "I love you."

"I love you too, *papai*. Now bite me." Grinning, Gabriel twists his head to the side and pulls his shirt down to bare his shoulder.

Liam pulls the beta to his chest and envelops him in a hug. "This'll hurt without the distraction of sex."

I snort. It hurts even with sex. But it's a pain that's worth it. Lust is easy. That's animal instinct. The rush of chemicals zipping through your body. It's love that's hard. That takes work and understanding. What endures beyond the hardships that come. Burdens are easier to bear when you're with the ones you love.

"I'm ready," Gabriel says, steeling himself.

Liam pulls Gabriel close, fitting his mouth to the weak scent gland in the beta's neck. Gabriel gasps when Liam bites, but he doesn't push the alpha away. He grunts. "Harder, *papai*. I can take it."

I know exactly when their bond forms. When Liam pulls away, his teeth are stained red. Blood trickles down Gabriel's chest, staining his crisp white dress shirt. Liam pulls him in again and laps at it, making it bleed more. Helping it scar and cleaning the wound with his special saliva made for this purpose.

"Fuck. Okay," Matthew says, slowly unbuttoning his clothes. "That wasn't too bad without all the growling. I guess we're doing this."

Gabriel prods gently at his bite mark at the base of his neck. He slides down so Matthew can fit between them. "You'll be fine."

"You don't have to if you're not ready," Liam says, offering Matthew an out.

Matthew shakes his head. "I'm not going to be the only one without a claiming bite."

Liam pulls Matthew in gently. Cradles him in his arms. He starts with kisses until Matthew's lean frame mellows. When he finally bites, all Matthew does is stiffen and breathe harder. Their connection joins the pack and I smile as I watch his eyes get glassy with unshed tears.

"That's it?" Matthew asks while Liam licks his neck clean.

I reach out and hold Matthew's hand. It's amazing to have the comfort of a pack bond again. To not be so alone and adrift in the world. But to be connected instead. Anchored and safe.

I'm satisfied in a way I haven't been in years. I press my forehead against Liam's arm and enjoy this special moment as our alpha tends to all of us one by one.

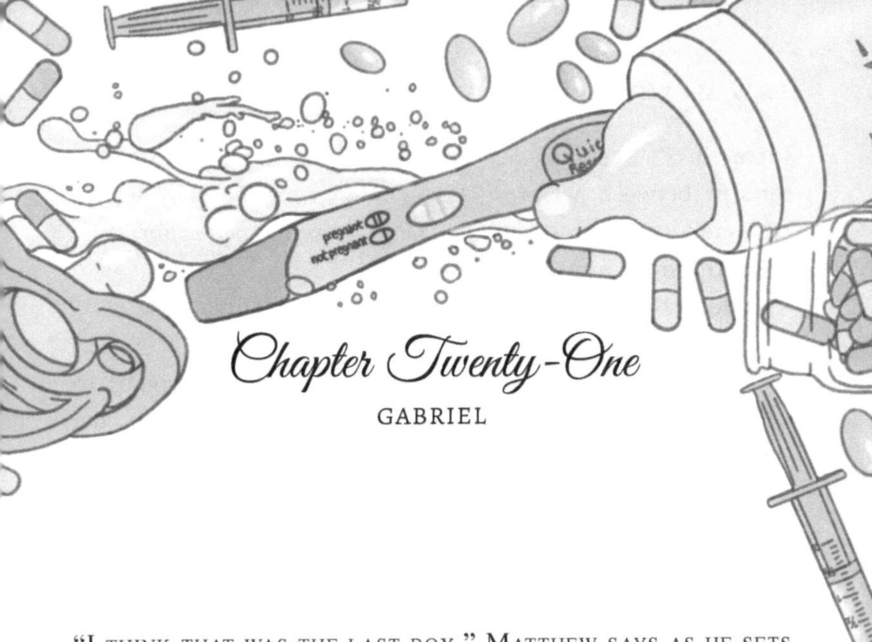

Chapter Twenty-One

GABRIEL

"I think that was the last box," Matthew says as he sets it down in the living room.

We've officially moved into our new house. Sort of. We still need to unpack. And we haven't touched the upstairs yet since we technically won't need the space for a while. After two weeks of furiously painting, fixing things, and hanging up blinds and curtains when I wasn't working a shift at the hospital, the downstairs area is done. It helps that the house was in great shape from whoever last renovated it.

"I'm too tired to unpack the kitchen and cook tonight," Matthew says. He puts his fists on his hips and surveys the mountain of cardboard boxes.

"Want to order food?" I offer.

"Sure. Chinese?" Matthew pulls out his phone to look at what's close to our new home.

"Sounds good. I'll take an order of beef and broccoli." I open the front door and yell outside, "We're ordering Chinese!"

Liam and Kat wander in from taking photos of the house to show our families. "Sounds good," she says. "I want chicken fried rice. Wait… I want shrimp. Or should I get the boneless spare ribs?" She rubs her baby bump and thinks, a wrinkle forming between her brow. "I can't tell what the baby wants. Definitely get egg rolls, though. Crap, I have to pee again." She heads off to the bathroom.

"You're ordering all of that, right?" I ask Matthew.

He types on his phone. "Yup."

Good. It never hurts to have leftovers when it comes to Chinese takeout. Especially with a pregnant woman in the house. Kat's appetite waffles as fast as her mood. Speaking of…

"We should let Waffles out of his carrier." Now that we're done going in and out, we can get her kitty situated. I shut him into the hall broom closet with the light on until we were done.

I retrieve Waffles' carrier from the closet and take it down to the basement where we've put his fancy litter box and his bowls. We'll need to cut a hole into the door for him but for now we can leave it cracked open.

"I'm letting Waffles out so mind the doors!" I shout up the basement stairs.

Waffles scratches at his carrier and meows. I open the door and he bolts out, pacing restlessly as he tries to figure out why everything's different. I scratch his back and show him where his stuff is, making sure his water is fresh. Then I pour some food into his bowl from his bin. "Here's your litter box and bowls. Have fun checking for mice in the basement."

He hunkers down to eat, crunching on kibble like he's lived here all his life. He'll settle in fine in a few days. I head upstairs, leaving the light on for him and the door cracked. We'll move his food and water into the kitchen once things are less chaotic, but for now, this'll do.

It's only a half hour before the delivery driver knocks on our door. I take the bags from him and give him a tip, then kick the door shut behind me. "Food's here!"

We spread everything out on the coffee table and pile onto

the couch, eating straight from the containers. A TV show plays in the background while we take a well deserved break. Kat vacillates between her food choices, taking small bites while frowning. When she side eyes mine, I make peace with sharing it with her.

"Are you sure?" she asks, hesitating to take it. She knows I'm in a cutting phase right now and trying to eat lean and healthy.

I kiss her temple and give her the plastic container. "Whatever the baby wants, the baby gets. But you can repay me after dinner if you want." I wink at her so she knows what I mean. It's been two weeks of nonstop work to get the house ready since we closed and got the keys. I'm ready for a night of fun.

"Deal."

I can't wait. The sun sets, casting the room in shadows since we haven't figured out all the light switches yet. Once we're stuffed and the leftovers are in the fridge, we get cozy on the couch. The TV show changes to an old horror movie. Part of the channel's line-up for something called Octoberween. On the screen, a young woman creeps through a dark house. She heard a noise and went to investigate because the house was supposed to be empty. Unbeknownst to her, a masked killer stalks her quietly through the house, a bloody knife held at the ready.

When there's a jump scare, Kat flinches, then laughs under her breath. On the screen, the killer corners the panicked woman. It's graphic and gory as he kills her. Kat groans and presses her face to my chest. I drop my arm from the back of the couch onto her shoulder and pull her closer. "Scared?"

"I usually like horror movies," she says. "I don't know why this one's bothering me."

She's right. Her books don't shy away from violence and sometimes gore. My hand strokes up and down her arm, making reassuring swipes. "You aren't usually pregnant. Pregnancy does weird things to a person."

Kat cuddles me and hides from the horror movie, and I'm not unhappy with this situation at all. She's soft and warm. Her breath tickles the hair on my nape, ghosting over the healed mating bite on my neck. The movie's scene changes to another young woman. This one's with a man. They're alone, making out in a car parked outside. Too absorbed in touching and fondling and kissing each other to notice the masked killer heading their way. The image jumps from the bloody, dripping prop knife to the girl straddling the guy in a bouncing pantomime of sex. I mistake a spike of arousal in the bond as my own until I hear a sound that's not the movie. A zipper being undone. A sigh.

Liam and Matthew are kissing, their clothes askew. Liam works a hand down Matthew's waistband and tips his head to nibble down the beta's neck. Another echo of arousal bleeds between us through the bond and my cock stirs.

She must sense it too. Kat lets out a whimper as the movie plays on, unwatched by all of us now. My cock strains my pants. The blanket falls away as she runs her hand down my front. Drags my shirt up to touch skin. Her fingers trip down my abs. They tug the low waistband of my pants down, stroking down to the notches on my pelvis. My cum gutters, as she called them once in one of her books. Such a dirty phrase. So creative. I like the naughty way she thinks.

Kat wraps her hand around my base and squeezes. She can't stroke me with my pants on, though. I work them open, lifting my hips and shoving them and my briefs down so she can stroke my cock. Her grip is loose at first, then tightens while she works me.

It's the best upside of the bond, and I could kick myself that we didn't try it earlier. She knows the moment her tugging is perfect. When it's what I like. What's only okay. Soon Kat is stroking my cock like she's an extension of my arm. Working the skin of my shaft over my sensitive head. Using my dripping pre-cum to slick her hand.

Wet sucking sounds add to our pleasure. Matthew's head bobs over Liam's lap. He's gotten on the floor to find a better angle for blowing our alpha. Liam lays a hand on Matthew's curls and groans.

"Fuck, babe, that's good," Liam groans. "Don't stop."

She jerks harder until I stop her. "Ride me," I tell her. I want to come in her pussy, not her hand. Sink into the hot clench of her wet cunt.

Kat stands and pulls her stretchy leggings off and I shove my pants down to my ankles, lying back so she can straddle me. She hovers and I line us up, and then she sinks down, sheathing me. Her tight, wet heat squeezes me from head to root. Swallowing me whole. God, she's perfect.

Her hips rise, pulling mostly off me, then sinking down again. Taking all of me. I ruck her shirt up over her baby bump, caressing it gently. Holding her and keeping her steady.

"You make me feel so good," she says, coming down hard and grinding. Rubbing against me. I'll let her come. Let her use me. Then it's my turn. Kat chews on her plump bottom lip, her eyes closing in ecstasy while she fucks herself on my cock.

"I want to see your pretty tits," I tell her, shoving her shirt up more. Grabbing the underside of her bra and shoving that up too. Her big tits bounce free, uncaged. They jiggle with every thrust. I squeeze and press them together. Make her cleavage crease.

She's so gorgeous. So beautiful with her belly that's round with our baby. Her breasts are swollen and ready to fill up with milk soon. I squeeze them, pinching her nipples. Playing with them. Her pussy clamps down on me with every pinching tug.

And then I feel it. Dampness on my fingers. A bead of fluid that rolls across her nipple.

I bring my hand to my mouth and lick it. It's sweet.

"Turn the lamp on," I tell Liam.

"In a minute," he groans, bucking into Matthew's mouth. "I'm busy here."

"Turn it on," I tell him again. Because I know he'll be upset if he misses this. "Her milk came in."

Kat stops bouncing on my dick and gently touches the breast I'm not squeezing. "It's too early."

Matthew pops off Liam's cock so they can turn the accent lamp on. I squint at the quick transition from dark to dim, then refocus my attention on Kat's breasts. I squeeze her again. Her pussy clenches around me in response. And a droplet of milk gathers on the tip of her nipple, hangs for a moment, then drips.

"Fuuuuck," Liam groans. "That's the sexiest thing I've ever seen."

Leaning down, I lap at her nipple, licking the drop of breast milk up. It's so damn sweet. Exactly like her. I groan and squeeze her breast, swirling my tongue around her nipple and sucking. Her milk supply is thin and intermittent. More of a scattering of droplets than a stream. Kat's pussy clenches around my buried dick while I suck the breast milk straight from her glorious pregnant tits.

"I want to try it," Liam says, his voice husky.

I pop off her breast and move to the other one. Luckily she has two. Kat moans, her hips grinding against me as I lick her other breast, lapping up the trails of leaking breast milk that dripped while we fucked.

Liam and Matthew slide closer, and Liam palms her other breast. Squeezes it until the nipple beads with milk again. He leans in, his cheek pressed against mine, and licks.

Kat goes still, her back arching and her breaths turning into pants while we suckle. More. I want more of her sweet milk. I grab her hips and rock her on my cock, grinding her clit against my pelvis. Bucking into her so hard her tits bounce in our mouths.

Matthew goes back to sucking cock, working Liam's dick with loud wet sounds. Liam lets her nipple go with a wet pop and squeezes her breast, mesmerized by the way her nipples slowly leak.

"That's so fucking hot, kitten," Liam says. "Your milk is so sweet. As sweet as you. I could eat you right up."

"I'm close," she whimpers, her face and chest flushing. "Don't stop."

"Never," I tell her, moving her faster. Letting her find her pleasure while she uses my cock. I pinch her puffy pink nipple between two fingers, loving how she moans when I do it. How the pearl of milk swells on her tip. Drips onto her pregnant belly. I milk her, squeezing rhythmically. There's an art to it, I learn. To extracting the milk from her swollen breasts.

She whimpers, hips swiveling, tits swaying while she rides me. God, her pussy is so fucking good. All soft whimpers and feminine curves. Our perfect, beautiful pregnant omega. Liam was right. We're gonna keep her bred. She's never been prettier than she is right now. And I can't wait until her next heat, when it's my baby I'm putting in her belly.

Kat cries out as she shatters on top of me, her pussy squeezing tight. Trying to milk me like I've milked her. I wait for her to settle, for her to finish riding out her aftershocks. Once her hips still, I grab them again. Use them like handles to lift her up, almost off my cock, and pull her down again. Thrusting deep.

"Oh my God," she moans, her nails digging into my shoulders. Holding onto me as I buck into her, fucking her the way I want. For my pleasure, now that she's had hers. She says my name like a chant. Over and over again. Her eyes lock onto mine, and I don't let her gaze go. I keep her here, with me, in this special moment.

"That's right," I tell her, thrusting so hard that all of her delicious softness jiggles. "I'm gonna breed this sweet pussy."

Her cunt tightens down, so hard it nearly shoves me out. I force my way back in. Pull her down on my cock and thrust up at the same time until my abdomen tenses. My muscles strain, torn between breathing and rutting. My groin tightens. My balls ache. Warmth blooms deep in my pelvis.

"Come inside me," she begs, her walls clamping down.

I can't stop it. There's a moment of stillness, then an eruption of need. My groin pulsates. Fast thrusts become slow and deep. My cock spills inside her, making her hot, wet cunt slippery with seed. A few easy thrusts work the last of my cum from my system. Emptying into her pussy, right where it belongs.

Once I'm spent, we both sit there panting. We glance at Liam and Matthew, to see where they are. Matthew kneels on the floor, his back straight and his mouth open. Tongue sticking out to catch the lashes of Liam's spurting cum.

Liam grunts, his hand working his cock, stroking hard with rapid tugs. He fucks his hand and splatters the beta with semen until it hangs in thick ropes down his chin, dripping onto his chest.

That's the second hottest thing I've seen tonight.

Kat shifts, and my softening cock slips free of her channel, slapping against my groin with a wet plop. Slick and cum drip all over me as Kat sits on my lap.

Matthew licks the cum from his face, what little he can reach, and strokes his own cock. He whimpers, tugging faster.

Liam reaches a big callused hand down. He scoops up some cum, and pops his thumb into Matthew's mouth. Feeds it to him. Matthew's lips close and his cheeks hollow as he sucks. His reward is a deep, rumbling purr from our pleased alpha.

With a whimper and eyes blown dark with lust, Matthew comes into his own hand.

The movie ends and switches to an advertisement as we all calm down, settling now that our lust's been slaked.

Kat lays her head on my chest and I wrap my arms around her. She's cold now that we've stopped. Goosebumps pebble her skin. She lets out a sleepy yawn.

"Let's get you to bed, hmm?" It's been a long day after a long month. And while she has more energy in her second trimester, I still don't want her overdoing it. She needs lots of rest.

She groans instead of answering.

"What's wrong?" I ask her.

"I don't know if I can walk just yet. My legs are still trembly."

Well, that's not an issue at all. "Hold onto me." I dig my fingers into her ass and lever us both off the couch, ignoring her surprised yelp.

"I'm too heavy!" she protests.

I squeeze her round ass harder and walk with her down the hallway toward our new bedroom. "Nonsense." I lift more than she weighs at the gym.

I nudge the bedroom door open with my foot and carry her inside. Nested delivered our nest yesterday, but tonight's the first night we're going to be using it. I lay her down in it, taking a moment to appreciate the picture she makes. She's naked, flushed, with sweat dotting along her brow, and leaking cum. She's fucking perfect.

"Noooo," she moans, clamping her legs closed and bending her knees up. "I'm gonna make a mess on the new throw blanket."

Unable to see that sort of target and do nothing about it, I chuckle and slap her on the ass. "It's your nest, *meu docinho*. If we're doing things right, it's gonna get covered in all sorts of fluids. Besides, I thought it was your idea to break in the house by fucking in every single room? Did you think we'd exclude our nest?"

"I thought we'd put the blanket on the chair during sexy times."

She's cute, but ridiculous. There is zero chance in hell that anything in her nest isn't getting soaked in cum at some point. It's a *nest*. To appease her anyway, I go to the bathroom and dig a hand towel out of a box, wetting it and bringing it back to the bedroom to clean her.

I wipe her pussy down, cleaning the cum and slick from her cunt and her thighs. "Better?"

Kat relaxes finally, letting her legs fall and her body twist onto her side. She can't stay flat on her back much anymore. "Better. Thank you."

I lean over her and kiss her deeply. "You're welcome." I wipe myself down too, and toss the dirty towel into the laundry hamper that we haven't decided where to put yet.

Liam and Matthew stumble in, nude, their dirty clothes bundled in their arms. "I put the food up," Liam says. They drop their dirty clothes into the hamper too.

When they move to slide into the nest, Kat makes an uh-uh sound and wags her finger at them. "Go wash up."

Liam's eyebrows rise. "Really?"

"You're sticky, and it's our first night in our brand new nest," she says.

Matthew glances at Liam for direction, and Liam caves. They head into the bathroom for a quick rinse. I grin and watch her scoot up the bed and wiggle under the covers.

Alphas might lead the pack, but it's the omegas that control the nest. I stand at the edge and smile when she looks at me curiously.

"Am I fit for your nest, omega?"

Kat raises one eyebrow. "Of course."

I pull the sheets down and slip inside, becoming her big spoon as she finagles her pregnancy pillow into place and gets settled. Becoming her big spoon has become the coveted position. A small part of me wants to lord it over Liam. That I get to be it on our first night in our brand new bed in our new house.

There's a whisper of omega contentment in the bond I share with her through Liam as she gets comfortable and I settle in behind her. Liam and Matthew finish up in the bathroom and join us, sliding into the nest.

The bed is huge. One day soon, it'll be filled with children. Matthew will read them bedtime stories as we all cuddle them. I can't wait.

We end up huddled together in a puppy pile in the middle anyway despite finally having enough room to sprawl out. Maybe it's because we're used to sleeping this way now. Or we simply don't want to have any room between us now that we're bonded. There's something comforting about slotting your leg between another's and knowing they're completely safe next to you while you sleep.

Kat falls asleep first, but the rest of us lie there a bit in the dark. We enjoy the moment that seems so mundane but is really quite momentous.

I'm half-asleep when something jolts me awake. We're still getting used to the new house and all of its noises. I crack my eyes open and look around the room in the dark. Waffles is curled up and asleep at the foot of the bed. Liam is gently snoring. Matthew and Kat are sound asleep.

Then I feel what woke me. A tiny thump under my palm. The one resting on Kat's baby bump. A kick? I press a bit harder. Our baby girl kicks back, as if upset to have her space invaded. With a kick like that, I'm gonna get her to play football.

Grinning, I lay my head back down and snuggle her closer, inhaling the sweet cookie scent of Kat's hair. Her smell is thicker than usual according to Liam. A sign of a healthy omega pregnancy. It must be if even I can smell it this strongly as a beta. Our daughter kicks my hand again, then settles.

I can't wait to start working on our princess's nursery tower.

Chapter Twenty-Two

KAT

Tires crunch on gravel and the fine dusting of snow that has settled on the long driveway leading up to the ski chalet. I look out the window, letting out a squeal when I see who's arrived. I head to the door as fast as I can, which isn't very fast considering I'm eight months pregnant.

I throw the door open, cold air slapping me in the face, and head outside. "Jen!" I shout, waving at her. Her mates pull their luggage from the trunk while Jen pops her youngest on her hip and their eldest runs up the drive, screeching with excitement.

"Auntie Kaaaaat!" Bailey stops short a few feet away, staring. Her nose is already red from the cold and her eyes are wide. "Wow, you're big!"

Jen hustles after her, panting. Her warm breath fogs the cold air. "Bailey, remember? I told you that Auntie Kat is growing a baby in her tummy."

Bailey cocks her head. "That's a big baby." She glances around at the ski chalet and the quiet woods covered in a blanket of snow. We got here last night before it started. It was a pleasant surprise to wake up to. "I wanna build a snowman!" she screeches.

"After we get settled and you eat lunch," Jen promises her daughter. "Hi," she says to me.

"How was the drive?" I ask her, stepping to the side so they can enter. "Hi, Jake. Your room is the yellow one if you guys want to put your bags down. They're all labeled with signs on the doors."

"The drive was good," Jen says, putting her youngest down once the door's closed. She stoops down to unzip the toddler's parka and picks Bailey's torn off winter gear up off the floor. She hangs everyone's coats up on the pegs by the door. "It's nice to get out of town." Once the little ones are out of earshot, she leans in close and whispers, "I have their presents in trash bags in the trunk."

I nod. "Your mates can put them in the attic tonight once the kids are asleep."

Jen smiles and looks around at the place. "Nice. This is fun. Thanks for inviting us."

"Of course. I wasn't going to have Christmas without you. Are you sure your parents don't mind?"

Jen waves my concerns away. "They booked a discount cruise and flew to Florida after we told them. They're talking about moving down there. They can't keep up with the snow or cold anymore. Wow. This place is gorgeous. I can't wait to post photos."

The ski chalet we picked is amazing. It's not the one that Liam and the others normally rent. Now that our pack's bigger, we needed something with more bedrooms to fit all of our families.

This one is a sprawling two stories with a finished base-ment. It sleeps thirty since there are five bunk beds in the base-ment, eight bedrooms, and some of the sofas convert to beds. It's rustic, but luxurious. The walls are bare wood, the hearth is stone, and worn rugs cover the hardwood floor. The kitchen and bathrooms are upgraded, and the back wall of the chalet is nothing but floor-to-ceiling windows overlooking the mountain range outside. The second floor has a wide back porch with rocking chairs and steps that lead down to the back yard where the firepit and hot tub are.

"Oh, hi, dear. I'm Margaret. Matthew's mom. You're Kathleen's friend, right?" Matthew's mother asks, coming into the kitchen. "I'm making cocoa. Would you like some?"

Jen nods and unwinds her scarf from her neck. "I'm Jen, Kat's friend. Nice to meet you. And sure, I'll take a cup. Thank you."

"Me too," I say. Matthew got his cooking skills from his mom. Whatever she puts in it, it's the best hot cocoa I've ever had. We sit on stools at the counter while she mixes a huge batch of cocoa in a pot on the stove.

"I need to make the kids lunch," Jen says. "We brought snacks for the car ride, but they'll be hungry again soon. Is there a store around here?"

"We stocked the fridge yesterday," I tell her. "I got the mac and cheese and chicken nuggets they like."

"I'll make it," Margaret offers, whisking the cocoa. "Gives me something to do while the boys are out." Margaret pours three mugs of cocoa, adding marshmallows. She turns the stove off and puts the lid on the pot, then sets the cups down for us.

I blow on mine to cool it before taking a sip and moaning from pure joy. It warms me from the inside out and takes the chill off my hands. "I don't know what you put in it, but I want your recipe. Does Matthew know how to make this?"

"He sure does," Margaret says, smiling. "Want to help us with the cookies later?"

"Yes." I've heard about these famous cookies for months. I'm excited to try one myself.

"We're back!" a man shouts from the back door off the

mudroom. Liam, Gabriel, and Matthew come in following two older men. Liam and Matthew's fathers.

"We found the perfect tree while we were out," Liam's father says. "We came back for the ax."

"Is that allowed?" I ask. Don't you have to go to a Christmas tree farm for that?

"Not really," Matthew's father says, brushing snow off his shoulders before it can melt into his coat. "But everyone does it. As long as you only take the one tree, they never say anything."

"Found it." Liam walks into the kitchen with his coat open to his red flannel shirt. He hefts the ax onto his shoulder. With the beard he's been growing since November first, he looks every inch the mountain man ready to split some firewood.

I need to see this. There's no way in hell I'm missing watching my alpha cut down my Christmas tree while looking like *that*. After, when we're alone, I'm gonna climb him like he's the tree. "We'll go with you."

"Yeah, we will," Jen says, blinking slowly.

I'm not even jealous at the way she's looking at my mate right now. She and her pack are very much in love. But it's impossible to be female and be unaffected by how fucking hot my alpha is right now.

We drain our cocoas and thank Matthew's mom who's busy working on mac and cheese for Jen's kids.

"Do we need to tell your mates we're heading out?" I ask her as we slip off our stools.

Jen winds her scarf around her neck and we both grab our coats. "They'll figure it out. They're probably lying down and zoning out on their phones for a bit after the drive."

We join the men outside. The dads load a tarp and rope and the ax into the back of an SUV, but Liam surprises me by pulling out one of the four-wheelers. The ski chalet comes equipped with both four-wheelers and snowmobiles for all-season adventuring. He cranks it to life and it smells like gasoline. It rumbles loudly as he drives it over and grins at me.

"Wanna ride?" he asks me, waggling his brows.

"You're very pregnant," Jen reminds me. "Maybe we should go in the car."

"I'll just be sitting," I tell her, taking Liam's hand. "Take the car and meet us there."

I trust Liam. He'd never let me get on this thing if he thought there was any way I'd get hurt. He helps me get on in front of him, his long arms reaching around me to handle the controls. I grip onto the four-wheeler tightly. It rumbles, loud and rough. Liam revs the engine while it's idling and it thrums underneath us, the vibrations going right to my groin.

"We'll meet you there," Liam tells the others, taking off.

The wind is cold as it whips at my hair and face while he drives us down the gravel road. I lean back against his chest, enjoying having my alpha behind me. With him curled over me, I feel safe.

It's beautiful out here. The nearest neighbor is miles away down the mountain. We're staying at one of the farthest homes up here. It's quiet and peaceful in a way that can't be imagined from living in a city all your life. Even our new house, somewhat remote, doesn't compare.

A red cardinal makes a bright splash of color on a snow-coated branch. It takes off before we get close. The noise and rumble of the four-wheeler is too loud to not spook the wildlife. Liam slows us down and pulls the four-wheeler off the road, going into the woods a bit. There are tracks from other sporting machines here. It must be a popular off-road trail.

"Is this where the tree is?" I ask him, looking around, trying to spot it or the car the others are coming in.

Liam slows the four-wheeler to a stop. He kisses my cheek

and nuzzles me. His breath is warm on my chilled ear. His voice dips in a gravelly purr. "I haven't gotten to fuck you in days."

My heart beats faster in my chest, my pulse fluttering. The four-wheeler's idle engine revs, the rumbles going straight to my pussy. My hips move, grinding my pussy against the vibrating metal. Given enough time, I could come like this.

I'm so swollen down there all the time that I'm always horny. I thought it would go away in the third trimester when I was big and sore and tired of being pregnant. But one lusty look or growl is enough to make my pussy wet. And we haven't fucked in what seems like forever. There hasn't been a chance. Between packing and meeting everyone's families and settling into the chalet, we've been busy.

"No, you haven't," I say. Reaching back, I scratch my fingernails through his beard. The hair is coarse and thick. And he melts in my hand whenever I do this. "Bad alpha."

His low purr turns into a throaty, masculine moan that has my pussy sopping wet. Liam nips at my fingertips, then slaps my thigh. "Stand up, omega."

Are we really doing this here? Now? In the woods where anyone passing by could see us? It's thirty degrees outside. "You're gonna get frostbite on your dick," I warn him. But I stand anyway.

His zipper opens. "No, I'm not. Your pussy's too fucking hot."

I bite my lip and lift the hem of my parka up. He thumbs the edge of my high-waisted maternity leggings and jerks them down, taking my panties with them. Fuck, it's cold. My bare ass nearly freezes the minute he exposes me. Goosebumps rise along my skin.

Liam grabs my hips and pulls me down, lining us up and sinking inside me within a couple of thrusts. I moan when he stretches me open until he's fully seated.

It's a hard, fast fuck. Desperate and dirty. My ass claps against his groin as he fucks me from behind. I grip the four-wheeler's steering for support as he bounces me on his dick.

"Fuck, I missed this," he groans. "I missed fucking this perfect pussy. Needed this so bad. You have no idea how bad I've needed you, kitten."

My back arches and my thighs tremble with the strain of the position. Even with support. Even with him doing most of the work. I get so exhausted these days. But I'm never too tired for this. For my pack to show me how much they love me. "God, I missed your cock."

It's a perfect, beautiful cock. And it's mine forever now.

"Take it, kitten. Purr for me. Nice and loud. Let's scare the wildlife when you come."

He loves it when I'm noisy. So I stop holding back. I let him fuck all sorts of filthy, depraved sounds from me. His dick carves a hot path inside me with every thrust. I moan, and whimper, and whine. Babble nonsense as I beg him to fuck me harder. To come inside me. To fill me up with cum and stuff me with his knot.

No, wait. We don't have time for him to knot me.

"Don't knot me," I remind him. His swelling knot pops in and out of me. Catching on my entrance, only to be shoved back in on his next thrust.

"Fuck," he growls, his cock kicking. His knot swollen and bulbous inside me. "I got caught up in fucking you and forgot."

"Liar," I accuse him, smiling to myself. There's no real heat to the word. Not when his cock pulsates inside me. Filling me up. Bathing me in the pheromones my body craves.

"I can't help it," he groans. "Your pussy was made for my knot. It practically begs for it." Liam settles me on his lap and reaches around, wedging under my baby bump and groping between my thighs. Shoving my panties and leggings down further so he can touch my pussy.

I forget to be mad at him when he strokes my clit, making swirling circles. I'm soaking wet with arousal, my pussy stretched wide on his flared knot and big dick. It doesn't take much for me to pant like I'm in heat again, for my walls to clamp down on him and milk his cock for more cum.

God, it feels so fucking good.

I come with a wail, pussy fluttering, belly tightening. My orgasm ripples through me like a wave, leaving my abdomen firm and my nipples tight. They leak a bit, my milk soaking into my bra. I've had to put shields in the cups to protect my clothes.

"Good girl," Liam says, nuzzling me and purring while we both wait for his knot to deflate. Now that we're not moving, I'm freezing. My thighs are going numb and my parka only covers so much. I pull my leggings up as much as I can and try to soak up all of his body heat. My ass sweats where his skin touches mine. He's a furnace. Which is really useful when your alpha decides to dick you down in the snow-covered woods three days before Christmas.

"Tell me about our tree," I demand.

He leans his forehead against my back. "It's gorgeous. You're gonna love it. It's gotta be eight or nine feet tall. It's round and full. No bald spots. I've never seen a prettier tree."

"I can't wait. We should decorate it tonight."

"Sounds good, kitten. Shit, I forgot to bring something to clean you up with."

"I'm wearing slick panties," I tell him. I have to now. All of my cute underwear have slowly transitioned over to slick panties. The super absorbent kind that have full protection from back to front. When you have three mates who love to bend you over on a whim, an omega's gotta be prepared to get messy.

"Smart girl." Liam shifts, and with some effort, his knot

pops free. I stand with his help and Liam tugs my panties up while I fix my coat.

Despite the absorptive properties of the underwear, I still feel the squish of cum and slick when I sit back down. Liam fixes his clothes, then shifts the four-wheeler back into drive. It's not much farther to our Christmas tree. We take a shortcut through the woods and meet the SUV at a trail marker. Everyone is standing around the tree, waiting for us.

He cuts the engine and hops off, then helps me down. His dad hands him the ax they leaned against the tree while they waited.

Jen and I stand a safe distance away. "Did you get lost?" she asks.

I avoid looking at her and focus on the tree instead. "We took a detour."

"Where?"

"Onto Liam's dick," I whisper.

She snorts. "That's what I thought. Damn, girl. How are you still able to get it like that at eight months? In my last month with both my kids I could barely walk across my house without getting tired."

Liam pulls his parka off and hands it to Matthew. He's in just his flannel, undershirt, and jeans. He has to kneel in the snow to get to the base of the tree. The tree's branches hang low, nearly touching the ground. Once he's in position, he lifts a branch out of the way and starts cutting a notch in the trunk with confident swings.

"I mean… look at him," I say, unable to rip my eyes away from him. "That's a lot of motivation. Plus Gabriel's been making me take prenatal yoga classes for months."

"Hmm."

Liam moves to the other side, cutting a notch on the other

end of the trunk. He swings repeatedly, chipping away at it until there's a creaking sound. "Watch out!"

Everyone standing too close moves away as he makes the final swing. The tree lets out a loud crack, then falls into the snow. Liam hands the ax to his dad, then bends down and hefts the tree up onto his shoulder, dragging it behind him.

"Fuuuuck," I whisper. That's so fucking hot. There's something primal and satisfying about watching my alpha take down a tree and hoist it up onto his back like it's a sack of flour. My pussy clenches, a fresh bead of slick and cum soaking into my panties.

Jen snickers. "RIP to your vagina."

"Mmhmm." We join the boys at the SUV where they're busy tying the tree closed with rope and hauling it up on the roof of the car.

"Ready?" Matthew asks, waving us over.

Fuck. Yeah. It's tree decorating time.

We don't detour on our way back. I'm too excited to get the tree up. Matthew's mom bakes her famous cookies and ladles out hot chocolate while someone puts on Christmas music. My parents help bring up the boxes of ornaments and lights that the ski chalet provides. We plug the lights in, testing the strings and fixing a few broken bulbs.

"Why don't some of them light up?" Bailey asks from her perch on my knee.

"If too many are broken, the electricity can't flow through. They all have to work together to light up and be pretty. If we pop the bad ones out…" I carefully pry the burnt out glass bulb free, "we can put new ones in. What color should we put here?"

"Red!" Bailey pokes at the red replacement bulb from my palm.

I help her pop it into the socket. "Okay, let's plug it in and see if it works now."

Matthew shoves the light strand's plug into the outlet and the strand of multicolored lights light up.

Bailey throws her arms up and squeals. "Yay!"

"Cookies are done," Margaret says. "Can she have one?" she asks Jen.

"Please?" Bailey begs with wide eyes.

Her little sister toddles over at the mention of cookies. "Cookie?"

"Only one," Jen says. "Or you'll ruin your appetite for dinner."

Bailey gets wiggly, so I set her down, then stand up to stretch. Margaret gives them each a cookie, then asks if they want to help her decorate the rest and make them pretty.

Gabriel and Matthew take over the task of wrapping the lights around the tree while the others start putting hooks on ornaments.

Liam comes up behind me, wrapping his arms around me and tucking his chin on my shoulder. "You look real good with a baby on your lap," he whispers into my ear.

I hold onto his arms and lean against him. "In a month we won't have to borrow Jen's kids for practice."

He makes a satisfied rumbling sound in his chest.

"Cookie, dear?" Margaret asks. She holds up a cookie shaped like a bell. It's messily slathered in yellow tinted icing with a chaotic sprinkle of silver sugar crystals. It's ridiculous and perfect. "Bailey wanted you to eat the one she made for you."

I take the cookie and hold it up. "Bailey! It's so pretty. You made this? Wow."

Bailey beams with pride over at the kitchen table, then gets back to it. She sticks her tongue out as she concentrates on decorating cookies.

Margaret walks back to the kitchen with a smile on her face.

I take a bite of the cookie and let out a moan. "Oh my God. That's so good. Want a bite?" I ask, lifting it up for Liam.

He nips my earlobe between his teeth. "Oh, I'm gonna eat my fill of cookies," he promises.

I don't think he means the actual Christmas cookies. A blush heats my face. I turn around in the circle of his arms so the others won't see and pat his chest. "You'll have to wait till after dinner too. You don't want to spoil your appetite."

He laughs and lets me go. Just in time for us to help my parents start hanging ornaments on the tree.

Chapter Twenty-Three

MATTHEW

"Bye!" we say in unison, waving as the last car starts down the gravel driveway. It's been a fun but exhausting couple of days.

"I wish we didn't have to leave," Kat says, pouting. "It'd be nice to have the place to ourselves for a night."

She's right. It's been hard to find time for ourselves with so many people around. With this many people, someone's always around. The only time we've had for each other is when we make an excuse to sneak out. My ass is wind chapped. I'm tired of fucking outside.

"It's booked through tomorrow, isn't it?" Gabriel asks.

"Yeah," Liam says. "They had a five-night minimum."

"Can we stay?" Kat asks, her eyes wide and pleading.

"How's the weather look?" Liam asks.

I pull up the weather app on my phone. "Snowy. It says three to four inches."

"Oh!" Kat says, even more excited now. "It'll be the white Christmas we didn't get because it all melted in the sun."

Liam glances at the clear blue sky and his truck. I can see the wheels turning in his head. He had winter tires put on it last month. His truck is tall. It'll be able to clear four inches of snow easily, even up here on this mountain where it won't be plowed often. "Okay. We can stay."

"Yay!" Kat throws her hands up and pulls him in for a kiss. "I want to fuck on that bearskin rug in front of the fire."

"You heard the lady," Liam says, grinning. "Let's build a fucking fire."

I snort with laughter, not sure if he meant it to sound that way on purpose.

Gabriel and I follow them in, locking the door behind us in case someone turns around because they forgot their phone charger or something.

"I'll build it," Gabriel says, heading to the massive stone fireplace. He takes his time building a fire, angling small splits of wood and a larger log just so. He stuffs twists of newspaper between them, then grabs the extra long matches from the mantle. A flame bursts to life, and the fire catches the dry wood quickly.

"Christmas music," Kat demands.

I find a playlist we haven't listened to yet and hook my phone up to their Bluetooth speaker system.

"I'll be right back," Kat says, heading down the hallway that leads to the bedrooms. "Don't follow me. It's a surprise."

Liam turns to us and gives us both smoldering looks. "You should go prep."

I think those are the four most beautiful words I've ever heard. It's been days since we properly fucked. There's not a lot of impromptu anal happening in the woods. It's been hands or mouths only unless we're fucking Kat. And as much as I've come to love her tight, wet pussy, I really want Liam to blow my back out with his massive cock.

"Yes, sir," I answer smartly, ignoring his amused look. "Come on, Gabriel."

"She said we couldn't follow her. Our stuff's in the bathroom." Gabriel follows me anyway.

I grab my keys from the table by the door and slip into my coat. "I have an emergency bag in the car."

Gabriel looks at me funny. "You keep an emergency sex bag in Liam's truck?"

"Yeah." I shrug and unlock the door, then unlock Liam's truck with his fob. "I was a Boy Scout, remember? Always be prepared."

"I'm not sure this is what they had in mind when they coined that slogan."

I shrug. "You obviously never went on group camping trips as a horny teen. I got my first hand job in the woods from a cute boy named Adam."

"Really?" Gabriel asks.

"What? They told us to go find wood."

Gabriel snorts and shakes his head at me. I drop the tailgate down and climb inside, then open up the steel tool box built into the back of the cab. I grab the small black duffel bag from there and toss it down to Gabriel.

He catches it. "I thought this was your gym bag."

Jumping down, I turn and lift the tailgate and shut it. I give him a wry look. "When have you ever seen me go to the gym?"

He hums thoughtfully and follows me back inside. We find an empty bathroom in one of the other bedrooms. He waits on the bed while I go first, then takes his turn.

By the time we're done, my cock is semi-hard with anticipation. Gabriel adjusts his cock inside his gray sweatpants. He's hard too. I can't keep my eyes off his bulge. There's nothing sluttier than a man in gray sweatpants and nothing else. They *should* be modest. The pants cover him from hip to ankle. But the way they cling around Gabriel's half-hard cock showing off everything is absolutely sinful.

"See something you like?" Gabriel asks, a cocky grin on his face.

I tug him down for a kiss. Our mouths slide together, slotting perfectly. He kisses me until I'm breathless. When we pull away, there's a small damp spot on his gray sweatpants where the fabric's soaked up leaking pre-cum. I groan at the sight and resist the urge to grab him through his pants. If I do, we're not making it out of this bedroom. And I have plans.

"Come on," I tell Gabriel, threading my fingers through his and squeezing his hand. "I've got a surprise for us."

"A surprise?" his eyes light up. Gabriel can't stand having to wait for surprises. He's an instant gratification kind of guy. That's why I've kept my Christmas present completely secret from all of them.

That's also why I've been keeping it on me. I pat my pocket to make sure the small plastic bag is still there. It is.

We rejoin Liam in the big living room and we're just in time for Kat's surprise.

It's her, all dolled up. She's put makeup on and curled her hair and she's wrapped up in a big red bow. Literally. She's wearing a bodysuit made of sheer netting and a red satin bow. The ribbon crosses over her nipples, and the open cups of the sheer bra show tantalizing cuts of skin above and below. The ribbon's pointed ends come down over her baby bump. Another ribbon sash crisscrosses over her hips, making a V in the front. Like an arrow pointing straight to her pussy. She turns around, showing us the big red bow over her butt and the open panel below that. It's crotchless.

"Holy shit," Liam wheezes.

Holy shit is right. Kat's grin is smug. Like the cat who got the cream. She's so fucking cute.

A Christmas song, one about the singer wanting only one thing for Christmas, their lover, comes over the speakers with perfect timing. Kat walks into the living room and joins us by the crackling fire.

"Want to open your present?" she asks us, tugging lightly on the bow tied across her big breasts.

Liam gets down on his knees on the bearskin rug and wraps his hands around her thighs, pulling her closer. "I've been a very good boy this year."

"Have you?" she asks, tilting her head. "I don't know. You were pretty naughty yesterday. Teasing me all day long with random groping touches."

"I can't help it," Liam groans. "You smell so fucking good. I want to eat you right up."

"Then maybe you should," she says, carding her fingers through his hair. She squeezes and drags him forward, pulling his mouth to her groin. Spreads her legs wider.

While they're busy, I pull the baggie from my pocket and show it to Gabriel. "Merry Christmas," I tell him.

Gabriel looks at the three flat white pills inside. "What are they?"

"Quaaludes."

These innocuous white pills are sex in a bottle. Wildly popular in the sixties and seventies, there's a reason they became known as thigh spreaders. They're also the closest a beta can get to the pleasure of a heat or rut. Of course they got banned when the free love movement of the seventies lost ground to the war on drugs.

Gabriel's mouth drops open with surprise. "They stopped making those forever ago. Where did you get them?"

"I guess they still make them in Africa. One of the guys I work with at the bank got them from his hookup at a gay bear retreat. I bought three off of him. Sorry, Kat. I can try to get more later when you're not pregnant if you want."

Kat moans and arches her back, pulling Liam's head into a

better position while she fidgets. "That's okay, I'm good." She sucks in a sharp breath. "Really good."

"I'll get us a glass of water," Gabriel says, going into the kitchen. He comes back with a glass and downs one of the pills, then passes both to me.

I take one, swallowing the bitter pill down. I bring the third over to Liam. "Are you joining us?"

Liam pulls away from Kat's pussy and smacks her ass. "Go make a nest for us to fuck you in, kitten. Get cozy for your mates."

Kat drags blankets and pillows off the couch and starts building a nest on the bearskin rug by the fire. Liam takes the pill and water and stares at it for a moment, then looks at me. He grins. "Didn't think this was what the four of us would be doing today."

"It's more romantic here."

"For our fuck fest?" Liam pops the pill into his mouth and drains the water glass, setting it aside. "How long will it take to work?"

"About forty-five minutes," Gabriel chimes in. He's already slipping into the nest, getting cozy with Kat. Shoving the waistband of his gray sweats down so his hard cock bobs in the air between them. She's on her back, using pillows to prop herself up. He fists his cock and guides it toward her face. *Sneaky.*

But that's fine. I can be patient. And I like to watch almost as much as I like to participate.

Liam claps me on the back. "Kat first, before we start anal," he says.

Nodding, I follow him to the nest. Liam moves between her legs, palming her knees and spreading them. I take my place at the top of the nest, closest to the fire, to watch. The fire is warm against our bare skin as we disrobe and toss our clothes into a pile.

Liam runs his hands over Kat's rounded body, playing with her big red bow. "What a nice present. I can't wait to unwrap it." He reaches for the ends of the ribbon obscuring her breasts. Pulls them slowly until the knot loosens and the ribbon falls away.

Her breasts spring free, pink tipped and pointed. I palm one, enjoying how soft and squishy they are. They're fun to play with. I didn't know I was a boob guy before her.

"Open up for me, kitten," Liam says.

Her legs spread as she drops her knees to either side. Liam settles between her legs, his head dipping low. Going back to eating her pussy with long wet strokes.

Gabriel strokes his cock and angles it toward her mouth. She turns and opens for him without being told to. She's such a good girl. Her pretty pink lips part, wrapping around the tip of his cock, cheeks hollowing as she sucks and licks him while he squeezes his base.

I love seeing my pack like this. Undone with pleasure. Lost in one another. She reaches for me, groping blindly for my cock. I capture her hand and bring it to my groin.

Her fingers tighten, making a ring, stroking and fondling while she tries to multitask. Tries and fails, as Liam feasts on her pussy until she pops her mouth off Gabriel's cock to moan.

A good opportunity. I grab her chin and angle her lips my way. Urging her to suck me next. Her mouth wraps around me, and my hips thrust, fucking her face with slow, measured motions.

"You're so good at sucking cock," I tell her, praising her. Her eyes lift to mine and she takes me deeper. Closer to the back of her throat. I palm her breast and pinch the nipple, rubbing my thumb over the bead of milk that gathers there with stimulation. She's impossibly swollen. Her breasts are more than double what they were in the early stages of pregnancy. I knew pregnancy changed an omega's body, but I didn't realize it was this extreme.

"So good," Gabriel adds. He strokes himself leisurely. Keeping his cock warmed up. We have a long afternoon ahead of ourselves.

Her eyes flutter and she moans around my cock. What is Liam doing to her?

Liam rises from between her legs. He slaps her thigh with a loud crack of his palm. "All fours, kitten. The doctor said we have to stretch your perineum. Matthew, you're on the bottom."

Oh, fuck. This is my new favorite thing.

She whimpers but doesn't protest. What a good girl.

"Let me help." I pull my cock from her mouth and help Kat get onto her knees. She's delightfully helpless without us at this stage. Her baby bump is so big that she can't roll over anymore.

I take her place as the bottom in the nest and help her climb on top of me until she's straddling my lap. Liam fits my cock into her pussy. She's so wet with slick and saliva that I slide right in. Her pussy's swollen with arousal. She clenches me tight. I never knew pussy could be so damn good.

"Gabriel, up top," Liam commands.

He's the most limber of us for the most awkward role in this group position.

"Are you ready for me, *meu docinho*?" Gabriel comes up behind her and waits for her to say yes. Slowly he presses his cockhead to her entrance. Coats himself in her slick with restrained thrusts as he gently makes his way inside, his cock sliding along mine.

I grit my teeth, denying myself the urge to thrust while Gabriel seats himself beside my cock inside her tight, wet cunt. She gasps, her nails digging into my shoulders while she takes him. Droplets of sweat plaster baby hairs to her forehead as

Gabriel rocks. A gentle swaying of his cock inside her. Slip sliding up and down my shaft.

"Fuck," I curse, forgetting how to breathe. "That feels so goddamn good."

My hips twitch. I can't stop it, can't contain the small movement. Is there anything better than my dick sliding against Gabriel's while we're both inside Kat? I don't know how she takes it. What sort of omega resiliency lets such a small thing take so much cock? But God bless whatever force of nature designed them. I didn't know what I was missing.

"Liam, I can't," Kat whines, holding still. "It's too much."

"Shh." Liam shifts behind us all. Purrs, his chest rumbling with sounds that soothe her. "You can take it, kitten. You've done it before. And we need to stretch you so you don't tear. It's doctor's orders, remember?"

"I don't think this is what the doctor meant," she says.

Liam shushes her again and Gabriel presses in deeper, slowly. One agonizing inch at a time.

"Oh, God." Kat buries her face in my throat while Gabriel and I set a rhythm. One of us thrusting in while the other pulls out, then changing it all together. Both of us filling her. Stretching her pussy wide.

Despite her protests, she takes us like she's done this all her life.

"That's my good girl," Liam says between thick, rolling purrs. "Can you take a bit more? Just the tip."

Kat whimpers but doesn't say no. Liam presses closer, his legs brushing against me as he settles into position. Gabriel and I go still, our cocks buried deep, as he aligns his cock with her pussy.

She takes a breath that turns into a low, ragged moan as he works the head of his dick inside. Uses our cocks as the guide to her poor stretched cunt. He pauses, giving her a moment to adjust. My muscles tense with the restrained urge to thrust.

"Good girl," Liam croons. "That's the tip. I'm in. You're doing such a good job taking us, kitten. You can take some more." He doesn't phrase it as a question. His cock pushes in, making room for himself. Demanding it. "Don't fight us. Just relax and let us take care of you."

Once he's fully seated, he goes still. Lets her adjust to the intrusion of three cocks in one small pussy. A furrow forms between her brows. As if she can't understand how something so terrible can feel so good. But she's an omega. If she couldn't take it, her pack would never demand it. We'd never, ever hurt her.

I pull her face to mine and press our lips together, kissing the worry from her. Pouring our love into my lips. When she kisses me back, her breathing settled, I know she's ready. I pull my hips back and shove my way inside. Reclaiming my space inside her.

Her mouth softens with a swallowed moan and I twist her tongue up with mine. Distract her while we take turns fucking into her. It's a beautiful torment. The slide of their cocks along mine. The slippery fluttering of her overstretched pussy.

"Fuck, kitten," Liam groans. "God, you're so fucking tight."

"That's it, sweetheart," Gabriel says. "Take all of us."

We take turns, cocks thrusting, sliding along the shaft of the others. Hollowing out a space deep inside her as we stretch her pussy wider than it's ever been before. I lose all sense of time as the three of us fuck our omega in tandem. It could be minutes or hours since we started till I feel the bulge of Liam's knot begin to swell.

My groin tightens. A dull bloom of heat unfurling through me. Making my balls ache and my mind fog with need. The need to thrust. To cum. Until all of my focus narrows to the slide of my dick in and out of her. The way my head bumps along their buried cocks. Stroking one another. It's obscene.

"You like it, don't you, kitten?" Liam asks.

"I'm so full," she moans. Her thighs tremble.

"We're gonna cum in this pretty pussy. This is the rest of it," Liam promises. "You'll take it all."

His growing knot adds more challenge. Makes his thrust inside her harder to manage. That's what his knot is designed for, after all. To keep competitors out, rather than in. So that his seed can find a fertile womb. His knot squeezes the middle of my shaft and my abdomen tightens with the urge to come. To thrust up hard and fast and come first before he locks me out. It hurts so good.

Liam groans. A deep, filthy sound that makes her impossibly wetter. "Only a little more. You're doing so good, kitten."

"Liam," she whines. Despite her protests, her pussy clamps down on ours. As if it's hungry for what her body craves but her mind balks at.

"You need it, sweetheart. We've gotta keep this pussy nice and ready for how much we're gonna breed you."

That's all it takes for her to unravel. For the promise of the babies we'll put in her to make her come. She tightens down again. Flutters and squeezes. With a strangled moan, she comes on our cocks. Thighs quivering, her face flushed and her mouth rounded with surprise. Like she didn't know she could do it while three cocks stretched her pussy to its limits, but did.

His cock surges deeper. Faster. His knot raking against our cocks like a stroking fist. And he shows no signs of stopping. *He's not... Oh, shit. He is.* He's going to knot her while we're still in her.

"*Meu Deus,*" Gabriel groans.

I can't hold back. My orgasm surges through me as Liam's knot swells, milking the cum from me with each of his thrusts.

Gabriel tenses, fucking deeper. Wetness squelches between us. His cock shudders, pulsating.

Liam lets out a deep growl and fucks through his release. His knot pops, nearly crowding us out. I grab Kat's ass and buck up, pushing my cock back in. Pulling her down on it. Gabriel holds her by the shoulders, keeping her pinned between us.

And Liam comes, and comes, and comes. His thick cock swells, jerking. Balls emptying. I feel each pulsation and pump like they're my own. His knot blows her pussy wider, stretching her body to its limits. Pinching my dick to the cusp of pain. It's a beautiful agony.

Kat lets out a strangled whine, settling only with Liam's rumbling purrs.

Even when my cock softens, my body spent and satisfied, it doesn't slip free. His knot locks us deep. We're only moving once he's empty and done.

"That's it, kitten. What a good fucking girl you are. I'm so proud of you. Look at how well you took our cocks and my knot."

"Oh my God," she whines, pressing her forehead to my chest.

Gabriel and I kiss her. Rub her down, murmuring soft words of encouragement as we wait.

After a bit, Liam's knot shrinks and our softening cocks spill free with a deluge of fluids. Cum and slick leave all of us messy and the blankets of our impromptu nest filthy. The others collapse beside us and I ease Kat onto her side, covering her with the least soiled throw blanket I can grab. Her eyes drift closed and minutes later, she's asleep.

Our cuddle pile is cozy. My post-nut thoughts are slow and dull. Warmth rolls through me like a billowing cloud. Rolling over would be impossible. My limbs are uncoordinated and rubbery. I'm loose. Floating and free. And getting so fucking hard. My cock stirs, rising and stiff.

It's the 'ludes, I try to say, but nothing much comes out except a laugh. I'm warm and melty and giggly. The slide of the blankets against my skin and the grazing of someone's hand along my thigh is a sensual masterpiece.

Every nerve in my body lights up under the rough calluses of Liam's palm. His face dips to the hollow of my throat, his breath hot and his lips wet. He nuzzles me, his mouth finding my small scent gland. My healed mating bite. He takes the skin between his teeth, nibbling lightly, and I groan. Arch my back into him. His cock slides against me, leaving a trail of slick and cum behind.

He spoons me from behind. Rubbing, thrusting, his cock slides down between my ass cheeks. I bend my leg and give him access. Fingers probe, checking how well I prepped. How slick with lube I am. Scissor my hole open and pump. When his cockhead replaces his teasing fingers, I melt against him. Sink into the blankets, our limbs entwining as he fucks up into me. We come together as easily as breathing. Our bodies move together like the tide.

I can't tell the distinction between our bodies. Where he ends and I begin. It doesn't matter. We're intertwined in all the ways that do.

Liam grabs my cock and squeezes, his hips smacking against my ass while he fucks me from behind, spooning me in our nest that smells of sex and musk and pack. He groans while he bites me and fucks me harder. Cum splatters all over my stomach. Makes a puddle in the nest, leaving us slippery.

And still I'm hard. My cock doesn't soften. This second release is only the beginning. Hard, consuming need ripples through me. Like all the orgasms that have come before have only been a warmup for *this*.

Gabriel tries to stand and slips back down among the blankets, a giggling mess of uncoordinated limbs. He wiggles his way over, his eyes staring unfocused and his cock bobbing in the air. He brushes against us, sensual ripples of desire washing over me with every point of contact.

I take him into my hand. Feed him into my mouth and suck on his cock like it's dripping ambrosia. His natural scent is strong against my nose, his trimmed patch of hair rubbing against me with every bobbing suck. Masculine and lovely.

His abs tense as I stroke him. Study each dip and curve of his sculpted body.

Kat stirs, recovering, and watches. "Are you guys okay?"

I talk around Gabriel's cock, my words of reassurance muffled and indecipherable. Gabriel babbles in Portuguese. I think he's forgotten he speaks English. Liam does nothing but grunt and moan and groan.

His cock slams deep, his knot blowing inside me. Splaying my asshole open and stuffing me full as he pumps me with cum. Empties his balls into my ass. I cry out, Gabriel's cock slipping from my mouth in time for him to empty too. Cum lashes across my face. Coating me in white ropes of dripping seed.

And still Liam ruts me. Shallow thrusts that use my body to milk his cock. Works his knot in deeper and pulls out far enough to tug at my tight opening before shoving it all back in. Churning up the load of cum he's filled me with until it's frothy.

I lick the salty, musky cum off my lips and collapse, utterly spent and exhausted. Mellow and floating. I draw patterns in the cum dripping down my chin into my chest and giggle. My nipples tighten and my cock pulses with every sensual swirl. Heat blooms everywhere I touch.

When Liam finally pulls free, there's an audible pop. A gush of lube and seed dripping down my thighs, staining our nest. He smacks me on the ass, and shifts over. Tugs Gabriel into position on his hands and knees. No words or gentle commands. Only rough pulls and pushes. The actions of a rutting beast. He mounts the smaller male. An alpha gently asserting dominance over his beta.

I watch, dazed, marveling at the beautiful sight they make when Liam breaches Gabriel's asshole. Works his way inside and fists his hand in Gabriel's hair to make the beta arch his spine. Lift his ass up higher for deeper rutting.

Kat watches, wide-eyed with a lopsided smile on her face. I crawl my way toward her and snuggle into the pillows of her breasts. God, Kat is so perfect. Soft and squishy. Comforting. Does she know how amazing it is to cuddle her? I rub my cheek along her breasts and throat, pleased with the way she giggles.

Her fingers stroke through my hair, catching on tangles and working them free. My eyes roll up into my head. It's bliss. My cock hardens, my hips moving of their own accord. I push my dick between her rounded thighs and suck on her scent gland. I hump her until I come again. Semen making her thighs a sticky mess. Pleasure spasming through my body, somehow working my need higher instead of satisfying it.

Is this really what it's like for them? This infuriating, divine need for pleasure. The fear that it will never be enough? That pleasure might end you? Make your pounding heart burst from your chest from the strain? My mouth goes dry and my cock stiffens again. I whimper from need.

I lose track of how much I come. How many orgasms I have until my balls ache, empty and spent. Our limbs tangle with one another. Cocks probe holes. Liam fills me, again, while I rut into Gabriel. Pulling his hair and biting his neck like he likes it. Digging my short nails into firm, muscled flesh. I become a wild thing. Near feral in my need for *more*.

At some point we sleep, either through exhaustion or the drugs subsiding from our systems. I blink crusty eyes open and try to remember how to breathe. My body aches, but my mind is clear once more. Everything hurts like I've run a marathon and my mouth is dry. I'm parched.

Kat waddles back from the direction of the bathroom. Her hair is wet from the shower and she's wearing a comfy sleep shirt. "Mornin', boys. We have a problem."

Liam is awake in an instant, his sleepy, bleary-eyed smile replaced with unwavering, alpha attention. "What's wrong? Are you okay? Is it the baby?"

"We're fine, but..." She points to the floor-to-ceiling windows and the snowy winter wonderland outside. "It snowed a *lot* more than four inches."

We all pop up and look, the mood changing quickly. Snow drifts have piled high against the windows. At least twenty inches, maybe more. Outside is blanketed in crisp white banks of snow that sparkle like glitter in the sun.

"Shit," I croak, too dehydrated to really speak.

She sighs. "Yeah. After you guys passed out it started coming down fast. Something about a storm cell surge. I don't think we're leaving today."

She's right. We aren't going anywhere. Because we're snowed in.

Chapter Twenty-Four

GABRIEL

Liam writes an email to the owner of the ski chalet. He explains the situation while Matthew goes through the kitchen to make sure we're okay for the next few days. We have no idea how long it will take all that snow to melt.

"The meals might be weird but I can make this work for three or four days," he says. "I'm glad we bought extra groceries."

"Are there any cookies left?" Kat asks, asking the important questions as she joins him in the kitchen.

Matthew shoves the cookie tin inside a cabinet and closes it. "I don't see them. Why don't I make you some eggs?"

She leans against the island counter and rubs her belly with a wince.

"Are you okay?" I ask her.

"I'm fine." She waves me off. "The doctor said they're Braxton Hicks contractions. They go away after a bit if I rest or drink something or change position."

"I'll get you some water," Matthew says, pulling the filtered water pitcher from the fridge. He grabs breakfast supplies too and lays everything out for cooking. Then he pours a glass for her.

Sliding off my stool, I go behind her and reach around her heavy belly. I cradle it with my hands and lift. Take some of its weight off her back while she drinks.

"Oh my God," Kat moans, leaning back into me. She sets her half-drained glass down and places her hands over mine. "That feels so good. Maybe we can just walk around like this for the next three weeks."

"Two and a half," I correct her.

She picks up her glass again to drink the rest. "I can't wait to get this baby out of me."

Matthew pulls a pot off the pot rack and spreads vegetables on the cutting board. "I'll have breakfast ready in half an hour. Why don't you go take a hot bath?"

"Good idea," I agree on her behalf. She's already showered, but the hot bath will help her relax so the false labor pains go away. "I'll fill the tub. Come on."

Kat side-eyes me while we head to the bedroom. "You just want to stare at my boobs."

"Can you blame me? They're spectacular." I run the bath until it's hot and add some scented Epsom salts for her.

Once it's filled, Kat twists her hair up in a clip and I help her in. Her balance is iffy now that she's nearly due. I sit with her while she's soaking, my hand on her knee, while I pull up the local weather app on my phone.

It turns out the reason why we didn't think the storm would be so bad is because we were using the national app that came with our phones. Their prediction didn't take the elevation and wind into account. A bit of searching shows me there's a regional weather company that the residents use. It's supposed to snow off and on until this afternoon and then the sun will come out. Hopefully that'll start melting it enough for us to leave soon.

I tell Kat what I've read and she hums thoughtfully. "Hopefully the roads will be cleared tomorrow. The plow has to come up here at some point, right?"

"Yeah."

Liam joins us, shoving his phone into his back pocket. "I spoke with the owner. The people who were supposed to come after us had their flight canceled because of the storm. We're fine to stay until it's safe to leave. His plow guy will come dig us out once it stops snowing."

"Breakfast is almost done!" Matthew shouts from the kitchen. "Shit. Dammit. Liam, can you help me? The bacon's burning and I need to keep whisking."

Liam rushes out to help. The smell of bacon makes my stomach twist with hunger. After last night, I've earned it. I got a week's worth of cardio in one evening thanks to Matthew's crazy sex pills.

"Come on," I tell Kat, popping the drain up and reaching to help her out. Once she's standing, I wrap her in a fluffy towel and steady her while she steps out of the tub. "Let's stretch your perineum real quick while you're relaxed from the bath."

Kat chuckles darkly and clutches the ends of her towel more tightly. "Oh, no no no. I had enough stretching last night, thanks."

I grab her bottle of almond oil and pour some into my hand, slicking them together and warming it with friction. "We've skipped it all week except for last night. You don't want to tear, right? We'll be quick. And then you can eat and we'll lie down and watch a movie."

"Fine. Only a bit, though. My pelvis is sore from last night." She gives in and sits at the bathroom vanity, propping one leg up for me.

Kneeling at her feet, I massage her with light strokes. Work the oil into her skin and curls, checking that she hasn't torn. We were as gentle as we could be with her last night, as gentle as one can be while shoving three dicks into one vagina. She still sucks in a breath when I start to stretch her walls.

I add more oil, massaging it into her until she relaxes. Then I work my thumbs inside, gently rubbing. Working around clockwise, loosening her pelvic muscles like the obstetrician's diagrams instructed. Adding a third finger and pulling down toward the ground, getting the skin used to being stretched.

"How is that?" I ask her, checking in.

"Good. It's better now."

I work the oil in deeper still, twisting my hand to start on her front wall. My middle finger brushes against her cervix. It's soft and squishy. Thin, and slightly open. I stop, my back stiffening. It's not… I check her again to make sure I'm not wrong.

She's four centimeters dilated. A week ago, her cervix was closed.

I don't want to say anything. Don't want to panic her or the others. Some women are dilated for days, even weeks. It doesn't mean she's in labor. Still, it worries me. But she's not due for two almost three more weeks. Most first-time mothers go over rather than under. It's second babies that arrive earlier than planned. But what if her contractions aren't false labor?

I can't say anything until I'm sure.

"Did the contractions go away?" I ask, careful to keep my voice sounding normal.

"It's better after the bath, thanks."

That's not a yes. But I can't pry and arouse suspicion. The last thing I need is everyone getting anxious and panicking. The road will be clear tomorrow. Some women have early labor for days before going into active labor. It's probably fine.

Pulling my hand free, I wipe the excess oil off her and my

hand with the edge of her towel and stand. I bend down and kiss her gently. "All done."

She gives me a sunny smile and puts her comfy night clothes back on. By the time we return to the kitchen, Matthew has everything plated. We eat, devouring his bacon and eggs. I don't understand how he gets his omelets so fluffy.

"What now?" Kat asks, looking out the kitchen windows. A light snow falls onto the already tall drifts of snow that cling to the glass.

She needs to stay off her feet. Gravity and movement will only speed up early labor. "Movie marathon?"

Her eyes light up and she claps her hands. "Yes! I know it's past Christmas now but I want to watch all the sappy Hallmark Christmas movies I didn't see yet."

Liam kisses the top of her head and stacks our dirty plates together. "You got it, kitten."

We cuddle up on the couch and I queue up an entire day's worth of formulaic romance movies for her. Liam kicks Matthew out of the kitchen to do the dishes and he joins us on the couch. I lay snuggled up with her with my hand on the belly, pretending I'm feeling for kicks when really, if she's having contractions, I won't miss them.

We're twelve minutes into the first movie when I notice it. A tightening of her abdomen. Her belly lifts and firms underneath my hand.

I use my bent knee to hide my actions as I discreetly set the stopwatch on my phone. Not that Kat is paying attention to me. She's currently crying over the heroine's troubled bakery business. The one she started after her parents were killed in an accident. The love interest is the EMT who tried to save them, but she doesn't see that yet. She thinks he's addicted to her Christmas wreath shaped donuts. But he doesn't even eat them. He's diabetic so he gives them to his partner. He likes the heroine, but he's worried that she could never like him because of what happened… and now his EMT partner thinks he has a crush on her because of the stupid donuts. It turns into a three-way love triangle full of idiots who won't talk to one another.

When the stopwatch rolls past the five-minute mark, I relax a bit. Irregular, far apart contractions are the body's way of preparing itself for birth. Satisfied that it's nothing and grateful that I didn't alarm anyone yet, I kiss Kat's tear-streaked cheek and slide off the couch.

"I'm gonna get a workout in," I tell them, heading to the basement. I saw jump ropes in a kid's toy box down there and I'm itching to get in a real workout. It's been days of good food, treats, and family obligations with no real exercise other than a few short hikes and the one day some of us went skiing.

Once I'm covered in a sheen of sweat, I head upstairs to shower and change before lunch.

A different movie plays in the background now. Matthew's in the kitchen working on lunch. Liam and Kat are making out on the couch. He has one hand on her breast, massaging it gently through her shirt, and I can't tell where his other one is with the blanket in the way.

Shit.

Until I am absolutely certain that she's not in early labor, she needs to stay on pelvic rest. But how the fuck do I get them to stop fooling around with her without alarming them?

Matthew opens a cupboard and pulls out the bread. An idea pops into my head. While he's busy making sandwiches with breakfast's leftover bacon and some turkey we bought for the kids, I pull the cookie tin down and pop off its metal lid.

"Oh! There's a few cookies left. Want one, Kat?" I call out.

Kat pulls away from Liam, her face lighting up. "Really? Help me off the couch, Liam."

Matthew gives me an expression that says he's not happy

that I'm feeding her sweets before she's eating something nutritious. He takes her diet seriously. Kat waddles into the kitchen and takes the cookie from my hand, smiling at me in return as she bites the yellow star off the tree. Liam drops his head onto the couch and groans, as if being cockblocked physically pains him.

Big baby. He'll get over it.

"Don't eat too many before lunch," I tell her, kissing her forehead.

"It's Christmas and I'm pregnant," she says, defending her right to eat the rest of the cookies in the tin. There aren't many left. Only four, including the one in her hand. And I'm not wrestling a cookie out of a pregnant woman's hand. That's the surest way to lose a finger.

"Lunch is almost done," Matthew reminds us.

I help him plate everything. We eat and clean up, then go back to our movie marathon. By the third movie, my certainty that it's false labor is waning. Her contractions are more regular. I need to check Kat again. There'll be no hiding this for much longer if my concerns are real.

After washing my hands and fetching her oil, I convince her to let me massage her again. She's used to our fussing. We've all gotten a bit over the top with coddling her since she hit the last month and her belly really popped.

With my oil slicked hand, I massage her and check her cervix. Six centimeters. Her cervix is soft and thinning. She's progressing. It's only been five hours.

Dread pools in my belly. She'll notice soon. It's a miracle she hasn't figured it out sooner. Everything is going to get very real, very fast. And we're trapped up here, snowed in on a mountain, with the nearest hospital miles away. A strange, unfamiliar hospital with doctors we haven't met rather than the nice birthing center full of midwives that's half a mile from my hospital. The one with the second best NICU in the state.

Liam's gaze drifts from the movie to us. He squeezes his arm around her shoulder. "Do you need help with your massage, kitten?" he asks, his voice husky.

"No," I answer for her.

He gives me a confused expression.

I clear my throat and tug the hem of her night shirt down her thighs. "She's all done." I glance at Liam, then make a subtle nod toward the kitchen. His brow creases with a frown, but he makes an excuse to leave the couch.

On my way past Matthew's spot on the oversized sofa, I squeeze his shoulder and jerk my head toward the kitchen.

They meet me there. I run the faucet for noise control in case she can hear us over her movie.

"What's wrong?" Liam whispers.

There's no gentle way to ease them into the situation. "Kat's in the early stages of labor."

Liam's face pales, and Matthew's eyes get big. "What?" Liam says, a little too loud.

I make a face and mouth for him to lower his voice. She doesn't realize it yet, and there's no sense in panicking her before we've made a plan for how to deal with it.

"We still have some time, but it's happening," I tell them.

"What? How? It's too early," Matthew says.

I shrug. "Babies arrive when they want to. Ours wants to be early. I've been reading my old textbooks in case this happens. I never thought it would, but… well, here we are."

"Fuck," Liam curses. "The snow's still piled high. It's over halfway up the door. And the road…"

"What are we gonna do?" Matthew asks, looking to me for the plan. Because Liam is the alpha, but I'm the medical professional. In this awful scenario, I'm the one in charge.

"Boil as much water as you can and let it cool while covered," I instruct. "We need to clean towels and blankets. Wash them in hot water with a cup of vinegar, set an extra rinse, and dry them on the hottest setting. I saw a first aid kit in the bathroom but it probably won't be very helpful."

Liam's face hardens with determination. "I'm gonna clear the snow."

It's hours worth of shoveling. Even if he clears the path to the car, he still won't be able to make it out of the driveway. Not unless he stumbles across a plow attachment and figures out how to hook it up to his truck. But if it keeps him busy so he doesn't panic, then that's what we need. We all have our roles to play now.

"Are you guys making popcorn?" Kat yells from the living room.

Matthew looks at me for direction.

I nod. We need to keep her busy and calm.

"Yeah!" he yells back, going to the cabinet to grab the tinfoil stovetop popcorn the kids didn't eat. Matthew puts the popcorn on the stove, then takes down all of the pots he can find. He fills all of them with the filtered water from the fridge and turns on all four burners.

Liam leaves to change into his winter gear, pulling his boots on and zipping up his parka. He slips his hands into ski gloves.

"Where are you going?" Kat asks from the sofa.

He leans over the back and kisses her upside down. "I'm going to get a jump start on clearing the snow for tomorrow."

"Okay." She watches him leave, then glances at us. Matthew and I do our best to appear nonchalant and busy. The first popcorn kernel pops, startling the both of us. Once it's done popping, Matthew dumps the hot kernels into a large bowl and brings it to her along with a drink.

I settle next to her and pull her feet into my lap for a foot rub. We need her as calm as possible. An hour later, she drifts asleep only to be jolted awake a few minutes after with a grimace. My heart knocks against my ribs.

"Everything okay?" I ask her.

"I've gotta pee." She scrambles off the couch. Or tries to. I grasp her hands and pull her off the couch.

"Oh no," she says, going still. Her face flushes pink. Wetness drips down her thighs, splattering onto the rug and making a dark spot. "Wait, I still have to pee."

Shit. Her water broke. Swallowing, I cup her elbow and walk her to our bathroom.

"That's embarrassing," she grumbles.

"How do you feel?" I ask her.

She gives me an odd look when I help her onto the toilet and stay hovering. "Why does everyone keep asking me that today?"

There's no easy way to rip off this bandage. "Are you still having contractions?"

She thinks about it while she pees. "Off and on. They've gotten worse since I'm closer to the end. I thought resting would help, but maybe I need to walk around. I wish they'd go away."

"Well… they will. Sooner rather than later." I can't keep stalling. "You're in labor."

She blinks at me, then furrows her brow. "What? It's too early. And I think I'd know if I were in labor. Doesn't it hurt like hell?"

I shrug. "It's different for everyone. Pushing will hurt. But early labor isn't always that bad. We need to start timing your contractions."

I see the moment reality sets in for her and she realizes exactly what position we're in. "I can't be. It's too early. The birthing center… They said first-time moms usually go over their due date."

It's a helpless thing to stand here with no answers that will satisfy her. "Babies come when they come."

"I can't have the baby here," she argues, getting shrill. "Not now. Not like this. I don't know any of the doctors at the hospital here. If we can even get to a hospital. Oh, God."

"If you're done going to the bathroom, let's get you to bed."

"No." Her face creases with worry. "I want to go back to the couch."

She needs time to accept this is real and not going away. Kat cleans herself up and I walk her back to the living room. Matthew goes by with a mountain of sheets and towels nearly blocking his view. I snag one for her to lie on and lower her down onto the couch into her impromptu nest.

"Where's Liam? Does he know?" she asks.

"He's digging the truck out."

She whines and pulls the blankets closer, shoving them around her and getting comfortable. "That's not going to help if the roads are undrivable." She winces, and I cradle her belly. It's tight, raised, and firm with a contraction.

There's no need to be discreet anymore. I set the stopwatch and time her contraction while we both pretend to watch the latest holiday movie. Her contraction lasts less than a minute. I clear the time and reset it. It's five minutes and forty seconds until the next one. The movie distracts her while I keep time.

The side door off the kitchen opens and Liam bursts inside, stomping to shake the snow off his boots. "It's stopped snowing, but I don't see any sign of the plow yet. It might be a while before they get this far up the mountain. But I got the truck out."

"Be right back," I tell Kat.

Liam watches me approach him with trepidation. He bows

his head so he can hear me while I tell him everything in a low, calm voice.

"Her water broke," I say.

"Does that mean it'll be soon?" he asks, his expression grim.

"Hard to say. That depends on her and how quickly she progresses. But her contractions aren't too close together, so that's good. Could be tonight or early tomorrow."

Liam lets out a low growl and runs his fingers through his hair. "I don't like this. She should be in a hospital."

"I don't like it either, but it's not like we have much choice."

"I called for an ambulance," Liam says. "They said there's no way up the mountain until it's plowed. They called the city to have a plow sent from the highway department but I don't know when they'll get here. They said they'll come as quickly as they can."

The news is disappointing, but not unexpected. Ambulances are big and heavy, but there's not much that any vehicle can do against two feet of snow. "What about a helicopter?"

His face pales. "You think it's that dire?"

I shrug. "It doesn't hurt to ask."

Liam nods, grateful to have a task again. "I'll call them again."

"Out of earshot," I order. We don't need Kat getting more alarmed than she already is.

Liam shrugs out of his coat and boots and goes over to Kat, kissing her in greeting. He tells her he's going to take a hot shower to warm up.

What else? I think, looking around. If there's no way out, then we need to be prepared to deliver here. I raid the cabinets to see what we have. A bottle of vodka can help with disinfection. We can use hot towels from the dryer to keep the baby warm. Matthew boiled water and it's cooling now. We have sanitized towels and blankets to clean her. But there are a few more things we'll need. I rummage through drawers to search for anything useful and start making a pile. Trash bags, kitchen twine, and newspaper.

I raid the first aid kit next. There are bandage scissors and a bottle of rubbing alcohol. Sterile gauze and an oral syringe I can use to clean the baby's airway since we don't have a bulb syringe. It's not enough but it'll have to be.

I bundle everything onto the kitchen table and clean the scissors. Then I bring Kat a glass of water and remind her to stay hydrated.

When Liam returns, his grim expression tells me there's no helicopter coming. Not with the sun setting outside and the thick trees and deep snow. There's no good place for them to land. It was a longshot to begin with.

Matthew comes upstairs from the basement where the laundry machines are. "Any update?"

It's been an hour or two. Time to check her again. I wash up at the kitchen sink, scrubbing well, then go to Kat.

I kneel at her feet. "I need to check you, *meu docinho.*" I rub her massage oil over my hands and feel inside. Seven centimeters and thinner. She'll be in active labor soon. My hand comes away streaked with pink. The towel under her has a damp spot. She's still leaking fluid. I wipe my hand clean and fold the towel over itself before she can notice.

"Good job," I tell her.

Liam's phone rings and we all startle. I kiss her knee and follow him and Matthew outside.

Fuck, it's cold. I tuck my arms into my armpits and wait impatiently while he talks to whoever called him.

"I see. Thank you. Thank you so much. No, it's fine. I'll meet you there and guide them."

Meet them? How the hell is Liam going to meet them?

He hangs up and puts his phone away. "They got a plow and he's started working on the road, but the GPS is giving them weird directions. They don't see where the turnoff is for this private road."

We got lost when we first arrived too. The sign is small and easy to miss. If it's buried under a snow laden branch in the dark, they'll never find it.

"I'm going to meet them out there and lead them up to the house," Liam says.

"That's dangerous," Matthew says. "It's getting dark. It'll be pitch black soon, and you don't know the roads that well. Your truck will never make it, even with chains on the tires."

But Liam won't be swayed. "It's our best shot and you both know it. We need to do something. Now."

"How?" I ask.

He is full of determination when he says, "I'm taking the snowmobile."

Chapter Twenty-Five

LIAM

THE WIND IS BITING COLD, AND DEEP SHADOWS MAKE THE forest ominous. Snow drifts grow by the minute as a blanket of fresh snow settles over everything. The noise of the snowmobile shatters the quiet. Its weak amber lights make the snow banks glitter.

The wind blows and snowflakes land on me, melting into my skin and parka. I blink, wishing I had thought to grab ski goggles. And a snow jacket meant for adventuring, not a parka meant for commuting. Any of the ski gear, really. But I was too panicked, too focused on getting my mate help to take the moment to think.

An overloaded tree branch drops a clump of snow on me as I drive past. I flinch as some of it finds its way into my collar. Shivering, I tighten my grip on the throttle and keep going. There's no turning back. No giving into failure. My omega needs me, and I'm her alpha. It's my fault we're in this mess. My insistence that family tradition had to be upheld. My agreement that we could stay an extra day. That staying up in this mountain would be fine, so close to her due date.

If Kat and the baby get hurt because of this, I will never

forgive myself. If they die... *No. I can't think like that.* I won't let it happen. Everyone is depending on me, and failure isn't an option. Not when we're so close to having everything we've always wanted.

Thick drifts of snow make the snowmobile bob and dip in a stomach churning wave of motion. Navigating through the trees makes the trek difficult. I lost the road at some point, my brief familiarity with the area growing fainter by the moment. The trees are too close together for me to be on the road.

Nothing looks like I remember. Not with over two feet of snow obscuring everything. The thick white snow clinging to the evergreen trees would be pretty if I weren't terrified for all of us right now.

A jutting fallen branch and snow-covered rock make me dodge at the last minute and the snowmobile catches on a drift of snow. Rocking the machine and revving the engine does nothing. I'm stuck.

Fuck. Not again. I stand, thighs burning, and lean every which way until finally the machine gets unstuck and lurches into motion. Snow churns up as the machine's skis carve a path. It creeps its way into the edge of my boots as I drive the snowmobile to the right and maneuver around the bend in the drift.

Bringing the machine to a stop, I hold the camping lantern up and peer into the dark. The ground slopes down on my left, the snow pristine. Behind me, my path makes lines in the snow.

I need to find the road again. Try to navigate down the mountain without driving off it. The wind picks up, blowing snow around. I brush the worst of it off the machine so it'll stop dumping more of it into my lap.

Maybe I should turn around. Backtrack and follow my trail. How long has it been since I left the road? It can't be more than a few minutes, but when everything looks the same, it's impossible to tell. The forest is too dense and the neighbors are too far away to look for house lights in the distance to guide me.

Decision made, I turn the snowmobile around and follow the path I've made. The machine struggles to go uphill, nearly stalling on a buried rock or branch. Getting it out sends me right into the path of a tree.

The ground gives way, and my eyes widen as I lose control. The heavy snowmobile makes the snow covering the tree well collapse. Low branches slap at me as I brace for the impact and try to not be impaled. Something wet trickles down the side of my face. Breathing hard, I cut the engine and wipe my face. My glove comes away red with blood where a branch scratched me.

That was close. Way too close. I could have been blinded or killed. Broken my arm or leg. And now the snowmobile is stuck, wedged into a snow trap that forms when thick, loose snow makes an unstable ring around a tree with low branches.

If the snow were deeper, I might be dead now. Skiers get trapped in wells, the snow collapsing on top of them once they've broken through. If I'd been thrown and hit my head…

But I didn't. And now I need to get out. And somehow I have to get the snowmobile out too. I'll never make it on foot.

A couple of branches are what's keeping me from riding out of this tree well. I grab the thickest one and lean back on my seat, kicking my foot up to brace against it for leverage. It bends and bends until my muscles strain, my arms and back aching with the effort. Finally, it breaks with a loud crack. I nearly fall off the snow machine into the snow as the branch hangs limp.

One down, two more to go. I channel all of my rage and fear into escaping. Into breaking the branches holding me pinned. If I had an ax, a saw, a knife, anything, this would be easier. But I have nothing. Nothing but my two hands and determination driven by my threatened pregnant mate.

I grit my teeth and growl as I pull on the next branch while kicking it. My boot slips off, so I try again. Putting everything I have into it. It breaks off and I toss it aside, then reach for the final one. There's something primal and satisfying about ripping a tree apart with your own two hands.

Settling back into my seat, I angle the snowmobile and rev the engine, leaning forward to guide it up the edge of the snow well. It rocks and churns, trying and failing to move up and out. Falling snow pelts my face, my mouth, my lap. I shake it off and clamp down my gritted teeth and rock.

The engine sputters like it's threatening to die.

"Come on, you bastard," I growl, pulling the throttle and throwing myself forward. The machine hesitates for a moment, then lurches. It chews its way out of the snow well and I let out a loud whoop of delight as, once more, I'm underway.

My fresh tracks look old. That's how much snow has fallen. I'm not sure when it picked up again, but it's practically a blizzard. I can barely see anything but the falling snowflakes illuminated by the snowmobile's light and my lantern.

The engine rumbles underneath me and I worry about a slipped belt or some other mechanical failure that could leave me stranded. Leave me out here and my mates up at the house, isolated and afraid.

I pat the machine and wipe more snow off it. "You can do it. You hear me? Because we can't fail." I don't know if I'm talking to it or me. Probably both.

Following my old trail and backtracking takes ages. The snow tracks look old. As if they were made hours ago instead of minutes. The wind blows the snow into my face until it feels like stinging little daggers. I squint against the onslaught, but press on, following my old winding tracks through the wind-changed drifts. The battle uphill is rougher. The snowmobile's rumbles get rougher, and I will it to keep going. To not die on me and leave me out here alone and lost to freeze to death.

Am I taking too long? Will the ambulance still be there? Or have they given up and gone home to warm beds to try again tomorrow? There's no way to call them. To reassure them, I'm still coming. All I can do is keep trying, and hope, and pray. So that's what I do.

Dear God, don't let me be too late. I know I haven't been a very good Catholic. I don't go to mass or confession as often as I should. But if you see me through this, things will change. Please guide me. Give me the strength to keep going. Don't let this all be too late, or for nothing. Please save my omega. Please save my baby. I'll do anything you want. I'll go to mass. Go to confession. I'll read that damn book. Just give me a sign. Guide me. Please.

A scream in the woods makes me flinch and slow down. My heart pounds in my chest and adrenaline floods my system. *Was that a woman screaming?* My eyes dart around, looking for its source. *What the fuck was that?* Every nerve in my body is alight, and the hair stands up on the back of my neck. Fear makes me think it's Kat. That I'm closer to the house than I thought. Reality tells me it could be a bobcat or mountain lion. Mountain lions are rare up here, but sometimes there are sightings. This mountain is wooded enough. Would I even know if I was being hunted? Would some primal, hidden sense alert me? I scan the tree line for the flash of two reflective eyes and hold my breath.

A flash of movement in the distance makes me flinch. The creature screams again and peers out through its perch in the knot of a tree. An owl?

It should be hunkered down, warm and dry. Not perched at the edge of its nest and making noise. Not during a snowstorm.

There's no easy hunting in a storm. Better to wait it out when the hunt for food isn't so cold and wet.

The white and gray owl takes flight, and I only hesitate for a moment. What if this is the sign I prayed for? It flies off, moving away from my tracks. Nearly disappearing in the white out between snow-laden trees. My light only penetrates so far in the dark woods. I only have a second to decide. To choose between backtracking along my old paths or to press on toward pristine snow, following it.

It screams again; the sound echoing. And I make my choice. I rev the engine and take off, following it. Barely watching where I'm going as I try to keep it in sight. I avoid the trees, navigating between them and keeping my distance so I don't get stuck in another tree well.

Instinct tells me that if I get stuck again, I won't get out so easily next time. It's a strange thing, relying on instinct instead of reason. Navigating through nature. I'm a pub owner. I'm not the sort of alpha who likes to go on days' long hunting trips and sleep rough and reconnect with my roots. With my buried, irrelevant instincts.

The owl veers to the left, flying uphill, and my snowmobile cuts through the snow like its butter. It takes the steep incline fast and smooth. Hope buoys me for the first time since I made this crazy decision to come out here and lead the ambulance and plow. Made the crazier decision to follow a damn bird like it's a burning bush.

My snowmobile levels out, and I notice this stretch of snow is treeless. Is this the road? Did I cut across and find it again? I glance around, squinting to keep snowflakes out of my eyes as I hold up my lantern and peer through the dark.

There, down the incline, are my old tracks. There's a crack, loud and harrowing. A tree breaks under the weight of the snow. It must be rotted because it splinters apart and falls. It lands across my old tracks, sending snow flying from its branches and a rough landing.

Icy dread grips me. If I hadn't followed that owl, I could have been pinned under that. I would have been. Something deep inside me knows it to be the truth. In another lifetime, because of another decision, I could be dead or dying right now.

Follow the road, I remind myself. There's no time for dwelling on the fears of what might have been or could be still. Not when my family needs me. *Pull yourself together.*

The owl is gone, lost in the winter storm. Maybe returned, safe and sound, to its nest. Up is the house. Somehow, I know it. As if my instincts recognise something of this landscape. It's time to listen to that unflexed part of me. To let my alpha nature take over and guide me.

My thighs are numb from having snow dumped in my lap. My face burns with each harsh slap of the wind. Snowflakes coat the hair on my face and cling to my eyelashes and brow.

Ignoring the discomfort of my body, I press on. There's no stopping now. Not when I've found the road again. I'm close. I can feel it somehow.

Angling the snowmobile down, I pay attention to the trees. I follow the wide, barren path as it winds and curves. Until I see lights bouncing off trees. Amber and red and moving. The lights scatter across the unblemished snow. There's a deeper rumble that's not my snowmobile. A clanging metallic scrape and drag.

When I round a bend, I see them. They've gone past the turnoff, the ambulance waiting as the plow scrapes snow off the winding mountain road. The snow machine whips forward through the plowed area that's already filling with snow again.

I come up to where they can see me and let the engine idle. I stand, holding my lantern in the air, and wave it until they notice me.

"Hey!" I shout, trying to get their attention.

The ambulance driver sees me and backs up his rig. He rolls down his window and pokes his head out. "Are you the alpha that called us?"

"I am." I gesture behind me. "This is the turnoff. The house is up ahead about a quarter-mile."

"You drove out in this storm on *that*?" the driver asks. "You could have died."

I know. But I didn't. And there was no choice, not really. I'm the alpha and it's my job to protect my pack. It's the one thing I want more than anything in the world. To sit by the fire and hear Matthew read another of his favorite books out loud. To slow dance with Gabriel, when one of our songs comes on. To hold Kat in my arms again and feel our baby kick my palm. I want it all so badly, my chest aches like my heart's frozen solid.

I sit back down on the snowmobile and settle the lantern in my lap again. "I'll lead you guys up there. Call the plow and tell them to come back."

Then I turn around and lead them up the turnoff to the house.

I'll have to settle up with God tomorrow. But right now I have to get them to my pack.

Chapter Twenty-Six

KAT

"This is bullshit," I groan, my teeth gritted. The contraction makes me pant. When I'm able to breathe at all, that is. They come together quicker and last longer each time, my entire abdomen tensing.

"Do you want to lie down?" Matthew asks, hovering.

"No!" I wave them both away and lean on the marble counter. We've moved the nest into the kitchen for easier cleanup. Childbirth is messy.

"It says that walking, moving, and dancing can all help the baby move into position," Gabriel says, looking at his phone.

"What are you reading?" I ask him, frowning. The contraction passes and I suck in a deep gulp of air. I only have three or four minutes of sanity till the next one.

Gabriel shows me his phone. He's watching a video about childbirth. "Look. She's dancing between contractions to move the baby into place."

"You're gonna deliver our baby with a YouTube video?" I ask him, horrified.

"I *am* a medical professional," Gabriel reminds me. "And I

read my old obstetrics textbook from PA school. But this video has tips and tricks."

Tips and tricks.

Matthew and I share a knowing look.

Where the fuck is Liam?

I glance outside the kitchen window. We've turned every single light on in the house so that it's nice and bright. So that maybe if Liam gets lost, he can find his way back to us. It started snowing lightly again a half-hour ago. The wind blows snowflakes around, obscuring the view. How well can he see? The woods are dark. All he has is the light on the snowmobile.

I hate the idea of him out there. Alone in the dark. Maybe lost in an unfamiliar wood covered in snow. The landmarks we've come to know over the past few days have been obscured by snow and shadows. Only a small, weak light to guide him. What if he drives off the side of the mountain?

"He should be here," I whine. I bend over the counter and press my sweaty face against the cool stone.

"I know," Matthew says, rubbing my shoulders. "He'll be back soon."

Another contraction hits me. I lean against Matthew for support and press a hand to my hard, tight abdomen.

"Three minutes apart," Gabriel says. "Kat, I need to check you to see how you're progressing."

I'm dreading what he'll find. Part of me wants to pretend this isn't happening. But I know I can't.

They help me down into my shitty nest on the kitchen floor. Matthew supports my back by sitting behind me while Gabriel washes his hands again and checks the baby's progress.

"You're fully dilated," Gabriel says. "There's the head."

"He needs to be here," I groan.

Matthew moves his hands up and down my arms, soothing

me. "I know, honey. He'll come back soon with the ambulance. Then we're gonna get you to the hospital."

It'll be too late by then.

The next contraction comes with the vague urge to push. I grit my teeth and breathe through the discomfort. I need to move. Need to find a better position or get on my knees or… God, I don't know. I don't know what I want, and nothing is helping. Something is different now. Instinct tells me we're out of time.

"We're not making it to the hospital," I say through clenched teeth. "The baby's coming. Right now."

"Remember your breathing exercise we've practiced," Gabriel reminds me.

"Help me kneel," I tell them.

We shift into a weird but comfortable position where Matthew sits in a chair and supports my upper body while I kneel in the nest and rock. It eases my back pain. Gabriel gets his stash of supplies ready, moving everything into reach. When the next contraction hits me, I cry out and cling to Matthew.

"There were supposed to be drugs!" I complain loudly.

Matthew uses a damp cloth to wipe the sweat from my forehead and rakes the damp strands out of my face as I labor. "You can do this. You're doing such a good job, Kat."

"Push when you have the urge," Gabriel says.

Tears prick my eyes. "I can't. I'm too tired." But the urge can't be ignored. It comes with the next contraction. The need to push is all-consuming, but my efforts seem weak and ineffective.

I try. Again and again. Until I'm screaming and my voice is hoarse.

"If you push, labor stops and you get a baby," Gabriel says.

I'll do anything to make it stop at this point. This wasn't how it was supposed to go. I was supposed to have a warm tub to labor in. A giant inflated ball for positioning. A calm birthing suite full of friendly staff to help us. Drugs shoved into my *fucking* spine.

A stronger contraction hits me along with a burning sensation, like someone's doused my vagina in flames. I let out a bloodcurdling scream through clamped jaws.

"Push!" Gabriel yells at me.

I'm trying. But there's nothing about this that's easy. My face heats from the strain, and tears collect at the corners of my eyes.

"I can't," I groan, my concentration slipping.

"Yes, you can," Gabriel says. "You've got this, Kat."

The urge to push wanes, and I get a minute or two to recover and breathe before the next one comes. I lift higher on my knees, resting my cheek on Matthew's leg as he gathers my sweaty hair up from where it's slipped out of its bun. The next contraction and urge to push is brutal. I can't scream or moan or yell. The searing pain and sense of fullness, stretched to my body's limits, muzzles me. My body shakes. And I push. Until my pelvis is a ring of fire. It's an agony the likes of which I've never known before.

"Push!" Gabriel orders.

I need this to be over so I push. And then there's relief. So welcome, I sob.

"I have the head. Push, Kat. One more and you're done."

One more. I can do it. But I'm so fucking tired. Giving birth is awful without drugs. How do people do this?

I push again and the baby slips free. The worst of the pain fades with her birth.

"I have her," Gabriel says.

Sagging with relief, I sit on my heels and twist. She should be crying, shouldn't she? Why isn't she crying?

Gabriel wraps her in the blankets we've been keeping warm

in a pile on the edge of the nest. He rubs her briskly, and then I hear it. She cries, and tears of relief roll down my cheeks.

"Give her to me," I sob. I need to hold her. To make sure she's warm enough and safe.

"Lie back," Gabriel says. "And I'll hand her to you. We still have to finish up here."

Matthew helps me recline on pillows and Gabriel hands me our daughter while he deals with the aftermath of birth. I barely notice the lingering cramps and contractions while he works. I'm too busy staring at our baby to care. She squints and frowns, as if the bright lights offend her. I stroke her cheek and marvel at our daughter.

She's perfect. My heart swells with a love so pure it floors me. I'm swamped with emotion and crying, which makes me laugh from the sheer relief of it finally being over. I'm delirious and completely overwhelmed.

"Hi," I greet her. "You caused a lot of fuss, little girl."

She works a hand free of her towel and I grab it, rubbing it with my thumb. Five tiny fingers with tinier fingernails. She's chubby and perfect despite coming early. Her dusky coloring turns pinker with every cry.

Matthew wets a washcloth and wipes her down. She hollers at the injustice of being cold and wet and exposed to air. "She's so tiny," he says, his tone reverent as he palms her head.

I lay her skin to skin on my chest, then cover her with the towel so she doesn't get cold. "She didn't seem all that small while she was coming out of me."

"I've got the cord clamped," Gabriel says, wrapping the placenta in a towel and cleaning up the mess. "Want to cut it?" he asks Matthew and hands him the scissors.

"Where?" Matthew asks.

Gabriel shows him where to cut between the two pieces of kitchen twine he's wrapped tightly several times and knotted. I wish Liam were here with us for this. I hope he makes it back to us soon.

Matthew cuts the cord, and once Gabriel says everything looks good, they start cleaning the both of us up.

Our daughter hates her warm bath, but once she's placed on my chest again she settles down a bit. She ends up tucked into herself on her front, her little arms and legs pulled into her sides.

"You should feed her," Gabriel suggests, petting her wispy hair that swirls from the top of her head. "It'll help stop the bleeding."

"Okay, I'll try." The sound of her crying has made my breasts leak. I reposition her and lift a nipple to her mouth. She latches on, suckling weakly, then gaining confidence.

Gabriel lays new towels down and presses on my abdomen. I'm cramping again. But it's hard to care about the pain with our perfect baby girl in my arms. Matthew strokes her head and marvels at the shape of her tiny ear. Gabriel pauses in his work to stroke her back and adjust her covering.

The sound of metal scraping outside distracts me from her breastfeeding. My pulse leaps and I watch the back door, waiting. Where is he? If that's the plow, then why isn't he here? If something happened to Liam, I will never get over it. The scraping gets louder. Closer.

When the back door bursts open and I see Liam standing there in the open doorway, I burst into tears. He falls to his knees in our nest and stares, breathing heavily. His face is red and wind-chapped. His coat is covered in rapidly melting snow.

"You did it," he says, his eyes wide.

"We did," I say. "She's perfect."

He reaches for her, then notices he's still wearing gloves. Liam pulls his glove off and lays his palm on her head.

She lets go of my nipple and cries.

Liam jerks his hand away. "What'd I do?"

I laugh and take his hand, noticing how cold it is. He was out there for hours. "You're cold, she doesn't like that."

"Five minutes old and already bossing me around," he says with a grin. "She's gonna be a menace."

She is. Our little rebel princess. Coming early and defying all our plans for her. Nothing about her conception or our courtship was normal. Why would her birth be any different? We don't have anything she needs here with us. No diapers or wipes or clothing for her. No car seat either.

"Good job, Momma," Liam says, dipping his head so his forehead brushes with mine. Gabriel and Matthew touch me too. A hand on my leg and another on my shoulder. I'm surrounded by my pack and it's exactly what I needed.

Liam purrs, and our baby yawns, looking around with unfocused eyes and a frown on her adorable face. Now that she's eaten and warm, she's calm.

There's a knock on the door that jolts us all from our tender moment. Liam goes to answer it, letting two female EMTs inside. One of them talks into the radio clipped over her shoulder, "We're on the scene. I'll grab the OB kit and the stretcher."

The other one approaches us and kneels. "Seems like we're late to the party. Hey, Momma. Is this your first baby?" she asks.

"Yes," Gabriel answers for me. "She was thirty-seven and a half weeks. No allergies or significant medical history. She delivered the placenta intact and her bleeding's slowed. She's fed the baby once."

"All right," the EMT says. She's older and a beta from the smell of her. "So even though this was a good delivery, we need to get you two to the hospital to get checked out."

She reaches for the corner of the towel to check on the baby and a low growl bursts from my chest on instinct. My eyes widen and I choke the sound off, embarrassed. "I'm so sorry." The baby, startled, begins to cry.

"It's perfectly natural," she says, unflinching as she checks the baby out. "She's nice and pink, and those are some good, healthy lungs. Here's what we're gonna do, Momma. We're going to take the baby out to the truck and then we're gonna bring you out on the stretcher."

"I'll take the baby," the other EMT says after she returns with her kit.

It's hard to hand over my daughter. All of my instincts tell me to keep her close and safe even though I know these emergency responders aren't going to hurt us. I let them take her and watch her go.

"Let's do blow-by until we get a sat," one EMT says to the other. "Get a set of vitals. Bill can hold her and do the oxygen while we get Mom in the rig."

They're only gone for a few minutes, but it seems like an eternity until they come back inside. I'm transferred onto their stretcher and Matthew makes sure I'm covered with blankets. Then they strap me in and roll me outside through the path Liam cut into the snow hours before. The ambulance's lights flash quietly, cutting through the darkness.

"We can fit one person," an EMT says.

"Gabriel," Liam says. "Go with them."

Gabriel grabs his coat and shoves his feet into his boots, running after us and leaving Matthew and Liam to follow behind in the truck. After they load me into the ambulance, Gabriel hops in too and sits where they tell him to. They attach me to monitors and start an IV. Then they announce our departure to the hospital over their radio.

"Can she hold the baby while you drive?" Gabriel asks once we're on the way.

"Here you go, Momma." She hands our daughter to me and

sits the back of my stretcher up a bit. "Now if you haven't settled on a name yet, what about Lori?"

"Or Olivia," the other one says with a smile.

"What's the female version of Bill?" the driver asks from the front.

They laugh and bicker light heartedly. Each of them throwing out variations of their names that are more outlandish than the next as they try to come up with the best first and middle name combinations.

Gabriel holds my hand while we both stare at our little Christmas angel. "No, that's not her name."

Her name is Holly.

Jen holds Holly while the baby sleeps after a feeding. "I can't believe you went and had the baby without anyone knowing."

I chuckle. "It's not like we planned it."

She sighs and hands my daughter back to me. "Ugh. You're making me want another one. She's stinking cute."

I fix Holly's pink hat and move her to the crook of my arm, using a pillow to prop her up so I can watch her sleep. "She's kind of perfect, isn't she?"

Someone knocks and Matthew opens the door, checking first to make sure I'm not nursing before he opens it wide for the influx of our family. The hospital kept us for a few nights, but since we both have a clean bill of health and Holly's feeding well they're discharging us this afternoon. That didn't stop everyone from driving up to see us, though.

"Let me see my granddaughter," Liam's mom whispers,

leaning over my bed and smiling. One by one, everyone gets a peek and coos over how sweet she is. I'm not sure we can fit anymore people into this hospital room. It's a good thing that Gabriel's family doesn't arrive from Brazil until tomorrow.

"What's her name?" Margaret asks.

"Holly," Matthew answers his mother proudly.

We waited until she was born to pick a name. Holly wasn't on our list of potential names at all, but it fits her.

When the baby wakes up from her nap and starts to fuss, everyone heads out to get a cup of coffee from the cafeteria while I nurse her. Liam, Matthew, and Gabriel crowd around and watch, talking about what's left on their to-do list.

"I think I got the car seat base installed correctly," Liam says.

"Jen can double check it if you want," I offer.

"I'll finish baby proofing the house when we get home," Matthew says.

"You have months to do that," I tell him. "It's not like she's going to be crawling around anytime soon."

Matthew shakes his head. "I'd rather have it done and not have to worry about it. I'm just glad we had the entire house tested for lead when they painted. Are we forgetting anything?"

I motion with my free hand to the mountain of gifts covering every horizontal surface. "I'm sure whatever it is, it's in there."

Everyone went a bit crazy considering this is the first grand-child for all four families. And with the move and renovations, we never got around to having that baby shower.

There's a knock on the door and then a nurse enters holding paperwork. "Hi. So good news, you get to go home. We got your labs back and everything looks great. Just call your doctors to make your follow up appointments. I put some extra supplies in here," she says, handing us an enormous trash bag. It's full of diapers, wipes, and cream as well as stuff for me like witch hazel pads and a peri bottle and dozens of mesh underwear. "You can take anything you want from the room except for the linens. It's all gonna get thrown away, and I'd rather you have it than send it to the dumpster."

It's way more generous than I was expecting.

"Here's your discharge instructions and a list of emergency numbers. If you need anything, call." The nurse hands me a paper to sign, then takes out my IV and leaves me to change.

Gabriel holds the baby while I change into my clothes.

The drive back home isn't too long, and I sit in the back so I can make sure that she's okay in her carrier. I tuck the blanket tighter over her harness to keep her toasty warm.

Once we're home, Waffles meows incessantly as we open the door. Matthew gives him one of the baby blankets to sniff while the others unload the truck. Chelsea left a note that says she'll keep coming by to check on him until we call her and tell her we're home. I make a mental note to call her, then carry Holly to her nursery.

I can't wait to settle her into her bassinet. To unpack the rest of her stuff and use my rocking chair for the first time. We'll move it from our room into her nursery in a bit, but for now I want her close.

Humming, I clean and change her and put her into the tiniest onesie she has. Gabriel helps me swaddle her, and then I settle into my chair and pull my sweater up and pop my nursing bra open. She latches easily, sucking down milk. It eases some of my fears. She's lost a few ounces since yesterday, which they said was normal, but if her appetite is any indication then she'll regain it quickly.

Matthew brings me a drink so I can stay hydrated while breastfeeding, and Liam watches me nurse, a dopey grin on his face.

"What?" I ask him, unable to hide my grin.

"You're just so fucking beautiful," he says.

I don't feel beautiful. And I'm sure I don't look it. I showered in the hospital, but it's been an exhausting couple of days. My hair is up in a messy bun out of necessity because it's snarled and needs brushing. And I don't want to talk about the leakage. Or the fact that my belly still looks six months pregnant.

"How long before we can have another one?" he asks.

I shake my head. "Let me forget how much it hurt first." But I sort of already have. The pain is a fading memory, soothed by holding our baby. Feeding her and petting her wispy soft hair and watching her do everything for the first time ever, like sneeze or touch her cute button nose.

"She won't have a heat until she stops breastfeeding," Gabriel says.

"So that's… six months? A year?" Matthew asks.

"Yeah. You know, the doctor told me something really interesting," Gabriel says.

"What?" I ask.

"That you didn't tear or need a single stitch. I guess our massages and stretching exercises did the trick."

I give him an unamused look. "My vagina is off limits for at least six weeks."

Liam shares a look with the others. "That's okay. I think we can keep each other entertained. But for now, how about Chinese food?"

"Yesssss," I groan with excitement. "I want one of everything."

"Then you'll have everything you want," Liam says, pulling his phone from his pocket. He stoops over me for a kiss, then brushes a hand over our daughter's head and dials our favorite delivery place.

Waffles follows us into the room, sniffing curiously. He hops up on the side table next to my chair and stares at Holly. I pull the edge of her swaddling cloth down so he can see her face. "Here's your new sister. What do you think?"

Waffles purrs, sitting regally, and watches me nurse my daughter. I like to think that means he approves.

Chapter Twenty-Seven

GABRIEL

"I got the cabbages," Matthew says, showing off the round green heads of cabbage he bought. They're not to eat. The cold leaves go in Kat's bra to dry up her milk. Her supply dropped when we added solids to Holly's diet so we've decided to supplement with formula and go ahead with making baby number two. Holly turned six months two days ago. It's breeding time. "Do you really think this works?"

"Who knows?" I say. "But it can't hurt."

"Do they go in the fridge or freezer?" he asks.

Uhhhh… Hmm. "Let me look it up."

Liam pokes his head into the kitchen, a giggly baby girl on his hip. "Oh, good. You got them."

"The internet says they go into the fridge until she's ready to nurse, then the leaves go in the freezer for after," I say. "It should dry her milk up in a few days."

"And then how long before she goes into heat?" Matthew asks.

I think about it. "Hmm. Two to four weeks. Her body will be ready to breed again once her hormone levels drop. Omegas are hyperfertile."

My groin tightens in anticipation. It'll be her first heat with all three of us. I can't wait to breed her.

"Are you excited?" Liam asks.

"You know I am," I answer with a grin.

"Now, we have a very important task to get back to, don't we, Holly? Those bubbles won't blow themselves." Liam carries her back to the living room.

Holly babbles at her Daddy, as if she's answering his question. I follow them and watch. Liam dips the bubble wand into the bottle and blows them over Holly's head. She grabs at them, her movements slow and uncoordinated. When she finally manages to catch one and it pops, she giggles with delight.

"I'm home!" Kat calls from the entryway. Waffles runs through the house, meowing and his tail quivering with excitement. He's joined a minute later by our dog, Syrup. A good name for our rescued Golden Retriever. She ruffles the dog's fur. "Hi, Waffles. Hey, Syrup. Did you two have dinner yet?"

"He did!" Matthew yells from the kitchen. "Don't let Waffles convince you he needs a second dinner. I'm putting him on a diet."

Waffles meows, as if in protest. But Matthew is right. The cunning cat has gotten a bit chubby. With four people to lie to and convince he hasn't gotten fed yet, he's sneaking extra meals from us. We need to hang up a flippable sign or something. Syrup sits and lets out a soft woof as if she agrees.

Kat picks Waffles up and pets him, then joins us in the living room. She kisses Holly's cheek. "Hi, baby. Did you have a good day with your daddies?"

Holly babbles in response, reaching for her mommy's loose hair and getting a good fistful of it. She's been grabbing at everything she sees lately. Being handed something to hold is the new favorite game. I root through the baby's toy box and find her plastic keys, then jiggle them to catch her interest.

Holly drops the hair for the toy and promptly brings it to her mouth for gumming.

"How did your writer's club meeting go?" Matthew asks, greeting her with a kiss.

"It was great!" she says. "There was a new writer there. We talked about marketing for a bit, then everyone hung out and wrote. I didn't get much done, the bookstore was kind of noisy, but it was nice to meet someone new."

Waffles meows and fidgets so she puts him down. I pull her in for a kiss and wrap an arm around her. "That's great, *meu docinho*. We got the cabbages. Are you ready?"

She pulls a bottle of pills from her purse and rattles them. "I called Dr. Fugo and picked up the prescription on my way home. I get blood work done in three days, and then he said it's okay to start the next cycle right away. He also said it should be an easy cycle since my hormones are already primed."

I can't wait.

WHEN KAT STARTS TO HAVE TROUBLE SLEEPING, HER BODY becoming restless, we know it's close. It starts on Friday so we stay home and wait. Make sure we have everything ready. Even before her temperature spikes and her face flushes with the hormone swing.

Auntie Jen takes Holly for a few days. The fridge is stocked with omega protein water. The nest is freshly laundered. And we all have a week of heat leave scheduled with our jobs.

We're as ready as it gets.

We're trying to watch a movie when Liam announces he can smell the change in Kat's pheromones. He says her pheromones get extra delicious, like someone's covered her vanilla cookie scent with a thick layer of drizzled icing.

Liam buries his face in her neck and sniffs her scent gland to make sure Kat's made the transition from preheat to heat. Kat arches between us, her hand clawing at my shirt. Trying to pull it off me to get to my skin. I lean in and give her a lick, tasting the sweat on her skin. Sometimes I wish I could taste her pheromones underneath it. That I was born with an alpha's senses.

"Is it time?" Matthew asks.

"Yeah. She's ready," Liam says with a husky voice.

My teeth nip over the pack bite in Kat's neck, and she cradles the back of my head, urging me on. "Instead, I let her go. Come on, *meu docinho*. We're gonna give you what you need."

I stand and lift her off the couch. She wraps her legs around me and whimpers. A damp spot grows on my shirt from where she rubs her pussy against me. Naughty girl. I squeeze her ass and carry her to the bedroom. Matthew tidies up the living room quickly and gets the dog settled in his crate, then follows us.

My foot nudges our bedroom door open, and I lay her down in the nest, taking a moment to appreciate the sight of her wiggling and writhing. She works a hand underneath the waistband of her comfy sleep shorts and starts playing with herself.

"What a pretty fucking sight you are," I mumble, running my hand over her bare leg.

"Gabriel," she whines. "It hurts."

"Shh." I hook my fingers in the band of her shorts and pull them down. She lifts her ass up to make it easier. Once she's bared, her legs fall open, showing us her pretty pussy. Her fingers never stop working as Kat rubs and strokes herself. Her wet pussy glistens with arousal.

I want to eat her up.

So I get on my knees and drop my head between her legs. Shove Kat's hand aside to finish the job for her while Matthew and Liam collect everything we're gonna need. Her fingers card through my hair and squeeze, keeping me from pulling back while I lick her pussy and lap up her sweet slick. As if there's any chance of me not making her come in my mouth.

I latch onto her clit, sucking the swollen bud into my mouth. Kat moans and writhes, her back bowing. My tongue moves in circles around it, working it harder. Making her pussy drip for me.

I lap at Kat's pussy, working two fingers into her and rubbing at her g-spot until she comes apart underneath me. Slick floods my mouth and I swallow her down.

Kat settles, her breathing more even and her movements slower as she basks in the afterglow of her orgasm.

I pull back, then stand up, wiping her slick off my chin and licking my fingers clean. "Ready for your shot?" I ask Liam.

"Yeah. Let's get this over with," Liam says.

I grab the bottle of rut blocker and alcohol pads and a needle and draw up a syringe of it. Liam shoves his pants down, and I palm his ass and scrub the skin clean. Then I give him the shot.

"It's like you're pouring fire underneath my skin. Fuck, that hurts," Liam complains.

I slide the safety mechanism over the needle and put it in an old, empty coffee can. "You'll need another dose in twelve hours."

"Damn," Liam curses. "I was kind of hoping that it would only be once."

"Not quite." I draw up the nine other syringes we'll need and set them aside. Enough to get us through the next five days. This is my heat, then Matthew, and then if she's up for it Liam will give her baby number four. A kid for every bedroom.

"I'll set a timer," Matthew says, tapping on his phone. Once that's set, he pulls the small baggie of quaaludes from his pocket. He talked his coworker into selling him more.

"Not yet," I tell Matthew before he can take one. There are only a few pills. "Let's wait until she's deeper into estrus. Don't waste them."

We put the pills aside for tomorrow, maybe. She's only just started her heat. She's not ready yet.

Kat's gotten naked while we were busy, then covered herself with a blanket. She's already snoring.

Grinning at how cute she is, I strip too. We climb into the nest and settle in to wait. Watch for the right moment. Her body will tell us when she's ready to start breeding.

We doze for a bit. It's the nipping of her teeth on my chest and neck that wakes me. I blink bleary eyes and glance at the clock. Two in the morning. Kat is hot to the touch and sweating. The baby hairs that frame her pretty face are stuck to her skin.

"You need a cock, *meu docinho*?" I ask her.

"It hurts," she whines and paws at me. Such a needy little thing.

I stroke my cock to life. Getting hard for her. "Come here, I have what you need."

I drag her hand onto my cock so she knows that relief is coming. She latches on, needing no instruction. Kat rubs my cock until I'm hard and dripping, then throws her leg over me and climbs on top. She notches me to her slick entrance and takes me in one swivel of her hips. She starts to ride, fast and furious in her pursuit of relief.

"*Ai, meu Deus*," I moan. "That's it, baby. Take my cock. That's a good girl."

Matthew rolls over and murmurs uncomprehendingly in his sleep. Liam rubs his eyes and watches.

Kat's pussy is a hot, wet dream. She takes me hungrily, her

hips rocking to meet each thrust. To take everything I've got to give her. Knowing that she's all mine this heat drives me wild.

I can't last, can't—when her pussy flutters and she moans with her orgasm I'm lost. I come with her, my groin pulsing. I fill her. There's nothing between us.

She purrs, and I'm satisfied. If she weren't happy, we'd know it. I settle my weight over Kat without crushing her until she drifts off to sleep.

Matthew's timer goes off. Kat whimpers with need again. I roll her over and nudge her onto her knees until her ass is in the air. The bed dips as I kneel behind her. Mount her like a proper bitch in heat. She grips onto the blankets, pushing herself back against my bobbing cock. Urging me to fuck her hard and fast from behind. The position's good and deep. Perfect for breeding her.

I press my hand to her back. She's burning up. Flushed with fever, her eyes dark and glassy when she turns her head to the side to breathe. She's lost in her heat. After this, we'll force some of her special water down her throat before we bathe the sweat and fluids off her. Cool her down some. I itch with the need to take care of her. To give her everything she needs.

For now, there's cum she can eat. Liam's cock is already hard, fluid gathering at the tip. Dripping. He watches us hungrily.

Kat eyes Liam's erection, intent and purpose flickering to life.

"Our omega's hungry," I tell him. "Feed her."

Liam crawls closer and fists his base, slapping his cock against her cheek to make it more plump for her. The thrill of him obeying my order, of taking the supportive role in this heat, makes my cock even harder.

Her mouth latches on with no prompting. She swallows him down, taking him to the very back. Her gag reflex is gone with the heat riding her so damn hard. Her ass arches higher, the smacks of our bodies meeting coming loud and wet, and her cheeks hollow as she sucks on Liam's cock. Trying to suck the cum straight from his balls. It's got everything she needs to keep her going for a while longer. All that good alpha nutrition.

The bathroom door opens and Matthew walks out, rubbing the sleep from his eyes. "Morning. I heard the alarm go off. Time for your shot, Liam."

"Let me come first," Liam says, fucking into Kat's slack mouth. Pulling back enough to make sure she catches a breath before shoving back in. Groaning while she works.

They're so pretty together it hurts.

"God, kitten. That's so fucking good," Liam says. "You're so good at sucking cock. Do you want some cream in your belly?"

My groin tightens with arousal and need. I've always loved his dirty talk. Loved how focused he gets when he feels good. I rut into Kat harder, getting lost in the sight they both make. In the feel of her ass against my thighs.

She makes sounds, trying to talk, but it's impossible with the cock in her mouth. Saliva drips from the corners of her stuffed mouth.

I lock eyes with him while we spit roast her. What a fucking way to wake up. My groin tightens with the urge to come. The need to pump my seed inside so I can plant my baby in her womb.

"She's so wet," I say, leaning a hand on her hips. Angling her for deeper thrusting. I pull my hand back and smack her on the ass. Again, and again. It ripples, her pale skin turning delightfully pink.

"Let's come together," I say to him. "Tell me when you're close."

His nostrils flare and he drops his head down to watch how

his cock churns in and out of her. Saliva makes it shiny. "I'm close."

"You hear that, *meu docinho*? We're both gonna fill you up. What do you think about that, hmm?" I push her hair back so I can see her face. Watch her suck Liam's cock. She looks up at him with big round eyes. Like she's pleading for a big load of cum.

My abdomen tenses. Flutters with my deep breaths. There's a dull ache blooming inside me. Need. Raw and primal. The need to give my omega what she needs. What her body craves. Good, healthy sperm. A pussy full of seed. And a belly full of Liam's protein. Protein water is all well and good, but in the old days an omega drank only from her pack.

"You ready?" I ask my alpha. I'm not sure I can hold back much longer. Not when Kat's pussy grips me with fluttering squeezes. The urge to empty my balls into her makes me near feral.

"Yes," I hiss between clenched teeth. "I'm gonna put my baby in you," I promise her.

The need overtakes me and my body acts on instinct. My pace slows, fucking her deep, using her pussy to milk my cock as I erupt in her too. Flood her slick cunt while Liam pumps down her throat. He pulls back a bit so his knot doesn't catch behind her teeth. But he doesn't pull it free. He makes her swallow around it. Keeps it there, spurting on her tongue, until he's sure she's swallowed every drop.

"How many times did she come?" Liam asks me.

"Twice."

"Make her come again," he says. "It'll make her cervix dip into the pool of semen. Shove the cum back into her if it dribbles out."

I pull back and study her pussy. Roll her clit under my thumb. Work her until she's panting and moaning. When she comes on my fingers, I scoop up what's trickled out of her and push it back in. I make her stay like that for a while. Give my seed time to work.

"She might not ovulate until tomorrow or the next day," I tell them. "But the sperm will live inside her for a bit. Ready for when she drops her egg."

Liam massages his knot, working out a final spurt of cum for her to lick up and swallow. When we're both done, Matthew reminds me it's time for Liam to get his shot. He keeps us idiots on track. I kiss him in thanks, then tell Liam to hold still for his injection.

She dozes in the nest, her hunger satisfied for the moment. She's still ass up, cum and slick dripping down her inner thigh. Making a mess of her and working our pheromones into the nest. We give her a half hour to soak up as much seed as she's going to, then Matthew runs the bath for her.

Liam carries her into the bathroom, and together they bathe her. I spend the time sorting through the pile of stuff we bought just for this heat. The inflatable knotting ring for my cock. Condoms with a special expandable base made for alphas just in case the rut blocker fails for Liam. And a tube of arousal cream called Nymph-o in case my cock gets tired.

Waffles meows and scratches at the bedroom door. I follow him down to the basement and get him settled, giving him fresh food and water and petting him. I feed Syrup and take her outside for a bathroom and play break. By the time they're settled again, Kat's bath is done.

Kat is stretched out on the bed, her damp hair spread around her. She fingers herself and watches while Liam and Matthew kiss and fondle one another. When I enter, Matthew gives me a sly look. "I prepped for you."

I grin. Let the fun begin.

I pause by the bed and run a finger over her knee. "Do you need me, *meu docinho*?"

She nods, her hips bucking as she tries to fuck her fingers. But they're not what she wants. Not what she needs. Too slim and gentle, when the thing she wants most right now is to be rutted into oblivion.

I lean into Liam and Matthew, kissing both of them and stroking their cocks. Squeezing their dicks together so they can fuck my hand. I thread my other hand through Matthew's hair and pull him away from Liam, breaking their kiss.

"Who do you want to be inside while I fuck her?" I ask Liam.

"You," he tells me with half-lidded eyes.

My heart pitter patters in my chest. I love it when he says he wants me. Needs me. The reassurance is always nice to hear. Their long shared history made me insecure at first. Made me feel like I had to prove myself. Justify my place in the pack as an extra beta. But now… Now I know they love me for me. Even though Matthew complains about how spicy I make my food and Liam thinks whiskey is better than cachaça. He couldn't be more wrong, but I love him anyway. We all have our flaws.

"Go prep," Liam tells me, his gaze heated.

He doesn't need to tell me twice. I let go of hair and cock so I can slap him on the ass. "Be right back."

In the bathroom, I get myself ready. Make sure I'm clean and lubed. I stare at my reflection for a moment, tensing my muscles. I wonder what our kid will look like. If they'll have her eyes and my bronze skin. Our baby's gonna be the cutest. I flex and stretch, getting ready.

"Time to go make a baby," I tell myself.

They're fooling around and touching one another by the time I'm done. I climb onto the bed, then I get into position between her legs. Matthew coats his hand in slick and gets me ready. He plays with my cock too much to be all business. I kiss his forehead, stroking his curls back, and pump into the tight ring of his hand. "And what are you going to be doing?"

"I'll fuck her mouth."

Good plan. His hand falls away from my hard cock, and I sink into Kat. She arches her back and moans as I bottom out. Her breasts ripple with every thrust. Her pussy squeezes me, begging for my baby. The baby I ache to fill her with.

Liam rubs a slicked hand between my cheeks. He finds my tight hole and presses the tip of his finger in.

Groaning, I throw my head back and keep fucking her. Thrust my dick into her pussy with each forward stroke and fuck myself onto his hand with each recoil. He adds another finger, working my asshole open. Scissoring it wide and getting me ready for him.

My balls ache and my cock is hard enough to break rocks. Liam strokes my prostate as he scissors me wide. Kat whimpers with each of my thrusts, and her whines and whimpers are almost enough to break my tempo and make me lose myself.

"Hold still," Liam orders. He brings his cock to my hole. Lines himself up and pushes inside. Makes me stretch and open for him. Slow and controlled. He tests my patience to be gentle. I need this. Need him to fuck me. Rut me raw and breed my ass while I pump Kat's pussy full to bursting and put my baby in her.

He sinks in past the tip and I stretch around him, my tight hole puckering. Thrusting slowly, he works his way deeper. Makes me open up and take him until he's buried to the root. To the base where his knot will grow and tie us together.

"Good boy," Liam tells me.

My body flushes with warmth. Sweat beads my brow. It's

taking all of my control to hold back right now. To wait until I've adjusted to him.

Kat whines, impatient. She bucks underneath me, as much as she can with my weight trapping her in the nest.

"Shh, *meu docinho.* Hush," I tell her. "You're gonna get what you need real soon. I promise."

"Yes." Liam pulls back and pushes into me. Makes me take him deeper, but there's nothing left to take. I've gotten all of it.

He braces a hand on my shoulder for leverage. And then he pulls back and thrusts again. No more warmup. No mercy. Only rutting. Our bodies slap together. I let it rock me forward, driving me into her. Setting our pace and rhythm as our bodies become intertwined. Kat's whimpers finally stop. Her mouth rounds open and her hips make circles while she rocks with us.

"*Meu Deus,*" I groan, dropping my head and giving into it. Letting my alpha rut me while I breed our pretty little omega.

"Are you just going to watch?" I ask Matthew.

Matthew finally joins us. He crawls into the nest. Guides Kat's head to the side and his cock to her lips. She parts them, taking him halfway down and sucking. Filling her mouth with cock until both of her greedy holes are filled. Later, once her pussy's nice and soaked with cum, we'll fill her ass too. All of us will fuck her at once while I get her pregnant.

I can't wait to watch her belly get big again. Watch her do her cute pregnant waddle. Get another ultrasound photo to add to our fridge. Fill another empty bedroom. Take her to her prenatal yoga classes.

"That's so good, babe. You like being full of cock, don't you?" Liam asks me.

"Yes, alpha." I pant. "I'm close."

He tightens his grip on my firm ass. Spreads my muscular cheeks apart to watch me take him so deep.

"You don't come until I do," Liam orders.

I groan. My thighs tremble. "Her pussy's fluttering. I can't…"

Liam's hand wraps around the back of my neck. Holds me in place and asserts his dominance over me. "Not. Yet."

He slows his pace, edging me. Ignoring my protests and foreign curses. Working me to a frenzy until I'm begging him for permission to come.

"Liam," I whine, desperate with need. Kat's pussy squeezes and grips me, her knees tight on my hips. Her body soft and plush and fertile. She doesn't need to lose the baby weight she complains about. She's perfect the way she is.

Matthew's already emptied himself inside her mouth. His spent cock twitches against his thigh with renewed interest, plumping from the scene we make. From the filthy things I promised my alpha if he'll just let me come already.

"I'm going to come inside you," he tells me.

Finally. "Please," I beg.

"And you're going to put a baby in our omega because I'm letting you."

Ai, meu Deus. Why does that make it hotter? I love it when Liam plays out my stern alpha fantasies. When he acts tough and bossy. "Thank you, alpha," I groan.

His knot swells, triggered by my submission. It teases at my tight ring with every thrust. He fucks me harder and need burns through me. Makes my balls ache with unspent seed.

Matthew catches my eye and smirks while he strokes his cock back to life with languid movements. Kat mewls, begging us wordlessly for relief. For a womb full of cum. For a baby.

"You'll take my knot," Liam tells me, not giving me the choice.

My asshole clenches around him while Kat's pussy clamps down on me. I can't take another minute of this. Of this perfection. "Thank you, alpha."

He growls, pleased, digging his fingers into my hips. Tugs my ass back onto his cock, fucking me deeper. Thrusting me forward into our omega. Fucking her good and proper. Until waves of relief pulse through me. Travel down my body like rings in a pond from a tossed stone. His knot swells and he shoves it deeper, pumping me full while it pops and stretches my asshole obscenely wide.

I come with a cry and a gasp for air. My spine stiffens, and my noises become strangled. I come inside her, each instinctual thrust of my hips tugging at his alpha knot in my ass. Pulling on it, stimulating me, rubbing my prostate. Milking me.

I collapse on top of her, spent and exhausted, and catch my breath.

Purring, he rubs me down. Soothes me with his rumbling chest and strokes of his palms up and down my heaving sides. Kat purrs too, her knees squeezing my hips. Keeping me inside her.

When I'm able to think clearly enough for speech again, I glance at Matthew. "How many times did she come?"

"Four."

I nod and sigh with relief. Thank God. Four's enough for now.

Matthew chuckles and grabs a protein water, encouraging all of us to drink as we wait for Liam's knot to subside. After all that edging, it takes him a while.

When we finally detach, I let my cock slip free of her. Matthew folds Kat's legs back and drags the pussy plug he bought her through the cum dripping down her ass. He shoves it inside her pussy, stoppering her up on the bulbous silicone knot. He plays with her clit and makes her come on it, her eyes rolling back in her head as she finally orgasms on the knot her omega instincts demand.

We fuck her unconscious, and she sleeps deeply. Properly filled and plugged.

Liam pulls out of my ass and pats my hip fondly, pausing to enjoy the faint bruises already forming on my skin. He lies down, exhausted and spent, and cuddles her. She purrs, her happiness settling the emotions of the room.

Hopefully we have at least half an hour to recover. She's satisfied for now, but our girl won't be for long. I've never seen an omega through her heat before. Never seen anything but porn. I wasn't fully prepared. Porn only gets the gist of it. None of the exhaustion. The marathon aspect of it all. It's gonna be a long couple of days. At least it's good cardio.

Matthew grabs another protein water and makes me drink half, and then he shows me the small white pill in his hand. "Open."

I open my mouth for him. He sets the pill on my tongue, and I swallow it. I drain the rest of the bottle and crumple the plastic in my grip. My throat bobs as I swallow it all down.

I can't wait for what comes next.

FOUR DAYS. THAT'S HOW LONG IT TAKES FOR HER HEAT TO break. For her scent to change. Liam pulls Kat closer until she's nearly on top of him and sticks his nose against her neck. Smelling her deeply.

"You're pregnant," he says.

Kat blinks a bleary eye open and rubs at her face. "Oh my God. I feel like I got hit by a truck. Between my thighs. Repeatedly."

Smiling, I laugh. "Good. That means I did my job right." I

squeeze her to me and I'm grateful that it's over. As wonderful as it's been, it's been equally exhausting. My cock and balls ache like they're about to shrivel up and fall off.

I cup my hand over her belly, where our next baby will grow. There's nothing to feel yet, of course, but it satisfies my possessive urge. I can't wait until her belly's showing. Until I can feel the baby moving. I've read that second births are often easier. The next two are gonna be a cake walk after this one.

"Really?" Kat asks, cupping my hand with hers.

"Yeah. I can tell," Liam says. "You're pregnant, kitten."

Leaning over her, I kiss her slow and sweet. Liam and Matthew slide closer, joining our cuddle pile. They take turns kissing her and feeling her soft, flat tummy.

The smile she gives us all is indescribable.

Twenty weeks later when we find out we're having another little girl, I tape up over a hundred paint swatches to decide what color we're painting the nursery.

Chapter Twenty-Eight

MATTHEW

I SPEND WAY TOO LONG LOOKING AT CABBAGE AT THE STORE. IT doesn't need to be perfect. We're not even going to eat it. But I want them to be extra special anyway. Because Marcia will be six months old tomorrow and Kat is worried about her age. Not that omegas don't have babies in their late thirties and early forties all the time. Especially with Dr. Fugo assuring us that he can increase her dose if this cycle doesn't take.

This cabbage needs to be perfect, because it's mine. It's to dry up her milk so she can get pregnant with my baby.

An elderly woman comes by, looking at the cabbages too. I make my selection before she can take the one I have my eye on. "Sorry, excuse my reach." I palm the vegetable and add it to my cart along with the other groceries we need.

I do the rest of our shopping and drive home in a daze. I drop the first bag on the kitchen counter and shout that I'm back.

Gabriel comes down, our youngest strapped to his chest in her harness. She hates being put down, and he likes talking to her in Portuguese while he works out. He says it's important she learns about her heritage so that she doesn't grow up speaking only English like he did until his teens. His immigrant parents wanted to assimilate into American culture as quickly as they could so they only spoke English at home. He didn't start speaking Portuguese until he went to Brazil to meet his extended family and his cousins made fun of him for not knowing his own language.

"Hey, babe," I say, ripping the paper bag open to get to the groceries inside. "There's more in the car."

He pauses to kiss me on the cheek. "I'll get the rest. You start putting them away."

Five minutes later, Gabriel nudges the kitchen door open with his foot. He's got six bags of groceries loaded in his two arms and the baby still strapped to him.

How the hell did he get them all in one trip?

I watch, wide-eyed, as he sets them down on the counter one arm at a time. They're not light. We go through milk and juice like crazy so I buy two things of each at a time. "Ooh, you got the cabbage," he says, waggling his brows at me.

My face heats with a blush. "Yeah."

Gabriel knocks his shoulder into mine. "Excited?"

I stare at the box of baby puffed crackers in my hands. "Yeah, but I'm pretty nervous too."

Gabriel rubs my shoulders until the tension melts under his digging thumbs. "You're gonna do great."

It's not that I'm worried about performance, per se. It's more like a fear that since Liam and Gabriel had it so easy, what if my turn breaks our streak? Kat's already so nervous about her age. What if this heat cycle doesn't take?

Kat comes in from the back from her writing room and starts helping us unload groceries. Syrup trots along behind her, getting underfoot as she waits for someone to drop food on the floor. The goofy dog loves hanging out in the kitchen when anyone's in here.

"How's the book coming along?" I ask her.

"Okay." She grabs the box of cereal the babies like and puts it in the cabinet with the others. "I have writer's block so I'm taking a break. I think I'm going to take the rest of the day off and recharge."

"Want to go down to the gym with me?" Gabriel asks, sliding a hand across her hip.

Kat gives him a suspicious glance. "That depends. What sort of exercise did you have in mind?"

Gabriel grins and lifts the eggplant from the bag of vegetables, stroking it. "I'll make sure you get your cardio in, don't worry."

She snorts and grabs the eggplant from him and mutters something about sexercise under her breath while she walks over to the fridge. He hands her vegetables to put away while I reorganize the soup cans in their turnstile. When they get to the cabbage, she studies it for a moment before putting it in the crisper drawer.

"I'll get started on dinner," I tell them once we're done.

"Let's go find Daddy so he can watch you," Kat says, pulling the baby from Gabriel's harness and cuddling Marcia to her chest. "Mommy needs to go do yoga."

"I'm gonna get changed," Gabriel says, unbuckling the baby harness.

"Dinner's at seven," I tell him.

He swats me on the ass on his way out.

Smiling to myself, I pull out the ingredients we need and find the recipe I saved on my phone.

LESS THAN A MONTH LATER, KAT'S HEAT HITS HER FAST WITH atomic clock precision. Her preheat is short this time. Only a day and a half. It must be from the higher dose of fertility meds.

"Are you sure?" I ask Liam as I pause while doing my tie.

Liam pokes his head out from under the covers where he's been eating her out under the pretense of checking to see if she's ready. "I'm sure." He slaps her right on her mound, making her gasp and push her knees together. "That's prime babymaking pussy."

"I'll call work." I call my boss real quick and tell him that I'm on heat leave and won't be in. So does Gabriel. Once we're both covered with work, I pull the tie from around my neck and undo the buttons of my shirt.

"Let me get one more lick," Liam says, wrenching her knees apart. His head disappears between her legs again and he tugs the sheet over them to keep her warm.

"We need to… to…" Kat moans, distracted. "Need to call Jen and—oh, God—have her get the kids."

"I'll call her," I reassure her.

Gabriel slips from the bed. "I'll go pack the kids up."

Jen doesn't live far away so it's only an hour until I help her buckle the kids up in her car and watch her go, their stuff loaded into the trunk.

Gabriel pats me on the back. "All right, Mattie. You're up."

My heart pounds in my chest. I am. I've been half-hard since Liam said those perfect words this morning. I don't have the breeding kink that our alpha does. But even without it, there's something extra special about knowing that I'm the one who will be knocking up our omega.

Kat is coming against Liam's face when we return, her fingers twisted in the sheets and her hair spread out in a tangled halo on a pillow. She's perfect.

I never thought we needed a fourth member of our pack. A

woman. An omega. Never felt that urge that rides Liam so hard to breed or makes Gabriel glance over his shoulder at a woman with a nice ass.

I'm glad that Kat proved me wrong. Proved how much our pack needed her. The mother to our two beautiful baby girls and —hopefully—another bundle of joy in nine months. Having two small children has proved challenging at times. But now that I know them, have read them bedtime stories and snuggled them and smelled their perfect newborn scent, I couldn't imagine us having any other sort of life.

"Did your alpha make you feel good?" I ask Kat, gripping the edge of the blanket and pulling it so I can see him. Liam's on his stomach, his head nestled on her thigh and his hips which flex as he humps a pillow. Poor guy. I can't imagine the hell he's going through. Smelling her in heat and knowing she's off limits to him.

Because this heat, she's mine.

"Mmhmm," Kat hums, basking in the afterglow of her orgasm while Liam tries to find his with a pillow covered in her scent and slick. A poor substitute for her hot little pussy. But it's all he gets from her for the next few days.

Gabriel stabs a needle into a glass vial and begins making a bunch of rut blocker shots. Even he's not immune to the sights and sounds and smells of our fertile, needy omega. His stiffening cock fills out his tight briefs.

I've already decided how I'm going to handle this. After spending hours reading stories on message boards, I know what I want. How to increase our chances of conception.

I go straight for our drawer of toys and pull out the knotting ring. It's bulky and awkward to put on, which is why Gabriel never liked it and only used it once. But I found the perfect solution. I grab the black leather garter I bought for this and buckle it around my leg, feeding the knotting ring's inflation bulb through it. I test it to make sure it's working, then release the valve. The air whooshes out and it deflates.

It takes some lube and patience to get the thick band of extra silicone onto the base of my penis. Once it's on, my cock is slightly harder. Looks a bit more engorged to me too. I'm nearly as big as some alphas. With the fake knot, I don't think she'll be able to tell the difference once she's delirious with her heat.

Liam slides out of the nest at Gabriel's prompting to get his first shot.

Kat watches me approach her with interest. Her eyes flick up and down my body, savoring the sight of my ruddy cock and the black ring and holster.

"You know I love you, right?" I ask her as I kneel on the bed and crawl into the nest.

Her eyes are extra shiny in the light. Glassy, her pupils big and black. Her pink lips part and she licks them, fidgeting. She nods, but doesn't answer. Heat makes her less talkative, keeps her thoughts muddled and distracted between lulls. But she shoves the blankets down and her knees fall open, displaying her pussy. She's wet and pink and oh so ready for me.

"Good. Remember that," I warn her. "Because I'm about to fuck you like I hate you."

Surprise makes her eyes widen, showing off the whites. Grinning, I grab her ankle and pull. Tug her down the bed. Startled, she yelps. Alphas are aggressive. I've been fucked by Liam enough to know how hard our alpha likes it sometimes. Helped him fuck Gabriel or Kat stupid too.

I'm going to rut her into the nest and dick her down so good that she forgets my knot is silicone.

I pull her down the nest until her legs are hanging off the edge. Precariously perched. She bends her knees and lifts her hips on instinct to keep her balance. Spreads her pussy for me. Exactly how I want her.

Perfect.

I notch my cock to her entrance and shove inside. No warmup or gentle preparation. No slow, easing thrusts. I bottom out inside her and make her body adjust to me. Her nostrils flare as she breathes in deep, adapting to me and my blunt intrusion. She gets wetter. Fresh slick soaks me and makes my rough entry smoother.

"You like that, Kat?" I ask her, thrusting hard. Making her tits bounce and her thighs quiver. "You like getting fucked hard and fast like a perfect little slut? Yeah, you do. Your pussy's already strangling my dick, begging for my knot."

Kat mewls and tucks her legs up tighter. Stops focusing on her balance and relies on me instead. Gets lost in our fucking and trusts me to catch her if she falls. I slam into her. Fuck the air out of her lungs and the thoughts out of her pretty head.

"Fuck," Liam whispers.

"Meu Deus."

I pound her relentlessly. Until her nipples are hard buds and her pussy quivers on my cock. I keep fucking her through her spasms, her aftershocks, not stopping. Merciless. The knotting ring is tight. It makes me slower to come. But I don't mind trying all that much harder.

"Listen to how wet that pussy is," I say, reaching a thumb between her folds. Finding her clit and rubbing it until her back bows. If I weren't gripping her tightly, she'd damn near levitate off the bed. "It wants a baby, doesn't it?"

Kat tries to speak, but can't. She's too busy panting. Too busy coming on my cock as I ruthlessly fuck her cunt and stroke her clit. She comes again and I fuck her through her orgasm, not pausing. Not letting her come down or catch her breath. Her pussy clamps down like a vice, trying to strangle my orgasm from my cock. Anything to make this harsh claiming end. Because her body knows it's mine.

There are benefits to always watching her. Observing and taking mental notes. I know what she likes. What they all do. And I don't have any qualms about giving it to her. They're too gentle for her. Too sweet considering what she really wants, what she craves, what she writes about. To be loved like our precious omega, the mother of our beautiful children, and to be fucked like our dirty whore. Our perfect omega fuck doll.

"You're such a slut for cum, aren't you, baby?" I ask her, not expecting an answer.

My thrusts bounce her up the bed. It's only my hold on her hips that keeps her exactly where I want her. After she comes again, I leave her clit alone to play with her breasts. Grabbing them, squeezing. Spanking them. I bring my hand down hard on her nipple and delight in how she squirms underneath me. How her pussy grips me, urging me to come. To fill her pussy. Breed her raw and put a baby in her belly.

I guess I do have a bit of a breeding kink. Maybe theirs rubbed off on me. Or maybe it's because right here, right now, with her, it's actually possible. The thought of her belly growing with my baby makes my groin tighten. My engorged cock throbs around the knotting ring. My balls ache to fill her. There's no holding it back anymore.

Chasing the feeling, I fuck her until she screams, and when that familiar tingle coils deep inside me, I let go. Hurdle over that precipice. My whole groin pulsates, shooting cum in thick pulses. I have just enough thought to pump the knot up, thrusting deep and spilling inside her until the knot's too big for me to pull free anymore.

"Mmm. Fuck," I groan, leaning over her to catch my breath. Sweat drips down the side of my face and lands on her stomach.

"That was good, baby." But she still needs to come again. To increase our odds of making this baby. I massage her clit, rubbing circles. Working her up again until she's writhing on my silicone knot. She orgasms, walls fluttering, her pussy squeezing like a vice. Trying to milk the fake knot for more cum.

I shudder and my hips twitch. It's too much. I'm too over-sensitized. But she doesn't care. Her body clamps down on my buried cock, and I don't come again so much as she sucks another spurt of seed out of me. Dredges it out of my balls like some sort of cum vampire. It's her delicious revenge for my brutal pounding.

Fuck. Is this what it's like for Liam? Goddamn. I don't know how he can stand it without going insane.

I leave us tied together and collapse on top of her, pinning her down in the nest. My face pressed between her plush breasts as she breathes fast, regaining some awareness. Her legs wrap around me and keep me locked in, her heels digging into my ass. As if she's worried I'll pull out. That's nice. It's like she wants to make sure my sperm finds her egg.

I kiss her chest over her heart, and we lie there until we're both somewhat recovered. She falls asleep, her body already exhausted from her heat. It doesn't matter that she just woke up. She'll sleep and fuck and not do much of anything else for the next four days or so.

Liam shoves a protein water at me, his eyes sparkling with amusement.

I take it and gulp it down, draining the entire thing in two swallows. This is gonna take a lot of protein water. I'm glad I bought an entire case. I toss the empty bottle toward the trash, not caring if it misses.

"That was… Wow." Gabriel says, his tone impressed.

Recovered, I pry her legs from around me and turn the valve

that deflates the fake knot. I slide her up in the nest so she won't fall and hold my hand out toward them. "Plug."

Someone puts it in my hand. I work it in between her cum slicked folds and glance at the clock. In half an hour, I'll take it out and we'll give Kat her first bath. But for now… I pat her tummy and wish my little swimmers good luck.

Once she's cat napped and she's gotten all the good stuff out of my hot load, I pop the plug free and let Liam pull her from the nest. Gabriel and I run her bath and gather up her heat wash supplies. Liam sits our sleepy omega on the toilet so she can pee.

"Prep her ass with the bidet. I have plans for that too," I tell him.

We check that the bath water's not too hot or cold. She's running a fever from the heat so both would bother her. I check the water temperature against my wrist like I do with the babies' bottles.

We add scent-free heat wash to the bath and mix it until it's sudsy. Liam picks her up and puts her in, lowering her down. She wakes up once the bubble-covered water covers her.

"Shh," Liam says, purring until she settles.

Gabriel and I wash the sweat from her hair and spray leave-in conditioner into it. Then Liam washes the rest of her, running her sudsy loofah over her body. Using his hand between her legs where she needs it extra gentle. I get a bottle of protein water in her while she's getting clean and then we dry her off and bundle her up for snuggling.

Kat dozes off and on until she finally stirs around noon. I wake up to her tongue swiping across my chest. She licks her way to my neck, lapping at my scent gland. Her sharp, dainty omega fangs graze over my healed bite mark.

"Need a cock, baby?" I ask her.

She hums while she licks me. I find the cleaned knot ring in the bed and stroke my cock to life. Putting the ring on without lube is less pleasant. It catches on my skin and I wince.

"Let me borrow some of that," I tell her, slicking my hand up on her pussy. I use her slick to lube up my cock and get the ring into place. Then I slap her on the ass. "Okay, get on top."

This is perfect. Kat straddles me and I line us up. She sinks down, taking me halfway, then grunts. As if she's disappointed she didn't get all of my cock in one go. She lifts up again before dropping her ass down. The stretch of my cock makes her sigh and her hips grind down on me.

"Gabriel," I say, patting blindly on his side of the bed. "Fuck her ass."

"What?" Gabriel says sleepily. "Oh. Okay." The bedding rustles as he gets up. I hear the click of a cap and the rhythmic slap of skin against skin as he lubes up his hand and makes himself hard. He gets into place behind her.

I palm her ass, spreading her cheeks for him. Helping him see her tight hole. He gets her ready, stretching her with his fingers first. Lubing her up.

Her hips swivel and I tighten my grip. Pinning her down until she's gone still while he gets himself seated.

"You can take it, *meu docinho*," he tells her, working his cock inside.

Kat's back arches as he fills her ass while I'm deep in her pussy. We stretch her wide and stuff her full. Fill both holes. Once he's inside, I start to thrust. Use my grip on her ass to work her on both of our cocks.

Kat moans, rocking with us. Fucking herself on our cocks now that she's warmed up and ready to go.

"*Meu Deus*, she's so tight back here."

"I can feel you fucking her," I moan, thrusting slowly. Building up a rhythm. Finding our pace together. "Your cock is rubbing against me."

We fuck her slowly until she stops whining. Until her shocked noises turn to moans. Then we fuck her for real. Alternating. Surging together. Making her take us however we want.

"You're being such a good girl for us," I praise her, spreading her ass cheeks for him. "Bend her arms behind her back," I tell him.

"Fuck." Gabriel curses, but does it. He twists her arms back and pins them down while he fucks her in the ass.

Kat gets wetter. Slick rolls down her body, dripping onto me. She likes it. Likes being our perfect, dirty slut.

I let go of her ass to grab her face, angling it toward me. Making her look. "Yeah, you like that. You like having a cock in both of your slutty holes."

Kat shudders. Her face and chest flush. Her pussy spasms, and she comes.

And I can't help but to follow her. To hear the strangled noises she makes and surge up faster. Chase the tight spiral of my own release. I come so hard I forget about inflating the knot, but Liam remembers. He takes the bulb and pumps it. The cock ring tightens on my shaft as it swells, plugging up her pussy.

I tug her hips down and grind her onto my pseudo knot until it's buried. And Gabriel fucks her still, his cock rubbing against me through her fluttering walls. Pushing past my buried knot. Shoving in deep as he uses her ass until eventually he's close too.

"I'm going to come," he warns us. His cock jerks inside her. Kicks against mine through a thin dividing wall. Stuffs her ass full of cum until both of her holes are nice and soaked.

"Pull out first," I tell him. I don't want his cum dripping onto her pussy when it's not plugged up. This baby's mine.

Gabriel listens, pulling out and collapsing on his side. I tighten my arms around Kat and roll us, flipping her so she's under me. My silicone knot is still buried deep, locking her womb up tight for me.

She barely stirs. I've fucked her asleep again. The gnawing hunger of her heat satisfied. At least for now.

We stay like that for a bit. With me half on her. Pinning her down in the nest. Covering her with my body. She loves it. Finds safety in being covered and smooshed. Her primal need for protection's been met.

Alphas no longer battle to the death over omegas, of course, but the hindbrain needs what it wants. Instinct can't be reasoned with. Kat sleeps, and I lie there, soaking in the soft curves of her face. The way her baby hairs curl on her sweat-beaded brow. The gentle rise and fall of her chest and the absolute certainty Kat must have to sleep this soundly in my arms. Safe. Cherished. Protected.

I kiss her forehead and deflate the knot, pulling free once it's released its air. The plug goes in her cum slicked hole. Our cycle continues.

Liam comes in his hand and smears his satisfied alpha pheromones on her chest. Rubbing the scent into her tits. Coating her in his perfume so that Kat sleeps deeper. She curls on her side, and I tuck a soft blanket over her while my sperm go to work.

I curl around her and bury my face in her hair. Gabriel and Liam join us, taking this moment to nap. We'll have to get up. Get clean. Force water down her throat. But for now, there's only peace. Only comfort and pack. I hook my arm around her under the blanket and rest my palm on her belly.

Three days later when Liam sniffs her and pronounces her pregnant, all I can do is give them a thumbs up. There's no moisture left in my body to coat my mouth so I can speak. My eyes are gritty, and it takes effort to keep them open.

I crash and sleep for fourteen hours straight.

Chapter Twenty-Nine

KAT

THE WAY LIAM KEEPS LOOKING AT THE POWDER BLUE ONESIES covered in pastel cartoon dinosaurs tells me what he's thinking. He adores our three daughters, but I know how much he wants a boy too.

I reach out and touch the one with the green stegosaurus pattern and consider it. A boy would be nice. "You know, I asked Dr. Fugo if there's any natural way to choose the baby's gender."

Liam's grip tightens on our shopping cart. "Really?"

"They can do that?" Matthew asks.

"There's research that says diet and timing can make someone more likely to have a specific gender," I say.

Now Matthew looks interested. "What sort of diet?"

"Foods rich in sodium and potassium for a boy rather than magnesium and calcium."

Matthew makes a thoughtful sound. "So no more chocolate during preheat."

It's a small price to pay if it works. As much as I love the onesie, it feels like bad luck to buy it early. Like it'll jinx things.

I leave it on the rack and throw a yellow one with lambs on it into our cart instead.

Liam grabs the baby shampoo and bedtime lotion the girls like from the cardboard display and adds them to the cart. "What's the timing thing about?"

"Something about how boy sperm swim faster so you want to wait until closer to the end of the heat," I say.

"Interesting." Liam seems thoughtful for the rest of our shopping trip. Matthew loads our cart up with potassium rich foods. Leafy greens, avocado, potatoes, and bananas. And of course our traditional cabbage. Lily's six months old and eating solids. This next baby will be our last one. After baby number four, I'm getting an IUD. Each birth has gotten easier and faster since Holly's surprise entry, but still. Four kids are enough. We don't want to become outnumbered.

We pick up the prescription Dr. Fugo called in on the way home. When we get home, Gabriel is passed out on the couch in a cuddle pile with all three girls. Our youngest, Lily, is curled up on his chest. They're good nappers. Their favorite show, the cartoon with the dogs, is still playing in the background. There are toys and stuffed animals everywhere. It's like a bomb full of plastic shrapnel went off. We bring the groceries in and put them away as quietly as we can.

Waffles' excited meow and Syrup's rapid tail thumping wake them. They're excited we're all home. I pop Lily on my hip and put the bananas away. Then Matthew waves me away, saying he'll finish, then get started on dinner.

After dinner, the kids have tub time. A quick nighttime feeding for Lily. Then teeth brushing and, finally, stories. The others each take a kid while I put our littlest down in her crib and make sure her baby monitor's on. By nine, they're asleep.

I collapse with my pack on the couch, watching some TV show that's mostly forgotten about. Matthew brings me two frozen cabbage leaves. I crunch them and shove them down my nursing bra and shiver as they make my sore nipples harden.

"I'm always sad to see them go," Liam says, eying my breasts. They're not as full as they are when my milk production is higher or right before a feeding. My supply always drops off quickly once the babies start eating solids.

I snort. "You're just sad you can't touch them for the next five days." No breast or nipple stimulation outside of Lily's feedings. It's firm bras and cabbage leaves and ice packs for me for the next couple of days.

"Can you blame me?" he asks. "They're glorious when they're full of milk. Still, it'll be worth the sacrifice." He puts a hand under the throw blanket and palms my stomach. Leans in close to me and drops his face next to mine. "I can't wait to put my son in you," he whispers into my ear.

"We should practice," I tell him. "Make sure we remember how."

It's harder to find time alone, all four of us, with three kids. Two of us can sneak off easily for some adult time, but it's difficult for all of us to disappear together now. It'll be easier once they're all in school. Jen thinks I'm crazy for having so many close together, but at my age that was a necessity rather than a choice. And I love my girls. I can't imagine a life without them anymore, even when it's hard.

Liam kisses my throat, making his way down to my mating bite. He nibbles it, making my scent gland perfume. "Good idea, kitten. Let's get that pussy nice and ready for your heat because once your fever spikes, you're not getting any dick until it's time for me to get you pregnant."

Part of me is excited. It's going to be an edging like no other. But the rest of me is worried that it might literally drive me insane.

My future self is probably gonna hate me for this.

MY PREHEAT LASTS ONLY A FEW HOURS. IT'S GOTTA BE THE extra strong meds, or maybe my age. I've heard that heats get more unpredictable with age before they eventually stop altogether.

"Liam," I whine, gripping onto him. My hips swiveling to work myself on his fingers. But fingers aren't what I want. "Please." It hurts. The endless cramping. The bottomless need. The constant river of slick flowing down my thighs, soaking into the nest.

"Sorry, kitten." He doesn't sound sorry at all.

I growl and reach for his dick.

Liam chuckles in response, and Gabriel grabs my wrist, pinning my arm above my head. I growl louder, jerking my arms to test his grip. Gabriel's grasp tightens. Fighting them is useless. They're all bigger, stronger, and more determined than me.

My previous resolve to hold out as long as I can is a faded, distant memory. I need a dick in me and I need it now. I might die if I don't get it.

"Keep growling at me, hellcat, and I'll let Matthew take over."

What sort of alpha leaves his omega in heat without dicking her down into the mattress first? I growl louder still. Jerk harder against Gabriel's restraint, trying to get loose. To pounce on him and make my alpha put his cock in me.

Liam shakes his head and pulls his hand from my pussy, leaving the nest. Leaving me? Panic makes me whine. No, I need him. I need his safety and his knot. His protection. Where's he going?

Matthew comes into view, eying me thoughtfully. Always thinking. Calculating. He leans over, blotting out my view of my alpha. "Don't worry." The beta grins. "I'll keep her distracted."

With his dick? I perk up at the hopeful thought.

Matthew strokes me between my legs. Spreading my slick around. Making sure I'm nice and wet. My belly cramps with need, and fresh slick trickles out, telling the beta that I'm ready. Ready for fucking. Ready for breeding. That once they put a cock in me I'll stop fighting them.

Instead, he plays with me. Fucks two fingers in and out of my needy pussy. Adds a third. But it's still not what I want. It's not a cock. A knot. Nothing else will sate my body's terrible craving. Still, the pumping of his fingers helps. It eases some of the ache and awful cramping.

My hips move with him, fucking me harder on his fingers. Making wet, filthy sounds.

He pulls his hand free before I come, ignoring my disappointed whine, and brings it down on my pussy with a smack. I jolt, let out a yelp, and bring my bent knees together to protect where I'm most vulnerable.

Matthew grasps one of my legs and wrenches it open. His hand comes down on my mound repeatedly. Sharp smacks that make my eyes cross and my swollen clit throb. Warmth blooms between my legs as he spanks my pussy. Slaps right over my empty hole and clit.

I can't take it. It's too much.

Wiggling, I fight Gabriel's hold. Where is Liam? My head swivels, searching for him in the dim room. He's kneeling on the nest, his beautiful cock in his hand. Stroking it. Pre-cum dripping down his knuckles and soaking into the sheets. *Wasting it.*

I whimper. Slick trickles in thick ropes down my ass. My core clenches with every smack of Matthew's palm. Despite my irritation, my body likes it. Likes any sensation that gets it closer to coming. Even if it's not exactly what I want.

"If you come while he spanks your naughty pussy, I'll put my cock in you," Liam promises.

Yes. My labia swells, engorged and warm from the spanking. My clit swells too, erect and sensitive. Matthew focuses his fingertips on it. Spanks it lightly until my hips roll into every hit. Need tightens, aching and awful. I need relief. Need a cock and a knot and some fucking relief. I gasp, and moan, and wiggle uselessly under Matthew's heavy hand.

"That's it, sweetheart," Matthew says. "Let go. Let us make you feel good until it's time to fuck you. Can you come from having your pussy spanked?"

It takes a minute for his question to penetrate the fog of my heat. Can I? I close my eyes and nod, breathing heavily.

"That's our good girl," Matthew says, slapping my mound harder. Tapping over my clit. "You're being such a good omega, Kat. Such a good slut taking her spanking so well. You were naughty earlier when you tried to mount Liam while he was sleeping."

Did I do that? I don't remember it.

"That's okay, sweetheart," he continues. "We know you're sorry. That's why we're gonna let you come."

Come. Yes. I need to come. Pinned between my two betas, I let go and surrender while Matthew disciplines my naughty pussy. Spanks it until my breath catches in my chest and I flush with heat. Tension coils in my pelvis.

"That's it. That's our good girl. You're taking your pussy

spanking so well," Matthew croons. "Come for me, sweetheart."

I come against his hand, a strangled moan rattling through my throat. My back arches, and Gabriel's hands tighten. He pins me down harder until I stop pulling against him. My channel clenches, slick dripping down my ass. It soaks into the bedding.

Matthew palms my swollen, hot mound. My pussy spasms against his hand, tight and swollen. Throbbing. "Good girl. Now bend your knees to your chest for your reward."

I bend my trembling legs up and wait. He slides away, and Liam takes his place between my thighs. Fists his cock and rubs it up and down my pussy. Spreads my slick around and taps his head against my clit. Drifts lower, notching against my entrance. Teasing my hole.

Yes. Yesssss. Oh my God. I need it.

He presses slowly inside, and all the breath rushes from my lungs in relief as I sigh. The stretch is glorious and long overdue.

"Liam," Gabriel says in warning.

"Just getting slick," Liam answers. He thrusts in slowly. Too slow for what I want. He buries himself to the root until I've taken all of his big, alpha cock. "Trust me." He pulls out. Not halfway to push in again, but all the way out. I whine from the loss of him as he notches lower at my ass. His slicked up head presses against my asshole and pushes in slowly.

Nooooo. Not there. He can't give me a baby there. I like it when my betas fuck my ass, but not my alpha. Whining, I fidget. Try to twist and contort and pull away. What if he doesn't realize he's fucking the wrong hole?

"It's your fault, pretty kitty," Liam says, pushing into my ass. Shallow, controlled thrusts. He palms my hips and keeps me still underneath while Gabriel still has my arms pinned above my head. "You're the one who made me promise not to fuck your sweet pussy for three days. To edge you."

I don't think I meant *this*. This is torture. "Liam," I groan, my voice rough with lack of use. From all the screaming I did earlier.

He bottoms out inside my ass and starts rocking in and out. Slow, measured thrusts that don't satisfy my heat.

"Do you want your pussy plug, *meu docinho*?" Gabriel asks.

I nod. Yes. Anything to fill this void.

"I have a better idea," Matthew says. He gets out of the nest, and I hear rustling sounds. He takes something into the bathroom and runs the tap. A moment later, he's back. He's holding the vibrating butterfly toy, the one they gave me as a mating present. We use it on our rare date nights out.

Matthew pushes it into me and palms the remote. It buzzes to life, the butterfly's wings vibrating my mound while its feelers tease my clit. Its bulbous body curls inside my pussy. Too small to be satisfying. Too large and vibrating to be ignored.

This is fucking worse. It's like starving for days and then having one bite of ice cream.

I choke on a sob. Unshed tears gather at the corners of my eyes. Liam fucks me slowly. Gently. His big cock stretching the wrong hole.

"Hmm. This might have gone too far. I can grab the condoms," Matthew says.

Yes. I nod. He should grab the condoms and fuck me.

"No, she made us promise," Liam says. "We don't know if the spermicide might make the cycle fail."

"Kat did say she refused to go through with a shitty heat more than once," Gabriel says.

I'm a fucking idiot. I can't do this, not even once. Why did I think I could stand it?

"We're almost there," Liam says, still rocking. He leans over me and uses his thumb to wipe the tears from my eyelashes. "Twelve more hours, kitten. You can bear it. We're almost there. Don't give up. You can take it."

His soft, sweet words fill me with rage. My lips peel back from my teeth and I clench them together, hard. Growl. A primal need to hurt him as badly as he's hurting me now by not fucking me face down in this perfect nest I built for him. In our bond, he's sweet and sorry. A gentle balm that does nothing to soothe my irritation.

Matthew clicks a button that makes the toy buzz harder, faster. Makes my hips rise up and fuck my ass deeper on Liam's buried cock. His cock rubs against the toy in my pussy through my wall and finally—fucking finally—there's a break in my all-consuming need. A brief flash of relief.

Liam grunts, feeling it through our mating bond. His hands tighten on my fists and he pulls his hips back and slams them into me. His cock slides against the bulbous toy. Pushes it up, rubbing it against my sweet spot.

I gasp and go still. My focus shifts. My growl stutters into a hesitant purr.

"Is that what you want, kitten? You want me to pound this tight little ass?" Liam thrusts hard again. Bounces me on his cock. "That, I can give you."

And he does. He fucks my ass hard. Harder than they've ever fucked me back there before. Matthew cranks the toy up and it doesn't take long for me to come. For my body to clamp down on everything stuffing me full.

Liam groans, his thrusts slowing. His cock pulsing. Coming inside me and wasting good alpha seed in the wrong hole. He pumps my ass full and sits there, his knot on the outside, breathing hard as he squeezes it with his hand.

"God, I wish I could fuck her mouth," Gabriel says.

"Are you crazy?" Matthew asks. "She's half-feral right now. She'd bite your dick off."

"What a way to go," Gabriel jokes.

The toy stops buzzing, but my need's only half-satisfied. The silicone toy's not enough. Liam pulls out, leaving me emptier. Cum drips down my ass, wasted, and soaks into the absorbent bedding.

"It's still not enough," Liam says, looking down at me thoughtfully.

"We should have bought that fucking machine we looked at," Matthew says.

Liam rubs the back of his hand over my body at different points. "Her heat's gotten worse. She has to be ovulating."

Yes. I'm ovulating. He can fuck me once I've ovulated.

"We agreed to wait until seventy-two hours," Matthew reminds him. "To be sure."

"It's up to you," Gabriel says to Liam. "How badly do you want to have a boy? I can stop giving you your rut blocker."

Liam eases my legs down and lays his palm on my belly. "Sorry, hellcat, but I'm not fucking your sweet pussy until you're ready for me to give you a son."

"Let me check her," Gabriel says. "Switch with me."

They change places, Matthew holding my wrists over my head while Liam watches and Gabriel slides between my thighs. Gabriel pulls the toy from my pussy and tosses it aside, then fingers me. His middle finger presses deep, tapping against my cervix. Checking my readiness for breeding.

"She's soft but mostly closed. She hasn't ovulated yet. Could happen in the morning."

With a sob, I give up struggling. I don't know how much more of this I can take.

Liam purrs, distracting me with kisses. He rubs his cheek against mine, scent marking me. "Just a bit longer, Kat. You can be patient. I promise you it'll be worth it when you hold our baby boy for the first time. I promise. You can do this."

I'm not sure I can. Rage and desperation fade away to resignation. The worst of my need's been fed, like cracking a valve to vent a boiling pot. But I'm still heated. Still full of bottomless need.

"We're going to help you go back to sleep now," Liam promises. Instead of fucking me, my alpha pulls out my pink knotting toy. He inserts it into me. Dimly, I'm aware of my body spasming around its vibrations. Of the fake knot inflating, stretching me. It helps. But it's not really the same. There's no warmth to the toy. No pulsations or throbbing. No cum drenched in my pack's pheromones spurting into me.

But it's enough to sleep. For a few hours of sweet oblivion.

They take turns washing up, and then someone wipes me clean with a damp rag. They drag the blankets over me. My limbs get heavy, and they let me go so I can curl up on my side, my legs tucked to my chest. They cover me with more soft blankets and stroke my hair. Liam purrs for me.

I sink into a fitful sleep.

"NUH-UH, SWEETHEART," MATTHEW SAYS, GRABBING A FISTFUL of my hair. He tugs, prying me off Gabriel. "Naughty girl."

I whine, annoyed. My eyes crack open, gritty from sleep. Matthew manhandles me onto my belly. Slaps me on the ass with his other hand, his grip in my hair still firm. "Get on your knees. Let Gabriel check you."

"What time is it?" Gabriel asks, his voice sleepy.

"Does it matter?" Matthew asks. "She's in heat. It's fuck o'clock. Ass up, omega. That's it."

I lift my ass until it's as high as I can go. Gabriel moves behind me, his fingers a blunt intrusion into my pussy. Made possible only by the river of slick my body's pumping out like crazy. He taps his fingertip against my cervix.

"It's time," Gabriel says, his hand pulling free with a wet sucking noise.

"Thank fuck," Matthew sighs. "Liam, get your ass up and put your cock in her."

"I'm up," Liam says, groggy. "What time is it?"

"It's fuck o'clock, alpha," Matthew says. "Now dick your omega down good before one of us does it for you so we can finally get some real fucking rest."

"So grumpy," Liam mutters.

"We've been wrestling a half-feral omega for three days. I'm *tired*," Matthew whines. "My arms ache. She nipped me yesterday. I didn't sign up for cardio or abuse."

Gabriel chuckles "Go take a break, babe. Eat something that needs cooking and take a hot shower. These two don't need beta babysitters anymore."

"I should probably be offended," Liam says under his breath. His palm lands on my ass, rubbing it. "But we're all tired, aren't we, kitten? You most of all. You've been so patient."

I whine, annoyed that he's not fucking me yet. My pussy's *right there.*

Liam strokes between my legs. Smears my slick and teases my clit. When the head of his cock rubs between my puffy lips, I want to cry.

"Such a good girl," he says, pushing into me.

The slow thrust of his cock in my pussy after three days of bitter denial makes my thighs tremble. He pushes all the way in.

Hits my cervix. The stretch after having nothing but toys and fingers in there is perfect.

Oh, God. It feels so fucking good. I moan as he pulls out and thrusts in again. He purrs for me. Deep and loud. The sound of a satisfied alpha. The vibrations rumble in his chest and his cock almost rattles inside me.

More. I need more. Whimpering, I push back against him. Drive him deeper until it hurts a bit. He's so big, his cock stretching me wide. And I haven't had a cock there in three long days.

Liam chuckles. "I was gonna take it slow to get you warmed up, but that's not what you want, is it?"

No. I want to be dicked down. Knotted. Bred. Like a proper omega.

Liam pulls out, ignoring my groans. He changes position, crouching over me. Lowering himself in a squat until his dick lines up with me again. He feeds it back into me, then grabs my hips and starts to thrust.

Rapid, hard, and rutting. I orgasm on his cock, fast and unexpectedly. My walls clamping down, trying to milk a knot that isn't there yet. To make him come and breed me.

"I love how needy you are for my hard cock," he says. "Come for me again, kitten. Show me how much you want me to put this baby inside you."

My pussy spasms as he talks dirty to me. Telling me how he can't wait to fill my womb. To watch my belly swell and my breasts get big. To suck the milk from my big tits. It drives me wild when he talks like that. It's too much. But there's no choice but to take it. I'm pinned under him. There's no moving an alpha once he's started rutting.

"You're so wet for my cock, kitten. Because you know this pussy's mine. That I claimed it with my cum. And I'm gonna keep claiming it forever. Keep filling you up. Keep you pregnant."

His thrusts and dirty talk make me come again. And still he doesn't stop. He fucks me and keeps talking until his breathing's hard. Until he grunts and moans with every surge of his cock.

"So slick. You like it hard, don't you, hellcat? Like getting put in your place. On my cock. Whose pussy is this? That's right. It's mine. It's my pussy and I'm gonna breed it raw. You're gonna drip come for a week straight."

He slaps my ass with a hard crack of his palm, then grabs one of my arms and twists it behind my back. Pins it to the small of my waist and changes our angle, somehow fucking me even deeper. Until it feels like he's trying to fuck his way right into my womb. I come again. Deep, pulsing waves that make my belly cramp and my pussy flood with slick. Easing his rough claiming.

"Fuck, your pussy got tighter. Wetter. Did you come again, kitten? That's good. You're being such a perfect cum slut for me. Are you ready to take it? I'm gonna make you a mother again."

I can't speak. Can't think. All I can do is lie there underneath him as his knot starts to swell. As his pace slows down and his dick pulses. He groans like my pussy's squeezing the life out of him. His knot pops, fast and wide. Locking his sperm up tight so it has nowhere to go but inside my open, fertile cervix.

"What a good girl," Liam says, stroking me. "That was a big load. I saved it for you. Come on my knot, kitten. Let's get you pregnant."

Liam gets on his knees behind me. His knot tugs against my pubic bone where we're tied together as he settles. He covers me and wraps a hand around my front, searching for my clit. Fingering me when he finds it.

"That's a good girl, kitten. Take some more. You can fit more cum in that tight pussy, can't you?"

He doesn't give me a choice. Liam fingers my clit until I come on his knot. Walls fluttering, milking out one last pulse of semen. Again. Another, until my groin's overstuffed and uncomfortably full. I whimper and come again. Until his balls have to be empty, drained dry. There can't possibly be anything left in them after that.

"Fuck," he groans, rubbing me down. "I came so hard, I think you're gonna have twins."

My eyes flutter shut. It's impossible to keep them open. Calm now, I purr. My heart is perfectly satisfied.

"Go to sleep, kitten. That's my good girl," he whispers in my ear. "Let my sperm do their job. Daddy's gonna make you a mommy again."

I fall asleep with his knot in me and a pussy full of cum. It's the deepest, best sleep I've had in forever.

"WHO WANTS TO GO OUTSIDE AND WORK ON THE GARDEN WITH me?" I ask the girls.

"Me!" Holly races to the back door.

"Hold on," I tell her. "You're not ready. What do we have to do before we go into the garden?"

She freezes and ponders it. "Put on boots." Then she plops onto the ground by the door and pulls her yellow rubber boots from their spot by the door. She sticks her tongue out while she concentrates on pulling them onto her feet by their pull tabs.

"Good job, baby," I tell her once she's done. "Now you're ready." I switch out my sneakers for my gardening shoes. Then I put Lily into her harness on my back and carry Marcia on my hip. Holly runs ahead of us and waits at the gate for me to unlatch it for her.

The kids have their own play garden full of sensory toys. Small plastic shovels and rakes, smaller plastic nursery pots and a tiny functional watering can. They don't do much more than create a lot of mud, but that's fine. It's good for kids to get dirty. Together, we check on the marigold seedlings we planted last week.

I sit Marcia down with her sister in their fenced-off garden so they play while I check on our vegetable garden. "Oh, look," I tell Lily. "We have our first tomatoes." I brush the leaves aside so that she can see the budded green fruits that will ripen soon. Lily babbles, talking to me in her baby talk while I point to different plants. I tell her what they are and what their fruit will look like once they've ripened.

Once the vegetable patch is pruned and tied back into submission and fertilized, I join the girls in their play garden.

"Look at my flowers, Mommy," Holly says with pride. She squats and holds the watering can above her marigolds. There's no water in the can right now, but she pretends to water them anyway.

"Wow, they're so beautiful, baby. You've done a good job taking care of your flowers."

"I know." She drops the watering can and moves on to scooping dirt into an empty flower pot with her plastic shovel.

I hold back my snort of laughter. I love her confidence. "What are you making now?"

"More flowers."

Pulling out the packet of seeds I bought at the store today, I show them to her. The flowers are pink, her favorite color. "Should we grow these ones?"

"Yeah!"

I show her how to pack the dirt, and make a divot with her finger. How to put a few tiny seeds inside and cover them with soil. Then I fill her plastic can from the hose and show her how much to water them. "Good job. It'll take a few days for them to grow. We'll check on them again tomorrow, okay?"

"Okay."

"You know, babies are a bit like seeds," I tell her. "They grow in a mommy's tummy like flowers grow in a flowerpot. I'm growing you a sister or brother right now."

"A baby?" Holly tilts her head and thinks about it. Then she drops her plastic gardening toy and points to my stomach. "In there?"

"Yeah."

"And it's gonna come out when it's big?" she asks.

"Yes."

"Wow," she says, blinking while she thinks.

"Do you want a sister or a brother?" I ask her.

Holly's silent for a bit as she thinks some more. I give her time to process it. "I want a brother. When will the baby come out?"

"Not for many months. They take time to grow."

Holly nods. "Like my flowers." She stares at my stomach. I wonder how much, if at all, she remembers about my last pregnancy with her sister. "How does a baby get in there?" she asks.

"Umm..." I cup my stomach and take a second to think of an age-appropriate answer for that. "A mommy and a daddy put it there when they love each other."

"Okay." She looks toward the house, distracted. "I'm hungry."

"I bet Papa's working on dinner. Let's go have a tubbie and

get in pajamas. But first, can you put your garden toys away please?"

"Okay." Holly grabs her plastic shovel and brings it to her tool basket. I pick Marcia up from where she was scratching in the dirt with a twig and pop her on my hip while Holly runs to the kitchen door.

"Boots!" I shout, reminding her to take her garden boots off. She runs back outside and sits down to pull off her muddy boots.

By the time she's done, I've met her at the door.

"Daddy put a baby in Mommy's tummy," she tells her papa, Matthew.

"Yeah?" Matthew puts his macaroni and cheese-covered spoon down in the spoon rest. He glances at me, wide eyed, for direction.

"I told Holly that babies grow like seeds in a mommy's tummy."

"What do you think about that?" Matthew asks Holly.

"I want a brother. I have sisters," she says matter-of-factly.

"We won't know if it's a boy or girl for a bit," I say. "Come on, let's get washed up for dinner." I take her hand and lead her toward the stairs so she doesn't get distracted and get mud everywhere.

After baths and dinner and bedtime routines, we finally have some time for ourselves.

"I heard you had the birds and the bees talk with Holly," Liam says, snuggling me closer on the couch.

I put my hand on his stomach and my head on his shoulder and tuck my legs up under the blanket. "Not in depth, but yeah. I read that it's better to talk about it before the baby's born. I doubt she remembers my pregnancy with Lily. She was too young."

"I can look for a kid's book," Matthew offers. Reading to

the kids is his favorite. He says he wants them to love books and reading as much as he does.

"That's a good idea," I say, smiling.

"I'll have the real birds and bees talk with them all when they're older," Gabriel says. "And the dynamics talk when they hit puberty."

"Thank God," Liam says. "I wasn't looking forward to that."

"What time is the doctor's appointment tomorrow?" Gabriel asks.

"Five," I answer. "Can you make it?"

"One of the other PAs is coming in early to cover the rest of my shift," Gabriel says. "I'll be there."

The next day passes in a hectic blur until Chelsea knocks on the door in the afternoon. Waffles and Syrup both come running. "Hi, Chelsea. Come on in. I stocked the soda and chips you like. Help yourself to whatever's in the fridge. We won't be out too late tonight."

"No worries," she says. "I'm always happy to baby and pet sit."

I take a minute to catch up with her. "How's grad school? You're almost done, right?"

"Good. And yeah." She tucks her long hair behind her ear. "Only one semester left after this one."

I'm glad for her, but also terrified to lose her. She's been a blessing to help us whenever Jen is busy. "Have you thought about what you're doing after?"

"I want to start my own company," she says.

"So you're staying here?" I ask, hopeful.

"Probably. There's nowhere else I really want to go."

Before I can ask her what kind of business she wants to open, she scoops Waffles up and starts talking to him like he's a baby. Waffles eats it up, purring. She carries him into the living room where the girls are watching an animated musical and coloring.

"Chelsea!" Holly yells. "Do you want to color with us?"

"Of course. Do you have pink?"

"We have lots of pink ones." Holly digs through her crayon box and pulls out every shade of pink she can find.

Gabriel brings Lily down from changing her and gives the baby to Chelsea to hold. Our babysitter grabs a piece of paper and starts drawing flowers and hearts and cat-eared anime girl doodles.

Chelsea glances at the TV. "Is that Rapunzel? She's my favorite. I like her dress."

"Because it's pink?" Holly asks, scribbling across her own paper.

I lose track of the rest of their conversation while I check that we have everything. My phone, wallet, new insurance card, and Liam's keys. We head outside, locking the door behind us, and make the short drive into town.

"Fill this out with any changes," the receptionist says, handing me papers.

I take the clipboard and fill out the all too familiar paperwork. Our ultrasound tech is new, a beta named Ashley. By now, this routine is familiar. But that doesn't stop my pack from being a nervous wreck. Liam is nearly crawling out of his skin. Today is the day we find out the baby's sex.

"Okay, that's everything I need. I'll grab the doctor." Ashley sets the probe in the holder and steps out.

A few minutes later, our obstetrician comes in. "Hello again," he says, smiling. "So are we ready to find out the sex?"

"Yes," Liam says, sitting on the edge of his seat.

The doctor sits down and adds more jelly to the probe. He puts it on my abdomen and finds the angle he wants. Then he smiles. "Congratulations. It's a boy."

Relief and happiness wash through me. We did it. All of that hell I went through was actually worth it.

"A boy," Liam repeats. "It's a boy?" He stands up abruptly and does a fist pump. "A boy! Finally. Oh my God." Then he fists his hands in his hair, leaving it crazy looking. He leans over the screen, invading the doctor's space. "Are you sure?"

I laugh as my alpha loses his mind. "Please excuse him. Our other three kids are girls."

"I'm sure," the doctor says.

"Liam, sit down," Matthew says, pulling at Liam's shirt.

Liam sits, his expression stunned.

"He's hardly my first eager dad," the doctor says kindly. "I sent the pictures to the printer. I'll give you all a moment. Kathleen, you can make your next appointment with the girls at the desk on your way out." He drops the probe on a hook and leaves.

Gabriel wipes the jelly off my belly with a tissue and pulls my shirt down over my abdomen. "We should give Liam a minute so he doesn't faint."

I look at my deliriously happy alpha, my pack, and the ultrasound screen with baby number four on it, and I think about how this all started with one small clerical error on some paperwork.

That was one hell of a meet-cute. Maybe I should put it in my next book.

Want to keep reading?

Join the Newsletter and get the bonus epilogue in your inbox
https://books.bookfunnel.com/alexisbosborne

Also by Alexis B. Osborne

OMEGAVERSE

Omegas of OAN

(Sci-Fi Omegaverse)

Omega Swipes Right

Omega Revealed

Omega for Rent

Omega Rescued

Heatverse

(Contemporary Why Choose Omegaverse)

Heat Clinic

Rut Bar

Breeding Clinic

ALIEN ROMANCE

Outer Limits Quadrant

Engineering Fate

Doctoring Fate

Interpreting Fate

Sagittarius Quadrant

Ice Planet Prison

Mate for the Alien P*rn Star

Author's Note

Thank you so much for reading Breeding Clinic! When I started this book the only thought I had was a fertility clinic and how difficult an infertility journey would be for an omega since omegas are typically hyper-fertile. As someone who struggled through the pain of fertility treatments and loss, I wanted to write a fluffy, low-angst book to give Kat the happy ending I dreamed of. Life doesn't always go as planned and sometimes we have to play the hand we're dealt, but thanks to books, readers get to live a thousand different lives. I hope that Breeding Clinic gave you all the fluffy, steamy, warm fuzzy feelings. And I hope that if you've also gone through divorce, that you realize endings can mean new beginnings and our past doesn't limit our future.

I'm not sure what I'll be writing next! I have a few ideas percolating and a bunch of rough drafts in various stages of development. I'm probably going to flit about between them and see which one grabs a hold of me and refuses to let go.

If you've made it this far, please consider leaving a review. Reviews are author hugs!

For updates, new release alerts, teasers, sales info, freebies, and bonus content delivered to your inbox about once a month, join my newsletter. To stalk me on social media or visit the shop, you can find that at www.alexisbosborne.com.

-Alexis

About the Author

Alexis lives in New York with her wife and step-son and a small horde of furry beings. She began her love affair with books at an early age, and began writing for fun in High School and College. She fell in insta-love with the strange and unusual at an early age. When she's not reading or writing she can be found painting and making subversive cross-stitch. Her favorite fairy tale will always be Beauty and the Beast. Alexis loves all things fantastical, alien, and weird. She will never forget the gorgeous glory that was the late, great David Bowie.

www.alexisbosborne.com